THIS
HOUSE
WILL
FEED

THIS HOUSE WILL FEED

MARIA TUREAUD

KENSINGTON
PUBLISHING CORP.

kensingtonbooks.com

KENSINGTON BOOKS are published by

Kensington Publishing Corp.
900 Third Ave.
New York, NY 10022

All Kensington titles, imprints and distributed lines are available at special quantity discounts for bulk purchases for sales promotion, premiums, fund-raising, educational or institutional use.

Special book excerpts or customized printings can also be created to fit specific needs. For details, write or phone the office of the Kensington Special Sales Manager: Kensington Publishing Corp., 900 Third Ave., New York, NY, 10022. Attn. Special Sales Department. Phone: 1-800-221-2647.

KENSINGTON and the K with book logo Reg. U.S. Pat. & TM Off.

Library of Congress Control Number: 2025945759

ISBN-13: 978-1-4967-5541-4
First Kensington Hardcover Edition: February 2026

ISBN-13: 978-1-4967-5543-8 (e-book)

10 9 8 7 6 5 4 3 2 1

Printed in the United States of America

The authorized representative in the EU for product safety and compliance is eucomply OU, Parnu mnt 139b-14, Apt 123
Tallinn, Berlin 11317, hello@eucompliancepartner.com

For my grandparents.
Nancy, Sheila, Christy, Haulie.
Without your past, there would be no future.

A Note from the Author

This book portrays one of the worst tragedies (and, some argue, genocides) of the nineteenth century—An Gorta Mór (the Great Hunger), known simply in America as the Irish Potato Famine. The population of Ireland halved as a result, from an estimated 9 million down to just 4.5 million. As such, **depictions of extreme starvation, desolation, death (including instances of child death), possession, use of slurs, cannibalism, suicide, and murder appear in these pages.** This book includes epigraphs, most documenting eyewitness accounts (from Irish, British, and American observers) and should be read with caution.

As an Irish author, born and raised, the researching and writing of this book dredged up—for me—a generational trauma that we as a people have not truly dealt with. Therefore, I suggest any native Irish readers to approach with a steady heart and the heady knowledge that our great-great-grandparents were forged in steel, and *you* are the freedom and legacy they dreamt of.

THIS
HOUSE
WILL
FEED

Chapter 1

Ill fares the land, to hast'ning ills a prey,
Where wealth accumulates, and men decay.
—Oliver Goldsmith, *The Deserted Village*

Ennis, Ireland. February 1848

The taste of my brother's flesh still haunted me.

Eat it, my brother, Michael, had said. *Live, Maggie.* For one of us had to. Extended in the last breath of impending death, his offer had smarted of desperation and the Devil himself, but God above bore witness that I fought to shake it away and bury it six feet under. 'Twas hard to forget what I'd done, when daily duty led me to the dining hall of the Ennis Workhouse, not a quarter hour past staff mealtime, air heavy with the taunt of stewed meat only the masters could enjoy.

But inmate number 1-3-4-0, of the Ennis Union, had work to do.

An icy draft toyed with the candle flame, shifting the shadows as I forced the brush back and forth over the cool stone floor. The workhouse was my life now—the raw judder of numbed knees, sweat coating my brow as I scoured and scoured. And yet it didn't seem to matter how hard I worked, for the cold had a way of seeping into bones, freezing the very marrow that kindled with a sliver of hope. Of tomorrow. Of the bright, burning dawn.

But hope was for the masters.

Leaning into the task, I winced and pushed the brush left, then right. Left, right; left, right. The matron would have no call to chastise me, no reason to halve my rations or double my debt. This was my penance, so I scrubbed and scrubbed. Day in, day out. Left: *I'm*; right: *so*; left: *very*; right: *sorry*. Until the task became part of me, as natural as the memories I'd buried away. A fever dream of what if and should-have-could-have. Except it was daylight, with no hope of waking from the nightmare beyond these bricks and mortar—like there was no hope of finishing this floor.

The supper hall of the workhouse stretched from wall to wall, a sea of black slate that bred exhaustion just looking at it. Sighing, I sat back on my heels and glanced up. Just a moment of respite. A fortifying breath to prepare myself.

Vaulted ceilings reached for the dark gray sky above; charcoal stone walls rose high before a trellis of curved beams slashed toward the ceiling, the clean-picked rib cage of a monstrous carcass. Stained-glass windows stretched above what was probably once an altar, its elevated stage now used to seat the esteemed workhouse officials and supervisors.

Right now, 'twas silent, save for my brushing. Calm. Peaceful. Everything my mind was not. Lord, but I yearned for true quiet.

"Margaret O'Shaughnessy, 1-3-4-0?"

The loud address whipped through the silence, cracking along the damp stone floor like thunder. Pursing my lips, I tightened the threadbare, workhouse-issued cloak around my skeletal frame and slowly struggled to my bare feet.

At least I could stand. At least I could turn. I had been on death's door when I was delivered through the gate by a rare Samaritan of the matron's acquaintance.

"Maggie," I corrected, my voice still rasped and torn from the constant thirst that came from starvation.

There was a little more meat between brittle bones and scaled skin than there had been when I'd arrived. But when I'd risked a glance in the sliver of broken mirror another inmate had smuggled into the workhouse, I still saw a gaunt, sickly thing. Skin, pallid with a greenish hue. Eyes, sunken in the darkened hollows of a waked corpse. Cheekbones, sharp enough to cut fresh-baked bread.

At the thought of bread, my stomach groaned with want—as if unused to going without. Fickle organ. Worse than new-money businessmen peacocking their trinkets, better than their neighbors for the few shillings more.

"Maggie then," came the tight-lipped response, and I forced my wary eyes to meet those of the matron. God above, I was grateful—so grateful—to have a roof over my head and some food in my belly, but something about the matron sent chills down my spine. Perhaps it was the cut of her steel-gray gown, a fashionable habit well-fitted above a corset pulled too tight. Or maybe 'twas the shadowed angles of her face, the severe bun at the back of her head, the crooked nose, eyes set too close together, or the irises so dark they may as well have belonged to a raven, scavenging for scraps. Perhaps all those things, but in that moment, as I glanced at her, bathed in shadow as the glow of a stained-glass window depicting the Sacred Heart illuminated her back, a sinister crimson nimbus lent a hellish quality to her presence. "You'll be coming with me, inmate."

Old Maggie would've raised a brow, asked question after question to ease the curiosity sure to get her in trouble. But new Maggie—new me—had lost that passion somewhere between watching my entire family waste unto death and burying every last one of them. Well, no. That's a lie. A turn of phrase. There came a point when weakness meant I could do naught but pull filth-stained cloaks over stiffening faces before whispering a prayer to the Blessed Virgin, hoping no starving dogs roamed the roadside that became their graves.

"Yes, maum," I responded, bobbing a curtsy before scurrying to fetch my scrubbing brush and bucket.

"You won't be needing that," the matron snapped. "Run along to your mat and fetch anything sentimental. Leave the rest. I expect to find you in the hall beyond the office in five minutes."

Surprise rippled across my skin until it puckered like a freshly plucked goose on Christmas Day.

"Am I being moved, maum?" I asked, fear creeping its way into my blood. Moved was better than the gallows, especially when the only real way out of here was with either bailiff or mortician.

"You're to see the workhouse master, Maggie." For a moment, something in her eyes softened, but the moment passed, and she barked, "As fast as you can. Now."

My heart fluttered as I turned on my heel and hurried out of the supper hall. I'd never met the workhouse master. Seen him from afar, sure, with his nice clothes and round belly. The hunger didn't touch the Anglos. Why would it?

My eyes widened as I reached the long mile—a dark, wood-paneled hallway with nary a candle to light the way. What if the workhouse master knew of what had transpired on my journey here? I hadn't told a soul, hadn't dared. But there was nothing else he could possibly want with the likes of me—a waif who'd traveled a great distance to give up all dignity and live in life-long debt to a foreign crown.

A girl who shouldn't have lived.

"Michael? What do I do?" I whispered the plea to my dead brother as a tremble rippled through my knees, up my legs, before settling into a knotted ball in my gut. All that struggle only to hang. My lungs failed my heart for two breaths, but I forced them to work. Forced myself to breathe. One step. Two. Until I reached the end of the corridor and glanced out the window.

I clamped my jaw shut and looked out onto the rock-covered yard dotted with hundreds of waifs. That was another thing to be grateful for—my appointment to floor duty. It was a sign of favor, and few women were afforded the luxury. It was better than the laundry or the yard. Those in the yard chiseled, they carried, and worked so hard the food they earned wasn't enough to keep death from calling. The Toonagh quarry sent the rock each week, availing of the free labor. I was certain I should've felt something as I watched. Old me would've. At least a pang of guilt as a boy leaned against a massive boulder for a moment's respite. Or a lurch of fright as a man dropped the heavy stone he carried—too close to bare feet for comfort.

Thing was, they were naught but walking graves to me. Specters who clung to the scraps they were thrown, while the world beyond the walls perished and died.

And if the workhouse master had discovered my crime, I'd be worse off than those below. I couldn't spare an ounce of pity. I had to save it and will it into strength for myself.

I turned away as a supervisor unleashed his whip on the body of a fallen child. If they weren't already dead, they soon would be. I couldn't muster pity for them either, because there'd be none for me.

Closing my eyes, I took a deep, shuddering breath before taking a right toward the female dormitories. As my bare foot touched water, I scowled. Another burst pipe, which meant our sleep mats were drenched. At least ample moisture would keep the fleas at bay, though it would likely bring fever come morning.

Clucking my tongue, I splashed my way to my own mat.

The matron had said to gather my sentimental things. I had eleven, all carefully placed in the small burlap sack I'd carried from Kilrush to Ennis—safely hung from a flimsy rack alongside my blanket. Leaks happened more often than not.

I grabbed the sack and peered inside.

My mother's wooden beads—worn and smooth from frantic decades of the rosary.

My father's shoelaces—to remind me of the journey.

Pieces of my sisters' filthy dresses, ripped from each as they died, one by one, on the road. *Aoife*. I breathed in. *Síofra*. And winced. *Mary*. Oh God. *Martha*. I squeezed my eyes shut. *Nancy*. I breathed out.

Michael's handkerchief. *Breathe*. John's cap. *Breathe*. A wooden toggle from Patrick's shirt. *Breathe*.

And a lock of hair from baby Crofton—born soon after the first blight struck and named for our landlord in hopes he would show us mercy.

But he did not. And they were dead. They were all dead. And I was about to join them.

Hot tears stung my eyes as I reached for the iron door handle of my assigned dormitory.

It was all I had left. Not much, by any means. Nothing to leave a legacy, a mark, or a reminder that they, or I, had ever lived.

With a shake of my head, I opened the door. It was time to face my fate.

The matron stood tall and stiff, a pillar of shadow and brimstone as I approached, and I gripped the burlap sack tight with hands that shook. The rough-hewn fabric scratched my skin, the only reminder this was real—despite the death knell a-clanging in my ears.

Time was up. Father had said we simply borrow time to stay the reaper. Stumble one step ahead. One meal beyond his reach. But the reaper had just come calling, hand out, for debt owed and interest due.

I didn't dare open my mouth to ask what was amiss, for if I did, I'd scream my throat raw as sure as the day was long. Instead, I watched as the matron rapped on the master's door. As she tilted her head toward the thick, stained wood. Waiting. Waiting. And then she nodded. He must have replied.

But I couldn't hear a blasted thing over the rush in my ears: an ocean of blood crashing against a storm-weary shore.

"English only once you're within. Chin up, Maggie," said the matron, rolling her own shoulders in case I'd forgotten how to stand. What language to speak. How to be. How to exist as a nothing and no one before a master.

As if I could forget.

And as the matron stepped from the shadow to push in the door, I molded my back, forcing it straight as if about to serve my own mistress, Lady Grace—as she had liked to be called— and followed the matron inside.

The office was a cave with no windows. A cavern of black so bleak, I'd not seen the like since the potato rotted where it grew—the only crop we could grow for ourselves, the only food we ever had to eat—and passed through our disbelieving fingers as a dark, inedible sludge.

There were no beeswax candles here, only the impossibly bright glow of oil lamps, made all fancy and delicate like the ones that had lit the darkest afternoons in Lady Grace's parlor.

A painting broke up the boring wood paneling—a fierce-looking man in a high-necked white shirt with white cravat choking a well-fed throat. A lord, I supposed. But the man sitting behind a desk fit for a king was certainly not he. He scribbled and scratched, fingers blotted with ink as he ran a free hand through a generous cropping of hair.

His clothes were crisp. Well-laundered and kept, though not new. Local fabric at that. Wool, perhaps. My brother, Michael, would never stop talking about fabrics, describing their wins and woes in minute detail until we'd beg Father for a story. Anything to get Michael to shut his hole.

Jesus wept, but I could hear him now.

That's good Dublin wool, Maggie. Expensive enough, but

not out of reach for a comfortable man of the Town. Now, if I were to show you his lordship's woolens, you'd see at once the gulf between them, and know his lordship a man of great station.

I squeezed my eyes shut at the memory. Of my constant reminder to him that Colonel Moore-Vandeleur was only a mister, not a lord. Not high-born aristocracy like his wife, Lady Grace. But Michael would always roll his eyes and say, "What matter that, when he's a-lording over most of Clare, and you and I the richer for being polite."

The matron cleared her throat, stirring me from the past. "As requested, Mr. O'Brien. Inmate 1-3-4-0, O'Shaughnessy, Margaret."

The master didn't look up. Instead, he stilled his scratching and swapped the fountain pen for a pair of spectacles that had seen better days.

"What's your place, inmate?" he asked, a thin, nasally preen that set my teeth on edge. There was a trace of London in his English, but he was Irish-born for sure. Educated across the sea then. I opened my eyes.

"Kilrush, sir."

A grunt. He rose and turned to sift through a filing cabinet that lined the wall, then returned with a rectangle of cardboard, a ream of paper within.

"Kilrush," he repeated, though more to himself than me. He thumbed through the file, licking his inked thumb between pages, and I fought the urge to remind him. But the ink now staining the corner of his wafer-thin lips made him less . . . intimidating. Less the master.

"O'Shaughnessy." Murmuring, he seemed to find the right page, then glanced up at me, his beady eyes skimming from the tip of my crown to my dirtied bare toes. "Margaret, you said?"

"Yes, sir." I bobbed my head, the movement stiff and odd, as if more than two years had passed between duty and now.

He took up the pen and made a note on the paper. "Family?"

I paused, but only for a beat. "Dead, sir."

"In what union?" he asked.

I winced. "I don't know, sir."

"What do you mean you don't know?" Pursing his lips, he glanced at me and circled the air with his pen. "What poor union did they perish in? Which workhouse, girl? What district?"

"They perished on the trip, Mr. O'Brien." The matron stepped forward and placed a gentle hand on my shoulder. I would thank her for that small kindness later. "From the Kilrush union, by way of Kildysert, then Ennis."

Mr. O'Brien's wispy brows drew together. "Why not come straight to Ennis?"

My throat tightened, but it seemed he didn't need or want an answer.

"No mind. I'll pray to thank your destitute family for absconding their burden on Her Majesty's charity," he said, burying his nose in his notes. I didn't know why I felt nothing, for I knew I should. But New Me would bite her tongue, so I did.

"Age?"

"Nine—" I broke off and pressed my lips together. "Twenty-two, sir."

"Are you certain?" he asked, a sneer in his inflection. No. I wasn't sure. But time had passed both fast and slow since that first summer, and I had aged a decade between.

"Yes, sir."

He put down his pen, then spoke into the shadows beyond my shoulder. I raised a brow.

"Will she do, Your Ladyship?" he asked.

I didn't whirl—for I was beyond childish surprise—but I did stiffen. There was a rustle, one I knew all too well. The crisp newness of fresh-pressed taffeta afore an outing, and a whiff of lavender blended with foreign spice.

"She's the right height." The woman's voice rolled over my skin, a deep alto drizzled with warm honey that could spell fortune or ruin on a whim. And yet there was something unrefined about it; it lacked the nasaled clip of all the well-to-dos that had swanned through the Moore-Vandeleur estate at one time or another.

Click-tap. A pause. Click-tap.

The hair at my nape snapped to attention as she neared, her perfume wafting in the draft as I fought the urge to turn. To ask why my height mattered.

"It's as I was told. She'll do, Mr. O'Brien." The woman's skirts brushed my bare feet as she approached. She held a cane in her left hand, lazily dragging it forward with each step as a gentleman might. And as she came into view, my brow furrowed.

The lady wore a black gentleman's frock coat, cut in the back to accommodate the frill of the charcoal taffeta bustle skirt that cascaded from rump to floor. A ruffled charcoal bodice peeked beneath her lapels, swimming up the length of her neck before pillowing in a cloud of black lace. A simple golden charm—three swirls, connected to a central branch—adorned her throat, held in place by a length of black ribbon. Her dark hair was swept up, a severe style I'd never seen before, and tucked into the black top hat perched on her head.

It was bold. Daring. Like her eyes. I thought they could have been a smoky dark blue. But in the dim light of the master's office, shadowed by the languid sweep of black lashes, I could swear they too were charcoal.

I knew I stared, but I couldn't glance away. Even as she stepped before me, a half-smile lighting her pale face. She didn't need the powders and kohl that Lady Grace had always insisted upon. By no means young, yet I couldn't place her age.

"Leave us," she said, shooting the words over her shoulder at the master. I shivered, from chill or fear, I knew not.

His face flushed as the woman raised a black, lace-gloved hand and gestured for the door. He was dismissed, and the arch of his brow screamed displeasure.

"Th-there's still the matter of her debt—" he began, but the woman cut through his words with a sharp rap of the cane against the concrete floor.

"Later," she snapped, her eyes locked on mine. They were both cold yet warm, and my heart raced in tandem with my thoughts as I wondered what this woman wanted with me.

"I must insist, My Lady. We also discussed compensation for silence in this matter."

My guts turned to water as his words sank in. What in the name of God did he mean?

"And you will be compensated," the lady said, a dangerous edge creeping into her voice as she turned in his direction. "Though what value would you put on a life when that soul spends their days toiling for naught but a cup of gruel and a place to lay their head? I'm sure she's repaid her debt to the state ten times over. See my man in the courtyard. He has your purse."

With a curt bow, the master backed out the door, and I didn't blame him. I wanted to follow. There was a charge in the air, the kind of shift that warned of a coming, violent storm. But there was nowhere for me to go. Nowhere to take cover.

Not as the lady turned her attention back to me. Not as those dark eyes gleamed as bright and dark as a selkie's.

I swallowed, forcing a lump down my throat.

"Margaret, is it?" she asked, and I found I could do naught but nod. "Do you prefer that name? Or do you go by another?"

"M-Maggie." Wincing, I cleared my throat to steady my nerve. "Maggie, that is, Your Ladyship."

"Maggie," she repeated, nodding. "Very well. Tell me, Maggie. What is it you desire most in the world? If the wrath of God, and the British Crown, weren't determined to wipe this country and her people off the map, what is it you would want?"

Danger settled hard and heavy in my stomach, filling my heart with dread even as I opened my mouth. As if I had no control of myself. "A house. A few acres. Land in my own right that could never be taken, and food enough to never know hunger again."

"And?" she urged, leaning forward, the scent of her perfume overwhelming my senses as the truth slipped, unbidden, from my lips.

"Revenge."

She smiled, a wide grin that brightened the room.

"Good. Excellent. Well then, Maggie. I have a proposition for you."

Chapter 2

There is such a tendency to exaggeration and inaccuracy
in Irish reports that delay in acting on them is always
desirable.
—Sir Robert Peele, prime minister of the United
Kingdom, 1845

"Please. Take a seat."

I pursed my lips, following the sweep of her ladyship's hand
as she pointed toward the master's chair. Was she jesting? "I-
I'm fine here, Your Ladyship. Standing, that is."

"Ah." With a curl of her lips, her ladyship clasped the curved
silver handle of her cane with both hands and rapped it on the
floor before her. "You prefer to speak as equals. Eye to eye. I
like that, Maggie. It shows character. Though, do know I was
merely concerned for your health."

She pivoted, her dark gaze affixed on the portrait that stood
witness above the master's chair.

"I don't envy him. Inherited quite the calamity from Peele,"
said her ladyship, taking one step, then another toward the
master's desk, dragging the cane as well as any dandy who took
luncheon with Colonel Moore-Vandeleur. It was enough to remind me of another cane. Another dandy. Another time. I
shuddered.

"Lord John Russell, prime minister of the United Kingdom

of Great Britain and Ireland. Tried his best, poor chap, but bungled everything, if you ask me." She gestured toward the portrait, paused, then turned to face me. My heart leapt in my chest as she perched on the edge of the desk, and I stood that little bit straighter. "I won't keep you in suspense any longer. First, the terms. You said you wanted land, a place you can call your own. I can provide that. I have a need that requires what I hope will be your full cooperation. In exchange, when your task is complete, I will gift you a cottage with five acres on my land."

Five? I pursed my lips. There wasn't a landlord in Ireland with five spare acres to rent, never mind give away. Every inch was accounted for. We toiled the land for the landlord, who sold every ounce of our labor to the markets in England. Even now, they were sending food across the sea while we died in ditches. In exchange, most got a quarter acre. Barely enough space for a one-roomed home and a patch of potatoes. "Did you say five acres?"

Her ladyship nodded slowly. "I will be frank. The land isn't disposed to cultivation, save the blaggarding potato. But sheep should thrive."

"I don't understand." With a shake of my head, I took a step forward, then thought better of it and rocked back onto my bare heels.

"You don't have to. Just know it's yours if you agree to our arrangement."

This smelled of the Devil himself, come to deal with the soulless wretches who yearned for anything but existence. I was one such soulless wretch. My crime was proof of that.

"Lady—" I stopped. I didn't even know her name. She smiled.

"Browne. Or, Lady Catherine. Whichever you prefer."

I nodded. "Lady Catherine. You'll forgive my asking, but how can I be sure you'll keep to these terms?"

"Ah! You *are* a clever one. Good, good!" Reaching into the

dark depths of her coat, she produced a folded sheaf of papers. "I have it all here in this contract. I can, of course, read it to you."

There'd be no need for that. My eyes slid from the contract to meet her steely gaze. "What must I do in exchange?"

Placing the document on the desk, Lady Catherine stood. "I need a girl to pose as my daughter, Wilhelmina. I have six months before a bevy of lawyers arrive at my home to prove that she is, in fact, dead. Our goal is to convince them she is *not*. In that time, I expect you to learn how to hold a conversation with these learned men, and how to comport yourself as Wilhelmina in society. Her husband, the Earl of Norbury, passed last year, and his family have heard rumor of her own passing. If they can prove it, Wilhelmina's inheritance will revert to the old earl's great-niece, and I will be left destitute while her money-grasping husband milks the situation to fill his own coffers. I've put it about that Wilhelmina is sick with her grief, but I've stretched her mourning period as far as decorum allows. This is, of course, no great matter to you. However, there are four hundred souls under my care. Good people. And though I am no great landowner, I will not see them suffer if I can help it. We're the same, you and I. Born and bred and sick of the suffering."

A chill wended its way under my smock, and my father's words echoed in my mind: *An Anglo would sell his soul to own the flea-bitten shirt off an Irishman's back. And any aristocrat in Ireland is not only Anglo, but well and truly British.*

"Think of it, Maggie," her ladyship continued. "A simple task in exchange for your own freedom. The opportunity to pull the wool over the eyes of the very people who refuse to do anything but dig mass graves and export Irish-grown food to feed their own people."

Nothing about this arrangement felt right. I was no idiot . . . but I needed to sit before I fell from lack of blood. It drained from my face all the way to my toes with each word she spoke, until I shivered where I stood. I took a step, and another, being sure to keep distance between us as I circled the master's desk. She followed my movements, her dark gaze locked on mine as I carefully placed a hand on the chair and lowered myself into its forbidden depths. I couldn't speak. Couldn't ask permission to sit. Could do naught but tear my eyes from hers and glance at the contract that lay within arm's reach.

It couldn't have been for nothing. All this, everything that had happened—it wasn't enough to be alive, to survive. It had to be for something. For it was all my fault. Everything.

From my father's wan face as we were turned out of our home, to his silent tears as we laid eyes on the hundreds of bodies crawling over each other outside the Kilrush workhouse. To the scalp my father and neighbors had dug—a hole in the ground large enough for the twelve of us to huddle within, with naught but branches to keep out the rain—certain Colonel Moore-Vandeleur would recant, would forgive, would invite his prized land agent back to work. We had to stay near. Stay close, lest he came looking. Until baby Crofton died in my mother's arms, and her with no energy to weep. And by the time Father realized we had to try and make it to Ennis, we were too weak to travel but a little every day.

That's when the dogs came baying. And it was all my fault.

"You appear piqued," said her ladyship, but I still stared at the contract. Breathing in, then out. Gathering my thoughts. A home, independent of a master, of relying on the whim of another. A place I could call my own. A place where my family could live in memory. A tangible thing to atone for my sins, where I could finally put them to rest, where they could finally *be* at rest.

"I have . . . I have questions," I said softly, closing my eyes against the sting of tears.

"I'm sure you do." And with a rustle of taffeta, Lady Catherine strode toward the door. "I'll call for tea and answer any concerns you may have."

What of Wilhelmina's friends? Wouldn't they know I was not her? What if we were caught, what would happen to me? What of this land—would it truly be mine, or would I still have to pay rent, either to her or a middleman?

I grilled her, and her ladyship had a ready answer for everything.

Wilhelmina had been brought up in France and had no acquaintances in Ireland. As a result, she was more French than Irish, and the gamble had paid off when Wilhelmina married the earl. The ceremony was a private, family affair—as the earl was ailing—and the only other witness besides Lady Catherine had been the earl's old friend, Lord Croyden, also deceased.

Lady Catherine abhorred high society and made it her business to rarely appear, so few of her circle would have met Wilhelmina as an adult.

If we were caught, Lady Catherine had the means to get me away safely, and she alone would bear the legal brunt. However, if the law discovered the deception, it would mean no land for me.

If all went well, the land would be mine, without rent or middleman—with one condition. If I ever felt the need to sell it off, I needed to sell it back to Lady Catherine.

"That's it?" I asked.

Lady Catherine had dragged a chair from the back of the office so she might sit opposite me. It was strange, sitting in the master's chair, a contract clutched in my hands as if I were the master and she the wretch.

"That's it," she said with a nod. "If you'd like, we can go through the contract point by point until you're satisfied."

"No need," I murmured. I'd already scanned the words as she answered my questions. Everything was written in simple language. It was straightforward and followed everything she had said. "And this will stand in a court of law?"

"It will."

I turned over the page and squinted. "Whose signatures are these? Ah . . . never mind, My Lady. Their titles are here."

Esquires. Solicitors. The document had been notarized. It was sound.

"You surprise me, Maggie."

I glanced up from the contract to find her brows arched to her hairline. God's blood! I flushed. "Where did a tenant's daughter learn to read?"

"Land agent," I corrected, smoothing the contract over the desk. "My father was a land agent, My Lady."

"And . . . you were turned out?"

Her face paled in tandem with my own rising shame. I took a deep breath. "Yes, My Lady. My eldest brother and I were lucky enough to work in the Big House until that . . . happened. Her ladyship educated me in English speech and letters, as I had an aptitude for it."

Silence fell, a thick void of unanswered questions I imagined she wanted to ask. Why would a landlord turn out a land agent? Why would a lady of the house take it upon herself to teach a servant to read? For a moment, I thought all my distrust and delay would end in Lady Catherine calling for the master to find another girl. A different wretch to save—one who didn't belong to a turned-out land agent, for he must have been disgraced in some way to have lost his livelihood. I'd said too much. Revealed more than necessary.

The master's fountain pen lay discarded on the smooth, dark wooden top of the desk, and I reached for it, chest constricting.

As my fingers grasped the cool metal barrel of the pen, Lady Catherine whipped out her hand and covered mine with hers. I froze, my heart hammering faster than that of a hare in flight.

"Look at me, Maggie," she said, her voice barely a whisper.

But I couldn't. This was it. After offering the world on a platter, she was about to take it all away.

"Look at me," she insisted, a dangerous edge creeping into her voice that compelled the servant in me to scrape my eyes from the pen. To draw them upward. To meet her gaze. "They take, and take, and treat us like dogs. But they'll never win if you can shut them out of here."

With her free hand, she slapped a palm over her heart.

But she *was* them. Didn't she understand that it mattered not where she lived or died? She was Anglo-Irish—an Irish-born British aristocrat and well-to-do. Certified so by her title. Forgiven her birth by the queen herself.

And we were naught but animals to them. Working livestock that needed to breed bodies in order to keep the breadbasket of the British Empire in working order.

"Are you amenable to the terms laid out before you?" she asked, patting my hand before pulling away.

My chest caved inward, and I released a breath on a gust that threatened to blow the contract from the table. If this woman wanted to believe we were the same, if she thought overlooking my family's disgrace was a gesture of solidarity, then I certainly wouldn't stop her.

I quickly twisted the cap from the pen, dipped it in the inkpot, and scratched my signature along the line.

"Yes, My Lady," I answered, replacing the cap as my stomach flipped over. For better or worse, I would become Wilhelmina for this woman. And when the deed was done, I would earn my freedom.

Chapter 3

On the roadside there were the humble traces of two or
three cabins, whose little hearths had been extinguished,
and whose walls were levelled to the earth. The black fungus, the burdock, the nettle, and all those offensive weeds
that follow in the train of oppression and ruin were here . . .
I could not help asking myself, if those who do these
things ever think that there is a reckoning in after life,
where power, insolence and wealth misapplied . . . will be
placed face to face with those humble beings, on whose
rights and privileges of simple existence they have tram-
pled with such a selfish and exterminating tread.
—William Carleton, *The Black Prophet*

My heart still thundered as we stepped onto the cobbled courtyard, the sun, obscured in swaths of heavy dark clouds, hanging so full and low one could almost touch their wisp-like
webs. Mist spat from their depths, the kind that kissed the skin
and whispered against fabric afore night brought the bad lung.
My sister, Síofra, had suffered on days like these, and Mam always kept her indoors, a-stirring the food over the fire to keep
the priest from our door.

The workhouse stood large and silent behind, and I dared not
look back for fear the souls of those who went in, only to never
leave, would reach as one through the huge wooden doors and

yank me back. My chest constricted as my palms went slick. May God rest them and keep them. *Blessed are those who hunger and thirst for righteousness, for they shall be satisfied.* Taking a deep breath, I closed my eyes.

I did not know these people and could spare them no more than a parting prayer, for freedom ebbed on the breeze. *My* freedom.

"I've instructed your man to use the back gate, Your Ladyship. We've cleared it of vagrants so you may leave unmolested."

The master bowed as Lady Catherine adjusted her gloves, a single brow arched as she glanced over her shoulder. "Vagrants, Maggie. Aren't we so very lucky to not have to run them over in my carriage? Why, Mr. O'Brien, how very thoughtful of you to clear our path of the good and honest subjects of her majesty the queen, whose crime is naught but being Irish. May you never know a day's hardship, sir."

The hair at my nape stood to attention as I glanced between the master and Lady Catherine. If she expected a nod of agreement from me, she wouldn't find it. Not until we were clear of this place. Instead, I fiddled with my burlap sack and focused on the carriage.

There was naught much special about it, though mayhap wider and taller than most I'd seen. But the horses . . . they were a sight to behold. Six of the finest beasts I'd ever laid eyes on. Black as tar, and identical—crimped manes cascading over glistening withers, their fetlocks adorned with blue-black curls.

"Your Ladyship, we do our best with what we're given, I assure you," the master protested.

"I'm sure you do, Mr. O'Brien. Cormac? Can you help our guest?" she called, before turning to me. "Go on, get settled, and we can be on our way."

I nodded, clutching the burlap sack to my chest, unwilling to relinquish it to the man who emerged from the opposite side of the carriage. My brow rose. Odd. He didn't wear livery of any kind. Only what a farmer might—a swallowtail coat over a plain linen shirt, woolen knee-breeches, well-darned knee socks, sturdy shoes, and an old, misshapen felt hat atop his head. Though travel-worn, he appeared clean enough, without a hint of shadow on his face.

"Miss," he said, his voice a gentle lull as Lady Catherine continued her conversation with the master, "this way now."

Puffing my cheeks, I strode forward, one foot in front of the other. The man—Cormac—opened the carriage door and pulled down the steps as I approached, pulse racing. Freedom. The carriage meant freedom.

"It's a ways, Miss, so there are extra cushions for your use," he said, offering his hand, as if I were a somebody. As if I didn't wear a filthy smock that reeked of damp and death. The gesture stilled me to the bone, and I dared glance at him. My eyes met his—a strange hue that reminded me of Colonel Moore-Vandeleur's prized whiskey, but viewed through crystal. Amber, perhaps, and . . . familiar, somehow. Not yet thirty, I surmised. The sharp peaks of his cheekbones sloped into deep hollows below before curving outward to form a fine strong jaw. Old Maggie might have admired him, for he was handsome. But New Maggie knew better. Handsome faces tended to spew pretty lies, especially when those lies fueled interest and desire.

"Thank you, Mister . . . ?"

His cheeks pinked. "Cormac will do, Miss. There's a flask waiting for you within." Nodding into the carriage, Cormac glanced at his extended hand. "'Tis a drop of vegetable stew. I wasn't sure what ye might be needing."

My stomach turned over from want. I couldn't remember the last time I'd tasted stew. Maybe the summer before the first blight. God, when was that? 1846? No. 1845.

Right. I grasped his hand, and my cool, skeletal fingers were at once swallowed by his warm, sturdy grasp. There was strength in it. The kind that came from good health. I pressed my lips together. The famine hadn't touched Cormac.

"You may call me Maggie," I offered, stepping up and into the plush velvet interior.

"Nay, you'll be 'miss' while in earshot," he said, stepping up after me.

My eyes widened, and I glanced out at Lady Catherine as Cormac squatted next to my bench.

"Blankets, here." Opening a door in the floor, he pulled out two heavy velvet blankets, followed by a cylindrical container. "You might want one over your shoulders. The cushions are there. And here." He handed over the cylinder. "It's likely cold, but I figured you wouldn't mind one bit."

He smiled then, and a dimple appeared in each cheek. It was so . . . carefree. So foreign and strange that I couldn't bring myself to return the gesture.

"Thank you. Yes. I'm sure it's perfect," I said.

He nodded, then pulled a matchbook from his pocket and pointed toward an ornate metallic orb that hung from the roof, tucked against the window. "I hope ye don't mind a bit of incense. Her ladyship is most fond of it."

"Not at all," I replied.

Without another word, Cormac lit the incense, stepped out of the carriage, and waited for Lady Catherine to take her leave of the master.

While I stared at the cylinder clutched between my hands, afeared to open it, lest it be the last drop of food I'd ever eat.

At some point, I fell asleep.

Lady Catherine was happy enough to let me sip at the stew and stare out the window as the town of Ennis fell away. But the lull of the horses' clip, coupled with the rocking of the carriage, soon helped me drift.

Perhaps Cormac's fine features—or the taste of a proper

meal—prompted it, but I dreamt of *him*. Of Teddy. Of his sandy blond hair and eyes bluer than a summer sky. Of promises made. Of stolen kisses behind the summerhouse. It was always the same dream.

He brings a picnic and hand-feeds me bread, and cheese, and fruits I'd never known existed. But soon the loving gesture turns dark, and he keeps feeding and feeding until my eyes bulge with terror, and I can't breathe for want of swallowing. That's when he transforms into the Black Hound of lore and rips my spine out through my throat.

I woke with a start, my smock soaked through with fear-tinged sweat as my pulse flared. Gasping for breath, it took me a moment to realize where I was. My eyes darted.

Gray velvet benches and walls. Windows. Lady Catherine.

Her gentleman's top hat lay discarded on the bench betwixt her sleeping form and the wide world beyond the carriage walls. It seemed the sandman had taken my strange benefactress into his cool embrace, and I wished her better dreams than those granted to me.

Breathing deep, I closed my eyes. Of all the spirits haunting my past, Theodore "Teddy" Moore-Vandeleur was the one I wished to be rid of most. I hadn't dreamt of him in a while, but whenever I did, 'twas as if Teddy extended a hand through the miles between us, reaching into my mind to be sure I'd never forget everything he was. Everything we could have been.

The carriage lurched, bouncing as the wheels caught a divot in the road. I yelped, and Lady Catherine's eyes snapped open.

"Jesus wept," she muttered, snatching her cane from the carriage floor. In one fluid motion, she rapped on the roof before opening the window. "Cormac? What the Devil was that? I damn near flew off my perch!"

"Pothole, Your Ladyship," Cormac yelled, his voice almost lost to the roar of wind.

"Where are we?" she called.

I glanced out the window and furrowed my brow. Where were we, indeed? I could curse myself for a fool that I'd never even asked where we were going. But I supposed it didn't much matter so long as 'twas far from the workhouse.

As time lapsed, the scenery had shifted from a smooth patchwork of quilted green fields to one warped by high rolling hills. Houses dotted the landscape. Well, structures that were once houses. Even from the carriage, I noted the tumbled walls and the charred, roofless carcasses of what had once been some family's pride and joy. In the distance, I spied black smoke, the kind resulting from flame-charred thatch. A family freshly turned out by their landlord, most likely. If they were lucky, they could return beneath the cover of darkness and salvage a night or two more afore the constabulary found them and tossed them into the road. We'd done the same, taking refuge in our scalpeen—the shell of our home—before Da dug a scalp for us, in the mud, when the bailiffs came to tumble the walls of our house.

"Coming up on Ennistymon!" Cormac responded.

"A few hours yet." Sighing, her ladyship closed the window and settled back on her bench. "Hungry, Maggie?"

Tearing my eyes from the landscape, I glanced at her. "Oh, no thank you, My Lady. I saved some stew for later."

She nodded. "Once we're past Ennistymon, we've a long uphill climb. If you can sleep, you should, lest the boredom does us in."

"Yes, My Lady." I hadn't a fiddler's notion where Ennistymon was. "Where . . . that is, where are we going?"

"Ah." With a smile, Lady Catherine looked out the window. "Home, my dear. Gortacarnaun. Have you heard of it?"

"No, My Lady."

"A lonely spot, for sure, but a beautiful one." Reaching into her pocket, Lady Catherine smiled, revealing fine crow's-feet in the corners of her eyes. She pulled out a box and opened it.

Inside was a pipe made of gleaming black metal affixed with an ivory bit. "When my husband asked for my hand, I agreed, but on one condition—that we remain in Browne House for the rest of our days. I didn't want to be one of those landlords managing things from London. Old Charlie even gave up his seat in the House of Lords. Wait until you see the Burren, Maggie. You'll never wish to leave."

I straightened as Lady Catherine packed the pipe and struck a match into the chamber. I'd heard stories of the Burren from wandering seanchaithe, who came to Kilrush to pass on the old tales. They told of the Other Crowd—Daoine Uaisle from the Other Realm—who called it home. They'd said the land was desolate, made only for goats and spirits who liked to wander the limestone countryside. That it was nestled between mountains of loose shale and the gateway to Tír na nÓg—where the ancient Old Gods of our ancestors dwelled—the Atlantic Ocean. "The Burren? Then, we're still in Clare?"

"Oh, yes," she mumbled between kindling puffs. "I was born and raised here, and wouldn't leave. So Charlie agreed to stay."

"Does his lordship not think all this business odd? Bringing a stranger into your home?" I asked, savoring the heady scent of tobacco, and I was suddenly transported to happier times. Father used to smoke a pipe.

"If Charlie still lived, none of this would be necessary." Lady Catherine pursed her lips around the pipe bit and took a thoughtful drag. "I had a widow's pension from his eldest brother, the marquess. But the penny-pinching amadán only agreed to pay until Wilhelmina wed. After that, I was to rely on my own daughter's charity and the goodwill of her husband. The rest you know."

I shifted on the bench, unsure what to say. "Sorry for your loss" held no meaning for me anymore. "Do you miss him? His lordship?"

Lady Catherine shrugged and leaned over to crack the window. "We were happy, if that's what you mean. For a time, at least."

I understood that well enough. The carriage jolted, and I was thrown from the bench to the carriage floor.

"What in the . . . ?" Lady Catherine coughed, pipe smoke caught in her throat, as the carriage slowed to a near halt. She grabbed her cane and rapped on the roof as I tried to right myself. "Are you all right, my dear?"

"Y-yes."

With a scowl that spelled Cormac's doom, Lady Catherine flung open the window. "Cormac O'Dea! What is the meaning of this?"

The horses' whinnies pierced the air, and I felt the moment the wheels ceased turning. Within a breath, Cormac himself appeared at the window.

"I'm that sorry, Your Ladyship," he said, that soft, gentle voice now laced with urgency. I scowled. "But there's a bit of a to-do up ahead."

"A to-do? I'll give you a to-do if you don't explain yourself this instant." Lady Catherine's hand was already twisting the door handle.

"Are you all right, miss?" Cormac asked as I smoothed the velvet blanket over my knees.

Nodding, I watched as Lady Catherine opened the door and hopped down without waiting for Cormac to draw down the steps.

"There, m'Lady," he said, pointing in the direction we were traveling.

"Lord have mercy . . ." Lady Catherine trailed off, all color draining from her cheeks.

I frowned and slid from the bench to pop my head out the door. In the distance, a tall spire promised a town ahead. But in the fore, a dark mass of people blocked the road. They were . . . walking. Toward the town, perhaps.

No, walking was wrong. I'd seen this march before. The slow

forward shuffle of those barely able to move. Of those who should already be dead. Of those determined to persevere—if not for their sakes, then the sake of the child they carried or the one they couldn't leave behind.

I balled my fists as I watched them, my eyes falling on a figure sitting by the side of the road, wailing as she cradled the stiffening corpse of a child not three summers old. Even from here, I noted the bloated stomach and stick-like limbs of a child gone too long without food. I wanted to scream my throat raw, to beat my chest, to cry the tears I couldn't when it was I on that march.

There were hundreds of them, most naked, without a stitch to keep them from the wind and rain, their clothes long since sold to pay for lifesaving grain. But the famine lingered still, and we had naught left to sell. And no aid to be found. All we could do was watch cartloads of food drive by, guarded by the constabulary, bound for England. Our food, our labors, to be sent to market across the sea. Oh yes, England took care of their own. That much was certain.

"Is there nothing to be done?" Lady Catherine whispered, her gaze affixed on the same grieving mother I'd spied. As we watched, the woman lovingly lay the corpse on the ground, her wails turning to shallow gulps of air, and wrapped her own naked body around the child. She would be the child's shield in death, as she was in life. I pressed my lips together. That ditch at the side of the road would become their grave, unmarked forever. With no one to remember that they had lived. Just two more bodies for the dogs to gnaw.

"Not unless you have a mind to invite them all into your home, My Lady," I spat, aware of the tremor in my voice. My eyes narrowed, and I glanced from Lady Catherine to Cormac. "I take it Ennistymon boasts a workhouse?"

"It does." Cormac's throat bobbed as he spoke.

"Then we should find a way around the town." Without another word, I ducked back into the carriage and rearranged the blanket, yet again.

"Good God," Lady Catherine murmured, bracing against Cormac's hand as she hopped back into the carriage.

"God is gone, My Lady." With the kind of snort my mother would've backhanded me for, I looked Lady Catherine dead in the eye. "He died of the starvation Himself, and there's none now left to save us."

Except, perhaps, ourselves.

Chapter 4

It is a country where there is not enough water to drown
a man, wood enough to hang one, nor earth enough to
bury him.
—Description of the Burren by Oliver Cromwell's
second-in-command in Ireland, Edmund Ludlow
(died 1692)

Sometime in the last two hours, the landscape had shifted from
excellent farming country to a barren gray. Patches of grass appeared here and there, but the fields were all rock and shale,
with strange boulders precariously perched on narrow peaks—
how they didn't fall and roll was beyond me. The land was
good for livestock, Lady Catherine had said. But by God, the
seanchaithe had been right. This land was fit for naught but surefooted goats.

Brows furrowed, I shifted on the bench.

I'd learned why Cormac had offered extra cushions. With
naught but bone to chafe against skin, I'd begun to feel the ache
of every mile long before the sun went down.

It was full dark now and had been for some time, but the
moon shone full and bright against a backdrop of obsidian
pitch, the stars a smattering of glittering white as chaotic and
beautiful as a brush-spattered painting. Silhouetted against the
moon, wind-bent trees grew short and narrow, their branches
forced to grow backward as if reaching away from the strong
gusts that battered the coast. This was the Burren.

For miles, we traveled without sight of a candle or fire, despite passing plenty of houses along the way, doors flung open. Abandoned. Everything was silent. Still. As if we were completely alone in the world, a carriage without purpose, a dark stain against a gray landscape, intruders rattling in the night.

Lady Catherine was asleep once more, but I hadn't been able to settle since meeting the march outside Ennistymon.

I scowled. Surely I should've felt something beyond fear the wraiths might slow the journey. God above, if Da could see me now, he'd say I was well and truly lost. Had he not fought every day to keep moving? Had he not done his best to stay alive so we might have the fortitude to go on? But none of that strength was forgotten. That's why I sat in this carriage, because to live was to win. This was my rebellion, and my promise to my brother, Michael. I would survive.

Compassion and guilt could come later, when those who survived rebuilt the country. When we came back from the brink of extinction one more time. Oh yes. Father had often told tales of old Cromwell, God rot him.

I stared out the window. Even the walls dividing acreage were different here. At home, rounded rocks fitted together like puzzle pieces, with grass and vines growing within and without each crevice until the walls burst with life. Here, long jagged slabs interlocked horizontally and vertically, an intimidating portcullis sprouting from the ground.

A low-lying fog crept from the shore, its tendrils curling around each hoof as the horses hauled us onward. To our left, the land fell away, sloping downward toward the crashing waves of an angry sea. And in the distance to our right, great shadowed mountains warned that the world I once knew was now far behind. Let the past stay there, then. I had work to do.

I placed my temple against the cool window and looked as far ahead as I could manage. How could a place so barren hold any sliver of maybe? A place where only the forgotten would wander in hopes of being found. But I didn't want to be found. Because, I supposed, part of me didn't believe I deserved to be.

Squinting into the night, I straightened. A dim glow in the near distance spelled people, and sure enough, a dark shape appeared. An occupied house, for sure. At last, signs of life. Light spilled through the cracks of the door and shutters, promising the heat of a roaring fire within, and as we passed it, my heart skipped a beat. People. Family. Life. We passed another, and another, then rolled into what must have been the center of a village. A modest spire reached toward the stars, and the road opened into a market area.

We continued uphill. More houses. As we turned a corner, the waist-high rock walls gave way to the kind of imposing stonework I recognized. These were the walls of an estate, cut stone with mortar, built so high none could see over the top. It was the same kind of wall that surrounded Kilrush House, the Moore-Vandeleur's estate.

This must be Browne House.

"My Lady?" I called, but Lady Catherine didn't stir.

Cormac turned the carriage to the right—the walls curved inward—and slowed the team to a trot as we drove beneath a stone archway. There was no gate. I frowned. Odd, that.

We rumbled up a short drive, a few lone trees standing sentry amid wild lawns. No team of gardeners then. This was a far cry from the manicured field of green that carpeted the Moore-Vandeleur's drive.

But all thought of the sprawling style of the Moore-Vandeleur estate fell away as I caught my first glimpse of Browne House. It was a strange monstrosity—five stories high and narrow from the front, with long-fingered vines of ivy slowly strangling its façade, brick by brick.

It seemed alive somehow, its semicircular windows on the top floor serving as brows above large, rectangular eyes. A wide stone staircase swept from ground to entrance—a tongue rolled out in welcome to the hungry, double-doored maw on the first floor. Ready. Waiting to devour me whole.

Dread coiled deep in my gut as the carriage rolled to a jolting halt, and with the final rock of wheels fully spent, Lady Catherine's eyes opened.

"Home at last," she murmured, stifling a yawn with one hand as she reached for her top hat with the other. "Are you hungry? The house is surely asleep, but we could manage bread and cheese."

Hungry? Wasn't I always hungry? But not now. Not as I faced the reality of what I'd done—abandoned the memory of what had passed for an unwritten future that could well destroy me. It would've been more honorable to die as the others had. At least I'd been there to hold their hands at the last, but who was left to hold mine? I shook my head. Whatever lay ahead was atonement for the unholy bargain struck on the backs of those gone forever to ensure my survival.

My gaze slowly shifted from the house beyond the window to Lady Catherine's sleep-hazed eyes and lifted my chin.

"Thank you, My Lady. But I think I'd prefer to rest."

"And rest you shall." Lady Catherine smiled. "Cormac can show you to your room, and we can reconvene when you rise."

The unknown might terrify me. But I'd faced it before . . . and there were worse things than death.

Chapter 5

Out of the unreal shadows of the night comes back the real life . . . a world in which things would have fresh shapes and colours, and be changed, or have other secrets, a world in which the past would have little or no place, or survive, at any rate, in no conscious form of obligation or regret, the remembrance even of joy having its bitterness and the memories of pleasure their pain.
—Oscar Wilde, *The Picture of Dorian Gray*

The summerhouse was always in bloom—ferns and orchids, amid rare lotus flowers acquired from overseas. And it was there, beneath the glass-roofed heat, that my love would promise the world.

"I'll always find a way to be with you, my Maggie."

"And I, you." My Teddy. My heart.

"Eat, love," he said, smiling, offering a quivering sliver of something, perfectly cooked, speared with a golden fork. "To strengthen you."

My lips parted, and as the juicy tang of fresh-charred meat touched my tongue, I knew.

'Twas the flesh of my brother, Michael.

I woke with a jolt, gasping with terror as the watery light of dawn spilled over my face, forcing the sleep from my eyes. God blast it! Teddy again. I clutched a fist against my chest to still my heart. With a scowl, I settled back into the pillow, and froze. Pillow? There was nary a pillow to be found at the work-house. My pulse ignited, and I bolted upright, heart hammering in the hollow of my throat. Where in the blazes?

Eyes wild, I glanced at my surroundings, and the events of the day before flooded back in a rush of bone-weary accep-tance. Browne House. Lady Catherine. God above in Heaven and all the saints.

The footman . . . Cormac. Yes. He'd ushered me up a back stair the night before, by the glow of a sad candle pilfered from the vast kitchen, and I'd promptly fallen into bed. A damn sight better than any bed I'd ever been lucky to call mine. I glanced down. It was so large it could sleep my entire family head-to-toe. Running my hands over the plush, pink duvet, my fingers tingled at the feather-like touch of . . . was that satin? My eyes widened. Surely it was. I'd helped Lady Grace dress often enough to remember the feel of it.

I glanced up, and textured pink wallpaper winked back at me. There was something old about the room. As if the wallpaper—now pastel—was once vibrant, hints of former brightness dark-ening grooves around dull yellow birds frozen mid-flight along the walls. My back ached as I shifted—twenty hours in a car-riage would certainly cause an ache—turning to take everything in. My brow furrowed. It was a child's room. A dollhouse stood in one corner. In the other, a rocking contraption styled like a horse. Floor-to-ceiling shelves filled with shiny, gargoyle-ish dolls bedecked in styles I'd never laid eyes on before. A girl's room.

To my right, atop a nightstand, a fresh bouquet of snow-drops had been placed in a glass vase, their drooping blooms a weight of snow threatening to slide from their stems. And next to the vase, an ornate incense burner sat, freshly used as if lit the night before.

I frowned. I didn't remember Cormac lighting any incense,

but a deep inhale drew notes of jasmine, and . . . perhaps lemon? The same scent that had permeated the carriage the day before.

A shiver wound its way up my spine as my ears caught the faint hint of a laugh drifting from my right, beyond the vase, and I snatched the duvet close to my chest before whipping around. Whatever blood flowed through my body rushed to my toes, leaving me cold and breathless as my eyes searched for its source, but all I found was a large window, the bench below the sill as empty as the rest of the room. Breathe. It wasn't like me to fall victim to bouts of fancy.

The frame of the window was old, dark-stained, and cracked, but as my eyes wandered, I squinted. There was something there. In the center of the frame, above the window.

Pulling the duvet tight around my shoulders, I slipped out of bed and padded toward it. An etching? My brows furrowed as I stared. Three perfect spirals originating from a singular source—one pointing skyward, one to the east, one to the west. It felt familiar somehow, but also not at all. And as I stared, an icy draft filtered through the cracks in the window, chilling me to the bone as I slowly reached out to touch the carving.

"Saints!" a voice exclaimed.

I yelped, yanking my hand back into the confines of the duvet as I whirled on my bare heel. I hadn't heard the door opening.

"Step away from that drafty window at once!" A woman. A woman wearing the black dress of a housekeeper, hair braided and twisted into two loops that framed a stern face awash with horror. I swallowed. "Blessed Mother, would ye look at yerself, a-dirtying her ladyship's duvet. Step away, I said. Ye'll catch yer death of cold."

Christ Almighty. What if it had all been a dream? What if I'd gone sleepwalking and wound up in some grand house? It would be the barracks for me, and no way back to the workhouse. My eyes widened.

"What was that eejit Cormac thinking? Not waking us to scouse ye of whatever flea-bitten diseases ye carry from that awful place ye came from? We could be dead in our beds afore the Lord's Day, and ye bringing plague into the house." With a final grunt, the woman placed a bucket and floor scrubber upon the slate hearth of the fireplace. "Come in, Beth, and light the fire afore the girl perish. And then burn the sheets and anything she's touched."

A younger woman—younger than I—entered the room then, her eyes glued to the floor as she quickly did the housekeeper's bidding. Another black dress, this one adorned with the white apron of a serving girl. But in the heartbeat it took to glance at the girl, the housekeeper was on the march. Toward me. I straightened my spine.

Scritch. Scritch. Scritch. The girl struck a flint over and over— no precious matchbook for the serving staff—waiting for a spark to catch hold of the kindling. I knew that fear—of performing duties with my overseer present. As frightening as Lady Grace used to be, the head housekeeper struck terror into the heart. And this housekeeper was bound to be no different. *Scritch. Scritch. Scritch.* My jaw tightened with each strike, until at last, a familiar fizzle echoed through the room, and relief flooded through my tightening muscles. I glanced at the girl and spied the ghost of a smile as she snatched the bellows from their hook, triumphant.

"Ye'll be wanting food, I'm sure," said the housekeeper, lips pursing as she yanked the duvet from my shoulders. The wheeze of bellows met my ears, breathing life into the juvenile embers that sparked in the fireplace. The housekeeper froze, eyes affixed on my filthy gray chemise. Or rather, affixed on the outline beneath. A flush stormed from my chest to cheeks, and I thought how nice it must be. To not go without. To not know what was happening beyond these walls. To not fear the reaper from one hour to the next. Crossing my arms across my chest, I glared at the housekeeper.

"Jesus wept," she breathed. "Yer naught but a corpse."

"Aye." My jaw clenched.

She stood frozen a moment more, then her gaze shifted to my face, my hair. "Her ladyship must see something of Wilhelmina in ye, but I'm stretched to find any resemblance, girl. Sure, all we can do is feed ye up for now. Ye can call me Aggie."

"I'm—" I began, but Aggie held up a hand.

"Yer Lady Wilhelmina," she said, each word clipped and weighted with the death knell of my former life. "Whoever ye were, it matters not a whit. There's work to be done. Good work, mind, that will save hundreds of lives. Beth?"

I bit my lower lip as the girl, Beth, hopped to her feet.

"Have the bath brought," Aggie ordered, glancing over her shoulder. "But ring for it, mind. We'll both need a scrub and new clothes when we're done here. Don't want to spread Lady Wilhelmina's miasma through the house."

Lady Wilhelmina. For I was Maggie no more.

"Leave yer garment in that bucket." Nose crinkled above a disgusted frown, Aggie pointed at the iron bucket that Beth had brought when three other maids had shuffled in with the bath. Steam rose from the water. It had been so long since I'd washed, never mind washed in hot water, that I had no qualms stripping before this stranger.

Pulling the filthy chemise over my head, I tossed it in the bucket as Aggie undid the bun at the top of my head. I should've warned her the minute I saw her reach for the brush, but it took naught but one sweep through my lifeless, stringy hair for her to realize her mistake.

"Saints above," she muttered, eyes wide as a clump of hair came away in the bristles. "What in the . . . ?"

"'Tis from the hunger," I offered, as she stared at the strands.

I'd long since abandoned my vanity. Doomed it to a time before.

Aggie shook herself and set down the brush. "'Tis a wonder ye've anything left atop yer head. I was going to comb ye for lice, but there's likely naught for them to take hold on. Here. Let me check for fleas."

With a heavy sigh, I lifted my arms and stood still. This routine was as familiar to me as my own mother's embrace, a weekly ritual at the workhouse. With warm hands, Aggie turned me slowly, inspecting my skin for bites. Lady Catherine had plucked me a day past lousing, so I doubted Aggie'd find hide nor hair of a telltale welt.

Facing me now, Aggie straightened, eyes drifting to my abdomen. Her brows drew together as she stared, and I closed my eyes.

They were still there, the stretch marks. The only sign I'd once dreamt of a bright future, one filled with love and laughter with a good man at my side, and a child at my hip. Pah! How wrong I'd been about everything. Teddy had never intended to marry me. Not that it mattered, for our babe was born cold. I opened my eyes. I was glad of it now, for if I'd known what was to come, I might have grieved less and planned more.

"Married?" Aggie asked, meeting my gaze.

"Dead," I replied. It was true enough—everyone that mattered was gone. And it wasn't likely I'd cross paths with Teddy ever again. Last I'd heard, he'd wed some chit of an heiress from Dublin while I'd grieved our son. The boy I hadn't even laid eyes on, whisked away by Lady Grace's midwives before the words "the child is dead" had even reached my ears.

Diarmuid. That's the name I'd chosen for my sweet boy—whether Teddy wished it or not. In the end, my letters went unanswered.

"The light of Heaven to your husband. Child too." Pressing

her lips together, Aggie gave a sharp nod toward the bath. "In ye go."

Aggie scrubbed the workhouse from my pores, working the bar of lye and horsehair brush over delicate skin until it screamed blood red, aflame with pain. And by the time I was dry and dressed—in a loose cotton day dress peppered with sunflowers, and undergarments, to boot—Beth had returned with a tray of black pudding, toast, and a dish of tea.

Eyes widening, my mouth watered as Beth placed the tray on the table next to my chair. Christ above! When was the last time I'd seen black pudding? Surely 'twas years, likely in Lady Grace's parlor. We'd never had it. Pigs were for selling, not eating. How else were we to pay the rent?

My stomach growled, but I knew not to dive in. Not to eat my fill. My stomach couldn't handle it. Even broth had been difficult to keep down those first days at the workhouse. How strange that an empty craw would reject food, yet it did. And I had no intention of vomiting.

Instead, I slowly cut a sliver of the blood sausage, pierced it with a fork, and brought it to rest beneath my nose. Salt. Pork. Spice. My eyes closed. Iron. The faint tang of blood that held it together.

I brought the black pudding to my lips and let it crumble on my tongue, savoring the delicious flavor and its decadent warmth as it slid down my throat. I'd have a slice or two more, but I didn't dare touch the toast. It never kept the hunger away for long and only drove it home ten-fold.

"There'll be liver for supper," Aggie said. "We must get ye to full strength as soon as possible. And when yer done here, I'll bring ye to her ladyship in the library."

"Oh, I'm done." I pierced a second slice of pudding and popped it into my mouth.

"Oh no, yer not, ye must—"

"Take my time lest I heave." I stood and placed the fork on the tray. "I promise to eat my fill at supper."

Pressing her lips together, Aggie nodded. "Right then. Follow me."

I followed in Aggie's wake, stepping into her shadow as she led the way out the bedroom door.

"This is the fourth floor," she offered, sweeping her arm in an arc. "The family's resting quarters. Her ladyship sleeps at the other end of the hall."

I glanced around. Two windows stood at each end of the corridor, but little good they did. The hall was dark, with deep red wallpaper inlaid with black, velveteen fleur-de-lis. This wasn't the sophisticated gold and cream of the Moore-Vandeleur house. This was old. Firmly settled in a time gone by. Black-painted portrait frames lined the walls between golden sconces, their canvases depicting stern men and tightly laced ladies. Some sported the powdered wigs of the last century, some the chevalier costume of the Stuarts. Below the wallpaper, as if propping the portraits, black-painted wainscoting lined the lower half of the hallway, darkening it still further.

"Servant stairs is through there. Leads straight to the kitchen and servants' quarters," Aggie said, pointing to a hinged panel to our right. If she hadn't said, I might have never known the wall hid a door. "Not that ye should ever use it. Yer Lady Wilhelmina now, so best be acting like it."

I tried not to let it bother me, that small loss of self, but it would be worth it in the end if Lady Catherine was true to her word. My gaze drifted from the hidden servants' door to another, a little farther down the hallway to our left. It was strange. Out of place. A heavy, velvet curtain lay, hooked to one side, and I supposed 'twas meant to cover the monstrosity from prying eyes—usually that would be the case. But with the curtain swept aside, I saw the door, its hinges eaten almost clean through by what looked like centuries of neglect, leaving naught but a trail of blood-red rust behind.

Affixed upon it, a series of locks and bolts glinted, their new-minted iron stark against the black-painted grain of the door. They stepped from top to bottom, ladder rungs haphazardly nailed to the wood. And right now, each and every one was unlocked. What in the name of God? Were they to keep people out . . . or to keep something in?

Screeek.

The little hairs on my arms stood on end as the twist of a rusted doorknob set my heart a-hammering. Staring at the door, I halted.

"A-Aggie?" I called, my voice a tremor, skittering over a tongue that felt a tad too large for the word. Surely she heard it?

Aggie glanced over her shoulder, right as the door creaked open to reveal . . . Lady Catherine, emerging back-first.

"Christ!" I exclaimed, hands flying to my mouth.

Lady Catherine wore a black, floor-length bustled skirt. Its rustle promised of silk whispering over the finest cotton petticoats money could buy. A high-collared man's shirt was tucked into the high-waisted band, but she wore no coat today. No adornments, beyond that simple golden charm dangling from a black ribbon at her throat, with a braided bun wound like a viper at the back of her head, soft ringlets bouncing afore and aft her ears.

In her hand, a kerosene lamp dangled, its light casting shadows on the space within, and I caught naught but a passing glimpse before she doused the lamp and hung it from a hook inside the room before shutting the door.

"Mistress Lynch," Lady Catherine snapped, not turning. One by one, she slid each bolt shut with definitive clicks, then turned an ancient-looking key—near its end of life if the teeth-shattering grating was anything to go by—into the final lock. "You know better than to dally by this door."

"Yes, m'Lady," Aggie answered, bobbing a curtsy.

With a flick of her wrist, Lady Catherine unhooked the curtain, and it fell back into place, concealing the door with a whisper that fought against the screaming draft—an echo that drew to mind a huddle of weeping women. Folly and fancy.

This was no time for silliness. Straightening my spine, I bobbed a curtsy of my own as Lady Catherine turned, a bright smile curving her lips.

"You look somewhat refreshed. I'm that glad." She glanced at Aggie, and the ghost of a frown flitted across her ladyship's face. "Tea in the library, Mistress Lynch. I'll see to my new charge."

"Yes, m'Lady." Another curtsy, and Aggie spun on her heel.

"Oh, and Lynch?" Lady Catherine called, the frost in her voice enough to freeze the marrow of my bones. Aggie paused, not daring even a glance over her shoulder. "If I ever catch you dallying in this hallway again, I'll have to refund your deposit."

My palms went slick as Aggie stiffened, and the air thinned until it was difficult to breathe. I forced my gaze to the floor, knowing that's what my old benefactor, Lady Grace, would have wanted . . . but a glint caught my eye. There, near the hem of Lady Catherine's gown, was the charm she wore around her neck, its black ribbon still hooked through.

Without thought, I bent and snatched it up, presenting it in my palm for her ladyship to retrieve.

"You must have dropped this, Your Ladyship," I murmured, glancing at her, but Lady Catherine still glared at Aggie's retreating back. I tried again, this time louder. "The knot must have loosened. Lady Catherine?"

With a start, she turned her attention to me, eyes widening as she spied the charm nestled in my outstretched palm. Her face paled, and she quickly plucked it from my palm.

"Don't you *ever* touch this again," she hissed, taking a menacing step forward. The warning was laden with such venom that it took all my strength not to take a terrified step back. "This is not yours."

"O-of c-course n-not," I stammered. "A-apologies."

"Now." She retreated a step and tied the charm around her neck, her voice suddenly warm where it had chilled the soul but a moment before. "Let me show you around the house."

God above and all His saints, protect and guard me.

And as I followed in Lady Catherine's wake, I secretly made the sign of the cross.

Chapter 6

Ghosts are troublesome things, in a house or in a family,
as we knew even before Ibsen taught us. There is only
one way to appease a ghost. You must do the thing it asks
you. The ghosts of a nation sometimes ask very big
things and they must be appeased whatever the cost.
—Patrick Pearse, Christmas Day speech, 1915

"And this is the library."

I trailed Lady Catherine as she led the way from the ornate
dining room, across the black and white checkered tile of the
foyer, toward a pair of doors to the right of the sweeping staircase. The staircase was grand, branching in two at the second-
floor landing—one arm leading to the drawing room, the other
to the master's study. Or, I supposed, Lady Catherine's study.

"I expect it will become a second home to you in the coming
weeks." Lady Catherine threw a smile over her shoulder as she
opened the door. "It's not as grand as some, but it serves its
purpose."

I'd never stepped foot inside the Moore-Vandeleur library,
so I had nothing to compare this one to. My eyes swept over
the book-lined partitions, floor to ceiling, as if the walls themselves were fortified with naught but leather-bound brick.
Brick that absorbed all light, despite the great bay window facing the front of the house. Deep red wallpaper bloodied the

walls, dripping in sheets from above, where a coffered ceiling depicted cherubs in each of its intricately chiseled squares.

Lady Catherine's heels clacked over the smooth, dark wooden floor toward a great desk.

"Come, come," she said.

I followed, heart pounding as Lady Catherine took her place in the master's chair and promptly propped her feet on the polished, wooden surface of the desk. There had been no more outbursts from her, and no mistakes on my part, but I feared it would take time to settle into my new role.

"Now. To business." From a fold in her skirt, Lady Catherine produced a pipe and brought it to her lips. "There are a few things to go over."

Bending forward, Lady Catherine swiped the side of her heeled boot. *Scritch.* The hiss of a match rent the air, and the sweet scent of sulfur was soon replaced by tobacco smoke as Lady Catherine lit the pipe.

Another scritch, and she touched a fresh-lit match to an incense box that sat next to the inkwell of the desk. White smoke billowed forth, melding with the gray of her pipe, tobacco mixed with the same jasmine and lemon scent that wafted from the box in my room.

She glanced at me. "Don't mind me. I like to cover the pipe with my favorite blend. The staff keeps it burning throughout the house, morning and night. Do let me know if it begins to bother you."

"Not at all," I replied, watching as the smoke steadied from a bulbous cloud to a thin, concentrated reed. The incense had been packed in a pattern, winding in thin spirals between metallic dividers, its burn now slow and steady.

Lady Catherine nodded. "Then to business. We don't get any visitors, generally, isolated as we are, but the guest wing is always kept in a state of readiness—that's the third floor, dear. The second floor was Charles's domain, so I do all my business from here, the library. And though I daren't venture to the study or drawing room, I realize sitting here with me all day could be a stuffy inconvenience, so you're welcome to make yourself at home there. That said, you have the run of the house until you've fully recovered your health." Lady Catherine took a long drag, then released the smoke on a breath.

I nodded, head swimming—from pipe or incense, I knew not.

"With the exception of the attic, that is. That's where I was departing when we ran into each other upstairs. You noted the locks, I'm sure. The floor is unstable up there, and I'm the only one with access for fear of injury. You understand?"

Another nod, despite the cool draft that warned caution. But I shrugged it away as Lady Catherine continued.

"In the meantime, I expect you to eat your fill and exercise your mind. To pass as Wilhelmina, you'll be expected to maintain polite conversation in company, and we'll have to work on your elocution—refine your English. Then there'll be some rudimentary French, as Wilhelmina was educated abroad."

My chest tightened. Speech, yes. But French? "I'll do my best."

"I know you will. Do sit." She spoke around the pipe, then took another drag before releasing it. Bobbing a curtsy, I took the chair opposite as Lady Catherine gestured toward it. "Now. The sea air will no doubt serve you well, so I insist on walks in the garden. When you've acquired a sufficient level of health, you may accompany Beth to the village."

"Yes, m'Lady."

Lady Catherine raised a brow. "Mama."

"Pardon?"

"Mama, dear. You must leave the past where it belongs for the time being, and you will call me Mama from this day forth. You must give no indication that you're not who we say you are."

Mama. Mom-aw. The English way of saying it. I closed my eyes and begged the Lord above that my own Mam— Mammy—could forgive me this sin, as she'd forgiven all others.

What in the name of God had I gotten myself into? I'd come here hoping to bury my ghosts, not confront them head-on.

"Tea, m'Lady."

My heart skipped as Aggie spoke from the door.

"Ah!" With a smile, Lady Catherine swung her legs from the desk and reached into her skirt pocket. "Right here, Mistress Lynch."

In one smooth movement, Lady Catherine produced the key used to lock the attic door and opened a drawer.

Silver tinkled against porcelain as Aggie strode forward. "I took the liberty of adding a couple of scones, m'Lady. For the young mistress."

My mouth watered at the thought. When was the last time I'd tasted Mam's flaky scones?

"Excellent, Lynch." Placing the key in the top drawer, Lady Catherine glanced at me as Aggie set down the tray. "Sugar?"

"Oh, no . . . that is, no thank you . . . Mama."

Aggie poured two cups as I stared at the scones. Already cut, and slathered in creamy, golden butter. I knew I shouldn't eat. Not so soon after breakfast . . . but maybe a nibble. Surely that wouldn't cause my stomach to heave.

"I can handle the milk," Lady Catherine said, waving toward the door.

"Of course, m'Lady." With a curtsy, Aggie turned on her heel, the twirl of her skirt brushing my arm.

"A dash?" Lifting the delicate porcelain jug, Lady Catherine lifted a brow.

"Please," I replied, before twisting in my chair. "Thank you, Aggie."

She froze mid-stride and slowly turned. Lips pressed together, Aggie glanced at Lady Catherine before offering a nod in my direction.

Thump!

The sound echoed through the library, freezing the blood in my veins. My eyes widened as Aggie whipped her head toward the wall of books to my right, and a tingle shot up my back when I spied a slim volume sprawled on the wooden floor. I pursed my lips as the pulse at my throat startled to life, a horse whipped from walk to sudden canter. Surely, the book couldn't have simply fallen, and it certainly wasn't there before.

"Blessed Virgin," Aggie muttered, bringing a hand to her forehead to make the sign of the cross.

Without another word, glance, or attempt to put things back to rights, Aggie scuttled from the room, and I rose from the chair.

"Your tea, dear?" Lady Catherine tapped a silver spoon against the saucer beneath her cup, but my attention was firmly fixed on the fallen volume. "Don't want it to get cold now, do we?"

"One moment. I'll just pick that up." I approached the leather-bound book, its jacket sprawled open, pages flipped over. I furrowed my brow and dragged my eyes to the shelf. Where its counterparts were tightly packed before, one now tipped over where this lone jumper once was. Spirits didn't bother me. Never had. What was Ireland if not death's waiting room? It was a comfort to think life went on in some way. That maybe, somewhere, my family might be looking on from afar.

Bending, I plucked the book from the floor and quickly placed it back on the shelf.

"All this fuss," Lady Catherine said with a snort. "Don't let the staff's contrariness infect your rationale. You'll hear talk of some 'woman in white,' I'm sure. It's all nonsense. Superstitious, the lot of them. There's likely a lean on that bookcase. Lord knows, the place is old."

Pursing my lips, I glanced at the golden letters declaring its title, only to find it wasn't a book at all.

Tenant Registry 1828–present.

A quick scan of its counterparts revealed this was not where an accounting journal should be kept. Left and right, books on animal husbandry and agriculture sat in proud order, their spines cracked from dedicated study and hours pored over pages.

"Which one was it?" Lady Catherine asked.

With the middle finger of my right hand, I pushed the journal as far back, and as deep, as the shelf allowed, and with thumb and forefinger, I pulled the title to the right forward.

"*On the Management of Bees,*" I replied, offering a polite smile over my shoulder, despite the cool sheen of sweat that slickened my palms. Why on earth did I lie? "You maintain hives?"

Lady Catherine's eyes widened in surprise, and she set down her cup. "God above. Perhaps there *is* a spirit haunting these halls."

She laughed then, loud and hearty, but something about the pitch set my teeth on edge. Without thinking, I reached for the book to the left of the almost-concealed journal, and pulled that forward to match the title I'd called out.

"My dearly departed Charles once set his mind to raising bees," Lady Catherine offered as she tempered her amusement.

"Ah, I see," I said, forcing a bright smile as I pinched the two books together, to fully conceal the journal.

"Perhaps his spirit played a little trick just now to remind me of all the wonderful time we spent together," Lady Catherine continued.

"Perhaps—" I began, but all thought of making polite conversation ceased. My breath misted as a sudden chill rippled over my skin, and out of the corner of my eye, I swore I spied the flap of wings—a translucent bird in flight, gliding toward the specter of a familiar male figure before ducking behind a book shelf. Eyes widening, I turned, but there was nothing there.

Except the strange echo of a long-forgotten memory that only I could hear.

Eitilt, eitilt, squawk!

And that was the last I remembered, afore suddenly, and completely, crumpling to the floor.

Chapter 7

When you gain her Affection, take care to preserve it;
Lest others persuade her, you do not deserve it.
—"Advice to Her Son on Marriage," by Irish poet
Mary Barber (1685–1755)

September 1845: Before

At first, I thought the bird beautiful, a clever, colorful creature that brought joy. A macaw, of the parrot family, the bird's feathers reminded me of a dandy—a bright saffron shirt beneath a deep blue overcoat, complementing a powdered white face, his dark eyes encircled with black patterned lines, like the illustration of a zebra I'd once spied in one of Teddy's schoolbooks.

Saffron and blue, the same colors carried by Brian Boru at the ancient Battle of Clontarf . . . and the proud colors of our county—Clare. There might be symbolism there if one believed Lady Grace had a propensity for deep thought or philosophy, but alas, she did not. A pleasant coincidence only . . . though pleasant was not a description anyone might use to describe Lucy.

Nicknamed "Lucifer" by the rest of the staff, Lucy was given a wide berth. I wouldn't dare allow Lady Grace to overhear such a cruel thing, for her beloved Lucy had traveled halfway across the world from its native Amazonian jungle, only to roost in the oft-times dreary sun-room of Kilrush House—quite the adjustment, I'm sure. For if a bird could suffer from loneliness and melancholia, Lucifer was a prime example—biting, clawing, beating with wings so strong he'd once knocked me off my feet. Nor could I blame him. Weren't we both plundered conquests of an overreaching empire? Both beings of sunshine wallowing in a darkness that swallowed our souls.

But Kilrush House could never dampen our light, not truly. I had found my joy, my smile, and I would help Lucifer find his, for even the weakest shaft of sunlight cuts through rain-filled clouds.

Lady Grace thought the bird had a great fondness for me . . . though, given the bandage wrapped around my forearm, "fondness" to Lucifer, meant "maim, don't kill." And thank God for such small mercies, as I was made his companion, and he mine—two curiosities to be paraded before company whenever guests arrived.

Ah, and here's Margaret with Lucy. She's the girl I took under my wing, you know. Great propensity for letters and language. Margaret, speak for Lady Marlborough. You'll hear naught but a faint wisp of their savage tongue in her pronunciation.

"Their," as if Lady Grace wasn't an Anglo, born and raised in the very country and among the people she so casually hated. *Savage.*

Beast. Devil. Lazy. Ignorant. All spat in the same breath as "Irish."

"Tusa agus mise, Lucifer," I said with a sigh, gently stroking the soft yellow feathers of his breast. You and me . . . it was always he and I.

Squawk!

"Ba mhaith leat a eitilt?" I asked, glancing out the window. Of course he wanted to fly. And I wanted to join him, flying far from the sun-room, over the garden, all the way to the summer-house, where my smile—my light—lay bottled. A captured beam encased in glass, to be consumed in measured bursts whenever circumstances allowed. But my Teddy wasn't at home, and I'd no way of knowing when he might come back from whichever piece of land he was prospecting with his father, my master. Soon, Teddy would return to Dublin to resume his studies, and I'd be left waiting once more, anticipating his correspondence, sporadic though it was.

"Eitilt, eitilt, *squawk!*" Lucifer shook out his wings, and I instinctively pulled my hands toward my chest, for fear he'd accidentally peck my current injury.

"No Gaeilge, silly goose," I said in English. "Lady Grace will have me dismissed if you don't speak the Queen's. If you're a good boy, I'll ask the falconer to put you on the long leash so you can spread your wings." At least I got to leave. Unlike Lucifer, and the rest of the staff, my brother Michael and I didn't live in the Big House. Our father was the Moore-Vandeleurs' land agent, a position granted to him thanks to a distant oath— Colonel Moore-Vandeleur's father had been saved by my grandfather during some political skirmish at Dublin Castle during the Wolfe Tone rebellion, and he had promised our family a good living in recompense and gratitude. It meant employment for us all, and the luxury of returning home of an evening.

Squawk!

I turned to my charge, and smiled. "Beautiful boy. I bet you miss your home. Here."

Digging in the pocket of my apron, I produced a hardened treat, and Lucifer happily—and gently—took it from my fingers.

"Maggie!"

I whirled, heart racing, ready to explain that it was naught but a crust of bread, and dear Lucy would be just fine—

"Michael!" I let out a shuddering breath and almost choked on my own relief. "You frightened the daylights out of me."

"Arra," scoffed Michael, eyeing Lucifer. "Still have both yer eyes?"

Squawk!

Lucifer ruffled his feathers, training that dark, beady gaze on my brother.

"Stand down, darlin'," I whispered, running a gentle finger over the crest of the bird's soft head. "I must away, but I'll be back soon. And I'll follow through on my promise."

"It's an animal, Maggie," Michael said with a snort. "A mean one at that. Come on quick, afore his lordship or her ladyship need anything else. We'll be able to catch the start of the céilí if we hurry home. Mam said there'll be lamb stew tonight. Mr. O'Shea lost a few to an auld fox and sold one to Dad."

"Stew?" My eyes widened. It had been quite some time since last we'd acquired honest-to-goodness meat. Colonel Moore-Vandeleur had upped the livestock quota—again—last year, and with more animals earmarked for the landlord, the less there were for those who raised them.

"I must away, beautiful boy," I said, smiling wide, stomach a-fluttering with the prospect of marrow-rich broth.

"Maggie! *Squawk!*"

Shooting a glance over my shoulder, I spied Lucy shuffling along the perch, promising to hop to the ground and follow us home.

"I'll be back on the morrow, silly goose. Stay there now, lest Lady Grace accuse me of thieving ye."

"Lord above, it doesn't know what yer saying." With a roll of his eyes, Michael spun on his fresh-cobbled heel as Lucifer let loose another indignant squawk. "Come on quick, let ye! I promised Eileen Mangan that I'd ask her to dance, and I don't fancy the clip 'round the ear I'll get if we're late."

" 'Tis worse than that you'll get if Eileen Mangan's father

catches ye behind the church again," I said with a laugh, following my brother from the room.

"And what will his lordship do when he catches you and the young master?"

I lashed out with my uninjured arm and slapped the back of his head.

"Ow!" he protested. "I don't approve, in case it matters at all."

"Keep yer voice down," I scolded. "I love him, Michael."

For Teddy's father couldn't know of the promises made between us just yet.

But when the time was right. Yes. The timing had to be perfect, or all my hard work would come to naught, and I'd lose the love of my life.

The music rose with the moon, bowstrings sawing through notes as local fiddlers threw themselves into the melody with fervor, driving it through the gathered crowd, an unending fever no poultice could break.

"Yoop!" I called, laughing from the candlelit edges of the dance floor of the parish hall, stomping my heel along to the beat as the feet of the set-dancers flew "around the house." When I was younger, I feared the dancers might levitate off the ground and make it all the way to Heaven. And sure, how would they come back?

A low drone emanated from the uilleann piper, and the laughing couples on the floor quickly shuffled into position to begin the Fourth Figure as the fiddlers took swigs of porter. Ten sets of eight dancers each quickly took shape, and I was parched just watching them.

"You not dancing, love?"

A wooden cup of non-alcoholic blackberry cordial appeared to my right, and I turned with a smile.

"Thanks, Da," I said, gladly taking a sip. My father wore his Sunday best—a fine, wide-brimmed felt hat, a swallowtail coat above shirt, waistcoat, knee breeches, and woolen, knee-high socks.

"Has no one asked ye? Síofra wouldn't mind a set. One of ye can dance the man's part," he said, taking a sip from his own wooden cup. Da didn't drink the English porter. In fact, he didn't drink any kind of alcohol. Some thought him cold because of it, but Da was always aware of the important position he held as land agent, and he took being Colonel Moore-Vandeleur's record keeper—and translator—for the tenants very seriously.

"She's out there with Paudie Connolly," I said, nodding toward one of the far sets.

"Arra!" With a scowl fit to raze all of Kilrush to the ground, Da knocked back the rest of his blackberry cordial. "How many times must I warn her off them Connolly boys?"

"At least once more, it seems." He elbowed me for that. "Ooft!"

"And you, Miss? You can't be thinking of cleaning bird shite for the rest of your life, surely? You should be using that education of yours to teach or some such."

I chuckled and looped my free arm through his. "And where would I teach, Da? I'd have to go to Ennis or the like to find work, and I couldn't leave you and Mam for a position I'd not be able to keep once I wed."

"That's a while off yet," he said with a smile.

Heat prickled my cheeks, and I brought the cool wooden cup to my skin. Not as far off as he might think.

"Yer flushed," he noted, brow furrowing as he turned, concern tugging at his lips. "Have ye caught something from that bird?"

It took everything I had not to roll my eyes. Every sniffle in our house was attributed to poor Lucy, as if he carried every illness known to man and lay in wait to breathe them onto me so I might spread the miasma to the village. "No, no, I'm grand. Maybe 'tis just the crush of people. The humidity doesn't help."

That summer had been especially hot. Thunderstorms had plagued us for months, with no relief. No clearing of the air. Just damp, sticky humidity that caused havoc on the drying. Mam complained every day that she could get nary a shirt dried for the frequency of the downpours.

"All right." Da raised a brow and plucked the cup from my hand. "Go get some air for yerself, if you can. I'll try and pry Síofra from that lad of the Connolly's."

"Good luck." With a laugh and a bright smile, I turned on my heel, weaving through the boisterous crowd as I meandered toward the door. Men and women alike bobbed their heads and removed their caps as I passed—*the land agent's daughter, the eldest, Maggie, educated by Lady Grace, if you don't mind*— and there was a smile for each of them.

"Oh, Maggie!"

I wasn't so much tugged on my sleeve as I was yanked backward.

"Jesus wept," I muttered, glancing over my shoulder. It was Mrs. Leary, a babe tucked under each arm and another clinging to her skirts. Married four years, and only six and twenty, the stress of homemaking had already etched itself around once-sparkling blue eyes. "Mary! Wisha, how are you?"

"I'd be much better if I could find my husband, but c'mere, I have a favor." She leaned in, and I followed suit. "Is there any chance ye could put in a good word for my Jimmy with your Da? 'Tis only he wants to get digging the spuds tomorrow after hearing all the talk from Dublin, and he'll be late with the quarterly rent."

The "talk from Dublin" might as well have been about some far-off foreign place as far as I was concerned. Da said to pay it no mind. That a few failed potato crops on the east coast were naught to worry us here in Clare, and should the worst happen, we'd been through it before and would get through it again.

"I'll be certain to let him know, but make sure Jimmy still talks to Da about it. Da mentioned something about getting all the digging out of the way in one shot." Likely to ease everyone's minds, so they could all get back to work, lining the Moore-Vandeleurs' pockets.

"Oh, I'll make certain he will. If you see him, tell him I'm looking for him." Without another word, Mary Leary disappeared into the crowd and I finally made my escape, emerging into the twilit dusk.

Taking a deep breath, I settled my hands on my hips before striding around the side of the hall. I'd find Da and relay Mary O'Leary's message once I returned to the fray. But for now, I would breathe, and not worry about failing crops or Síofra's choice of suitor, or Michael being gelded by Eileen Mangan's father.

There was only one thing I needed to puzzle out, and that was how Teddy planned to announce our secret engagement to his father.

I wasn't worried about Mam or Da, for so long as Teddy convinced his parents, mine would gladly follow suit. One of their daughters? Marrying a landed Anglo? It was the stuff dreams were made of, and I'd dreamt and planned since I was old enough to understand what a marriage truly meant, and what a good one could do for my family.

My parents would just be bothered that I settled so young. They had this idea that I should be twenty-three or four when I wed, so I might better know my mind and be sure of what I want.

"Bah!" Hands came around my waist as the deep voice yelled in my ear, and my pulse set off at a gallop. "Did I frighten you, lovedy?"

"Teddy," I exclaimed, turning in his arms, my heart now pounding in my ears. I gave his chest a light thump with my fist, and he laughed—a beautiful, honey-sweet laugh that lit up that handsome face.

"Forgive me, forgive me," he begged, bending to plant a light kiss just beneath my earlobe. "Oh, I missed you."

"I missed you too," I said with a sigh, melting into him before quickly pushing away. We were a secret, a clandestine smile that only we two shared. Glancing around, it didn't appear we had an audience, but prying eyes were everywhere. I took four steps back and drank him in, cheeks heating as I fought against the grin playing along my lips. "You're back."

Nodding, he took a step forward, and another. "I'm back."

"But leaving for school soon." I took a step back, and he advanced once more. *Reach me. Touch me.* What might have started as a calculated plan to marry leagues above my station had melded to all-consuming love two years since, and my skin prickled with anticipation as I bit my lower lip.

"Yes . . . but surely you won't let me go without a proper send-off?" Another step forward.

"Perhaps I will. Mayhap I fell for another while you were away, neglecting my heart." This time I stood my ground, and my love—my heart—silenced me with a deep kiss.

"Silly poppet," he murmured against my lips, kissing me once more before pulling away, taking my hand in his. "There is only ever I for you, and you for me, wife of mine. Come."

A thrill ignited within every time he called me by that title, "wife." It promised the world, and so I had already given all that was precious to me in return.

"I'm not your wife yet," I breathed.

"Shall we abscond to Limerick? Find a drunken minister in that great city, and elope?" he asked, a smile toying with the corners of his lips.

"Will you be able to stand up to your papa when he seeks an annulment for marrying without his consent?" Teddy's face fell, but I squeezed his hand. "Stop, breathe, and think, my love. I want to be with you as much as you want to be with me.

But we must stick to the plan. Trust me. Then I can stand beside you and give you courage."

"Prove it," he countered. "Show me how much you missed me."

"Where?" I asked with a smile, not truly caring so long as it was with him.

"Where else? The summerhouse," he replied.

To make love among the flowers, to affirm our promises, once more, beneath the stars.

And the woes of the world could simply melt away.

Chapter 8

I grant this food will be somewhat dear, and therefore
very proper for landlords, who, as they have already
devoured most of the parents, seem to have the best title
to the children.
—Jonathan Swift, *A Modest Proposal*

Present: February 1848

"There she is." My eyes fluttered open to the sound of a rustle, and before the realization that I was in my borrowed bed took purchase, Lady Catherine's concerned face hovered over mine. "Poor thing. I fear I overtaxed you on your first day."

The press of a damp cloth moistened my forehead, and I frowned.

"I was going to call for Dr. Brady, but it seemed you were simply sleeping." Lady Catherine said, voice soft and gentle as she retracted the cloth. I raised myself onto my elbows and glanced around. We were alone—thank God. I didn't wish for an audience. She perched on the edge of the bed. "It appeared you were having a nightmare."

Nightmare? I pursed my lips. No. Not a nightmare, but a vivid memory that had played out in dreamscape. A sweet memory at that. Every breath, every touch, every detail, immaculate—as though not just a memory, but I was there, transported through time. Even the injury sustained from Lucy smarted something fierce, and I glanced at my arm. Naught amiss.

"Will you please be quiet!" Lady Catherine snapped the command into the empty space to my left, and I whipped around . . . but there was no one there, sending my heart into a skitter.

"M-mama?" I stuttered, slowly turning around to face her.

Brows furrowed into eyelids, lips downturned, she stared at the shadowed corner next to my bed while clutching the charm at her throat.

"Mama?" I attempted again, this time clearly.

Her glare slid to meet wide-eyed fear, and like match to candle, she smiled, transforming all distress into kind benevolence once more.

"Take some time to rest," she cooed, reaching out to smooth the hair at my temple. "If you wish me to call Dr. Brady, I'll do so gladly."

"No, thank you." It took everything in me to stay still, to not recoil at her touch.

"Nightmares are windows into our souls," she said, pulling back of her own accord before pushing to her feet. "It's best to face them. Lean into all those feelings, else we shan't heal from our hurts."

"Yes, Mama." What did this woman know of hurts?

"I know more than you think."

I froze. "Pardon?" I hadn't said that aloud, surely?

"About dreams and nightmares, dear," she replied, smoothing her skirts. "Rest now. I'll have Aggie fetch you a tray to avoid any more fainting spells."

But as she swept from the room, I could swear a woman's voice whispered from the shadows with which Lady Catherine had conversed.

Feed me, it said. *Set me free. Help me.*

But I could barely help myself, and I had to stay the course.

Three months later

I took breakfast in my room, morning tea in the library, lunch in the dining room, afternoon tea in his lordship's drawing room, and supper on the terrace with Lady Catherine—when the elements allowed.

Desolate couldn't quite begin to describe the weather. There was something otherworldly and wrong about the way the rain fell here, as if God above thought the Burren might sprout grass if He sent enough water to drown the rocks. An hourly flood to wash away the crags so life might spring from their depths.

Wind howled constantly, screeching through cracks in the windowsills, enough to require a blanket over the shoulders, and a chair close to the fire.

Most days, when I was done practicing Wilhelmina's flowing script or reviewing her old schoolroom vocabulary cards—doing my best to mimic the stiff-upper-lipped clip of the Anglo aristocracy—I spent time between the library and rummaging through the old records in his lordship's study, mesmerized by the view beyond the window, where the violent Atlantic met Irish soil.

The ocean, naught but a stone's throw from the road, running parallel with the estate boundary, was wild, a dark, roiling mass of seaweed that thundered upon the shore in a froth of seafoam. An army on the attack, its onslaught constant and terrifying. I oft wondered how the long curraghs thrashing through wave and wind ever made it back to moor unscathed. Yet they did. I watched them leave every morning from the window overlooking the shale-covered coastline, and as they came ashore, their teams of two worked to secure the crafts farther up the beach.

I hoped it was worth the trip, wherever they were, and whatever it was they did.

When the dreary gray of wintery spring's constant downpour gave way to the watery sun of almost-summer, I could spy clear across the bay to the land beyond. Galway Bay, Lady Catherine had informed me, and the trio of islands in the distance—stepping stones into the Atlantic Ocean—were the Aran Isles.

Today was no different as I stared out that study window, a leather-bound journal marked "1832" nestled in my hands, three months past my arrival.

I smoothed the bodice of the borrowed, pale blue day dress, and marveled at how quickly I'd improved my health. Lady Catherine had spared no expense to ensure my recovery. It was a kindness I'd never forget, and tucked away from the destruction beyond, it was easy to believe that the eradication of my poor countrymen wasn't happening. That these last three years of famine and disease might have all been but a dream.

Easier still when the staff ate well and none complained of hardship in the village. It drew to mind a divine barrier, one affixed around Browne House and Gortacarnaun beyond. That those therein were blessed with ignorance.

God forgive me, but I was glad.

I glanced out the window to gaze at the rocky beach. Two curraghs bobbed to shore, and I watched the men aboard unload their haul afore upending the long, slim crafts to berth them.

Figures awaited in the rocky bluffs near the roadside, baskets propped on hips, ready to barter for whatever it was the men had hunted. Fish, maybe. Or crab.

With a sigh, I turned my attention to the journal. Thus far, I'd only found rent and accounting records on the shelves of his lordship's lavishly adorned study. Unlike the library—where the shelves created walkways and aisles—bookshelves lined the burgundy-papered walls, and a grand, dark polished desk sat proudly in the center. No wooden floors here, however. His lordship seemed to have had a preference for black marble.

Burgundy and black striped velvet curtains framed the large window, where I now sat, settled into the black leather Chippendale, perfectly placed to enjoy the view.

As I thumbed through my new find—tucked away on the lower shelf of the bookcase farthest from the door—a smile teased the corners of my lips. At last, an account devoid of eye-crossing mathematics. If I were to be Wilhelmina in truth, acquainting myself with her deceased father was paramount. What child would know nothing of her da?

June 12th 1832
  The walls whisper her name, over and over, and I fear the worst. Cut off as I am from the world at large, I fear none have heeded my call. Isolation, it appears, has erased my very existence from the memory of those I once relied upon.

June 13th 1832
  I have taken to sleeping in the drawing room, lest she appear in the night. Yet Cate has absconded to the girl's chamber. I cannot understand how she bears it, for I cannot unsee the horror of four nights since. Those round blue eyes, unseeing. Cate has forsaken me, and I have forsaken myself, for my mind wanders.

As I read, my brow furrowed, and Lady Catherine's flippant comment regarding a supposed haunting flitted through my mind. Had his lordship believed the stories too?

"Another soft day, Miss."

My heart leapt against the confines of my bodice as I whirled, journal slipping through my fingers, dropping to the floor with a thud.

"Christ, Beth. I didn't even hear you."

"Arra, ye were away with the faeries again, Miss." The young, quiet serving girl who'd lit the fire in my room on the day of my arrival—Beth—smiled, and my eyes slid to the tray she carried. "I figured you'd take your tea here, so I gathered it afore Mistress Lynch could say aught about your contrariness."

"Mistress Lynch would do well to keep her opinions to herself." I arched my brows, doing my best Lady Catherine impression, and Beth chuckled.

"She's nary so bad," Beth noted, setting the tray atop the end table, perched next to the Chippendale, before pouring a dish of tea.

"No, indeed. Aggie's been kind to me." I turned my attention back to the shore. "Will you take a cup with me, Beth?"

"Oh no, Miss." Glancing out the window, Beth bit her lower lip. "I must bring in flowers from the garden for drying. You know her ladyship insists on keeping the incense lit morning and night."

I smiled and took a sip of the scalding-hot tea. I'd long since thought the incense might have brought about the fainting spell that first day—at least that particular blend. Lady Catherine had refrained from adding the "healing herbs" she claimed required some level of getting used to, and I'd had no such incident since. "I'm surprised there's a flower to be found in the garden with all the incense she burns."

Beth's breath hitched, and she gripped the sideboard.

I followed her gaze. "What is it?"

"Naught."

I glanced at her and noted the flush creeping across her cheeks. "Well, it's not nothing."

Turning, I squinted through the window. The crowd on the shore were dispersing, but then I noticed the horse-drawn cart rumbling along the road. I couldn't see much from our vantage point, but it certainly appeared to be full of goods.

"Friend of yours?" I asked, my lips curling.

With a shake of her head, Beth took a step backward. "I should see about the flower drying."

"Oh, come now. I didn't mean anything by it." My brow furrowed as Beth placed a hand against her forehead.

"It's silly, really, Miss. Just Cormac back from Galway."

Cormac. The footman. Gods above, that's right. I hadn't seen him since my arrival. "Ah! Mr. O'Dea? Has he been in Galway this entire time?"

"You've met him, then?" Beth asked, her eyes bright as she glanced my way. "He's ever so kind. And always brings the maids something on his return from market. He's new, came here last year, and her ladyship sends him off to sell her goods. She says he gets the best prices, but it means he's away a bit."

I smiled. I couldn't even remember what he looked like. But one thing was certain. Cormac O'Dea had an admirer.

"Yes," I said. "He's very kind indeed. I wonder what trinkets he brought home for you this time."

"Maybe a length of ribbon!" Beth exclaimed, and for the first time I wondered how old she truly was.

And the urge to warn her of the dangers of slick-talking men took hold.

The house—like Beth—was abuzz upon Cormac's return, and in the disarray, I managed to squirrel some supper to my room. Lamb stew, with hearty chunks of fresh meat, slow-cooked in herbs and broth on a bed of onions and carrots. My mouth watered, as if scent alone could substitute taste. Just a few more steps and I could set down the tray. A few more steps and I could sit by the fire. Eat. Close my eyes and count my blessings.

It was a strange thing, eating. Going weeks and months without, there was a kind of resignation. As if the body knew there was no food. As if it knew to switch off the hunger so one might conserve enough strength to simply exist.

But at the workhouse—with half a ladle of watery broth and a chunk of stale bread to get us through twelve-hour days—it was like the beginning all over again. Each day brought the pain.

As if the meager rations had woken the hunger, and the stomach demanded more.

But now, months into my strange new role, I never went without. If Aggie wasn't shoveling food in my direction, there were trays waiting around every corner, my palate's desire a mere bellpull away.

And I welcomed it. I grazed through the day—a prized heifer with an acre for my own pleasure.

Little and often. Never enough to get too full. For if I was ever fully satiated, I might forget who I was, and my true purpose. This was not my life. This was but a stepping stone to independence. A cottage of my own and a few acres to sustain me. No rent. No landlord. The life my father dared dream for all of us. Dared so much that, when Teddy had crossed my path . . . I shook my head.

Setting down the tray, I caught sight of the vase of fresh flowers by my bed. Beth was militant when it came to those flowers, both cutting and drying. Every day, without fail, a fresh bouquet appeared—roses, bluebells, foxglove. But never had a day gone by without an unusual bloom I'd never laid eyes on until my arrival. Each day it sat boldly, with pride of place, in the center of the bouquet, its white drooping trumpets hanging from vine-like stems. Beautiful. I could smell its uniquely sweet, heady scent from here. Jasmine, with a hint of lemon. Not quite unlike the overpowering scent of Lady Catherine's incense.

Mam would've loved them. She was a great lover of flowers. My chest tightened, and I settled in front of the fire before carefully loading my spoon with the hearty stew.

My eyes closed as the savory notes struck a delicious melody that danced over my tongue. Good God. If I never again woke come morning, I'd die happy knowing this was my last meal.

I didn't even miss the absence of quartered potatoes. To be fair, when all this was over, I never wanted to see a potato again.

Or smell one.

Then again, I'd said the same of meat not too long ago, and yet now I ate it with gusto.

A shudder rippled over the nape of my neck, and I slipped a throw from the back of the chair to drape over my shoulders.

"Not now," I whispered, stiffening as the telltale crackle of oncoming lightning thickened the air in my chamber. I hadn't seen an apparition, exactly, but felt a sort of presence. Often. Mostly when alone. In the dark. In the quiet. And yet I was not afraid, for it brought comfort; and it was not the feminine presence I thought I'd encountered when I woke from the fainting spell, but masculine. Like the specter I thought I'd spied, with the bird, in the library that first morning. As familiar to me as my own reflection.

"I'll read to ye tonight, Michael."

That's how I'd started to fill the void of silence—reading aloud when the house settled in for the night. It wasn't that I was frightened, but something about my spectral visitor screamed protection and loneliness, as though they knew me and had never moved on for fear I'd not fulfill my promises. Who else could it be if not my brother? So I welcomed him. Though, why he hadn't appeared to me in the workhouse was a mystery.

With a shake of my head, I tucked into the stew, silently chewing between bites.

Tap, tap.

My heart leapt in my chest, and I almost dropped the spoon. "God above!" It wasn't like me to be given to flights of fancy. It was just a soft knock on the door. "Enter!"

It opened, and in bustled Aggie, her color high, a twinkle in her eye. "I thought ye might have escaped to yer room. I've brought ye a fresh-pressed nightdress."

Breathing deep to calm my pulse, I offered a smile. "That was kind of you, Aggie."

"Yes, well. Ye were up afore cockcrow this morn, and I

thought ye might retire early if the opportunity presented it-self." Without a glance at me, Aggie busied herself laying out the new nightdress before fetching the bed warmer from its hook. "Mr. O'Dea's returned from Galway, and her ladyship does like to make a fuss of him to learn news and gossip."

"It was a good trip?" I asked, as Aggie strode toward the fire to scoop hot coals into the bed warmer.

"It was, by all accounts."

"Mama will be pleased." It wasn't strange anymore, calling Lady Catherine "Mama."

"Hmph." With a grunt, Aggie turned on her heel to warm the sheets with a handheld brazier, and I pushed myself from the chair. "Let me just get the bed ready, and I'll help ye dress. There's a chill in the air tonight."

With a smile, I pulled the throw tight 'round my shoulders and stepped past the shelf of old dolls toward the window. It was full dark now, and with the light of the fire and candles be-hind, I could see almost naught of the land beyond the glass. But I knew what was there.

Where the third-floor window overlooked the ocean, my fourth-floor room faced the harsh, gray landscape of the Bur-ren—a vast plateau of jagged ravines, knitted closely together with shallow grass that hid the depths of the canyons beneath. I fancied that mayhap a mythical giant once punched the endless sea of rock, sending hairline cracks throughout the land. Some cracks were slender enough to bridge with the ball of one's foot, others still just wide enough to twist an ankle if one were care-less. But some could trap livestock; others, people.

It was a constant warning from Beth. That once I was able to venture beyond the walls of Browne House, I be ever so careful if I chose to walk the land. To step only on the rocky slabs. To keep my wits about me. To never risk stepping on the grass.

"Pull the drapes to shut out that draft, Wilhelmina," Aggie advised. I glanced over my shoulder and watched as she swept the bed warmer beneath the duvet. That's what I liked about Aggie. She never let me forget who I was or where I came from. She never called me "Miss" or referred to me as the "Dowager Countess" when we were alone. Not like the others. She was Aggie to me, and I, Wilhelmina to her. Though I wished she'd call me Maggie.

I untied the drape with one hand and turned to gaze out the dark window one last time before shutting myself away from the outside world.

The moon was high, fighting through a band of fast-moving clouds, but there was nary a star to be seen. Naught but the twinkle of a—what was that?

From the corner of my eye, I caught movement on the rocky plain in the distance. My brows drew together as I squinted into the night. What in the blazes?

With quick hands, I pulled the drape shut, trapping myself between velvet and glass, to shut out the fire's glow.

Greenish lights. Many of them. They bobbed along with speed, then halted, swaying in the dark as though swinging from the hands of multiple people.

A shiver rippled over my skin, and the little hairs at the back of my neck sprang to life as a sudden chill froze the blood in my veins. My breath misted the air as if it was still the coldest depths of winter, and I was caught outside. It fogged the window, but I quickly wiped it away.

Holding my breath, I stared hard into the night.

I'd once read of insects that could light up the night, but surely these luminosities were too large—not to mention those insects lived in far-off places, not the likes of drab Ireland. From this distance, I thought they might be lanterns, their height from the ground hinting that they were being held aloft by riders. But what could riders be doing out there, without a road to be found and naught but dangerous ravines for company?

I'd also never seen a greenish glow coming from any lantern.

The lights turned as one, flitted forward in tandem, then

pulled sharply around. The synchronization sent the hair on my arms into full salute as the lights quickly accelerated off down the land, away from the house.

I stared, a knot of dread coiling in my gut as the lanterns bobbed farther away, until Aggie pulled back the drapes.

I yelped, pulse pounding in my throat as I whirled.

"What in the name of God are ye doing?" she asked, glancing out into the night.

"N-nothing," I stammered, fighting for breath as my chest tightened.

"Aye, well. Come away from the draft, and let me undress ye for bed." But there was something in her expression, in the way she pursed her lips, the way her eyes squinted into the darkness.

Something I couldn't quite put my finger on.

Just as I couldn't quite understand what those lights were or where they'd come from.

Or if the voice that reverberated within my mind was mine, or another's, as Aggie lit the bowl of fresh incense atop my nightstand.

Beware the fog.

Chapter 9

I was led by a hatred of England, so deeply rooted in my
nature that it was rather an instinct than a principle . . .
The truth is, I hate the very name of England. I hated her
before my exile and I will hate her always.
—Irish revolutionary Wolfe Tone, *Autobiography*

October 1845: Before

The weather broke at last, at the end of September, and we had
a few great days for drying, which allowed a quick launder of
the bedclothes before we locked ourselves away from the brisk
bite of winter.

Well, not Da, Michael, or myself. We'd still have to slog and
trudge our way to the Big House, no matter the road conditions. But the thought of the rest of the family bundled away in
the house—a prickle of hibernating hedgehogs—brought a
smile to my face.

Wearing a freshly laundered uniform—a crisp black dress
over a starched petticoat, with grease-shined leather shoes (a
luxury for those lucky enough to work in the Big House;
everyone else went barefoot) and hair braided into a bun at the
back of my head—I happily swung my basket of just-plucked
wildflowers, despite the blanket of dense, bluish fog that carpeted the ground as I made my way toward the Big House. The

flowers were for Teddy's young brothers, Hector and Crofton. The little boys loved to sit quietly in the sun-room while I kept Lucy company, and I thought, mayhap, we could craft crowns made of daisies to while away the time.

Teddy. I frowned. We'd spent every evening together since the night of the céilí, but alas, our parting came too soon. It always did. He'd left for university almost seven days hence, and my guts were twisted with worry. Busy as he was, he rarely wrote when occupied in Dublin, but the time to force his father's hand was fast approaching. I would have to put pen to paper soon and insist he return to Kilrush for Christmas. God only knew the hurdle that was ahead.

"Is that you, Maggie?"

I pivoted to the left and righted my frown to a smile before waving. Not that she could even see it. Mary Leary reminded me of a ghost, silhouetted as she was in the fog. 'Twas just luck I recognized the crooked tilt of the Leary's gate. "Morning, Mary!"

She quickly made her way toward me, broom in hand, the freshly thatched roof of their one-roomed stone home glistening with dew in the background. A pretty picture if one had the talent to paint. I, however, did not.

I hadn't noticed the night of the céilí, but with her apron tied high, it was quite obvious she was with child again.

"Mary, ye never said—oh!" Jimmy Leary, Mary's husband, stumbled through the red-painted half door, stuffing his long work shirt into his pants. A flush stained his ruddy cheeks when he caught sight of me outside the gate, and I offered a wave.

"Wisha, good mornin' to ye, Mistress O'Shaughnessy," he called.

Mistress . . . hearing it prompted daydreams of one day being an actual mistress, wed at last with permission from Teddy's parents. But for now, it was just a cursory title, used only to keep my father—the O'Learys' overseer—placated.

"Good morning to ye both. When does the digging start?" I asked, knowing full well that today was the day, and that Da had secured the next two days for the entire tenantry to bring in the only harvest meant to sustain them and their families. The bad weather had caused delay, but we could wait no longer.

"As soon as I can get over to the Maloneys' place. Hopefully the sun peeks out soon to burn away the fog," Jimmy replied, turning toward Mary. "We'll be circling the farms, love, so we'll be here after noon."

"Go on then, let ye," Mary said with a laugh.

Grinning, Jimmy hopped along the short, narrow path—wedged between packed potato patches—from the front door to the gate, pecked Mary on the cheek, doffed his cap at me, then sprinted in the direction of the Maloneys'.

I glanced at Mary, who stared at the vegetation that rippled in Jimmy's wake, dispersing some of the fog that seemed to settle on its leaves. An ominous blanket that boded ill. Worry weighted her brow, as it should. I'd noticed the same issue in our own crop. The plants should have been a bright verdant green . . . instead, they had turned from spring green to a faded, pale brown in the last few weeks. But that wasn't all.

"Yours didn't bloom either," I said. A statement of fact. Not a single flower had sprouted at the end of summer, an event that always signaled the last month or so before harvest, and Da had mused that the warm, hot summer might be the culprit. If the potato crop failed, the next year would be hard. Last year brought a poor yield, which meant overall farm production was down. Malnutrition and weakness were the bane of productivity, after all.

Our families tended to be large, so we had enough hands to work the Moore-Vandeleur land, but that meant food was scarce, as options were limited. We could either buy what we needed—the exact same produce we personally harvested for the Moore-Vandeleurs, if we could afford it—or grow our own crops on quarter and half acres. But with the Anglo landlords raising rents all over the country, most of us survived off what we could grow. And given we could only utilize the ground within our rented walls, the potato was the only vegetable anyone grew.

Why? Because the potato produced six tons of food, enough to sustain a family for an entire year.

With all the talk from Dublin of another failed harvest and the lack of bright white flowers sprouting long, golden cones of pollen, my stomach was in knots.

"Don't worry," I called brightly, as Mary placed a gentle hand over her growing belly. "We got through the bad harvest last year. We'll get through the next."

Nodding, Mary snapped out of her stupor and clasped the broom.

"Aye. All will be well. Though"—she trailed off, furrowing her brow—"do ye smell that?"

Pursing my lips, I sniffed the air. Nothing but crushed grass underfoot, and a hint of wild rosemary. "Smell what, Mary?"

She shook her head and swatted the slab of rock before her feet with the broom.

"Naught. Just a strange sickly smell brought on by the fog. Like slurry, but not. Something so rotten it's almost sweet."

I furrowed my brow. Surely it was slurry, but Mary would certainly know the difference between fermenting manure and whatever it was she smelt.

"Ah, never ye mind," Mary said, waving a hand in front of her face, as if to dispel the scent. "'Tis likely the babe in my belly. Me auld nose gets awful sensitive when I'm with child, and even the waft of fresh baked bread can make me nauseous.

I'm keeping ye, Maggie. Head on away afore Lady Grace repri-
mands ye."

She was right. The morning was stretching on, and Lucy
needed company. But something she said struck me.

A sensitive nose. My mother was oft plagued with a sensitive
nose during pregnancy and was about to give birth for the tenth
time, God willing.

Yet I smelled nothing. I was now absolutely certain of the
child currently growing in my own womb. Perhaps I wasn't
far enough along yet to experience the nausea or the smells?

I don't know when it happened, though it was likely before
Teddy went to inspect neighboring land with his father, but
we'd been as intimate as a married couple since the end of June.
Years of planning, of turning childhood friendship into something more, of becoming everything to him and he becoming
everything to me, culminating in the final blessing of creating
life together—the final step in a plan that had become ours, not
solely mine.

I could hardly contain my relief and triumph, but had wished
to be certain before telling him. Now, my stomach flipped over
as seeds of doubt took hold—will he have the mettle to hold
firm against his lordship? Or worse, what if he didn't still love
me the way I loved him?

My lips curled, and I waved a hand. "I'll be off then, Mary."

"Aye, have a good day."

"I'll pray for an excellent potato yield," I called, springing
into a brisk walk. Everything I ever wanted was within my
grasp. I only had to reach for it.

"What's this?" Michael asked, pointing to my head as we
headed away from the sun-room and down the opulent main
hallway of Kilrush House. Huge floor-to-ceiling windows provided light from our right, offering stunning views of the mag-

nificent lawns, immaculately landscaped with interspersed statues and rockeries—a luscious pavilion fit for a king, overlooking the Shannon Estuary. On a clear day, like today, one could see clear across the estuary to Scattery Island and County Kerry, and it wasn't unheard of to spot a dolphin or two taking an inland detour from the vast ocean to the west.

Mirrors lined the left-hand side of the hallway, deflecting sunlight onto the gold-inlaid ceilings, smoothly arched, like something from the Continent.

I reached a hand up to touch my head, and my fingers brushed daisies. "Ah! Hector and Crofton made them. What do you think?" I twirled, and Michael snorted.

"Airs and graces is what I think. Their lord and ladyship have been too kind to ye. Master Teddy too. I fear they've given ye notions of grandeur."

My cheeks heated. Airs and graces indeed. Wasn't he given as much attention by the Moore-Vandeleurs as I was? "Nonsense. Yer just jealous of my lovely crown."

"At least it isn't another bandage. That bird has it out for you, mark my words." Michael elbowed me, and I whacked his arm.

The door to Colonel Moore-Vandeleur's study banged open at the end of the hall, and my heart leapt into my throat as I automatically backed into the windows before sinking into a curtsy. Michael followed suit, melting into the glass as he bowed. Two still statues of obedience and deference, begging to not be noticed. Not be seen.

Boots marched forward with agitated steps, and I didn't dare look up. Instead, I found a whorl in the grain of the marble floor and focused on it.

"My Lord!" A voice called, and the hair on the back of my neck stood on end. Da.

"God damn it, Junior!" Colonel Moore-Vandeleur roared, and I felt Michael stiffen beside me. We both hated that his lordship still referred to Da as "Junior." His name was Michael too, like his Da before him—who died long ago—which now made our da senior, and my brother junior. "What does this even mean?"

"We did discuss the possibility, Your Lordship—" Da began, but the sound of ceramic shattering on marble cut him off . . . and succeeded in exacting a gasp from me.

"Do you even *understand* what this means?" Colonel Moore-Vandeleur shouted. "Christ above! How many tenant homes do we have living on less than a quarter acre?"

"At the estate? A couple hundred," Da replied.

"You fool! All together."

Da hesitated for a moment, then cleared his throat. "About fifteen hundred, Your Lordship."

Colonel Moore-Vandeleur chortled, then a great booming laugh shook the windowpanes. But there was no humor in it; instead, it weighed the air in tones of disbelief and despair.

"Do you know how much money I've spent developing this town?" Colonel Moore-Vandeleur's question required no answer. We all knew. His father, a kind and generous man, had spent a fortune building Kilrush from the ground up, from the port to the homes, the main square, the roads, the Protestant church. The port allowed well-to-do tourists from Limerick to cross the Shannon so they might avail of all we had to offer before continuing to Kilkee to enjoy the beachside amenities. And the current Colonel Moore-Vandeleur had continued his father's good work, so he could continue to thrive from the great relationship between the townsfolk, his tenants, and his many enterprises.

He'd even facilitated the building of a workhouse, a small prison, and a Catholic church, making Kilrush a town of note.

"Your Lordship, I—" Da began, but the sound of angry bootsteps cut him off. *Thud, thud,* closer to where Michael and

I stood, and for a moment I feared he would stop to take his wrath out on us.

Thud, thud, his step echoed, away from us, down the hall from whence we came, and the knot in my chest loosened so I could breathe once more.

"Da," Michael called, sprinting forward once it was clear his lordship was gone.

I glanced up, and my chest tightened once more.

Da, my big strong father, appeared so small in that hallway, his felt hat in hand, squeezing the brim with two blanched fists amid a mosaic of shattered vase shards.

Small and . . . old. For the first time in my life, the brightness that shone through his eyes seemed to have died, deepening the wrinkles of his face, inviting shadows to hollows I'd not noticed before.

With a deep sigh, Da looked over at me, then at Michael, before placing the hat back on his head.

"Take your sister home, Junior," he said quietly, but not in Irish, in English. Alarm bells rang between my ears. We spoke Gaeilge at home, like everyone else, reserving English for the Big House and when needed to translate between the tenants and the Anglos. Speaking English now . . . he meant for his words to go unheard by any prying ears. Some of the staff had enough English to get by at the Big House—mostly those in a supervisory role—but few would've had a strong understanding. Da grabbed Michael's shoulder. "Go down the main drive and use the Ennis road. Don't cut through the side gate. Stay away from the farmland. Stop for no one. When ye get home, gather everyone inside and bolt the windows and doors. Can I rely on ye to not frighten everyone?"

My heart raced as he gave his instructions, and I finally willed my body to move, my feet to work, before quickly joining my brother and father.

"What has happened?" I asked, in English.

"Disaster," he whispered, training his eyes on the ground. "Complete and utter disaster. But not a word of anything ye see or hear on yer way home, lest ye upset yer mother in her delicate condition. Understand? I'll break it to her as gently as I can when I get home."

Michael and I nodded in sync, and I bit my lower lip.

Disaster meant one thing, and one thing only.

For the second year in a row, the only crop we could grow to sustain our families must have had another poor harvest.

"What was all that his lordship was saying?" I asked, hurrying to keep stride with Michael's long legs. He kept a punishing pace, heeding Da's words as solemnly as a priest's sermon.

The breeze picked up suddenly, ruffling the slowly changing leaves of tall oak trees caged behind the high, imposing wall surrounding the estate.

"I think he's worried about the poor rates," Michael replied, grunting as he kicked at a loose stone. "Remember what happened back in April?"

My eyes widened. His lordship had evicted a few hundred families from their homes, then made Da and the bailiffs burn the houses and level the remnants.

From what I understood, according to Teddy, there was a law in place that stated for every home on less than a quarter acre of land, the landlord had to pay four pounds to the government if the family sought poor assistance—food and government-run work projects—from local authorities. And the crops on his lordship's land in Moyarta fared worse than ours last year, which led him to evict those most likely to seek aid and level the houses so he could say the homes didn't exist . . . and therefore he wasn't required to pay the poor rate.

"You think he fears having to evict more people because of another bad harvest?" I asked. That was the picture Teddy always painted of Colonel Moore-Vandeleur—a benevolent man who sought to continue the family's legacy of goodwill toward the people under their care.

Of course, he was benevolent. Hadn't he forgone marriage matches until he found a woman comfortable raising Teddy as her own? Not just as the heir of the house, but with the kind of love only a mother could give. There was a huge gulf in age between Teddy and his siblings as a result—and the only reason I dared hope that our marriage could go ahead. For Teddy's birth mother, his lordship's first wife, had once been a tenant, like me, raised above her station to become Mrs. Moore-Vandeleur. His lordship must have a fondness for us and would surely look favorably upon our union. I wouldn't have dared such a plan otherwise—I wasn't a complete fool.

Michael was slow to answer, as if mulling my question and weighing the information. But surely a good Christian man, Protestant or not, Anglo or not, would worry for those less fortunate, those who depend upon him? "Perhaps."

I was about to ask him to elaborate, but the fast-approaching rattle of a cart set my heart racing.

Ahead, the road curved off to the left, winding around the Moore-Vandeleur estate toward the village of Lissycasey on the Ennis Road, almost eighteen miles from us, away from the town of Kilrush. Da had said to stop for no one, and I prayed to God whoever approached didn't feel like chatting.

"Keep yer head down," Michael said, as the rattle reached a crescendo of thundering hooves and screeching wheels. The *fzzt* of leather reins against a horse's back drove my gaze upward. Nobody traveled this winding road at such a clip; it was far too dangerous.

The horse's ears lay flat against its skull—a fine beast, half-draught, half-Vanner by the looks and height of it, its black-and-white coat shimmering with sweat as it barreled around the corner. I thought for sure the cart behind would tip, but the driver leaned toward the wall-side of the road, and the cart stabilized.

"Rith amach as seo!" The driver roared, pointing at Michael and me before sweeping an arm toward Kilrush, behind us. For a moment, I wondered if he wanted us to dash away so he wouldn't run us over, but then he spoke again: "Fanann an diabhal i mo dhiaidh!"

Ice wound up my spine, freezing the breath in my lungs. *The Devil waits behind me.* The man was terrified and running from something.

Surely not illness? Something like that crept upon us, case by case, until we all remained indoors for fear of the miasma.

With another slap of reins against the horse's back, the driver drove on, and Michael whipped out an arm to push me behind him as the cart sped past.

"Jesus wept," Michael murmured, grabbing my hand. "Come on. Let's run."

Without another word, I hopped into a jog, debating the irony of running toward whatever the driver had been fleeing from.

But I didn't have long to wonder, for the moment we turned the corner, where the road would soon straighten and rows of tenant houses would dot the fields, the wind shifted, and we were blasted by a stench that stopped us in our tracks.

It hit the back of my throat, rotten eggs and sulfur, mixed with the unmistakable scent of sewage and mold.

Michael gagged, and my stomach roiled.

"What in the name of God is that?" Michael spat, covering his nose and mouth with his arm.

I shook my head, desperately pressing my lips together for fear I'd vomit.

A scream rent the air—a long, keening wail heard only at funerals, and the hair at the back of my neck stood on end.

Was this the "devil" the man warned us of?

A woman stumbled from a field to our right, onto the road, bent forward, and threw up.

"Mary?" My eyes widened as I recognized her, and I quickly broke away from Michael to assist. "Mary!"

Wiping her mouth, Mary Leary glanced up, the whites of her eyes so bloodshot, the blue of them glowed.

"The crop!" she cried, voice hoarse.

I wanted to tell her it was all right. That we'd get through it. That we'd plant again in the spring, and that my da would do his best to intervene with his lordship.

But the words died in my throat as Mary held up her hands.

"The fog. 'Twas the fog," she wailed, staring down at the thick, black sludge that coated her fingers, stretching like webbing as she fanned them out.

"*What* was the fog, Mrs. Leary?" Michael asked, placing two strong hands on my shoulders—whether to support me or himself, I'd never know. "And what's that smell? And why in the name of God are ye covered in tar?"

A chuckle emanated from the depths of Mary's chest, and fear gripped my soul.

"It came with the fog, the smell. And it turned the spuds to rot." Mary laughed now, straightening as she threw her head back.

Michael stepped back and pulled me with him.

"Come to your senses, Mrs. Leary," Michael snapped, voice shaking. "What are ye talking about?"

The laughter suddenly stopped, and Mary leveled a wild stare at both of us.

"Spuds," she said, holding up her hands so we might better see the tar.

"Spuds?" I echoed, furrowing my brow.

Mary nodded. "This is it. *This* is the crop."

Michael and I stared at the rotten sludge for what felt like a good minute, and I couldn't for the life of me figure out what she was trying to say. Then Michael grabbed my hand and jerked me into a walk, without a single word to Mary—who had started chuckling again.

"Home. Now," he hissed in my ear. "Like Da said, not a word to Mam or anyone about this."

I nodded, mute, and allowed him to drag me toward home, all while glancing over my shoulder at Mary Leary, who still stood, laughing, staring at her hands.

Chapter 10

The doubts I felt were the first stage of the process of forgetting; but in this place my heart rises up once more and cries out for revenge!
—Alexandre Dumas, *The Count of Monte Cristo*

Present: May 1848

That night brought another memory, dreamt in detail like the first. *Beware the fog.* Things I'd worked so hard to forget. Things I'd buried deep, brought to mind as morning's first light filtered through the drapes. Things that had haunted the very fabric of my being for years, replaying now as Beth helped me dress. As I broke my fast. As I sat through Lady Catherine's lessons.

Beware the fog.

That voice. Had the voice brought on the dream—the memory? A warning delivered on a breath of fear?

"You seem piqued," Lady Catherine noted, as I scratched out Wilhelmina's signature for the fiftieth time that hour. "Should I send for Dr. Brady?"

"What? Oh, no. Thank you." Setting down the fountain pen, I brought the heels of my palms to both eyes, blocking out the library for one, glorious moment before drawing a breath to form the sounds of the accent I had to speak in. "Only a restless night, I'm afraid."

Silence. I lowered my hands to find Lady Catherine's lips pursed. She wore the same ensemble she wore every day—a man's shirt tucked into the waist of a floor-length bustle skirt, her trusty pipe clutched in her hand.

"You poor thing." With a rustle of taffeta and silk, Lady Catherine rose from her chair and strode around the dark wooden desk to where I sat. With a smile, she brought a hand to my forehead, then glanced at my work. "No fever. And your script is getting closer to Wilhelmina's each day. You should rest. Read in the garden, perhaps? The air will do you good, and the rain has let up."

Tension left my body at those words. There was nothing I'd prefer than to venture beyond the thick stone walls of this old house. But it was only a matter of time before I'd have to put these lessons into practice. My pulse raced at my throat. Lady Catherine informed me that she'd received a letter not two days since, from a Dublin solicitor, demanding that Lady Catherine set a date for their inspection. "Shouldn't I try singing that melody again? I fear if I'm asked to entertain, it'll be certain I'm not who I say I am."

"Nonsense. Your health comes first. Besides, we can always still beg the excuse of the grieving widow." Grinning, Lady Catherine straightened and glanced out the window. "Such a fine day. God knows we won't see many more until midsummer."

"But the letter—"

"Hush now. It's all empty threats and intimidation. We have time. Besides, your elocution is passing fair, and you could certainly read aloud for company." Lady Catherine turned and placed a gentle hand on my shoulder. "Thank goodness your former mistress took it upon herself to teach you your letters."

My chest tightened as a slow flush bloomed across my cheeks, and I frowned. The past was the past, and the future loomed ahead.

"Perhaps . . . you had that nightmare again?" asked Lady Catherine. "However you are feeling—whatever emotions it stirred up—you should mull them over. Confront them."

I stiffened. "Oh no, Mama. I'm perfectly fine. I assure you."

The gentle hand on my shoulder suddenly tightened as Lady Catherine's fingers dug into my skin.

"You must confront them," she hissed, jerking me around to face her. My palms went slick as I pursed my lips. These strange outbursts were few and far between, but I'd quickly learned to agree, to say whatever it was she wanted to hear. To bow and scrape like the nothing I was—a terrible mimic wearing fine clothing.

"Yes, Mama," I whispered, gathering courage to meet her gaze. My heart raced in my chest as I forced myself to glance at her—eyes swallowed by darkness, frown lines etched deep, face contorted with anger that distorted her features 'til I wasn't sure I was looking at Lady Catherine at all.

Whipping out her other hand, she grabbed my second shoulder and gave a hearty shake.

"It's for your own good. For your vengeance," she hissed, before glancing over her shoulder. "Will you *please* be quiet!"

Pulse racing, my eyes slid beyond her hunched form, but—once again—naught was there. A chill gripped my very soul as I wondered if her ladyship was afflicted with delusion. Isolated as she was, here on the edge of the world, it wouldn't surprise me at all.

Her grip loosened, and she took a deep breath as she turned back to face me.

"What I meant to say was, oft times, we allow wounds to fester, until all that's left is hatred so bold, we are consumed by thoughts of vengeance, dear." Lady Catherine released me and straightened. Her eyes were bright, the darks of them so wide they swallowed the dark blue ring around her pupils. A shiver ran up my spine, sending a flash of ice to my core.

"You needn't worry, Mama," I replied. Steady. On Lady

Grace's worst days, I'd always maintained composure, and I would do so now. If this woman was afflicted, I would do all in my power to soothe her, for my future depended on her favor. "The only revenge I seek is that of which I informed you: to have a place of my own and land to sustain me. That's my vengeance, Mama. Naught else."

A shudder ran over Lady Catherine's shoulders, and she shook herself before clutching the charm at her throat. I watched as she closed her eyes, as her chest heaved. And as her eyelids popped open, a bright smile lit up her face, melting all trace of anger from her features.

"And you shall have it. I'll have Mistress Lynch bring you a tisane this evening. A sleeping draught to help keep any dreams at bay. That should help. Oh, and I'll have the soothing herbs added to the incense in your room."

Pursing my lips, I fought against the hammering of my pulse and rose. "Thank you, Mama. I'll take your sound advice and get some air."

"Good." With a nod, Lady Catherine made her way around the desk, opened the top drawer, and pulled out the key to the attic. I knew it on sight now. Not only from its intricate design, but from the length of lilac ribbon looped through the ring. "I have a few things to attend to, so this works out perfectly."

"In the attic?" I asked, eyeing the key as she slipped it into her skirt pocket.

Lady Catherine paused, then brought her strange, dilated gaze to mine. "That, my dear, is none of your concern."

And without another word, she swept past me, through the library, and out the door.

As the voice of the feminine presence—the same one who whispered from the shadows when I awoke from my fainting spell—reverberated through my mind.

Maggie, you must set me free.

*   *   *

Breathing the salt-tinged air was exactly what the doctor ordered. But despite the clear sky, with sunbeams beating down to erase any evidence of the rain that had plagued us since my arrival, I couldn't help but pull my shawl tightly around my shoulders.

Something about Lady Catherine's mercurial demeanor sent a coil of dread to my gut. It was as if she weren't quite there sometimes. Overtaken, perhaps. An illness of the mind was one thing . . . but then what of the spirit? Was it the "woman in white" Lady Catherine had once mentioned?

With a heavy sigh, I rounded the front of Browne House, my borrowed shoes crunching on crushed stone as I strode beneath the bower that led to the walled gardens. It was quite possible that a spirit was trapped in the house. Perhaps the real Wilhelmina. My chest tightened.

Mam had once told me that when the dead passed, it was best to say your goodbyes quickly and tell them to pass on, to rest in peace. That sometimes when grief overtakes the living, the dead cannot move on, and become stuck, affixed next to the grieving loved one who refused to let them go.

A mother's grief . . . that I understood all too well.

I shook my head—brushing away the macabre—and glanced about. I'd never actually been to the gardens, but I assumed they'd be no different from the well-kept lawns and regimented rose beds of the Moore-Vandeleur's walled garden. My brows arched as my eyes swept over the ancient beauty of dappled gray stone—weather-washed and bird-stained pillars covered with climbing roses. There were no straight lines here, and the pillars stood in a proud circle, a sundial in their center.

The lawns were curved—in need of a cut, but not completely overgrown—and interspersed throughout were wild beds of foxglove, butterfly bushes, betony, fuchsia, red valerian, crocus, hydrangea, roses, and—my God—thousands of the beautiful white trumpet flowers that always found their way to my room.

There was no rhyme nor reason to the planting. As if the seeds simply grew where they fell, a cacophony of color that would have sent Lady Grace screeching to the gardener.

But the gardens of Browne House boasted naught but nature and lusciousness—everything a garden should be.

I smiled, and strode forward, noting the gardener's cottage in the back right corner. It was partially hidden behind five-feet-high hydrangea bushes—blue and pink and white blooms of a size I never thought possible. Each bloom spanned the width of a dinner plate, almost consuming the gardener's path, and I wondered how they were able to move their equipment in and out of the pretty storage shed.

I'm sure that even if I hadn't been cooped up within the walls of Browne House for months, I still would've thought this the grandest place in the world.

"Afternoon, Miss," a voice called, and I whirled on my heel as my heart nearly jumped up my throat.

"Jesus, Mary, and Joseph," I exclaimed, eyes narrowing as I homed in on the intruder. "Mr. O'Dea! You gave me a right fright."

With a nod, Cormac set down the wheelbarrow he held and removed his hat as I fought to breathe. "I'm that sorry, Miss, but when ye didn't stir at the rattle of the barrow, I thought ye might be lost in yer thoughts. Better a startle now than a scream when ye finally spied me, in my opinion."

I nodded. I'd have afforded another the same luxury.

"In truth, I *was* lost." I brought my hand to my heart, as if the gesture might steady my thundering pulse. "Away with my thoughts, that is."

"This place does that to people," Cormac said, taking hold of the wheelbarrow once more. "I'll not be in yer hair. Only fertilizing, as the weather's fine."

"Oh, that's quite all right. Mama thought it best if I took some air." Pursing my lips, I noticed he was dressed for labor—a good linen shirt paired with dark woolen knee breeches, darned stockings, and sturdy boots. He looked more a tenant farmer than a footman. Then again, I wouldn't want to sully my good clothes if asked to ferry manure around. "You're delivering fertilizer to the gardener?"

He smiled and pushed the wheelbarrow forward. "I'm the gardener, Miss."

"But I thought you were the footman?"

"Gardener, footman, horse hand, goods negotiator, land agent, overseer. A jack of all trades, I suppose. Whatever her ladyship needs, I provide."

"Oh." My brows drew together of their own accord. I knew the staff was sparse—a third of what the Moore-Vandeleurs employed—but it seemed odd that Lady Catherine wouldn't have need of separate people to fulfill the roles. He was only one man.

"Not many souls come this far afield to visit," he offered. "Her ladyship trusts me with most of her affairs, and I'm paid three times the salary."

A flush stained my cheeks, and I busied myself with finding a bench to perch upon. "I didn't ask, Mr. O'Dea."

"Ah," he said, a wide smile lighting his face as he set down the barrow near the farthest flower bed, "but ye did."

My eyes widened at that, and he chuckled.

"Ye wear yer thoughts on yer face, Maggie O'Shaughnessy."

Maggie. Me. My own name. How long had it been since I was myself? My chest tightened. "It's Wilhelmina now. Her ladyship wouldn't like to hear me addressed as, well, myself."

Pulling a short spade from the depths of the wheelbarrow, Cormac nodded before shoveling a measure of manure. "Apologies, Miss. I didn't mean any offense."

I watched as he spread the fertilizer and breathed deep to

gather my thoughts. Maggie. When all this was over, could I ever be Maggie again? Could I ever face all that had happened without the guilt of knowing that I'd dishonored my family to survive?

"Reading, are ye?" Cormac called, and with a start, I realized I still held a book in my hand.

"Mama thought I could read aloud. But if that will bother you, I'd be glad to sit and admire the flowers."

"What is it?" he asked, moving on to the next flower bed.

"Pardon?"

"The book. What is it?"

"Oh, um." I hadn't even looked when I'd grabbed it on my way out of the library. But now, I turned the leather-bound tome over, to read the title. "*The Divine Comedy, Volumes One, Two, and Three.*"

I glanced up, and Cormac stood frozen, his lips parted as he stared at me. "What?"

"Well . . ." He trailed off, then barked a laugh. "Not exactly light reading, that."

"Oh?" I frowned, and opened the cover. "Is it not a comedy?"

"Certainly not." With a shake of his head, he went back to shoveling. "Have ye not heard of Dante's *Inferno*, then?"

"No."

"That'd be volume one, and 'tis about a dead man navigating through the nine circles of Hell."

"Oh. Well." With a scrunch of my nose, I closed the book and placed it on the bench. "Not exactly the kind of thing I'd need to know for a meeting with the solicitors."

"No, indeed." With a grunt, Cormac took up the barrow once more and wheeled it closer. "Besides, if it's convincing them ye need, titled ladies might talk about novels—enough spare time for fiction and all that. Though, her ladyship isn't one for novels herself. Howld on there. I might have something."

Setting down the barrow, I watched as Cormac hopped toward the gardener's cottage, before being swallowed by the hydrangeas. He certainly didn't strike me as the novel-reading type. Then again, neither was I. If only because I'd never read one before. So far, Lady Catherine had me read pamphlets on housewifery and a few philosophical texts that I couldn't decipher—all in the name of improving my speech and comprehension.

I glanced at the book I'd pilfered from the library and sighed. The nine circles of Hell didn't seem at all appetizing.

"Here ye go."

I looked up, and there was Cormac, book in hand.

"I picked it up in Hodges in Dublin on a trip for her ladyship," he explained, holding it out as he approached. "A little less reality might be just what the doctor ordered, given what's happening in the country."

I smiled as I took the book, but Cormac's gaze had shifted to Browne House.

"I suppose you'd argue we're living in one of those circles of Hell," I said.

He glanced at me. "Are we not?"

"Not here," I replied. "Not within these walls, at least. We're fed and sheltered," I reminded him. He pursed his lips and shoved his hands in his pockets.

"There's that."

"What else is there?" I asked, turning my attention to the book. Its pages were bound in light brown leather, its title etched in silver script. "*The Count of Monte Cristo*? What's this about, then?"

"Ah." With a shrug, Cormac backtracked to the barrow and continued fertilizing. "Vengeance for a deed most foul."

"And this is light reading?" I chuckled and opened the book.

"'Tis about a man who is betrayed by an aristocratic friend, for the crime of loving the same woman. And when he escapes the prison he's sent to, he assumes the identity of a nobleman to enact his revenge."

A chilled breeze ruffled the shawl at my throat. I'd had a bellyful of noblemen and aristocrats. Enough to last a lifetime. But was I not assuming the identity of a nobleman myself? Noblewoman, at least. "And you think I'll enjoy it?"

"I hope ye do. 'Tisn't the kind of romances the ladies of leisure might frequent. But it might be enough of an escape to help ye forget all ye've been through. At least, for a time."

"Did you? Enjoy it, that is?"

He paused in his work and threw a smile over his shoulder. "I did. While reading, I was both prisoner and pirate, and relished the comeuppance at the end. But I won't spoil it for ye. Is her ladyship teaching ye well?"

"Pardon?" I asked.

"Her ladyship," he repeated, taking a moment to lean on the spade. "We had a kind landlord that allowed the family's tutor to teach the tenants' children their letters, and I was lucky enough to be one of those children. But it seems ye've caught on over-quick, so I thought her ladyship must be a great teacher."

"Oh, well, yes. I suppose she is." No need to divulge my entire life's story to a stranger. God knew, I didn't want to get into details I'd prefer remain buried. "She's been very kind. And evidence of her kindness continues to impress me."

He nodded, then glanced away. "I hear she is. Kind, that is. If it weren't for her, and this job, me mam and dad would have to take ship to the Americas. And me along with them."

"You *hear* she's kind? Sounds to me like saving your family is evidence enough of that."

"Aye, well." Puffing his cheeks, Cormac rubbed the nape of his neck. "There's still something not quite right about this place. But her family is certainly kind, and I'll never say a bad word about her ladyship."

"You know them well? Her family?"

He turned, cocking his head to the side before forcing a smile to his face. A ripple of recognition took hold as I held his gaze, but it flittered away as he shook his head. "I suppose ye could say that. She's a nobody, like you, and I. A tenant farmer's daughter, elevated by his lordship, may he rest in peace. And now, she's the best of landlords. The people here are lucky to have her, though most aren't so fortunate. Lucky his lordship loved her and wed her, so she could care for them when he was gone."

I pressed my lips together as my brows knotted above narrowed eyes. A keening ache rose in my chest, a wail I swallowed down, down, 'til all that remained was the memory of promises made and the labor that followed.

My son.

Our son.

But Teddy hadn't kept his promises to me—the daughter of a tenant farmer. And suddenly, her ladyship and I were the same. Two women promised the world—one living the life she'd hoped could be hers, the other a specter of what could have been, living a lie to appease the other.

"God bless her," I murmured, making the sign of the cross. I didn't fault her ladyship. Not a whit. But the rage that bubbled up my throat was sure to suffocate me if I let it. With a shake of my head, I cleared my throat. "What an incredibly fortuitous rise in station."

"Maybe there's truth to rumor, and it has something to do with whatever goes on in that attic." Cormac jerked a thumb toward the house, and I turned to follow its direction. A large, round window on the upper floor. "Have ye seen her that lives up there yet? The woman in white? The spirit? 'Tis why I don't stay in the house. I prefer the gardener's cottage."

Laced with respectful fear, his words forced a cool sweat to my forehead. I stared at the window, an all-seeing gaze that crept over my skin, raising the little hairs of my arms. The silhouette of a person quickly ducked out of sight. Was Lady Catherine there? Watching?

If she was, she wouldn't like to hear such silliness.

"Whatever do you mean?" I asked. "Are you alluding to the supposed haunting?"

A flicker of shadow darted across the window as Lady Catherine went about her business in the attic, and I shivered.

"Never mind. Nothing to worry about," he replied.

It certainly didn't sound like "nothing," but part of me didn't want to dig any further. I had thought mayhap the spirit could be Wilhelmina herself, tethered here by the grief of her mother. But when I thought of the account of a haunting in Lord Browne's journal, that theory dissipated on the wind. Wilhelmina was recently deceased, and Lord Browne had passed a long time since.

"Shall I read aloud?" I asked, averting my eyes from whatever stared down at us from the attic.

"Oh!" Cormac glanced at me, his eyes alight. "Would ye?"

I nodded and flipped the pages to the first chapter. "*Marseilles: The Arrival. On the twenty-fourth of February, 1815, the look-out at Notre-Dame de la Garde, signalled the three-master—*"

But as I read, the crunch of shoes on gravel echoed through the garden, and I glanced toward the bower. The blood froze in my veins as Lady Catherine's black silk skirt came into view, followed by the lady herself. Eyes wild, I sharply glanced at the attic window. There wasn't a hope on God's green earth that she'd made it from the attic to the garden in less than a minute.

Which begged the question: Who had been watching? Or what?

"There you are, Wilhelmina. Ah, Mr. O'Dea," called Lady Catherine. She strode forward, her face etched with worry. "I'm afraid I simply can't work, given my fear that you've over-extended yourself."

With a frown of my own, I set down *The Count of Monte*

Cristo and rose from my perch. "Th-the air is already working wonders," I said, my eyes flitting toward the large window on the upper floor, brows drawing together as yet another shadow crossed from one side to the other.

"I've seen to the soothing herbs myself and would feel much better if you went to rest in your room." Lady Catherine said, running a hand over her immaculately styled hair. She glanced at Cormac—who had gone back to his work—then pulled me aside. "Are you certain you don't wish me to call Dr. Brady? It would be no trouble at all."

"No, thank you, Mama." I shook my head, heart racing as I glanced back at the garden. The beautiful colors now seemed naught but dull parodies of the bright wonder I'd thought it not long ago. I feared what might visit with the incense, what buried memories might scratch toward the surface.

"Very well," said Lady Catherine with a sigh. "Do let me know if you change your mind. Stress can wreak havoc on the health. But you needn't worry. Your studying is going well, and we'll get through this, you and I. Together. I promise you that."

But I held no stock in promises.

Not anymore.

Chapter 11

January 1846: Before

Mary Leary died two days after we'd met her on the Ennis Road, hands covered in sludge, laughing like a bean sidhe.

And she wasn't the only one. About forty people had collapsed, and three people lost their lives shortly after the digging. The coroner was called from the far-off town of Ennis, and he declared they'd perished from overexposure to a noxious gas emitted from the rotten crop.

I understood now, though I didn't then, that the tar-like substance in Mary's hand had been, quite literally, potatoes.

Da said the minute they began harvesting, the smell overpowered most, but when they noticed the off-gray color of the spuds, many grabbed the vegetables to inspect, and with a single touch, the potatoes simply turned into stinking piles of sludge in people's hands.

Reports from Dublin stated it was a kind of disease brought

on the air, likely a kind of fungus, and the hot, humid summer had provided the perfect environment for the spores to take purchase in the ground, destroying the entire crop.

It wasn't just a bad harvest, it was total annihilation.

But we would be fine. Not just us, but the tenants. For Da had convinced Colonel Moore-Vandeleur to offer paid work to those at the greatest risk of not surviving the winter—enough so they could maintain strength so as not to disrupt the spring farming season.

But that didn't stop a number of families from seeking government assistance, resulting in a new slew of evictions and house tumblings, lest Colonel Moore-Vandeleur had to pay the poor rate.

It made me sick to my stomach, but Teddy assured me his father was heartbroken. It was just that his lordship had spent a sizable fortune on improving the town, and he couldn't afford the poor rate if he was to continue offering paid labor to those strong enough to take it.

Last year had brought low profits for his lordship, apparently, and avoiding the poor rates was the only way to secure funding for the coming year.

"Settle, Maggie," Teddy murmured, squeezing my hand.

Settle? It was almost February, in the year of our Lord 1846, and I could no longer hide the babe. Four months gone, and in five or six more, Teddy and I would welcome our child into the world.

I laced my fingers through his, but he pulled his hand from mine with a shrug.

"No need to appear completely shameless. It would give the wrong impression, don't you think?" he said.

I bit my lower lip as we stood, outside the door of my home—Teddy, almost ready to return to Dublin after his Christmas break, steeling ourselves for what lay ahead.

When I'd written to tell him of the babe, he'd replied brightly, excited for this new chapter of ours, assuring me that none could protest with a child on the way.

And I'd been confident . . . then.

But now, with Teddy about to inform my parents and ask their permission to wed, I wasn't sure. Something akin to dread weighed heavy in my gut.

From within the home, my newborn baby brother wailed. Teddy had wanted to have this conversation with my parents right away, but I had insisted on sparing my mother the shock, lest it affect her pregnancy.

Dusk kissed the fields in hues of gray and blue, and soon, the Daoine Uaisle—the Good Folk, the Fair Folk—would take charge of the night, shepherding wayward men through the veil between our world and theirs, tricking them into leaving the mortal coil behind.

I shivered. I knew we had to wait 'til dusk to be sure Da was present, but I didn't like the idea of Teddy walking home at night. It was silly, I know. But with the failed crop—the blight, we called it—came whispers of the féar gortach.

"Hungry grass" was the only way to translate it for his lordship, who had heard the rumors and requested a full report from Da.

The tenants were certain the land was cursed, that the crops would continue to fail because an elemental spirit—a Daoine Uaisle—had taken up residence nearby and brought famine by way of a housewarming gift.

I knew it made no sense, for if the land was cursed, then the vegetables we grew for the Moore-Vandeleurs would have perished, and the grazing land for the livestock would have withered away.

And yet God could not have done this to us—we, the meek, for blessed be they. It was far easier to turn to otherworldly things for answers.

"Everything will be well," Teddy promised, knocking on the door before I could stop him. "Hulloa, the house!"

"Stop, breathe, think," I reminded him. "If things start to go awry, hold your words, breathe deeply, and think about the next thing you need to say."

"Your father is not mine." He smiled, and the tightness in my chest eased. "This conversation will go as planned. You'll see. I'll hold my own."

The top of the half door swung open, and Mam's lovely face appeared. Her brows—still dark, though her chestnut brown hair was now peppered with gray—rose when she saw Teddy, and her lips parted.

"Young Master," she announced, half-turning, likely for assistance from Da. Teddy had never come to our abode, not even when we were young children. Back in those days—before Lady Grace made Kilrush House her home—if we were to play together indoors, his lordship tolerated our presence in the summerhouse, and the summerhouse only.

Otherwise, we ran amok in the fields, bothering tenants with our antics.

A chair scraped within, and Da joined Mam at the door.

"Young Master Theo?" Surprise colored Da's tone, but when his eyes landed on me, he placed a gentle hand on Mam's shoulder. "Could you pour a cup of something for our guest, love?"

Mam's face twisted with confusion, but she nodded and stepped away as Da unlatched the bottom half of the door.

"Welcome," he said, ushering Teddy into our house.

"Thank you, Mr. O'Shaughnessy," Teddy said, brightly. As if we weren't about to confess that we'd conceived a child out of wedlock. That was my only concern: how they would receive such news. I didn't dare move just yet.

"Síofra," Da called, his eyes not leaving mine, "take your brothers and sisters over to Mrs. Lane for an hour, please."

"But it's full dark—" my sister began, but Da cut her off. "Now."

Da stepped forward, clearing the doorway for my siblings—Aoife, John, Mary, Martha, Patrick, and Nancy—who trailed along after Síofra like steps of stairs.

What's happening? Síofra mouthed as she passed, but I simply shook my head.

"Not you," Da said, grabbing Michael by the arm as he followed the others into the night air. "Back inside."

I squeezed my eyes shut to keep from cursing aloud. The last thing I needed was Michael's presence for this.

"Why?" Michael had no such restraint and blurted the question.

Boxing his ear, Da said: "Because when I'm gone, ye'll be the man of the house, ye eejit. And ye need to know how things are done."

Michael quickly retreated into the house, and I dared look at my father. He jerked his head toward the door, but I thought I'd faint if I tried to move. My heart hammered in my chest, and the pulse in my ears warned of danger.

"I know," Da said, leaning close so my curious brothers and sisters couldn't hear.

I glanced at him sharply, and he smiled—a thin, pained curve of the lips—as tears formed in his eyes.

"I hoped I was wrong, but I see that I wasn't," he said softly, wiping a hand over his face. "Come on, darlin'. The night air isn't good for ye. Time to hear what yer beau has to say."

"Oh, Da—" I murmured, voice cracking as I took the hand he offered.

"I love ye, my Maggie girl," he said, planting a kiss on the top of my head. "And so does yer Mam. Nothing will ever change that."

*   *   *

"You've not broached this with your father yet, I take it." Da's lips pressed together so tightly, a band of pure white skin blistered around them.

"Not yet, sir. But I have no reason to believe he would deny us," Teddy announced, folding his arms across his chest as he perched on Da's own stool.

He looked so out of place, so foreign, so *other* sitting there at the rough-hewn dining table.

Our house was grander than others. While most homes boasted a single room, where the family gathered to sleep on straw-stuffed pallets that barely kept the cold and damp of the stone floor at bay, we had four, and a loft.

The main living area—where a roaring open fire blazed before a sitting area and dining table. A small bedroom to the right of the entrance door, where our parents slept—on a bed, gifted to them by the late Mr. Moore-Vandeleur, Teddy's grandfather, on the occasion of their wedding. To the left were two small rooms. The first for the eldest girls—where I slept with Síofra and Aoife. And the second for the eldest boys, where Michael and John slept. The youngest children—Mary, Martha, Patrick, and Nancy, slept in the loft—a crawl space above our rooms, requiring the use of a ladder, where anyone over five feet couldn't even sit up straight.

The floor was stone, but Mam had been able to purchase a rug or two over the years, and to me—and most of the tenants—the O'Shaughnessy home was the lap of luxury. The kind of status most could only dream of achieving.

But now, with Teddy sitting there in his velveteen, full-length breeches—knee breeches were only for the Irish, a statement of us versus them, and only Anglos held the status and wealth to wear full-length trousers, waistcoat, pocket watch, fine tailed coat, and cravat, top hat in hand—our home and everything the tenantry looked up to us for felt wanting.

Mam hadn't spoken a word since we revealed our news, and I stole glances at her as Teddy took the lead. Flushed cheeks and glistening eyes met mine each time.

Michael's gaze, on the other hand, promised murder. If one could kill with a glare, Teddy would be six feet under before the sun rose.

"I can think of ten reasons why he'll refuse off the top of my head," Da said with a sigh.

"You feckin' *gowl*!" Michael exclaimed, slamming a fist against the tabletop. A thin wail sounded from my parents' bedroom, and Mam hopped to attention.

"That'll be the babe," she whispered, bobbing a curtsy to excuse herself. I watched her go and caught her pressing the back of her hand over her mouth.

Tears pricked behind my eyelids. I'd disappointed her greatly, I knew it in my heart and soul. But once the banns were called and the ring was placed on my finger, I'd make sure she'd want for nothing. I owed her that much.

"Michael," Da warned, as Teddy cleared his throat.

"I-I understand th-this has all come as a shock, but I assure you: once Papa learns of the babe, he'll c-come around to it," Teddy continued, dismissing Michael's anger with a flippant wave. "It was the route of least resistance."

"Wait," said Michael, leaning over the table. "I knew ye were meeting and such, and there was feeling between ye. But are ye really saying ye thought to *defile* my sister as some sort of way to strongarm your father to agree to this?"

"I-I . . . I . . . y-yes?" Teddy's brows drew together, and I winced.

"Stop. Breathe. Think," I whispered. He glanced at me and nodded.

"There's something wrong with him," Michael scoffed, turning to Da in disbelief.

Da held up a hand, briefly closing his eyes before giving his full attention to Teddy.

"I can't approve of this tonight," he said, and Teddy's confidence wavered. I could see it in the slight slump of his shoulders. "Return to me after speaking with your father. Then I will go to him, and he and I will discuss next steps. I will only offer approval if his lordship consents, and I will only speak with his lordship after you've confessed what you've done."

"Mr. O'Shaughnessy, I can assure—" Teddy began again, but Da was having none of it.

"If you are so certain, Young Master, then I wonder why you didn't speak with your father first," he snapped, rising from his stool. "If you think me fool enough to take this matter up with his lordship myself, out of the blue, then you are sadly mistaken. Our family's standing and survival relies solely on your father's good humor. And if you think I will overlook the gross imbalance of power you used to extort my daughter, you are very mistaken."

"Da!" I protested, eyes wide as Teddy uncrossed his arms.

"Ex-ex*tort*?" Teddy exclaimed, rising in a fury.

"Teddy, no!" I warned, but he did not listen.

"Have you forgotten to whom you speak, sir?" Teddy demanded.

My Da smiled, but that smile was not filled with happiness and hope. "Oh, I assure you, Young Master, I have not now, nor ever, forgotten to whom I speak. But for one so certain his parents will pay no mind in this matter, you are very quick to remind me—the father of the precious woman you promised the world to—of who your illustrious father is, and the connections that make you our master."

Tears sprang to my eyes, and I rose to my feet as Teddy jerked back, my father's words a slap to the face.

I reached for Teddy, lacing my fingers through his, and he turned. That beautiful face—the one I held so dear—was twisted with such rage that for a moment, a breath, I thought it possible that *he* was the elemental, the spirit that plagued the land.

Hard, cool eyes stared into mine, but in a blink, it was gone—the elemental, and the fury—replaced with something akin to resignation.

Drawing my hand to his lips, he gently kissed my knuckles, and turned toward Da once more.

"My sincerest apologies, Mr. O'Shaughnessy. I can assure you that Maggie is as precious to me as she is to you, and I will follow your instructions to the letter. I shall seek an audience with Papa first thing in the morning." Teddy bowed, and Michael scoffed. "A child is the surest way to his heart. And Father's fondness for my own mother—your own people—will guarantee success in this matter."

Da, on the other hand, nodded. "In the event that yer cast off as a result, our home is open to ye. I'll welcome ye warmly as a son of this house. Have ye savings to get ye by in Dublin? This is yer final year of study, is it not?"

All the blood drained from Teddy's face as Da's words sank in. "Cast off?"

"Yes," Da said. "Surely ye thought it a possibility? That his lordship would cut ye loose?"

He certainly had, for I'd brought it up in the past. Sometimes, during those conversations, I wondered if Teddy would hold true—could hold true—if that were to happen. But he had to, for I was his strength, and I would be his pillar. What may have begun as a calculated dance was now so much more . . . and I wasn't sure if I could go on without him by my side.

"That won't happen," I said, squeezing Teddy's hand. "All will be well."

"As ye say," Da continued. "But if it does, I assume ye'll both settle in Limerick. Join a practice there after graduation?"

"I-I hadn't thought about it," Teddy stammered.

"Maggie will be a great help to ye, thanks to yer stepmother.

She has the learning to keep the books in good order and won't be a burden to ye in society." Da nodded and held out a hand for Teddy to shake. "I look forward to hearing how the meeting goes."

Teddy stared at Da's hand for the space of two breaths, then shook it. "I won't let you down, Mr. O'Shaughnessy."

"Oh, it's not me ye'd be letting down. It's that woman standing next to ye."

Chapter 12

Death must be so beautiful . . . to forget time, to forgive
life, to be at peace.
— Oscar Wilde, *The Canterville Ghost*

Present: May 1848

"Da!"

The word scraped over my tongue as I jerked awake, the
blurred haze of slumber obscuring my sight. Where . . . what?
Da shouldn't speak to Teddy thus, nor should Teddy speak to
Da like that. I had to fix this, I had to—eyes wild, I glanced
about the room. The curtains were drawn, and it was dark, but
the shadowed forms of furniture slowly came into focus. My
heart leapt in my throat. This was not my room, not my bed.
My pulse fluttered as I flung back the covers and scrambled to
my feet.

A smoky haze swirled and dipped with the rapid movement,
and my gaze darted to the nightstand, to the incense burner—
still smoldering—beneath the vase of fresh flowers. Because
this was not my room, but Wilhelmina's, and I was now she.
With a great heaving breath, my knees buckled, and I sat back

on the bed, bouncing with the weight with which my body re-signed itself to reality.

It wasn't real, only a dream. A detailed, terrifying dream that replayed the memory with such vividness, I was sure I'd been transported in time. Everything I'd felt at that moment rushed back to me tenfold, gripping my gut before mercilessly twisting. This one was not like the others. It was far stronger. Far more . . . real. Forcing me to relive emotion in such detail that I had no choice but to remember every tiny detail.

I leaned forward and propped my elbows against shaking knees before burying my face in my palms. Lady Catherine had insisted I take to my bed. Yes, that was what happened.

But that was this afternoon. I straightened and launched off the mattress, making a beeline for the closed curtains before drawing them back. My eyes widened as the full dark of deep night stared back. I shook my head. Between the dream and the hour, disoriented didn't quite describe the muzzy sensation I couldn't shake. Squinting into the nightscape, I leaned forward, touching my forehead against the cool glass of the window.

I didn't want to remember; I didn't deserve to. I'd been taught that grief always barred the way forward, that wallowing stalled progress, that ploughing ahead was the only way to get through the darkness.

Bury it. Keep it down. Lock it away. Forget it.

Throw all your energy into whatever comes next, for the dead will not thank you for falling apart. I closed my eyes, lavishing the chill from the windowpane.

Why now? I'd done so well keeping it buried, keeping it down, locking it away—

"Because ye can't forget it, and ye shouldn't."

The blood froze in my veins as a voice—*his* voice—echoed through the room. Something gripped my chest, and building pressure fought against my lungs, desperate to expand. Breathe . . . I must—

"*Ye big eejit. Did we go through all that for nothing? Look where ye are.*"

"M-Michael?" I wasn't sure how I uttered his name, but it left my lips on a breath, a prayer, a hope.

I opened my eyes and forced myself to turn, though every hair on my body snapped to attention, the legs of a thousand insects clamoring over my skin.

"Is it you?" I asked, surer now as my eyes flitted about the chamber, scanning every darkened corner.

The moonlight at my back illuminated Wilhelmina's room, transforming the haze of incense into a sea of fog. Too much incense—more than I ever remembered burning before.

Turning was the most I could achieve, for my body would listen no more. Willing it to move would bear no fruit.

"Michael?" I called again, pulse racing in my ears as I . . . waited. Christ above, if anyone saw me. Standing, terrified, in my nightclothes, calling out to my dead brother, hoping that somehow, some way, he was—

The haze of incense shifted as a snaking draft ebbed through unseen cracks to grip its edges. But a draft would drag the smoke into a whorl, surely?

My eyes widened as I stared, and my lungs ceased their function.

One leg formed in the haze, then another, as a figure stepped through the fog. No, not through it, but . . . gathering it, pulling it into shape.

A scream died in my throat as a torso joined the legs, then arms, until at last a fog-formed likeness of my brother stood before me, tendrils of smoke billowing behind, hands of the dead reaching for him to drag him back through the veil between our world and theirs.

It smiled, *he* smiled, and my insides quaked with roiling fear.

"*I told ye to live, Maggie,*" he said, voice disembodied, echoing behind, beside, and before me. "*For that, ye must remember.*"

"I-is he with ye, Michael? Did ye find him, there, on the other side?" I whispered, asking the one question I didn't want an answer to.

My brother's likeness smiled and cocked its head to the side.

"*The child? Nay. For the sins of the father outweigh the goodness of the mother.*"

A laugh echoed somewhere in the house, and Michael's likeness whipped around to glance at the door.

"*She's trapped here,*" he said. "*That's why ye must remember. For to secure the future ye want, ye must save her.*"

"What do you mean?" I whispered.

"*The woman in white . . . here she comes.*"

He turned back again, but his form wavered, melding into the haze that bathed the bedchamber, but not before I noticed him gesturing toward the incense burner on the bedside table.

"*Remember it all, Maggie. The smoke will help ye.*"

"Wait, Michael. What do ye mean—"

But I didn't get the chance to beg him to stay, to answer my questions. For the woman in white's voice cut through my mind, each word slicing deep—straight into the center of my soul.

You're not the first to step in Wilhelmina's shoes, child.

My eyes rolled back in my head then, and the world around me disappeared.

October 1846: Before

Beyond the cool glass pane, the world continued turning, but mine had slowed to the heartbreaking terror of defeat.

I thought mayhap . . . nay, I was almost certain . . . that Teddy had forsaken me.

That window had been my only means of entertainment these past months, the reflection—a specter of my old self—my only company, and each day I fought against the vise that gripped my chest; breath . . . a struggle. Below, Merrion Square Park played host to chaperoned young women, promenading down straight, manicured pathways before suitors, their fine silk dresses screaming titled fortunes. And why wouldn't they? The park was for the exclusive use of residents of the square, and the square was home to titled families of the British court.

And I a cuckoo, locked away in the townhome of Lady Grace's own father.

I hadn't seen my family in eight months. Within two weeks of Teddy asking Da for my hand, I had been bundled into a coach bound for Dublin on February 7, 1846, with naught but a small sack containing fresh stockings and a shift.

Confusion gripped me throughout the journey. Why would I be better off surviving pregnancy in Lady Grace's city residence? Why could I not travel with Teddy, who was Dublin-bound for university? Why could I not bring one of my sisters for company?

Upon arrival, I was met by a fierce housekeeper, who spoke not a word during my entire stay. At least she kept me fed and watered—a prized heifer, set to calf.

Michael wrote, and so did Da, though my replies, outlining concerns about the wedding details, went unanswered.

His lordship had agreed to the marriage, under the condition that I gave birth in Dublin, where I would be provided the comfort and nutrition required to grow a healthy child, given the crisis caused by the blight. He'd even requested an audience before my departure, where he'd smiled so kindly and welcomed me to the family, before explaining that he would prefer I concentrate on the task at hand, and Teddy and I would be wed once I had naught else to worry me.

Truly, the gesture had been so thoughtful that it had warmed my heart and reassured me fully. I would be wed to the boy I loved, the boy who would make my family's fortune, the boy I'd set my hat at.

And yet . . . I had expected Teddy to at least visit in his free time, given our proximity, but he never came. At first, I thought his final-year studies must have been brutal to keep him from me. But my letters went unanswered, and I knew then that I was alone.

Stop. Breathe. Think. That's all he had to do when speaking with his father, and I couldn't help but worry that something had gone awry.

And so the months passed, with me only permitted to stare out the window at the hustle and bustle—so as not to garner attention from anyone, given my delicate condition and the unorthodox circumstances of our union.

Until Lady Grace arrived, breathing new hope five months into my confinement, ready to hold my hand for the imminent birth.

And pat my shoulders when the midwife announced that my child—our son—was dead.

Dead. Gone. This beautiful life I had created—*we* had created—dashed out before he could even know his mother's love.

And he had cried so very fiercely upon arrival, so fiercely that I'd laughed with relief, despite the bone-splitting pain.

Before he was whisked from the room to be bathed.

Before the midwife began working on drawing forth the afterbirth.

Before the physician who'd tended me throughout my pregnancy shuffled solemnly into the room and gently told me that he hadn't made it.

That he'd been born malformed, unable to function for long

outside the womb, and disfigured enough to cause distress if I were to view him.

In the end, Lady Grace took the reins and insisted they shroud him immediately. That it would be best not to see him.

And so my child was buried in a cillín, an unconsecrated burial site for unbaptized and illegitimate children, while I was recovering, before I had mind enough to ask the location of my babe's resting place so I might visit and pray. So I might lay a crown of daisies over the tiny mound of earth and tell him how very much Mammy loved him and loves him still.

Lady Grace had left for Kilrush House while grief gripped me, instructing that I should convalesce for a time, for she had found a new place for me with a family of her acquaintance so I might forget these terrible memories. I'd railed at that, explaining that we had a wedding to plan, that Teddy hadn't forsaken me, that ours was a love born of childhood and devotion and we would try again . . . but Lady Grace hadn't said a word.

And still the titled dandies promenaded.

And still Teddy did not visit.

And still he did not write.

For three months I convalesced, and waited, staring out that window, at the hope and blossom of new love. The possibility of a future worth living.

But that future was no longer mine.

My heart echoed with a keening wail that would not quieten, a knell so hollow I thought it would consume me whole.

Babes died. Often. And God forgive me in my misery, but so consumed with heartache was I that not once did I consider those worse off. Those who lost wife and child during the war of labor. Those who lost children they'd raised and nurtured.

The weight of circumstance settled heavy on my chest, an undeniable tug of disbelief and grief as I journeyed home, three months later.

As I disembarked in Kilrush town.

As I put one foot before the other.

As I slowly made my way down the Ennis Road, following the high, impenetrable walls of the estate. They taunted me. Mocked me. As if to say, "You reached too far, and God has taken all ye dearly love."

Anyone who passed doffed their caps or called their hellos, but I paid them no mind.

Home. I needed to be surrounded by those I loved, those who loved me. I needed Michael's poking humor, and Da's muted chuckle, and Mam's bright smile. Until Teddy and I could meet, so we could talk and heal and plan. Until I could ask him why he had abandoned me in that gilded cage and rally him against whatever obstacles had surely popped up. In the meantime, I needed the reassurance of a warm home filled with laughter.

But as I turned the corner, the one that straightened toward the fields, where tenant houses stood squat and proud, it hit me.

The smell.

And suddenly a warm home filled with laughter had leapt out of reach.

For the woes of 1845 were no longer a distant memory, because the blight had returned and destroyed whatever sliver of hope any of us had left.

Smoke billowed from the chimney of my house, and I was reminded of the fog that brought the devastation this time last year. How could this happen again?

Da had written of all the work they had done—turning the soil, removing all tubers and roots, to be certain the old could not contaminate the new. Effort and expense were put into the endeavor, driving most of the tenants to exhaustion—toiling by day for his lordship, toiling by night for the survival of their families. Da had even sold all our luxuries to distribute coin to the tenants so none would starve in the coming months, sure the new harvest would be fine—how could it not be?

I sighed, then spied a figure standing in the open doorway of my home, a gray shawl wrapped around thin shoulders, sweeping the dirt pile from the main room to the ground outside.

"Mam!" I called, waving as I jogged. Though the physical pain of birth had eased, my joints were stiff from eight months of lolling around, and with each thud of my feet against hardened earth, a judder ran from knee to hip.

"Maggie?" Mam froze as she caught sight of me, but within a breath, she abandoned the broom, picked up her skirt, and ran to meet me.

We collided, knocking the wind from my lungs as her stick-thin arms engulfed my waist.

"Oh, my darlin' girl," she exclaimed, shifting to cup my face in her hands and shower me with kisses, as if I were naught but a child in need of comfort. "Sweet girl."

Tears pricked behind my eyes as her own glistened, a contagion of sorrow and joy, felt wholly betwixt mother and daughter.

"Thank God, yer home," Mam whispered, glancing back at the house, where a curious babe crawled through the open door, drowning in linen, for the child was far too thin, with none of the cherub-like softness I would expect.

Come to think of it, Mam was too thin. Shadows haunted the hollows beneath her eyes; her cheekbones protruded. She was naught but skin and bone from eating just enough to quiet the hunger, and the guilt of having plenty these last eight months tightened my chest.

"Inside, Crofton!" she called, but the babe remained on the threshold, staring out at us with large eyes, sunken and weary.

"Crofton?" I repeated, brows furrowing as I stared at the

child. Mam and Da hadn't chosen a name for my youngest brother when I'd left. It was bad luck, lest the babe perish before a month old.

Wrapped up in selfishness, I never thought to ask what they'd named him in any of my letters home.

"For his lordship, for his good favor," Mam said quietly. "Come. There's broth in the pot. Ye must tell me of yer travels, and all the wonders ye saw."

"Mam," I began, voice cracking. But she pulled me back into her embrace.

"We grieve with ye," she whispered near my ear. "Let's talk it all through tomorrow. After ye've rested. After everyone's met ye. With today's disaster, yer da will be so very glad yer home."

There was no sign of Da, or Michael, as the afternoon stretched to evening, and evening to night. Mam and I did our best to plug any drafts so the stench of rot might spare us, but still it found its way into the house.

There was little for it to permeate, for the house was almost stripped bare of its furnishings. Rugs and blankets gone, sold off.

"We're lucky to have more land than the others," Mam said, making the sign of the cross. As land agents, our house sat on one acre, a bounty four times that of our neighbors. "Thanks be to God. Yer da put half to cabbage and half to carrot. Neither yield as much as the spud, so we've been struggling. At least we had the luxury of having items worth selling."

"Everyone else replanted spuds?" I asked, knowing full well the answer.

"Aye. Sure, what else could they do?"

Nothing. Only the potato could sustain them. Failure or success; feast or famine.

After putting the younger ones to bed, Mam, Síofra, and I all sat before the fire, mending clothes as we waited. And waited.

I embellished my Dublin experience for Síofra's sake, detailing lovely walks around Merrion Square Park—as I'd seen the fine ladies do from my window, my cage. And, now I realized, my prison.

But conversation soon turned to the kind of food I'd eaten, and my stomach growled at the thought, guilt-ridden and hungry.

I'd never gone without and had plenty of meat—a luxury at home. But after a single serving of the watered-down cabbage broth my mother had so excitedly placed before me earlier, I chose to keep all of that to myself and instead spoke of boiled vegetables served once a day.

Mam asked about the countryside and what towns I'd passed through, so I regaled them of all I could remember.

Anything to avoid mention of my loss. Anything but that.

Until, finally, the door opened, and Da and Michael stepped through, the stench of decay wafting into the main room.

"Gack!" Síofra exclaimed, covering her mouth with her arm.

But I hardly noticed, for there was Da, eyes bloodshot—from tears or noxious gases, I knew not—with the weight of the world etched into the lines of his face, hair freshly washed, and skin scrubbed raw, glowing red against the stark white of a freshly laundered nightshirt. They'd obviously rinsed away the lingering rot in the washhouse before entering.

"Maggie," Da breathed, thin face crumpling as he swiped a hand over it. "Oh Jesus, God, and all the saints. I thought—yer not supposed to be here."

I rose from my chair and rushed to greet him.

"I'm home," I breathed, burying my face in the hollow of his collarbone. Da's arms came around me and, for the first time in a long while, safety engulfed my soul, and the weight of grief lessened.

A third hand patted my head, and I pulled back to glance

over my left shoulder. Michael—also far too thin. I reached for him and pulled him into Da's safety net.

For nothing else concerned me in that moment. We were all together again, and it didn't matter what was happening out in the fields or up at the Big House.

With my family, I knew I could get through this, because where Teddy drew strength from me, I drew my strength from them.

Chapter 13

To whatever part of the world the Englishman goes, the condition of Ireland is thrown in his face . . . by every worthless prig of a philosopher . . . by every stupid bigot of a priest.
— *The Times* (London), March 22, 1847, on mounting criticism of England's treatment of Ireland

Present: May 1848

"Remove it immediately!" I commanded, drawing upon all my lessons to truly personify a dowager countess, to become Lady Wilhelmina. "It's bad enough that I must endure the stench when about my studies. But there is something *in* it, Mistress Lynch. Something that causes these restless nights."

Upon waking in a crumpled heap on the floor, below the window, I'd barely righted myself to standing before Aggie and Beth had entered the bedchamber to go about their duties. But between Michael's appearance last night, the strange words of the woman in white, and replaying those memories, an unease I'd not experienced in years bloomed dark and heavy in the deepest recess of my gut.

"Calmly, m'Lady," Aggie soothed, as Beth stood, wide-eyed, scrubber and flint in hand. "Ye suffered a nightmare?"

"A *nightmare*?" I scoffed before rolling my eyes and storming toward the bedside table. "There is something *in* this incense, Mistress Lynch, and I will not tolerate its presence in this room any longer."

Plucking the heavy dish from the table, I held it aloft for Aggie to take, but she stood firm, lips pursed.

"Be about yer business, Beth," she ordered, eyes never leaving mine. Beth nodded and hurried to breathe life into the embers still smoldering in the hearth. "Now, m'Lady. I'll inform her ladyship of yer request, but ye must get yerself ready for the day. If it's tired ye are—"

"What's all this fuss?"

Aggie's eyes widened as Lady Catherine's voice boomed from the open doorway, and the retort standing ready at the tip of my tongue slipped down my throat.

Lady Catherine stepped into the room, arms burdened with a long, ribbon-wrapped box, bringing with her a breeze cold enough to pucker my skin with gooseflesh.

Aggie turned and bobbed a curtsy. "I'm afeared Lady Wilhelmina passed a rough night, m'Lady, and wishes the incense be removed from her room."

Lady Catherine pursed her lips and glanced from Aggie, to me, to the incense burner, and finally to the box in her hands.

"What, exactly, is in it, Mama? The incense?" I asked, steeling myself as that dark gaze of hers met mine across the room. For the first time since stepping foot in Browne House, I was truly afraid. Lady Catherine's mercurial personality did naught to frighten me, for I could handle a difficult master. Spirits? Absolutely not. But what, exactly, did "you're not the first to step in Wilhelmina's shoes" mean? Did the woman in white mean I was not Wilhelmina . . . or something far more sinister?

"Why, jasmine, lemongrass, and some herbs Dr. Brady recommended, my dear." Lady Catherine pursed her lips, brows settling into bewildered worry.

"What herbs?" Something in the mixture brought on these vivid dreams. I was sure of it.

"Mistress Lynch," Lady Catherine snapped, sending Aggie's shoulders back as she straightened. "Wilhelmina will catch her death of cold standing there in her night things. Have her dressed at once, and remove the burner as she desires."

"Yes, m'Lady."

"What herbs, Mama?" I would not let her leave this room until—

"I came to gift this treasure to you," Lady Catherine interrupted, stepping forward to lay the box on the bed, a wisp of a smile tugging at the corner of her lips. "Perhaps I miscalculated the timing."

She straightened and addressed Aggie. "Be sure she dresses in this. I'd like to see it."

"Yes, m'Lady." Aggie bobbed.

"Mama, please. What are these miscellaneous herbs—"

But Lady Catherine whirled on her heel, and before I could finish my thought, she swept from the room.

I could not let this go. As much as I wished for naught but to do what I was tasked, receive my bounty, and leave, I was not one to ignore a warning. Not anymore. Especially not one made with great effort from the other side.

Perhaps it was the dream that strengthened my resolve. Reliving those fateful events so clearly, I could scarce believe how naïve and stupid I once was. I had ignored the warning signs then, but I would do so no longer.

"Ye look like a painting," Beth cooed, hands clasped together, eyes alight with pleasure. But I couldn't bring myself to admire the veritable fortune adorning my body.

The ensemble itself—unlike Lady Catherine's chosen outfits— comprised a singular outer dress, high-collared, with three-quarter-length sleeves edged in lace. A boned bodice with mother-of-pearl buttons woven down the center, ending in a point from which panels of silk looped to the floor. The main skirt was fitted beneath, atop a polisón—a type of frame that rested above my backside, protruding mayhap a foot and a half from my body—where layers of bustle waves were laced atop the skirt.

If I'd had my wits about me, I might have felt very fine, especially with the addition of white laced gloves, ringlets framing my face, and the little triangular bonnet fastened to the crest of my head.

Instead, I swept from my bedchamber—without a word of thanks to Aggie or Beth—and began my descent to the main foyer, all while praying.

"*Our Father, who art in Heaven . . .*" I recited the Lord's Prayer, knuckles blanched as I gripped the railing, palms scraping against polished wood as I made my way to the third-floor landing, then the second.

I thought I had changed for the better, from an inquisitive girl who saw the good in everything and everyone, to a woman who asked no questions, numb to the world, with the ability to get on with it. And yet I had no control over the rapid, shallow breaths that set my pulse on fire. Nor the tremor that knocked my knees together with each step I took.

It was fear, not dread. Danger, not fancy.

"*. . . And lead us not into temptation. But deliver us from Evil.*" I murmured, then tacked on a blessing. "Lord, keep and protect the souls of the dead. Michael shouldn't be here, 'tis wrong. May he find peace beneath your watchful gaze. The woman in white also. Worry most dreadful must have driven both to gather such strength to communicate between our worlds, so hold them in Your heart, and guide them into Your kingdom so they might find peace. Amen."

I stepped onto the checkered entrance foyer—a sea of black-and-white marbled tiles stretching right, toward her ladyship's parlor and the dining room. Ahead, to the heavy double doors. Left, toward the library, and behind to the kitchen.

I could leave. Right now. Stride across the vast entrance and set the golden chandelier above my head a-swinging in my wake.

Old Maggie might have. New Maggie would have. But I was no longer either in that moment.

I was Wilhelmina, and Wilhelmina needed to confront her mother.

With a pivot, I strode for the double doors of the library and pushed with the confidence of a child born to greatness. The sole heir to Lady Catherine's and my dearly departed earl of a husband's estates.

"Mama?" I called, sure to keep my back straight, my chin held high, heels clicking. Clasping my hands before my waist—as I'd oft seen Lady Grace do—I turned the corner of the thoroughfare between the bookshelves and—

"Mama!" I exclaimed. There, sitting on the cold wooden floor before the great desk, sobbing into her silk skirts, a white-knuckled grip on the charm around her neck, was Lady Catherine. My eyes widened, and without a thought I ran forward and promptly joined her, leaving all decorum—and trace of Wilhelmina—at the door. "Arra, what's wrong? What's happened? Are ye hurt? What is it?"

With all the care of an elder sister used to comforting siblings, I gathered Lady Catherine into my arms and held her. Shoulders heaving, she melted into my embrace, and for the first time since meeting this seemingly strong, confident woman, I realized just how small she truly was. How light of frame. How weary.

"I n-need t-to h-help th-them," she stuttered, pulling back slightly to swipe a sleeve over her eyes. Lips pursed, I glanced at her—eyes puffed and red-rimmed, spider-like blood vessels webbing their whites, tears glistening on cheeks, pooling beneath her nose, dripping to her lips.

"Who do ye need to help?" I asked, but she shook her head.

"I-I'm t-tired. I j-just w-wished to h-help m-my people."

"Come now. Let's get ye off this cold floor and freshen ye up." I rose and, with a gentle hand, helped her to her feet. "That's it. Let's get ye in yer chair and—"

"You hate me," she whispered, leaning heavily on my arm as I helped her circumvent the desk.

"That's not true." Wary of her, yes. But hate? Nay.

"Ye hate that I must help my people," she continued, dropping the façade of the Anglo-born noblewoman and slipping into a native Irishwoman speaking Hiberno-English. She heaved a sigh as I navigated her into the chair. "That everyone else must suffer because I wished to keep them safe."

What in God's name was she talking about? My brows drew together. Tea. A warm cup with plenty of sugar would do the trick.

"I'll call for tea," I said, but as I turned on my heel, Lady Catherine grabbed hold of my sleeve.

"I didn't know what I was getting myself into, Maggie," she hissed, bloodshot eyes wild with fear. The sight sent a tremor straight to the marrow of my bones. I swallowed. Hard. "She warned me, but I didn't listen. I didn't believe her, not even about the necklace. We need to end it. Before the new moon."

"Hush now," I soothed, pulling my arm back. "I'll return shortly. Let me find Aggie."

I took a step back, and another, when Lady Catherine suddenly screamed: "*I'm doing my best!*"

But the words were not directed toward me. She'd twisted her neck to speak into the shadows at her back—to the nothingness she always spoke to. Taking a breath, I turned on my heel and hurried from the library without glancing back, hopping into a decidedly unladylike trot as I crossed the foyer toward the kitchen.

I could have rung the bellpull, but God above, I needed to be away from whatever fit had overcome her ladyship. Comfort would only distract from my purpose, and mayhap that was the intent. I shook my head. Surely not. A tear or two to throw me off my inquest, mayhap. But the display within the library? It seemed genuine. An honest-to-goodness episode.

"Aggie!" I called, pushing in the door of the kitchen. Within the darkened room, a cook, three assistants, and a spit lad froze mid-work—illuminated only by the light of the raging fire—and glanced up the steps leading downward. At me. I hadn't stepped foot in the kitchen since the night of my arrival, and I'd never been introduced to its staff, but it was very clear—eyes staring with curious surprise—that my intrusion was not altogether unwelcome.

"Apologies, but where is Mistress Lynch?" I asked, comporting myself as Wilhelmina once more as I descended the stairs. I needed a cup of tea myself—or something stronger.

A throat cleared. "Setting things to rights upstairs." The cook, an older woman sporting the clean, beige uniform that told all her status, stepped forward. "Was there something ye were needin', m'Lady?"

"Tea, please. Plenty of sugar, and piping hot. Mama has taken a turn in the library."

The assistants—all women ranging from their forties to sixties—hovering near the cook glanced at each other, and the lilt of whispered Gaeilge met my ears.

Is she back to herself now?

I hope so.

His lordship did always say her ladyship made a deal with the Devil.

Aye, and when you deal with the Devil, the Devil always collects.

It's not the Devil she dealt with.

Heart racing, I pursed my lips, and in the clearest voice I could muster, I addressed the kitchen in Irish. "Who made a deal with the Devil?"

The chatter ceased abruptly, and a deadly silence settled heavy as the cook boxed each assistant 'round the ears before turning toward me.

"Please forgive them, m'Lady. 'Tis only a sign of how well ye've adapted to yer role that they forgot themselves. No one made a deal with the Devil." The cook waved the spit boy over, and the little lad—no more than nine or ten years old—hopped forward. "I'll send Eoin here to fetch Mistress Lynch, and we'll have the tea brought. Maybe a sup for yerself as well? Yer looking a bit pale."

"Yes. Thank you." I nodded, storing away this new piece of information for later. Deal with the Devil, his lordship—Lord Browne.

Placing my palms against the vast preparation table before me, I closed my eyes as the sounds of the kitchen sprang to life. The spit lad dashing up the stairs to find Aggie. An assistant, hurrying toward the fire, ladling water from the ever-boiling cast-iron cauldron. Another continuing their chopping. Another putting a tray together.

It soothed, the normalcy, and I breathed in tandem with the bustle. Slowly in, two, three . . . and out, two, three.

"Ye had a fright?" The cook's gentle question stirred me back to reality, and I opened my eyes.

She stood still, eyes trained on me, forehead crinkled with worry.

"I'm very sorry," I said, clearing my throat before straightening. "It was so very rude of me to barge in."

"Not at all." With a chuckle, the cook's bright gaze met mine, and she smiled. "Yer welcome down here any time ye need a moment to yerself."

"I thank you." Glancing from her, I watched as an assistant poured the boiling water into a porcelain teapot, over the well of tightly packed tea leaves. What was I to do? Surely Lady Catherine would be of no mind to discuss the incense after such an episode. Aggie would likely administer a sleeping draught, and—my eyes widened. "Do you know if Mr. O'Dea is to home?"

Cook shook her head. "He's abroad in the village, dealing with Mr. Hogan."

"Can someone direct me toward Dr. Brady's practice? I fear we'll need to fetch him."

Cook's eyes widened. "Aye, m'Lady. I'm sure Beth will oblige ye."

"Make it so," I ordered.

How had I overlooked such an opportunity? With Lady Catherine indisposed, a loving daughter would naturally call a physician to discover what ailed her.

And that meant an opportunity to hear about these "herbs" directly from the man himself. I would go straight to the source.

But as I turned to leave the kitchen and find Beth, the disembodied voice of the woman in white whispered in my ear.

Dr. Brady can't help you, child. To do that, you must remember.

And my arms broke out in gooseflesh.

Chapter 14

The moment the very name of Ireland is mentioned, the
English seem to bid adieu to common feeling, common
prudence and common sense, and to act with the
barbarity of tyrants and the fatuity of idiots.
—Sydney Smith, *Peter Plymley's Letters* (1807)

I hadn't anticipated how freeing it would be to step outside the
walls surrounding Browne House, to breathe the salt-tinged air
and close my eyes for a brief moment, forgetting all the secrets
held within its walls.

So many secrets. But one I would have the details of shortly,
and another was revealed—thanks to the chatterings of Cook's
assistants.

Whatever was going on here, it seemed Lord Browne—when
alive—knew something of it. I drew to mind the journal I'd
found in the second-floor study, and thought I should read
through it in more detail, as soon as possible.

If I was in danger—both the future I'd dared dream, and
bodily—I needed to know what awaited so I could face it
head-on.

"M'Lady, please wait," called Beth, struggling to keep pace
somewhere behind.

But I simply pointed toward the sky and ploughed ahead.
The weather would wait for no one.

I'd already been accused of causing Lady Catherine's episode. In Aggie's own words, I'd "thrown a fit over silly incense and sent her ladyship spiraling into a melancholic state," and I'd not be accused of not making haste.

At least Aggie had agreed. It was best to fetch Dr. Brady.

I balled my fists as a scowl took hold of my face. I was right to question the contents of the incense. I was right to be wary. But that didn't stop the roiling of guilt bubbling in my gut as I thought of Lady Catherine's tear-streaked face.

A storm brewed in the distance, and the rising damp churned the heady, grass-tinged tang of turf, weighing the salt-laden air with the promise of thunder. Squinting, I glanced out over the violent sea and beyond to the horizon. Not a bird to be seen. Good. When the birds flocked inland, we'd have only a few hours before the sky opened and God rattled the earth.

As the sound of Beth's determined steps crunched closer, the roaring ocean battered against shale-laden shore, pulverizing pebbled beach as rocks cracked together—the wrath of Old Gods who'd once battled for control of our isle, before being driven to a land beneath the waves. The jolt of each tidal push pulsated through my veins. *Boom*—wave in. *Crackle*—wave out. The sound of a hundred carts sliding on slack shale.

My new walking shoes pinched around the laces, but at least I wasn't the only one suffering.

Beth had a new uniform—that of a lady's maid.

My lady's maid, to be exact.

"I don't think tugging will do much to help loosen it," I noted as Beth caught up, finger hooked beneath the laces of her new ensemble. Gone was the black cotton U-necked dress and white linen apron, replaced with a high-necked gown made of dark, soft French twill draped over a frame made of stiff crinoline, as became the maid of a dowager countess. No apron, not while accompanying her ladyship into the village. Me. I was her ladyship.

There were things power could accomplish that ordinary people could not.

"Sorry, m'Lady," Beth mumbled, dropping her hand to clutch up her skirt. "It itches something fierce."

With a scowl, I kicked a stone down the road, but it didn't provide the release of frustration I hoped for. Instead, it ricocheted off the tufts of grass that grew down the road's center, untouched as they were by carriage wheels and the maintenance of man.

M'Lady. My Lady, my employer, my mistress, my better. A necessary evil, for now. I glanced at Beth, at her neatly coiled bun and the bonnet atop her head. The flush of her cheeks and the way she stared ahead, biting her lip, as if searching for something.

There's only one thing I'd be searching for. The shuffling graves.

"What is the condition in the village?" I asked, glancing down the road. It dipped around a downward-sloping corner, but all was clear from what I could tell.

"Sorry, m'Lady?"

"I fear I'm out of sorts, given events. Should we have brought alms for the villagers?"

"Oh . . . oh *no*, m'Lady. Not at all." With a shake of her head, Beth smiled. "What I mean is, her ladyship has always provided. We're very lucky to have her. As soon as the potato failed, she took food straight out of the Crown's share and distributed it to us, she did. Even wrote to the queen across the sea—to account for the poor yield. Told her majesty that the hunger hit us hard, and she had no one to tend the crops bound for England's shores. And when the potato failed again last year, she partnered with Lord Belmont and Lord O'Brien to start the green roads, so those in neighboring parishes might earn enough to purchase food. Though, God above, the cost of everything has made that scheme futile. What kind of gobdaw decides the solution to a famine is to sell back the food we labored to produce at ten times the normal price?"

An Englishman determined to kill us off, with the British Parliament's approval. I pressed my lips together and shook my head. The people of Gortacarnaun were lucky indeed. Landlords all over the country had simply evicted whole families when they were too starved and weak to work the fields, replacing them with strong laborers from Dublin and beyond. Or turned their hands to livestock, requiring a third of the laborers, which meant two-thirds of the families relying on the landlord were left at the side of the road.

Someone had to do something. Da had told us they thought the Act of Union, bringing us into the United Kingdom, meant an end to centuries of war and persecution. But, here we were, nigh on fifty years since, and the British used the treaty to steal our crops and continue to make it illegal for Catholics to own land or be educated at school.

Yet they called us barbaric savages, lazy, with naught between our ears to allow us to pull ourselves up by the bootstraps.

"Th-that—" I cleared my throat, or tried to. A lump had settled large and heavy. Breathe. "That was very kind of Mama."

Certainly not the action of a woman I feared might harm me.

"Oh, her ladyship is very kind," Beth gushed, as we reached the downward curve of the road. "Look at what she did for ye."

I forced a smile, chest tight with guilt, and turned my attention to the road.

Below, in the distance, the main street of the village sprouted from the rocky ground. Six large buildings surrounded a wide area of beaten soil that likely served as a marketplace, and from that life force, several lanes ran between where smaller thatched structures sprang from the earth. Business, industry, homes.

"Don't fear the people, neither," Beth continued. "Ye may not be the first fake Wilhelmina, but all of Gortacarnaun will swear blue that yer as bonny today as ye were as a child. We owe our very lives to her ladyship, and we'd go to the very ends of the earth to repay all she's done." Beth's eyes widened, and she clapped a hand to her mouth. "Oh, forgive me, m'Lady! Please don't repeat it, else I'll be discharged from the Big House."

As though my heart was a horse and Beth its rider, her words whipped my pulse to life. A cavalry charge that stormed the gate of my rib cage.

That was the second mention of such a thing—confirmed by a living, breathing person.

Not the first to step in Wilhelmina's shoes.

These shoes. The ones that now dragged as if slogging through rain-drenched muck. The tattoo of my heart rang hollow, a *thud-ump* that shook my bones and left me half-blinded as I stumbled along the road.

The wind picked up, an ice-cool breeze that floated in from the sea. I glanced to my right, at the storm-tossed ocean, and spied the first gull coming ashore as a semblance of a plan formed.

I needed to discover what had happened to these other Wilhelminas—in a way that would not incriminate poor Beth.

After interrogating Dr. Brady about the contents of the incense.

Chapter 15

In all countries . . . paupers may be discovered, but an
entire nation of paupers is what never was seen until it
was shown in Ireland. To explain the social condition
of such a country, it would be only necessary to recount
its miseries and its sufferings; the history of the poor is
the history of Ireland.
—Gustave de Beaumont, French magistrate, *Ireland:*
Social, Political, and Religious

"Oh look! It's Mr. O'Dea!" Beth called, and the enthusiastic
tremor in her voice pulled me back to the here and now. "Mr.
O'Dea! Yoo-hoo!"

I glanced ahead. Cormac stood near the end of the road, his
back to us, Beth's voice obviously lost in the churning wind as
he waved to the driver of a cart and mule headed toward the village. Leaning on a sharp, jagged wall, Cormac wore a short, black
stovepipe hat with a fine, dark, swallow-tail coat over tightly
fitted knee breeches paired with white stockings and polished
shoes. My brows arched. This was neither the livery I'd first
spied him in nor the garb he donned while gardening.

He looked . . . truth be told, he looked a fine Irish gentleman,
pockets weighted with coin earned as a middleman or land
agent. The sight felt wrong, somehow.

I shook my head as we neared and cleared my throat. "Mr. O'Dea. Don't tell me Mama's stuffed you into a new suit as well?"

He startled and kicked off from the wall before turning—lips parted as he ran a hand over the fastened buttons of the coat before offering a smile. "Her ladyship likes me to dress for business when I'm about her business."

"Ye look like a dandy," Beth said with a laugh.

"I'll take that as a compliment." With a bow, Cormac touched a gloved finger to the brim of his hat and tipped it before pursing his lips. "What brings ye beyond the walls? Is everything all right?"

I shook my head. "Mama took a strange turn, and I need to fetch Dr. Brady."

Cormac's brows drew together.

"Mistress Lynch did say Lady Catherine would likely be fine," Beth piped up. He glanced at her. "She's having one of her spells."

"Best to alert Dr. Brady all the same." My words may have been clipped, but if I was to play the concerned daughter in order to corner Dr. Brady, then I would admonish Beth as Lady Wilhelmina might.

Blushing, Beth nodded and took a step back.

"Ye can go back to the house," said Cormac. "If it's one of her spells, 'tis naught a sleeping draught won't fix. But if ye insist, I can fetch him."

A jolt ran through my chest.

"Yes, I insist. And I will fetch him myself, Mr. O'Dea," I snapped. "You said yourself that you're about Mama's business. Be about it."

Sharp. Too sharp. A muscle twitched along the strong line of his jaw as he fell silent.

"Mr. O'Dea. Forgive me, I—" I began, but Cormac cut me off.

"By all means, m'Lady." Wiping the cut of my words from

his face, he smiled, and with a bow, promptly offered his right arm. "It so happens my business has concluded, and as her ladyship's representative, I'll be sure to escort ye there, as befitting a woman of yer rank."

My eyes widened as he shot a wink in my direction.

"I'll have ye know I was the handsomest man in my parish, so I'll not embarrass ye o'er much." He raised his brows above those clear, whiskey-like eyes and nodded at his arm. "Go on. It won't bite ye."

My chest tightened as a wave of déjà vu swept over me. Not this place, nor the situation . . . but his words. Those same words, that same voice. I'd heard them before. I was almost sure of it. I screwed my eyes shut, desperately racking my mind for the circumstance of that memory.

"Breathe," Cormac murmured. "Are ye worried about her ladyship? Mistress Lynch likely has a handle on it. But I know ye want that reassurance. She'll be fine."

Between everything at the house, and my own mind rebelling against recalling what was just beyond reach, it was nigh impossible to simply breathe.

"Yer all right," Cormac continued. I opened my eyes and found he'd taken a step closer. "Everything will be all right."

His soft timbre washed through me, wrapping the part of me that wished to ignore everything and carry on as if all was well in a comforting embrace. I took his arm.

"Thank you."

"Shall we?" Cormac asked.

"Yes, please."

And without another word, Cormac set the pace, Beth following behind, while the beat of my heart echoed in my ears.

Keeping dip with the unknown ahead.

It was market day, and everyone stared as we walked into the village proper, heads swiveling like hounds on the scent, halting all business and conversation as we swept in.

My cheeks flushed despite the bite of the breeze, and I gripped Cormac's arm.

"Why do they stare?" I whispered.

"Yer Lady Wilhelmina, and they've not laid eyes on ye in a while. That's all," he murmured, gently disengaging his arm from my grasp before tipping his hat to the crowd.

I forced a smile to my face, but as I glanced around the village square and found naught but unblinking stares, my knees buckled, and I wobbled in place.

A tall, slim man stepped forward, his clothing a well-worn replica of Cormac's ensemble, but constructed of patched tweed and darned stockings. He removed his felt hat and bowed. "'Tis that glad we are to see ye, Lady Norbury. That our home be graced by yer presence once more. As the village representative, I'd like to offer our heartfelt condolences for yer loss."

Loss. I thought of my brothers and sisters. My mam. My da. My *self*. Me. Maggie. And my eyes burned with the fresh sting of tears. This man's words weren't meant for me, and yet they punched my gut like a runaway carriage.

"Mr. Hogan," Cormac whispered, close to my ear, jerking me back to the here and now.

"Thank you, Mr. Hogan," I said, loudly and clearly for all to hear. "It's . . . it's been difficult to bear. But I'm afraid this isn't a leisurely visit. I fear I'm in need of Dr. Brady."

And like that, the spell broke. Mr. Hogan turned toward the square. "Call for Dr. Brady!"

And suddenly the villagers came to life.

Cheers of "God bless ye, Lady Norbury" rang over the village, and invitations to take a sup of cordial accompanied insistent requests for me to stay for the céilí they'd planned for that afternoon.

"Well done," Cormac said with a smile, and I felt my cheeks flush with the praise. "Truth be told, ye bear a fair resemblance to Wilhelmina."

"Thank you," I said, loosing a breath to halt a bubble of

laughter from creeping up my throat. "I'll need to do penance for this deception."

"At least we're all in the same boat. Come, I'll escort ye to the good doctor's abode, though he'll come running the minute he hears he's needed."

Biting my lower lip, I glanced out at the marketplace once more. One thing was certain—these people weren't starving. On the thinner side, sure. But they were all clothed, with an air of general health I hadn't seen in a very long time.

"Where are they all from?" I asked, taking the arm he offered once more. "There's more here than the village can house, surely? Are they mostly Mama's tenants, or have they come from afar for market?"

"Nay, they're all tenants. Some from atween here and Caherbannagh, some live truer to Formoyle. They're a bit spread out, and they've grown in number of late. Caherbannagh and Formoyle were devastated with the hunger. There isn't a Christ living in either village; they're either dead where they lay or chanced to cross the Atlantic. Lady Catherine paid some of the lads in the village to put up a few houses there outside Formoyle for any neighboring tenants who wanted her patronage."

"The more I hear about Mama, the more respect I have." With a sigh, I shook my head. What in the name of God was going on here? An angel to her tenants . . . with possible murderous intent?

"Respect is fine and grand, but balance it with a good dose of wariness," said Cormac, pointing off in the distance. "Dr. Brady's isn't far. Right over there. And if ye don't mind me sayin', ye seem like ye might need a respite from whatever is going on in that house. After ye speak with the doctor, I'm happy to escort him so ye can stay for that céilí. I'll return with the carriage later. For the bit of craic, like."

For the craic. The fun. The merriment.

A sad smile slowly stretched across my lips. Never, in a single moment in the last two years, did I think I'd ever hear the term or partake again. My face fell.

"With Mama ill, I don't think that would be very appropriate."

"Appropriate?" Cormac shrugged. "Maybe not. But for yer own health? Yer sanity? Aye, at least think on it."

I would. At the very least, taking the air while organizing my thoughts could never be a bad thing.

"Lead on, Mr. O'Dea. I may have to take you up on that offer."

Chapter 16

A young man led Cormac, Beth, and me into the parlor of a neat, two-story home, situated on the outskirts of the village, overlooking the bluff. The parlor itself lacked a woman's touch, with its clean lines and bare walls, but the brown leather armchairs were of fine quality, and the fire roared within its hearth.

"He'll be right down." The young man fiddled with his suspenders, hopping from foot to foot as he glanced my way. He was perhaps my own age, either the doctor's son or an apprentice. "P-p-please sit. I-I'll have Mary bring some tea, Miss. Er, I mean . . . m-m-m'Lady."

"No need," I assured him, spying a portrait above the mantel. A stern gentleman stared down at us, steely eyes penetrating mine as I paced from right to left. Always watching, so coldly. "We'll be leaving shortly, I'm afraid . . . Tell me. Who is that?"

"P-pardon?"

I turned on my heel to find the young man's mouth agape.

Beth grabbed hold of my arm, and I glanced at her. "Not a

great likeness, is it, m'Lady? Sure, 'tis nary a bit like yer dearly departed father, may he rest in peace."

My heart leapt in my chest, and I quickly laughed to cover such a stupid mistake. Pivoting, I turned to scrutinize the portrait once more. "Silly me. Now that you say it, Papa's fierce stare is captured perfectly."

So this was the infamous Lord Browne. Rather unfashionable in his powdered queue and turn-of-the-last-century frothed cravat, if you asked me. But what gave me pause was the stern set of his jaw—not at all what I was expecting of the kind of aristocrat who would raise up an Irish woman through marriage.

"I'm here, m'Lady!"

Glancing over my shoulder, I spied Dr. Brady stumbling into the parlor, stuffing himself into a fine swallowtail coat en route. Disheveled, I thought. A two-day growth evident on his chin, muttonchops dangerously close to becoming a full beard. His hair also required a cut. Older than Lady Catherine, for certain.

"Please leave us," I ordered, gesturing toward the door.

As Beth, Cormac, and the young man made haste from the parlor, Dr. Brady's eyes widened, and he placed a palm against his chest.

"Please, sit, Dr. Brady." I swept toward the nearest chair and descended as though this were my parlor and he the guest. The audacity of it tugged deep in my gut, but I had to be Wilhelmina in this moment.

Scurrying, the good doctor took the chair opposite.

"Tea, m'Lady?" he asked, eyes widening as he spied the lack of refreshments.

"No, no. I fear this is not a social call, sir. Mama has taken ill, and I'd be greatly obliged if you could call on her." I watched his light blue eyes darken and the way his knuckles blanched as he gripped the arms of the chair.

"What has happened?" The question bumbled forth in a

rush, a breathy panic that told me naught but a physician's concern for his most illustrious patient.

"I happened upon her in the library in a melancholic state, sir," I replied. It was time. "I believe it is an ailment of the heart and mind, and I would advise you to bring along the wonderful mixture that Mama has been using to calm my own nerves."

As his brows drew together, my pulse raced.

"You know the one, sir? The herbs that Mama blends with her florals? The incense?"

"Ah!" His face suddenly brightened. "Yes, yes, of course. Chamomile and lavender, with a dash of sage. I believe she adds jasmine from your own garden?"

"And lemongrass," I prompted. I pursed my lips. "Nothing else, sir? I had thought to try and put the ingredients together myself, but I fear I wasn't sure of its contents."

"That's it," he confirmed. "All aid with melancholia and help with relaxation."

"What of deep sleep? Strange dreams, perhaps?" I leaned forward. "I fear the incense affected me so, and I do not wish Mama to experience the same."

The doctor's brows drew inward. "The lavender induces deep sleep, which could cause strange dreams. If you wish, I can omit it."

"Is there anything in the mixture that could cause harm?"

Dr. Brady shook his head. "No, m'Lady. It is quite safe, I assure you."

Blood drained from my face as I nodded. How could I have gotten it so wrong? Pushing to a stand, I prompted Dr. Brady to hop to his own feet.

"Very well, sir. We should be on our way. Bring along whatever you think might suit."

With a grimace, I swept from the parlor, skirts gripped in sweat-slick palms.

Cormac was absolutely correct. I needed a reprieve, lest I lose my own sanity.

* * *

The rain held off for now, and thank goodness for it. Cormac and Dr. Brady had made their way to the house, but Beth and I lingered in the village.

Naught. There was naught in the incense save common herbs and florals, and my accusation had sent Lady Catherine into that state. God forgive me, ungrateful wretch that I was. Perhaps this—the céilí and all its trappings—was the best medicine. A reminder that there was a world beyond the walls of Browne House. A reminder of the life I was determined to one day live.

After fetching cups of cordial for herself and me, Beth had found stools for us to sit on, and we were now settled outside the parish hall as the atmosphere built before us, painted on the air with a brushstroke of excitement.

Someone had whipped out a fiddle, and the people of Gortacarnaun promptly formed six sets—four circles of six couples—in the square.

The jig flew high on the wind, and my feet itched beneath the layers of my dress as I instantly recognized the step-formation of the Caledonian set.

The sets closed the circle by clasping hands, then launched into action.

In, and two, and a-one, two, three. Back, and two, and a-one, two, three.

In, and two, and a-one, two, three. Back, and two, and a-one, two, three.

As the music climbed, I closed my eyes and smiled, fighting the urge to add a "whoop" to the beat. Seated on the stool to my right, Beth let out a "heeyup," and I opened my eyes.

The sets broke the circle, then turned to their partners to dance at home, before the top two couples of each set whirled around each other.

Children giggled and clapped on the sidelines as adults kept time with their feet, joining with "heeyups" of their own, and I was transported home—my father's arms around me as we twirled around the Kilrush parish hall, giving it hell-for-leather as we danced "around the house" before relinquishing his spot to my siblings.

Aoife and Síofra both had two left feet, and neither could dance the man, so I'd had to learn how.

Now that I thought of it, neither could Michael, for that matter. He always danced the woman's role.

I glanced out over the crowd and smiled when I saw no fewer than three men dancing the woman's role. Michael would've loved this. His keenest pleasure had always been these kinds of gatherings.

Tears stung my eyes, and I quickly dabbed them with the lace of my gloved hand.

"Ye all right?"

I whipped around, only to find Cormac, returned from his task, on my right.

"You're back," I stated.

With a nod, he took the stool to my right-hand side and stared straight ahead with his arms crossed, shoes tapping the beaten earth at our feet.

"Like ye said, 'twas a bout of melancholy," he replied. "I brought the carriage. Don't tell me yer that moved by the dancin'. Are ye crying?"

I nodded. "Naught but memories."

"They have a way of doing that. The memories. Just creep up on ye when ye least expect them." As all couples joined in dancing "around the house," he let out a bellow of a "heeyup," and I laughed. "Ah, she laughs. Yer only jealous 'cause ye know ye want to dance."

"I do. It's just in the blood, I think."

"Do ye dance the set?" he asked, dragging his gaze away from the dancing.

I nodded. "But not today, methinks."

"Arra. There's nothing to stop ye. Sure, couldn't we say ye've been learning?"

"I'd rather not. Besides—" I jerked my chin at the sky. "I don't think it'll hold off for much longer."

Cormac smiled, then untangled his arms to clap his hands together. "All we're missing is a seanchaí. Nothing beats a bit of bad weather when there's stories to be tellin'."

"You enjoy spooky stories?"

"Ye don't?"

Chuckling, I offered a shrug. "I've found the last three years far more frightening than tales of Daoine Uaisle tormenting the human world."

"Can't argue with ye there. I often feel like we're guests in their world, though. The Daoine Uaisle, that is."

"As I've never run into one, I'll take your word for it."

His eyes widened. "Never? Not once? Not even a cool breeze where there shouldn't be one?"

"No, not them at least. But spirits? Those I've met a-plenty. And God knows there are many restless spirits roaming the land right now." I ended with a sigh, just as the third formation of the set began.

Cormac was silent a moment, and the earnest reprieve settled warm and snug against my chest. It'd been a long time since I'd had someone to talk to—*really* talk to. Not just in general, but about anything other than where the next meal would come from, and I wondered if mayhap I could ask his opinion on matters at Browne House.

"How many have ye lost?" he asked at last, his voice a whisper as I closed my eyes.

Their faces flashed through my mind one by one, and I sighed. "My mam, Da, all nine of my siblings, and—" I clamped my lips shut and stared down at my lap.

"'Tis all right," he soothed, straightening on his stool. "They likely haunt ye from morning 'til night. Ye don't need me reminding ye."

"My . . . my son." Once the words were spoken, a weight lifted from my shoulders, and I shuddered. I don't know what tempted me to divulge, but it felt fine. To speak of him aloud . . . at last. "My babe. They told me he was stillborn, and I never got to see his sweet face."

"Arra Jesus." Running a hand over his face, Cormac's brow furrowed. "I'm so very sorry for your loss."

"It's fine. He likely wouldn't have made it anyway," I whispered. "God knows I barely did, and I suppose I'm glad, in a way. That I didn't have to watch him suffer over time."

"The light of Heaven to him, and to all those we've lost."

"Amen." With a sigh, I glanced at him. "You mentioned your parents before. Are they in good health?"

He nodded. "Hale and hearty, thanks to the money I send them. Anything to keep them from taking ship, ye know? Me dad was o'er distraught at the thought of being buried in foreign soil."

"I can only imagine."

"With luck, the harvest this year will be well, and I can leave this wretched place."

A chill wound up my legs, and I glanced at him. "You wouldn't stay? Even earning all that money?"

"Not a hope," he replied, voice soft. "I'm here to save my parents from emigration, and that's it. The moment the tide turns, I'm gone. Homeward bound."

And another wave of déjà vu swept over me—of another time, another céilí, moments before the hope of starting anew shattered into a million glass pieces. The tide turns . . . something about turning the tide.

Boom.

I startled, hand flying to my throat as Beth squealed on my

left. She wasn't alone. My breath came fast and shallow as the long-promised storm announced its arrival. Thunder rattled the sky above, and dancers stumbled in their sets. I glanced up.

"I'll fetch the carriage." Cormac hopped to his feet.

"So soon?" The words were meant for no one, a whispered disappointment, but he heard all the same.

"Next time the weather's fine, I promise to take ye beyond them walls again," he said. My eyes met his, and I knew from the glint of determination in those whiskey-like depths that he meant it. "I'll not have ye lose yerself in that house. Ye can mark my words. Now get yerselves inside the hall lest the skies open, and I'll be at the ready."

The cloud that darkened my thoughts roiled as we rumbled toward home. It had rained heavily while we were within the hall, and the sickly sweet aroma of storm-tossed soil melded with the sharp scent of seaweed—flung from the ocean and crushed against rocks as the surf let its anger out on the land.

Tír na nÓg lay somewhere out in the dark abyss—the place the Tuatha Dé Danann, one family of Old Gods, had retreated to thousands of years ago. Storms were said to be their vengeance on the people who'd settled Ireland and drove them into the sea. Morrigan darkening the sky, Dagda's thunderous roar, Lugh's lightning spear, and the waves—a stampede of white horses, a cavalry charge that would suck any unfortunate soul beneath their seafoam hooves to meet Bilé, God of Death.

"Penny for yer thoughts?" Cormac's gentle voice was barely audible over the clatter of the carriage. The spit lad from the kitchen had been commandeered from his duty to drive us, and Beth sat with him on the driver's bench. Cormac, as my escort, had to be seen accompanying me in the carriage itself.

I was . . . tired. Exhausted, actually.

"The storm's not over," I said with a sigh, staring out the window at the shoreline. Fog rolled over the shale-covered beach, a sure sign the temperature had risen. The show had only just begun.

"Aye. 'Twas only the first burst earlier," he said.

I glanced at him. He sat on the cushioned bench opposite, his hat abandoned next to him, cravat loosened. He stared out the window, jaw clenched as he squinted into the distance.

He had a strong profile. A fine nose, with high cheekbones.

And again, that familiar-yet-unfamiliar feeling swept over me.

I shook my head.

"'Tis nights like these I wonder how our friend Edmond Dantès survived his escape from prison," he noted, turning, a sad smile ghosting his lips. "Are ye enjoying the book?"

It took me a moment to realize he spoke of *The Count of Monte Cristo.* "I am, thank you." With a shudder, I watched the angry waves and wondered the same. I couldn't imagine jumping into the ocean from an island prison and swimming miles and miles to shore. Not in Irish waters, anyway. "I'm sure the sea is warm and calm in France. Or at least, I imagine it is."

"Maybe one day ye'll find out." With a shrug, he glanced at me. "Yer bothered about Lady Catherine's condition, I think."

My breath released on a sigh. "I'm afraid we had a disagreement preceding her episode."

"Ye blame yerself. Don't. From what I've gleaned, these episodes happen every so often."

"What causes them?" I asked, leaning forward.

"Depends on who ye ask," he said with a shrug. "Maybe they're caused by grief. The true Lady Wilhelmina's death likely hit her hard, ye know?"

I did know. I knew all too well. A mother's loss lingered from morning to night. "Have you heard rumor that I might not be the first Wilhelmina, Mr. O'Dea?"

He glanced at me, brows arched. "Well, of course yer not. The real Lady Wilhelmina was the first."

I shook my head. "Yes, I understand all that. But is there any talk that I might not be the first faux Wilhelmina?"

Cocking his head to the side, a bright smile stretched across his face. "Arra. Don't be listening to all that kitchen gossip. As far as I know, yer the only impersonator."

"I didn't hear it from—"

"Whoever ye heard it from, pay it little mind. Get the job done, and get free of this place, Maggie. Like I will. Whatever they say, Lady Catherine will keep her word, no matter the rumors."

"You surprise me, Mr. O'Dea," I said, mulling over his words. "On the one hand, you refuse to set foot in the house and are ready to leave at a moment's notice. Yet, on the other, you insist upon defending her ladyship at every turn."

The carriage lunged, jerking me toward the edge of the bench. "Oh!"

Cormac sprang forward and grabbed my shoulders to keep me from winding up on the hard floor, as a muffled "Sorry!" wafted from the driver's seat.

"Ye all right?" Cormac asked, his eyes on mine.

"Fine, thank you." With a shaky laugh, I shook my head and scooted back, but Cormac moved with me, his hands still warm on my shoulders, his eyes so bright with concern. "The lad needs a few more lessons."

"Aye. Well." Realizing he touched me still, Cormac yanked his hands back as if burned, and I loosed a breath. Good. Because New Maggie wanted none of that.

"Why is it you warn me not to listen to rumor when you yourself told me of the woman in white?" I asked. What's good for the goose was good for the gander, after all. Why should I not listen to rumor when he did the same?

Running a hand through his hair, he turned his attention to the darkness beyond the window once more.

"Because it's not rumor. I saw her," he murmured, shaking his head. "And ye've seen her yerself, have ye not?"

His question hung in the air between us, and I bit my lower lip. "No?"

"Ye don't sound sure," he noted.

"It's — " I pressed my lips together, mulling over what to say. How much to say. "I haven't seen a woman, but a man. My . . . my brother."

"May he protect ye. 'Tis only a matter of time before she shows herself. Harmless, I'm sure. But I've ghosts enough up here." He tapped his temple before shaking his head. "They're enough to bear. For ye as well."

With a sigh, I fiddled with the lace of my left glove. "Who is the woman in white? Do you know?"

"Nay. But if ye want to fuel them rumors of yers, tell in the village says she's there because of her ladyship. Conjured up, apparently."

"*Conjured*?" My blood ran cold as the weight of his words settled across my shoulders. "What are you saying?"

Glancing at me, he shrugged. "Ye know the way people are. Wealthy woman, living alone. A bean draíochta dorcha. But sure, if she were a dark sorceress like they say, she wouldn't be needin' ye now, would she? She'd be able to spell her way out of legal difficulties and such. Maybe even bring Wilhelmina back from the dead. And others."

A chill gripped my spine as I grasped for something to say. Anything to change the subject. To transition to something else.

The carriage slowed, and I glanced out the opposite window, the one to my right, facing the Burren, and spied the high walls surrounding Browne House.

We rumbled on, silence falling thick and heavy for the space of what felt like a lifetime before Cormac spoke.

"What was his name? Your son?" he asked, the question so soft, I thought I might've imagined it. Until I looked at him and noted the pained furrow of his brow.

"Diarmuid . . . though he didn't live to be baptized." Saying his name, it did something to my heart, as if a deep crack had been galvanized against further sunder. It fluttered in my chest as I noted the way Cormac picked at his thumbnail. The way a muscle in his cheek shivered as his jaw clenched. And then I thought he might have experienced similar pain. "You . . . you had a child as well?"

He shook his head. Curt. A sharp slice from one side to the other. "Nay. But many brothers. I was reminded of them is all."

"What were their names?" I asked, my voice a whisper as the carriage rumbled to a stop before the entrance of Browne House.

For a moment, I thought he'd keep them to himself. As I had kept Diarmuid's name locked away for long, as I likely should've continued to keep it.

"Cormac," he breathed instead, scooting to the carriage door that faced the house. "There were five Cormacs before I came along. Not a single one lived long enough to be christened, save me. I fear sometimes I'm naught but a spirit myself."

The practice was not at all unusual, naming a live child for the one who came before, hoping the deceased would watch over and protect the new babe.

"I'm here because of that, Maggie. And I stay because of that. I'm the only child left to care for my parents, and I'll not let them board a coffin ship. Ye have yer own reasons. But at any time, if ye need to leave, ye tell me, and I'll get ye free of this place. I promise ye that."

Not another word passed between us as the spit lad opened

the door. As Cormac hopped down. As he offered his hand to assist my descent. And as he flipped his mood entirely, turning to Beth with a grin.

"Made it back without getting soaked?" he asked, eyeing her cloak and hood.

"Only a soft mist," Beth chirped, her palm upturned to the darkening sky. "We were right lucky—"

Boom!

Thunder growled through the air, and the horse team whinnied and stamped their disapproval.

"Woah, woah," Cormac soothed, striding toward the lead pair of horses. "I should get them safe inside before the rain starts again."

"Yes, of course," I said, glancing up at the sky. Lightning lit up the bands of cloud in great bursts as branches of light streaked across the sky.

Boom!

"Go on, inside with ye," Cormac urged, waving us toward the house as he pulled on the horses' harness.

Boom!

The wind picked up, ruffling the wisped curls beneath my bonnet. No. Picked up was wrong. It rushed past, like a wave on the shore, pulling the fog with it. I followed its path, watching as the fog swirled up the outer wall of the house. Up, up, up to the top floor. My heart thudded in my chest as the night lit up once more, and I tracked a streak of lightning tearing across the sky above the dark megalith of gray brick and dense ivy, bathed now in a blanket of thick haze.

It was bright. So bright.

And that's when I saw him. Michael.

Staring out the window.

The attic window. The same attic none but Lady Catherine had access to.

But . . . I squinted. He wasn't staring. His face twisted with pain and fear, and I watched as he slammed ghostly fists against the glass, as if screaming.

Screaming a scream only I could hear, as another figure stepped into view. Another spirit, this one a woman . . . in white.

Ye must remember, Maggie!

Over and over, Michael's words reverberated through my ears, and I watched in horror as the woman in white closed a hand around his throat, 'til his voice grew hoarse and his words turned to gasps.

My mam always said I didn't know how to leave well enough alone.

That curiosity killed the cat. But this cat had a few lives left yet.

"Beth?" I called, tearing my gaze from the attic window.

"M'Lady?" she asked, gathering her skirt to avoid the puddles.

"I think I'll need the burner, along with Mama's soothing herbs, tonight."

"After all the fuss this morning—" Beth began, but I scowled fit to frighten a bishop. "A-aye, m'Lady. I'll run and fetch everything."

As she hopped ahead to run the errand, I glanced once more toward the attic window, to find it now bare.

Aye. If Michael needed me to remember, then I'd do my best to appease his soul, no matter the pain the memories brought.

But tonight, I'd be ready and waiting, safe in my bed. For the only way to draw them out was kicking and screaming, pulled forth by the haze of that godforsaken incense.

Chapter 17

There were no more friendly meetings at the neighbors'
houses . . . no gatherings . . . no song, no merry laugh of
the maidens. Not only were the human beings silent and
lonely, but the brute creation also, for not even the bark
of a dog, or the crowing of a cock was to be heard.
—Hugh Dorian, *Donegal, 60 Years Ago*

October 1846: Before

"**W**here are ye going?" Michael asked from the dining table
as I emerged from the elder girls' shared room. Almost the
whole family sat—with only Da absent—ten pairs of eyes staring at me as if I had sprouted a second head since my arrival
from Dublin the day before.

Tucking in a loose strand that had escaped my braided bun, I
ran a hand down the bodice of my Big House uniform, brow
raised. Where else would I be going?

"To work." I crossed the bare main room to join them, lips
pursing as I realized Michael wasn't in his uniform. "Did his
lordship give ye leave for the digging?"

Michael's eyes widened, and he glanced from me, to the dark
brown bread in his hand before laughing. It wasn't a hearty
sound, but weighted with disbelief—enough to set my heart
racing.

"Michael," Mam warned softly.

"Arra, *Mam*!" Thumping a fist against the tabletop, Michael scraped back from the table and stood as the half door opened.

Da walked in, wooden cup in hand, thin steam rising from its contents against the brisk morning chill.

"Enough, Michael," Da said, handing the cup to Síofra. She took a sip and passed it to Nancy, who took a sip, then passed it on.

My brow furrowed.

"Change into regular clothes, Maggie. I have a job of my own for ye." Da looked tired, and I bit my bottom lip, trying to make sense of it all.

"Is it the wedding?" I asked, taking a step forward. Christ, I knew something was amiss, and it was a fair bold thing to march up to the Big House as if nothing had happened, but I had to survey the lay of the land. If Teddy and I were to work through the hurdles, I needed to know what had happened. For though a part of my heart had died along with our babe, I could forgive him for abandoning me in my time of need, if only he would explain. I could find a way to begin again. "I can't be working at the Big House if I'm to join the family."

"Jesus, Mary, and Joseph, give me strength," Michael swore, starting for the door. "Did ye lose yer brain along with yer babe?"

The air left my lungs, and the sting of tears burned my eyes.

A slap resounded through the room, and Michael stumbled into the table.

"Get out, and cool off." Da's voice cut through the wide-eyed din. In all my life, Da'd not once taken a hand to any of us. "And don't ye dare come back 'til yer ready to apologize to yer sister."

Pale-faced, Michael clutched his cheek, glanced at me, then nodded and left the house.

"A sup for Maggie, Mam," Da said, quiet again, pointing to the wooden cup that had made it to Mam. She handed it to Da, and he took a step toward me to offer it. "A sup, mind. Everyone needs to make do with this much, lest the pig grows too weak for market. It's our last one, and we need a good price to make rent."

I glanced into the cup, and my brows arched as the coppery tang of fresh blood assaulted my nostrils. Things were so bad we'd resorted to letting the only livestock we had left?

"Keep your strength up." With a warm smile, Da patted my shoulder before turning on his heel and disappearing into his and Mam's room.

"Drink up," Mam said softly, eyes glistening with tears as her lips curled into a weak smile.

I brought the cup to my lips.

And tipped it back.

But I didn't drink. They were in more need than I—I who'd been fed the best of everything these last few months. I who'd ached with loneliness, while everyone else ached with want.

Changed into everyday attire—a chemise worn beneath a gray woolen skirt and faded black bodice—I strolled, shawl clutched tight around my shoulders, on my way back from doing business. Da had gathered the tenants a week prior, and a plan was formed.

If the crop failed again, he'd use whatever coin he had left, buy supplies, and dole it out to get us all through winter. That was the job Da had for me—to purchase enough grain to last the season.

The market, spanning the length of the stylish main thoroughfare—four carriage-widths wide—from square to wharf, was busy, thick with people if not coin. Most bartered with pieces of fabric—some the very clothes off their backs. But most were there to stare down the vendors, hoping against hope that a charitable soul might part with a morsel or two to keep away the pain.

"Wella wisha, Mistress O'Shaughnessy."

I turned to my left, with a ready smile. 'Twas Bridie Moran, from Scattery Island, here to sell estuary-caught bass and flounder.

"Hello, Mrs. Moran. Soft day," I noted, referencing the steady drizzle that showed no sign of letting up.

"Aye, soft indeed," she said, throwing a glare at the thick clouds in the sky afore glancing back at me. "The rot came here again too?"

I nodded, and she sniffed the air.

"If I don't live to smell it again, 'twill be an ease to me." With a sigh, she gestured at her ware. "Can I interest ye in fish?"

My stomach growled with want, but I shook my head. "I'm that sorry, Mrs. Moran. 'Tis only I've spent the quarterly on grain for the tenants."

"Aye, 'tis hard times, and worse ahead." Bolstering her posture with two firm fists pressed either side of her waist, she stared me dead in the eye. "We'll weather this, Mistress O'Shaughnessy. Mark me. If the Crown turned Ireland into a labor camp to keep England fed so their own people could work in factories, it'll send aid. And surely a queen would have more heart than a king."

I bit my lip. By all accounts, Queen Victoria was a young woman of eight-and-twenty, fully ruled by her Parliament, so I wasn't sure if her having a heart would do much to sway the men who made the laws that caused this mess to begin with.

"God willing," I prayed.

She nodded. "Will ye be at the parish hall this evening? I hear his lordship called in a seanchaí."

A seanchaí? His lordship wasn't one to initiate entertainment for the town, so his calling in of a wandering storyteller must have meant a great celebration was in order for the family and the village.

My brow furrowed, but I quickly righted my face. "Given all that's happening, I wouldn't miss it."

And that was the truth. A lighthearted evening filled with joy might just be what the physician ordered.

"Make way!" a man bellowed, and I whipped my head around as the crowds parted, a wave of people jumping backward as a carriage barreled through from the direction of the wharf.

I stepped around Mrs. Moran's stall, but froze when I spied the crest of the Moore-Vandeleurs etched in gold upon the door.

"I said, make way!" The driver bellowed, as an elderly man fought with a mule laden heavy with sacks. The driver abruptly pulled up his two-horse team, jerking the carriage to a halt.

My eyes drifted to the closed curtains of the windows as the driver shouted for onlookers to help the man so they could be on their way, and a pale hand pulled the curtain aside as the obstacle was removed, allowing the driver to spur on the horses.

It was a second—just enough for me to catch a glimpse of his face, his handsome face framed with beautiful blond curls, and my heart purred to life.

If he was coming from the port, then he'd arrived by ship, and that meant one thing.

Teddy must have been abroad, and I, like a fool, had been sending letters to his university residence.

And now he was home.

My pulse ignited with vigor, and I knew exactly what I must do.

Without haste, I said my farewells to Mrs. Moran and ran to pen a note to Teddy and leave it in our correspondence spot in the summerhouse.

Whyever he was sent abroad as I labored, abandoned, in Dublin mattered not. For he was here at last, and together we'd find a way forward. Because I could not let all that work—or love—go to waste.

Tonight. Eight.

That's all I'd managed to write, with naught but the juice of two o'er-ripe blackberries on a swath of linen ripped from my chemise. All paper, lead, and ink had been sold off for the precious grain I'd procured—so I'd learned—and I had to make do with what was available.

I'd had no trouble getting in and out of the summerhouse, though part of me had hoped Teddy would simply be waiting there, hopping from foot to foot, in hopes that I'd show up.

But never mind that. Teddy was home, and we would talk, and he would explain everything.

For the first time in months, I felt like I could finally breathe, filling my lungs with hope and excitement so vast that I practically skipped my way to the parish hall that eve to listen to the seanchaí.

In the hall, I sat next to Michael, who hadn't spoken a word to me since his outburst that morning. But I cared naught, because all would turn right in the end.

" 'Twas a bleak summer." The seanchaí—an elderly man, dressed in rags, sporting a silver beard that melded into long, almost-white tresses dotted with burrs—sat upon a stool in the middle of the hall, hands clasped atop an old wooden cane that had seen better days. "Not like this one, or the last. Jaysus, despite the troublesome harvests, at least we had heat. I mean truly bleak—cold and miserable, the kind that turns bog to marsh, and no amount of drying would turn out turf."

A murmur rose, a wisp of ghostlike fog that gripped us all. We all knew those kinds of summers.

"Most of us know of the púca and the puiseógs—things we keep an eye out for every day. We know of the Daoine Uaisle, the bean sidhe, the Dullahan, the changeling . . . but not enough is said of the Old Gods of yore. And sure, 'tis maybe blasphemy these days, a-talking about Old Gods. But ye see, them Old Gods relied on our prayers, and our offerings, to keep them calm. To keep them benevolent. We soothed their wrath with fealty, but those times are long since gone, and the Gods gone with them. They gave up on us when we embraced Jesus, and some say 'twas to our detriment. But one hasn't given up on us yet; one stayed behind. And that, my friends, is the Cailleach."

The hairs on the back of my neck stood on end as a cool chill wrapped around my ankles.

"Ye might know her by many names, for each village in Ireland swears they have a Cailleach—an auld woman with neither husband nor children. A crotchety type that sees naught but the worst in everything."

The seanchaí waved a hand to dismiss these claims and glanced around at his audience before standing, leaning heavily on his cane.

"They call her a hag. A witch. But in truth, she is a goddess, tasked with turning the tide. In lore, this was associated with the melting of winter to spring—waving goodbye to the barren season to welcome the planting. But turning the tide is turning the tide, and the Cailleach can transform misfortune to fortune or fortune to misfortune."

Michael snorted next to me and leaned in close. "I think he's talking about his lordship."

I elbowed him, but couldn't help the smile that curved my lips. Jesting meant he was no longer angry. Though why he had directed his anger toward me in the first place, I knew not. We would talk after and clear the air.

"On my travels, I've encountered several stories associated with the Cailleach," continued the seanchaí. "In Kerry, there's the Hag of Beara—where a local tale ends with her face carved into a jagged boulder that all can visit. And even here, in County Clare, far to the north, where wildflowers bloom between rocky crags, there's Hag's Head, so named for the story of a doomed sea witch, whose face is eternally etched into the cliff-side. And sure, where there's smoke, there's fire. But surely a goddess was never truly a person. And yet, she's been here, turning the tide for many a century. From good to bad, and bad to good."

"How does she do that?" A child's voice broke the silence of the audience, and we all glanced in its direction. A little boy. I recognized him as one of the weaver's children.

The seanchaí chuckled and singled out the lad.

"If I tell ye, ye must promise to never seek her out, for the Cailleach—though she adores the Irish people—rarely offers respite for free."

"I promise!" The lad called, as his father offered a red-faced, so-sorry nod to the seanchaí.

"Well, if ye swear," the seanchaí mused, before turning slowly, glancing at all of us. "Do ye all so swear?"

"Aye!" we called.

The seanchaí nodded solemnly, and circled the room. "'Tis said that those with the Sight—ye know the ones, the folk with a healing touch, who can see things beyond our eyes—them, with the Sight, they can draw power from the souls of the wretched to call upon her and offer their bodies as vessels. Once taken, the Cailleach uses that person's corporeal form in order to turn the tide—that is, to grant whatever it is they need—in exchange for her swift release from duty."

Next to me, Michael chuckled.

"Shh," I warned.

"The price for such a thing is steep," boomed the seanchaí. "But then, 'tisn't like a deal with the Devil, where an instant exchange is made. No. The Cailleach works to turn the tide, for hers is a different kind of sorcery. Where the Devil manipulates the human world to garner material success for those who exchanged their souls, the Cailleach manipulates the Other Realm, calling upon the Daoine Uaisle to get the job done. And in times like these, I wonder."

He paused, taking a moment to glance at the sea of faces, watching, eyes wide, wondering what he wondered.

"Maybe 'tis a reach, but I do wonder if this blight is the work of a Cailleach, and she calling upon the féar gortach to rid the Irish on behalf of the British Crown. Bringing forth the hungry grass, their ghoulish lanterns flying over the countryside, to inflict the blight and bring the famine."

No one breathed, myself included. We'd gone so still that one might hear the rustle of a rabbit in the field beyond the hall. It was treason, what he'd insinuated—that the famine was the fault of the British. Treason against the colonizers. Against those who treated us worse than the livestock we raised for their tables. Against those who took and took and bled us dry, stripping us of land and homes and surety. Those who had turned us into chattel. Those who had promised that the Act of Union—bringing Ireland into the fold of a United Kingdom— would bring prosperity and autonomy to the Irish people, but lied. Treason against the landlords who gave homes to tenants, under the condition that they work their farms for free yet still come up with monetary rent so the Crown could say it was all fair and legal if the civilized world decided to scrutinize the barbarity of the practice.

"Though, of course, the féar gortach doesn't always take from the people. Sometimes, when the Cailleach is fed the right kind of energy, it gives abundantly. And that energy? 'Tis vengeance—"

A throat cleared, cutting off the seanchaí. "Thank ye, Mr. Ryan." A man stood, and I recognized him as Mr. Daly, head of the town organization committee. He would've been responsible for the seanchaí's presence. And if word of the treason made it back to his lordship, Mr. Daly would be the one to receive wrath and punishment. "That was a mighty tale. Can we get a round of applause?"

Reluctantly, we began to clap, and Mr. Ryan—the seanchaí—pressed his lips together.

"I haven't finished," he said, loud enough for us all to hear.

"But ye have." Mr. Daly said the words through a forced smile. "It's time for music. This is a celebration, after all!"

"What celebration?" I whispered to Michael, but Michael didn't have to reply.

"To young Master Theodore!" Mr. Daly called, gesturing to the musicians waiting in the wings. "May he live a long and prosperous life with his new bride at his side! Hip, hip!"

"Hooray!" The audience called, but I stilled.

"Hip, hip!" Teddy's . . . new bride?

"Hooray!" Had this celebration been called to honor me? A flush bloomed across my chest as my eyes widened. He must have gathered all his strength and circumvented whatever went wrong without me.

"Hip, hip!" Bows scratched against fiddle strings as the musicians prepared for merriment, but I quickly smoothed my skirts and schooled my face in anticipation of the attention that would soon be turned my way.

"Hooray!"

"To our new Mistress, Lila Moore-Vandeleur, formerly Miss Fitzgerald, from Dublin!"

And my heart stopped beating, to the sound of a congratulatory jig.

*   *   *

I ran, and ran, and ran. Michael had tried to stop me, but the Devil himself would've had trouble.

For a single moment—a fleeting breath—I thought they meant me. That I was the new bride, that Teddy was home from a stint abroad and ready to wrap me up in his arms, and there-there me before reassuring us both that he'd taken care of his father and we'd try again after the ceremony. Stupid, stupid, *stupid*!

I don't know when it had turned from calculation to love for me, but it had been years. Years of trying to be the perfect woman in his eyes, years since he was more than a means to an end. Somewhere along the line, he became all I could imagine, all I could see, all I ever wanted. But now? He'd left me so coldly, and I doubted he even cared for the loss of our babe.

Tears streamed from eyes that had finally opened, frosting reddened cheeks as they cooled in the icy night air. It was a brisk evening, but at least the rain held off. From the looks of the smattering of stars above, it would hold off for a while— thank Heaven for small mercies.

I wasn't sure of the time. Michael and I had headed for the parish hall around six, so it must have been around seven, but there was no longer a stretch in the evening. In summer, I reveled in the late sunshine, basking in its warm caress until well past nine at night. But with Samhain fast approaching, it was full dark already, and when winter gripped us fully, the sun would set at four in the afternoon, denying us light.

Denying us hope, or prospects, or anything but the chance to sit with our thoughts as night stretched never-ending until midmorning dawn. Dark when we rose, dark as we waned.

Dark when I mourned.

A cramp gripped my womb, and I slowed to a stop, clasping my hands tight against my lower stomach.

"Ahhhhhhhhhhh!" I screamed. Not from physical pain, but the undulating cruelty of this life. Christ above, if Teddy had wanted naught but a tumble, I, in my stupidity, would've granted it out of love. But to promise marriage? A life together? The things I had originally planned?

And then to make me grieve alone while marrying another?

I could see it clear as day now: send the mistress away to give birth so the townfolk would not know of it, marry a woman of better station, then return with his wife, and no rumors of an illegitimate child would ever reach her ears.

That was why he hadn't written—abroad or not, his letters would have found me even if mine hadn't reached him. That was why Lady Grace informed me she'd found a position for me at a different house. I'd waved it away out of hand because I had wanted to return home . . . but what if I was never meant to return? Teddy had cast me off. My brows drew together. His lordship had blessed our marriage, had agreed to it! He had treated me so very kindly when I stood before him. This had to be Teddy's doing . . . but why?

He couldn't have discovered that we began as a simple plan. I had never written it down or breathed it to anyone. I wouldn't have dared. Surely he knew how very much I loved him.

Breath steamed from my mouth as I straightened and exhaled. The moon might not be full or bright, but I knew exactly where I was—the gate of Kilrush House. To the left of the gate, the gatekeeper's lodge was dark, and though I hadn't seen the gatekeeper's family at the hall, they must have been present.

Good. Now I didn't have to circle the estate and gain entry through the gap in the wall near the east corner.

"Maggie! Where are ye?" Michael's call echoed from afar, and I whipped around, wild-eyed. He knew I'd been cast off. They all knew, and I the only fool among them, blinded by love and the hope of a better future. Not just for me, but for my own family.

No longer.

With a determined step, I marched toward the gate, flipped the latch, pushed, and slipped betwixt the ten-foot-tall iron-wrought entrance gates.

Before this disaster of an evening, I'd been looking forward to stealing away to the summerhouse to meet Teddy.

But now?

I dared him to show his face.

Chapter 18

The land in Ireland is infinitely more peopled than in England; and to give full effect to the natural resources of the country, a great part of the population should be swept from the soil.
—Thomas Malthus, English economist, in a letter to David Ricardo (1817)

Present: May 1848

"Bastard!" Rage roused me from slumber, and before the word had fully left my lips, I snapped upright, gaze blurred and wild as my eyes fought for purchase in the darkness. A thin layer of sweat coated my skin, and I slicked a palm over my damp forehead, to shove stray strands of hair up into my sleeping bonnet. The pulse at my throat pummeled against my collarbone, in tandem with panting breaths that threatened to send me into a faint.

Remember? How could I forget any of it? It's not like there was a void where the last three years hadn't happened, for God's sake . . . but the anger?

I slapped my chest over and over, willing my lungs to slow, to inhale deeply, calmly. To gather myself, my thoughts. To pull myself together.

Is this what Michael wanted? To remember the rage? The

emotion? But what good was that when I had a job to do and a future at the end of it: impersonate one young widow to attain a home, somewhere I could do honor to my family?

With care, I pulled back the duvet and swung my legs off the bed before checking the incense. Its steady burn told me it was in no danger of petering out anytime soon. Good. I stood and gathered the robe that lay ready on an armchair.

Anger and rage could do naught but plant a bitter seed in my soul, a seed that would bloom to hatred so fierce, I'd hate myself the rest of my life. Hate that I'd trusted a noblewoman after all I'd been through, hate that I'd done her bidding to receive a small fortune, hate that I'd be the only O'Shaughnessy to gain aught from such ill-gotten gains. But the puzzle pieces tickled the very back of my brain, urged on by the thunderous roar of the storm outside.

And my skin crawled with what-ifs as I threw on the robe.

Fzzt.

I whipped around at the sound to find a spark diminishing on the slate before the hearth. The fire was still lit—if not roaring, decently smoldering. In four steps, I grabbed the poker and went to work, adding three new sods of turf before using the embers to light a taper.

I needed to think. Touching the taper to a candle on the end table near the hearth, I smoothly picked up Cormac's copy of *The Count of Monte Cristo* and sank into the armchair.

I'd always prided myself on not taking to fancies, but my head swam with them as I stared at the plain, leather-bound cover. Michael was dead, and if his soul was uneasy, surely he would've visited me long before now. Why did he choose here to visit, of all places? I shook my head. Between Beth corroborating the woman in white's warning that I was not the first faux Wilhelmina, Dr. Brady claiming there was naught amiss with the incense, and Cormac mentioning the rumor that Lady Catherine might possibly be a dark sorceress . . . had I gone mad?

My heart skipped a beat as a thought froze the blood in my veins. What if I'd contracted some disease at the workhouse, and this was all but a fever dream? Eyes widening, I opened the book, isolated a single page, and sliced my index finger along its edge.

"Ow!" I exclaimed, before quickly examining the finger in the candle's glow. Tiny red beads pilled against torn skin, and relief warred with terror as I realized this was real. I was here.

Why on earth did Michael need me to remember my anger . . . or worse? Perhaps I *had* forgotten something. A detail so dark, 'twas best to forget it completely.

I stiffened. The seanchaí. In my memory, he had spoken of ghoulish lights in the countryside and called them the féar gortach.

Was that what I'd seen from my window?

Fzzt. Another spark. I glanced in its direction.

The fire roared in the hearth, dancing wildly as a howling draft screeched around the cracks of the heavy curtains.

Gooseflesh pimpled my arms, and I pulled the robe tighter. Distraction. I needed one.

With a shake of my head, I turned my attention back to *The Count of Monte Cristo* and found where I'd left off. If I could just lose myself in the pages, I knew I could settle my mind. And yet something about Edmond's story terrified me, and I feared it might fuel the rage in my soul. My darkest thoughts— the ones that should give me pause.

Vengeance. But Edmond Dantès's vengeance was purposeful. Calculated. Was I not also seeking vengeance in my own way? To live a quiet life, without a landlord to breathe down my neck . . . that was my vengeance. My final dance. The only power I had.

Scrrrreeeeeeeaaaaaach.

The wild wind blew, and I closed my eyes. It was naught. Naught but the scrape of a tree branch against the window.

Remember.

I froze, spine tingling as a chill snaked up my spine. Edmond Dantès. I needed to get back to the book. Yes.

I lowered my eyes, but the letters on the printed page blurred as I stared.

Maggie . . . ye're forgetting.

"I'm *not!*" Frowning, I slammed the book shut and rose from the chair by the fire. "I remember everything, Michael! What is it I must remember?"

My heart leapt in my chest as a new breeze ruffled the hem of my nightgown. My pulse hammered at my throat, an unending thrum of heat and speed that forced its way to my ears. They filled with a *whad-ump* that threatened to consume me, to devour me whole.

Creak.

I whipped around, eyes wide as I sought the source of the sound. In the firelight, the shelves of porcelain dolls seemed to stare, their painted gazes following as I took a tentative step toward the bed.

Crreeeaaaaakkk.

A shriek wound its way over my tongue, and I clamped a hand over my mouth as I glanced at the door. At the widening triangle of moonlight that expanded over the wooden door.

It was . . . opening. But Michael's voice came from behind—

Don't go out there, his voice whispered.

"Wh-who's there?" I called . . . at least, I thought I did. My body was so frozen I wasn't sure I'd said the words aloud. "Who's outside the door?"

There was no response. Nothing.

I glanced at the bed and bit my lower lip. It was best to simply listen to my dead brother's advice and dive beneath the covers 'til morning. Morning, when I could make a list of all the happenings with a clear mind. Morning, when daylight would bolster my courage.

But from the corner of my eye, a shadow darted beyond the

now wide-open door. From left to right. A swift motion accompanied by the swish of silk and crinoline.

"Beth?"

Heaving a shaky breath, I stalked toward the door, brows furrowed as I readied myself to lash out. To scold. To strike her with the broad side of my tongue and declare it wasn't amusing.

A jest, surely?

"You jackanapes!" I declared, stepping into the hall, ready to make Beth promise to never do something so awful again.

The shadow had moved from left to right, so I turned in that direction, certain she couldn't have reached the main staircase.

But it wasn't Beth.

A cool sheen of perspiration coated my brow as the woman in white turned to the side, and slowly walked toward the wall.

Lightning flashed through the window at my back, and her edges were no longer translucent, but solid. Her hair hung in muddy strands. Her body, modestly concealed by the ragged remnants of a dirty chemise—once white—now torn and bloody. But it was her eyes that chilled me to the bone.

Or the lack thereof.

They had been gouged from her face, and rivers of blood ran from the sockets.

A scream rose in my throat as her outline shimmered, a strange blurring of what was real from what was not, as she walked through the wall.

I couldn't breathe. My chest was wound tighter than a bowstring, threatening to crack beneath the pressure of my lungs.

Crying, a low wail that whispered of heartache and agony, drifted on the air, and my eyes locked onto the place in the wall through which she'd disappeared. My brow furrowed, and before I knew what I was doing, one foot dragged in front of the other, as if my mind needed to know. If I was right. If it was the same spot.

The curtain. The ancient door with its myriad of ancient locks.

You should have listened to him.

Her disembodied voice croaked in my ear, breath like ice raising the little hairs of my arms as I placed a shaking hand against the door to the attic. The voice was old, wheezing over rattling lungs, and so weathered I couldn't tell male from female.

But I knew for certain it wasn't Michael.

This voice grated like chains, a-clinking in the echoed chamber of a vast dungeon. A weakened prisoner in the throes of anguish.

Feed me, Maggie.

"Feed you what?" My voice was naught but a breath as I fought to steady the wartime drum a-pounding in my chest. It was naught. My mind playing tricks. Then why, for the love of God, did my neck turn? I squeezed my eyes shut.

A glacial hand landed on my shoulder. Hard. Fingers gripping my flesh until light flashed through my mind, fading until Lady Catherine's shape took form behind my closed eyes. She stood in a darkened room, with only the glow of a single candle for light, bent slightly to speak to the figure before her.

"What is it you want most?" Lady Catherine asked. The same words she'd asked me at the workhouse . . . but she wasn't speaking to me. The figure in my vision was a child. A little girl, bedraggled with grime, blond hair hanging in greasy threads. A shadow loomed behind Lady Catherine, something dark and eerie, the stench of rotted flesh emanating from the void. A flash.

"What is it you want most?" Lady Catherine asked again. This time speaking to another blond girl, older than the first, but in a similar state of despair. Thin, but tall, mayhap in the first blush of pending womanhood. The shadow behind Lady Catherine seemed more solid now. Taking form. A flash.

"What is it you want most?" The same question. This girl

was older still. Sixteen or seventeen, with the curves of a woman grown. Blond. Pretty. The shadow wore a long gown, a singular length of fabric.

"What is it you want most?" This scene I recognized, though I couldn't believe the wraith she spoke to—the sunken eyes, the sharp lines, skin so thin it was naught but a wisp of parchment. Me. This was me. And the shadow looming behind Lady Catherine was no longer a shadow, but a woman. She wore a long white dress embroidered with gold, with long bell sleeves and a golden belt shining bright on her hips. A waterfall of black curls cascaded down her back, and the golden crown on her head spoke of royalty. Of wealth. Of an ancient queen.

My eyes popped open, ready to confront whoever had grabbed my shoulder. Ready to scream. Ready to demand the meaning of this.

Except . . . there was nothing there.

Wild-eyed, I whirled on my heel, frantically searching the hallway for whoever had touched me, but there was nary a whisper of anything out of place.

The sky lit up once more beyond the window at the end of the hallway, throwing unnatural blue-white light through the glass, and a deep, dissonant, disembodied chuckle resonated from behind. From the door. The door to the attic. I recoiled, heart dropping into my gut as I slammed my back against the opposite wall of the corridor.

"*Our Father, who art in Heaven, hallowed be Thy name.*" Making the sign of the cross, I retreated to my bedchamber, reciting the Lord's Prayer over and over until I'd stepped over the threshold and latched the door. "*Thy kingdom come, Thy will be done, on Earth as it is in Heaven.*"

I tugged on the door for good measure and ran toward the window, so I might cool my forehead and drag myself back to the here and now.

My mind wandered to Cormac as I pulled the heavy curtain

aside. I envied him in that moment. His cottage. His distance from the house.

Leaning forward, I allowed the cool glass to counter my heat. To ground me. To help me breathe. Eyes shut, I continued the Lord's Prayer until my heart slowed. Until the chill in my bones was spurred by the draft, and not the dread that branched through my veins, a disease invading my life's blood.

Until I felt safe enough to open my eyes.

And wished to God I hadn't.

For there, in the storm-tossed plain of limestone crags and ravines, several greenish lights bobbed in the violent darkness, and my chest tightened.

They shot right, then halted, before swinging to the left.

Lightning flashed, a great sheet of bright light that turned night to day for the space of a heartbeat, but it was enough.

Enough to see the twisted limbs in the distance, and the eyeless figures testing the air for whatever it was they hunted.

In a blink, they turned again and ran off over terrain that even surefooted men wouldn't attempt to walk without full daylight. Chest tightening, I fought to steady my breaths, now shallow and rapid as my eyes told me that which my mind could not fathom.

The lights, they belonged to the Daoine Uaisle—just as the seanchaí had claimed, all those years ago.

His lordship feared her, Maggie. The woman in white's voice, clear now, devoid of all grit, echoed through my mind. *Feared her 'til the day he died.*

I shook my head. The woman in white, Lady Catherine, Lord Browne, and the lights—the féar gortach. They were all connected, I was sure of it.

What is it you want most?

Revenge. That's what I'd told Lady Catherine when we'd first met, and it was as true now as it was then. Not the rage-fueled kind that laid waste to my enemies, but to know that if

Teddy ever learned I'd lived—never mind that I lived well, and free—he'd cut his teeth on the knowledge. To know Colonel Moore-Vandeleur would be eaten with guilt. To know Lady Grace would succumb to one of her fainting spells.

But in order to remain safe long enough to receive my payment, and enact my own flavor of vengeance, I had to assess what kind of danger I was truly in. For nothing, and no one, would keep me from fulfilling my task. And God help anyone who stood in my way.

Chapter 19

I want to make England feel her weakness if she refuses
to give the justice we the Irish require—the restoration of
our domestic parliament.
—Daniel O'Connell, speech in Drogheda, June 1843

"How is Mama?"

Dressed and ready for the day—this time in a simple, powder-blue day dress—I walked with Aggie as we descended the stair-case leading from the fourth floor to the third. Yesterday's storm had lifted, and the sun shone bright through each window—a lit brazier that burned through sorrow and pain, darkness and shadow.

More's the shame, for good weather was scarce, and I should take advantage of the respite.

"Aye, she'll be grand," said Aggie. "Ye did a fine job fetch-ing Dr. Brady, m'Lady."

"The least I could do after causing such an episode," I replied, stepping onto the third-floor landing and rounding the banister to descend to my destination—his lordship's study. "Will she be fit for visitors today?"

"Visitors, m'Lady?" Without turning, I could just tell Aggie's brows had flown up her forehead.

"Me, Aggie. I'd like to see her."

"Ah. Well. Maybe. We'll have to see how she is."

I halted on the stair, causing her to stop short, skirts pressing into mine.

"Tell me, Aggie." Glancing over my shoulder, I found her in silhouette against the light from the landing window, a faceless shadow looming above. I shivered. "Does Mama experience such episodes often? Are they brought on by grief?"

"Stress," she snapped, stepping around me to continue her descent. "'Tis a great undertaking, what she's doing here. And yer own part will be over soon. Can ye not just carry on without causing a commotion?"

Pressing my lips together, I followed her.

"What, exactly, is my part?" I asked.

"Exactly what ye were told. Become Wilhelmina and fool the solicitors." Aggie reached the second-floor landing and placed both hands on her hips.

"What if I've changed my mind?"

Aggie whirled on her heel, eyes narrowed, brows furrowed so low her nose wrinkled. "Ye cannot do that. If ye knew what it cost us to live under her protection, ye'd—"

Clamping her lips together, Aggie glanced up at the ceiling, chest heaving.

I paused on the stair. "What do you mean by *cost*? Surely you earn a salary here at the Big House and have no rent?"

"Never ye mind," Aggie snapped, glaring up at me. "And do as yer told. It'll all be over soon."

My heart raced in my chest. That's exactly what I feared. When I didn't move or speak, she rolled her eyes and huffed.

"It was a long night for me, sitting by her ladyship's side. I'm that sorry I lost my temper with ye," she offered, by way of apology. "Let's hurry now, else your breakfast will turn cold."

"I'll take breakfast in the study," I replied.

Her eyes widened.

"The least I can do after yesterday is throw myself into education. You said yourself that I cannot abscond from my agreement, and it is my understanding there are lives on the line."

Perhaps even mine.

Without another word, I swept down the remaining stairs and brushed past Aggie, rounding to my left, toward Lord Browne's study.

Seated at Lord Browne's desk, I eyed the stack of journals before me. There were accounts for each year, beginning with "1803," and my head ached at the thought of reading through twenty-nine years of this man's life. But a quick scan of "1803" told me enough to rule out anything interesting in that year—he'd turned twenty-two, his father had passed away, and our Lord Browne had taken over the running of the estate.

"1804" through "1823" bore similar fruit—noting births and marriages of friends and family, accounts of affairs that drew heat to my cheeks, trips to London and the Continent, details of other homes owned, gambling debts owed, race horses purchased. But there was one very interesting fact. Mr. Hogan and Dr. Brady were once part of Lord Browne's inner circle. That accounted for his lordship's portrait displayed proudly in Dr. Brady's parlor.

Stifling a yawn, I stood and stretched before noting the time on the fine, mahogany longcase clock—ten past two. With a sigh, I gathered the journals I'd already pored over and began re-shelving them to the left of the door, brow furrowed. By my calculations, Lord Browne had turned forty-three in 1823—still unwed, with nary an intention to marry at all. I'd even found an entry claiming he would leave the title, and all estates and land, to a nephew of his in London.

Striding back to the desk, I plucked "1824" from the dwindling pile, and thumbed through, settling on an entry a few pages in.

February 17th 1824

Low I spied her again today, hair wild and dark, skirts gathered up as she waded in the shallows, gathering the periwinkles so many tenants cherish. Foul, slimy snails—it baffles the mind how one could lower themselves to consume them. And yet I couldn't tear my eyes from her. Hogan and Brady completed our party, and when I enquired her name, Hogan had it. Cate. Recently come from East Clare.

Eyes widening, I took a seat in the winged Queen Anne chair before the desk. Cate? As in, Lady Catherine? I turned the page. Nothing more. Another. Nothing. Scanning through, I stopped when the word "Cate" jumped out once more.

August 15th 1824

I cannot for the life of me understand this change of heart. Truth be told, I am a victim of an enchantress, and that enchantress is to become my wife. She has acquiesced most joyfully, and I am torn so fervently. This woman brings neither family nor wealth, nor breeding. And yet I would give her the world if only she asked. My brother thinks I've run mad, but Cate consumes my every waking thought, and I must have her. It would be a small thing to elevate her to Browne House staff and have her squirreled nightly to my chamber. And yet I cannot. It's as though my voice and body are no longer mine own, but hers, and I act with only her interests in mind.

October 2nd 1824

We have returned from a honeymoon most sweet, where Cate charmed the aristo set so thoroughly that none might guess the dung heap from whence she sprang—save for the barbaric butchering of the King's. My brother is most foul in his correspondence, demanding a copy of my last will and testament, lest I leave everything to a possible heir. He needn't fear. At nine and twenty, Cate will have trouble conceiving, and I highly doubt our union will bear fruit. For now, we take pleasure in each other's company. I predict her charm will outstay its welcome shortly, and we shall live comfortably as lord and nursemaid as I creep toward old age.

I rolled my eyes. Twenty-nine was hardly old enough to be set out to pasture—my own mam was proof of that. Didn't she give birth to my youngest brother at the grand age of forty-one?

I picked up "1825," then "1826," but it seemed Lord Browne had lost interest in his newly married status—beyond a few tiffs and a surprise pregnancy—until "1827."

March 1st 1827

The grief in my chest swells to such dimension that I can feel naught for the arrival of the child. Something is amiss. Cate and I quarreled over the will a week before the accident. How could such a thing occur? My brother, his wife, and their son—my heir—all gone. A broken axel and a steep decline through Hardknott Pass in Cumbria has left no survivors. How am I to celebrate the birth of our child when her first words to me upon my entering the birthing chamber were, "There are no obstacles now. You'll name her your heir."

But I had learned of the tragedy that very morning, and she in the throes of labor.

No one had told her.

July 14th 1827

I demanded Cate produce the key to the attic, for I must know what occurs beneath my roof. It has been brought to my attention that she is a Connors of Faha, which makes her some relation to Biddy Early. Every mechanism of this ill-fated relationship is finally falling into place—my falling for her in the first place, wedding despite my better judgment, a child produced in a barren womb, my heir's demise. I will not name Wilhelmina my heir, and no amount of sorcery will compel my hand.

Reports of strange lights crossing the rocky planes nearby have alerted the Lahinch constabulary, lest they be a band of those troublesome Repealers attempting to spread their nonsense to my tenants. Curse Daniel O'Connell and all his ilk. Praised as some sort of "liberator" in his efforts to dismantle the Act of Union and emancipating the Catholic Irish. I feared Canning would entertain O'Connell's nonsense, but Canning's benevolence extends only to Catholic aristos of England, thank God.

December 24th 1827

I have made Wilhelmina my heir. Cate brought the faerie lights to Gortacarnaun, and with them came a disease affecting my livestock and failure of my crops. We are ruined, and she delights, speaking of her "mistress" and all her "mistress" can do. I have no choice now but to acquiesce to her every whim, lest Cate convenes with this Devil and sees to my own demise. I fear I'll not last to see the New Year, and I refuse to hold the child.

April 20th 1828

The faerie lights still abound, and misfortune most foul continues. Hogan has made enquiries further afield as to their origins, but fear has gripped the tenantry, and all speak of a "hungry grass." Ruination of the land at the hands of beings from the realm of faeries.

Dr. Brady visits weekly to test the food stores—I fear she might poison it to be rid of me.

June 7th 1828

I held Wilhelmina at last, and for the first moment since Cate entered my life, a great sense of peace washed over me. Whether this is another magic of Cate's at work or simply parental fondness, I care not a fig. To have the babe's arms squeeze so trustingly around my neck, to feel the soft-ness of her straw-colored curls brush my cheek. She is a ray of sunshine I did not suspect I needed.

Hogan returned with tales of a being with the power to control the "hungry grass." I told him it's not a "being" I wanted, but the name of whatever Devil Cate has made a pact with.

Brady continues his weekly visits.

October 20th 1828

The harvest was good. The curse has lifted. Cate has been pleased with me since embracing Wilhelmina in my heart.

I no longer fear death, for we have reconciled.

January 5th 1829

Cailleach. K-eye-lock. Cailleach, Cailleach, Cailleach. The being is the Cailleach.

April 6th 1829

Don't go in the attic. That's her domain. Cate had warned me, but with the atmosphere now at ease, it had slipped my mind.

Dr. Brady came to set my leg. Cate told him it was a fall, but something pushed me down those attic stairs.

The staff whisper about ghosts, but there was nary a specter in this house before Cate and her sorcery. I think it's her.

June 19th 1830

I found the accounting record Cate had hidden away in the library she's made her own, but can't make heads nor tails of it. The key to everything is within, I am sure of it. The gardener informed me that new tenants all dealt with Cate, and that each had paid a price for "protection." What protection?

I know in my heart it is intertwined with her, the Cailleach. I have long since determined it best to allow Cate to practice her craft, but I wish to know the extent of it all. If not for my sake, for the child's.

Dr. Brady has prescribed an herbal mixture to be burned daily, to calm my nerves.

June 30th 1830

Cate found the accounting record in my possession, promptly retrieved it, and locked me in my study. No food, no water, for two days.

She came in the night, the Cailleach. Unhappy, me-thinks. Cate's hold over her grows stronger. She spoke of drawing power, and symbiosis, but I knew not what she meant.

Hogan reports the weather turned on the day Cate confined me. He feared the worst for the crops, but it turned again when I was released.

I believe the Cailleach talked sense into her, and for that I am grateful.

Chapter 20

If the people are forced to consume their oats and other
grain, where is the rent to come from?
—Letter from Captain Percival to Charles Trevelyan,
August 1846

I didn't need to read any more, for I had an idea what accounting record Lord Browne had found—the ledger that had leapt from its shelf on my very first morning as Wilhelmina. Whether Michael or the woman in white, something not of this world had made that particular volume fall for a reason. I might not know much about dark sorcery or folklore and the like, but there was one thing I could do.

Carefully reshelving the remaining journals, I hurried from Lord Browne's study and made my way downstairs to the main floor, heart racing with every step.

Death at Lady Catherine's hands would have been a simple thing to thwart. But supernatural goings-on coupled with sorcery? I was ill-equipped.

I thought back to the vision I'd had in the hallway the night before—the shadow looming behind Lady Catherine, the different girls, the repeated phrase. It reeked of wrongness, knotting my gut until I wondered why. Why so many? And did many Wilhelminas mean Lady Catherine's own daughter had died long, long ago?

First things first. A glance at the entranceway longcase clock to my right told me three more hours had passed—it was five o'clock.

Not long past the golden hour, dusk painted the foyer in hues of gray and shadow. Odd that no one had yet lit the chandelier, but I supposed Lady Catherine's disposition had sent the house into disarray. With a shrug, I made my way to the sideboard, situated outside the parlor, and made quick work of lighting a candle before crossing the foyer to enter the darkening library.

Where had I placed the volume? On which shelf? I was sure I had hidden it between something about bees, and . . . I couldn't recall. Either way, it should be near her ladyship's desk.

Holding the candle aloft, I turned the corner to make my way down the main aisle, and—

I halted, blood turning to ice as a silhouette, seated behind Lady Catherine's desk—in profile—came into focus.

"M-mama?" I called, mustering all I had to temper the sudden vise that gripped my chest.

Only for the fizzle of burning tobacco, I'd have sworn my imagination had run wild, but as the silhouette took a drag, it slowly turned.

"Over here, dear."

It was her, thank God. My heart fluttered as I neared, its rhythm countering each step. For though her flesh-and-blood presence should put me at ease, it hindered my current task.

"Shouldn't you be a-bed?" I asked, placing the candle upon the desk. "Why are you sitting here in the dark?"

"Ah," Lady Catherine said, voice unusually soft, glancing out the window once more. "I wondered if it might be over."

Taking the chair opposite, I pursed my lips. "Whatever do you mean?"

Turning her attention toward me, she smiled around the bit of her pipe. "Did you break your fast, dearling?"

"Mama . . . it's suppertime," I replied, my voice gentle, now certain she'd not yet recovered. Where was Aggie? "Shall I escort you to your room?"

"I can't hear her right now." Eyes bright in the light of the candle, Lady Catherine lunged forward, over the desk, and I reared back with fright. "I need her gone. But the means frighten me. Freedom . . . I suppose it's worth the price."

"Wh-what price, Mama?" I ventured, knuckles blanching as I grasped the arms of my chair. "Is it something I can help you with?"

"I think so." She smiled then, a bright, peaceful smile that illuminated her entire face. Sitting back in her chair, Lady Catherine closed her eyes and lifted an idle hand to absent-mindedly fiddle with the charm at her throat.

I glanced over my shoulder, toward the very spot where the book I sought had once landed on the polished wooden floor, and sighed. First, I needed to tend to Lady Catherine.

I rose and circumvented the desk to assist her.

"Come, Mama. I'll take you upstairs." But as my gentle hand connected with her shoulder, Lady Catherine stiffened and bolted upright, turning in her chair to rake her eyes over me.

"Wilhelmina?" she snapped. Gone was the gentle lilt from a moment before, replaced now with a no-nonsense tone that meant business. "What in Heaven's name are we doing in the library? In the dark?"

My brows drew together as her clipped question set my pulse alight.

"I found you here, in the dark, Mama," I replied, swiftly stepping back as she rose up from her chair. "You have been a-bed since yesterday. Since your episode."

"Episode?" she echoed, lips pursing. "My dear child, are you unwell?"

With a scoff, Lady Catherine whipped out a hand to touch my forehead, and I froze.

"No, Mama." My words were but a breath as I desperately

fought to understand what was happening. Could one snap out of an episode in the space of a blink? Was this usual?

"Cool to the touch," she confirmed, then glanced about. "Mistress Lynch is in need of discipline. How could she allow the house to go dark? Come, come. It's not safe to wander about without light."

With a firm hand, Lady Catherine grasped my arm, but I held steady—even as she moved to step around the desk.

"I came to borrow a book and happened upon you," I announced.

"A book?" Her brows furrowed. "There's little of interest here save records and papers. Have you suddenly sprouted political leanings?"

Forcing a smile to my face, I shook my head. "I had thought to educate myself on the estate itself and the land hereabouts. I remembered you noting that Lord Browne had thought to turn his hand to beekeeping. I sought to familiarize myself with the process, lest the solicitors steer conversation toward the running of the estate."

I held my breath as Lady Catherine stared at me, a quizzical look on her face. One beat, two—

"Very well," she said with a nod, before turning on her heel and striding toward the exit.

I loosed my breath, but quickly straightened as she paused halfway down the main aisle.

"Tomorrow morning, be prepared to demonstrate your overall progress." She threw the command over her shoulder. "And if everything is to my liking, I'll have Mr. O'Dea tour the land with you. Learning about the estate will only enrich your knowledge and impress the solicitors."

"Yes, Mama," I replied, counting each step she took as she continued toward the door.

Before grabbing the candle and scurrying to find what I came for.

*   *   *

I slept, tossing and turning, but not from things that went bump in the night.

Like Lord Browne, I could not make heads nor tails of the accounting record.

It recorded no figures, no sums, but names. Names of tenants and villagers, and it appeared she'd noted whether they were loyal to either her or Lord Browne.

At first, those under Lady Catherine's "protection"—for there was, in fact, a column citing whether each tenant or villager had subscribed to whatever that meant—were few and far between, even after Lord Browne's death in 1832.

But when 1845 rolled around, every inhabitant on Browne land, under Browne care, were afforded this "protection."

A frustrating goose chase is all it was.

Still, I'd schooled my face, broken my fast, and descended upon the library as Lady Catherine had decreed. And now I sat, patiently, waiting as her ladyship evaluated my work.

"The script is perfect," she murmured, setting aside the page and a half of newspaper articles she'd had me copy, all observations on the queen's proposed visit. Queen Victoria had apparently pushed back her promised visit to Ireland yet again, fearing for her own personal safety after donating the measly sum of two thousand pounds to the Irish relief effort . . . and blocking a ten-thousand-pound donation from the sultan of the Ottoman Empire. What was there to fear? Anyone with enough feeling left to care had neither will nor strength to harm her precious majesty.

"Your speech is adequate, script is adequate, and I'm pleased with your etiquette," Lady Catherine announced, steepling her hands beneath her chin. "I'll have Mr. O'Dea ready the carriage."

I had prepared for this. With naught gained from the accounting record, I thought to use this opportunity to examine the final lead I had left.

"Would it not, perhaps, be a more enlightening experience if I rode myself?" I asked, my gaze never wavering from her face. "That way I could really get a feel for the land, versus the scenery from a window?" My palms grew clammy, clasped in my hands as they were, but I kept my voice steady, even as Lady Catherine's eyes widened.

"My dear, have you ever ridden a horse before?"

"Of course, Mama."

"Not a bare-backed ploughhorse, child. Properly, with a sidesaddle and rein."

I pressed my lips together. I could ride. I could even hunt. Teddy had taught me. "Yes, Mama. I was taught as a child and was brought on the hunt often."

Lady Catherine's face paled as she leaned forward. "What, exactly, was your position in the house of the Moore-Vandeleurs? Because not once in my life have I ever heard of a grand family teaching skills to a tenant's daughter that are best taught to their own children."

There was a sharpness in the question, a sharpness that cut me to the bone. As if her words would flay me open and reveal me for the liar she thought me to be.

And yet . . . the twinkle in her eyes sparkled with mirth. I wished I could make sense of it—of her—but now was not the time.

"As I've said before, my father wasn't a tenant. He was Colonel Moore-Vandeleur's land agent, and as such, he secured the position of valet for my eldest brother. And when the time came, I served as lady's maid to his wife, Lady Grace. Lady Grace is fond of the hunt—"

"She most certainly is." With a smile, Lady Catherine sat back in her chair. "I met her once or twice, many years ago. A kindhearted soul, if memory serves. I should imagine she's also responsible for your knowledge of letters and numbers?"

A kindhearted soul, indeed. Lady Grace had been kind enough until that day. The day my world came crashing down, a runaway train that would take months to rein in.

"With such a gentle mistress, it must have been hard to leave service when you wed," said Lady Catherine.

My brows furrowed. "Pardon?"

"You were wed, weren't you? Mistress Lynch mentioned you may have been a mother." Lady Catherine's voice dipped low, laden with grief and kindness.

I placed a hand over my heart and nodded.

"I'm that sorry, Maggie," she whispered, reaching an upturned palm over the smooth wooden desk. An invitation. A moment shared between two grieving mothers who had lost everything. "There is no greater hurt in this world than losing a child."

Tears stung my eyes, and I reached out my hand to cover hers. She clasped it.

"You are strong, Maggie," Lady Catherine said, and I jerked in response. She had never, not once, called me by my name. Not from the moment I'd signed the contract and stepped foot in her carriage. My eyes widened as they met hers—determined, steely. "But never lose sight of who and what you are."

My chest tightened against the pounding of my heart. "A-and what's that? What am I?"

"A woman meant for so much more than whatever life has already thrown your way." With that, Lady Catherine released my hand and sat back in her chair. "I'll call Mistress Lynch and have her put together a basket for yourself and Mr. O'Dea. I do hope the rain holds off."

With a quick push, Lady Catherine rose from her chair and turned on her heel to inspect the weather beyond the window.

"Have Beth riffle through my trunk for a riding habit. You'll need to be properly attired."

"Yes, Mama," I whispered, knowing I was dismissed.

A woman meant for so much more than whatever life has already thrown your way.

It wasn't what she said, but the way she'd said it—with urgency and fire, in a way that screamed *listen to me.*

I didn't know if it was a warning or a cry for help.

But I had to push it to the back of my mind.

Because right now I had an opportunity to check the land for myself and determine if an idle group of tricksters could have ridden across the plain . . . or if the lights I'd seen had no explanation, beyond the féar gortach themselves.

Chapter 21

All knew that Irishmen could live upon anything and
there was plenty grass in the field though the potato
crop should fail.
—The Duke of Cambridge, from the minutes of the
Agricultural Society, January 1846

"Penny for your thoughts?"

Cormac's voice was almost lost over the whinny of my
horse, a fine, dappled gray mare with a light gait.

We'd been riding in silence since leaving Browne House. I'd
insisted on not taking the main road, but Cormac had been hes-
itant. After yesterday's storm, the way was saturated with mud,
but I needed to see for myself—if it was possible to ride around
out here in view of my bedroom window. If it was possible that
a person—or a horse—could be surefooted, even while a storm
raged. That perhaps there might be a road hidden from my aspect, so far in the distance that I couldn't discern it from the
tufts of grass sprouting between rocky crags.

I didn't tell him that, but at every opportunity, I'd ask if there
was a way through here or a way through there.

"Maggie?" Cormac said again, and I jerked my horse's rein
as I startled.

"Pardon?"

"I said, penny for your thoughts."

I glanced over at him. He sat astride a fine brown gelding, as fine as any beast owned by the Moore-Vandeleurs, but he wore a shirt and knee breeches better suited to gardening. Usual mucking-about attire. The contrast between horse and man was stark, but it suited Cormac—a humble man atop a fine horse.

"Apologies," I sighed. "I didn't sleep well last night."

"Ah," he replied, nodding as I shifted my gaze to the road ahead. "More haunts in the night?"

I chewed on that question for a moment, keeping a close eye on the road. It was naught but a cleared strip of land, shored up with crushed stone. But the grass had swallowed the makeshift paving, providing a carpet of verdant splendor. To our left lay the open crags and rocky pathways of the plain, and to our right, more of the same. With each clip of the horses' hooves, hope and excitement condensed to a nagging chide that rang through the back of my mind.

There was no way a person—or a group—could've been traveling this particular road. The lantern lights had been far too close to Browne House. It simply wasn't possible.

"Maggie?" Cormac coaxed. "Yer gone away again."

"Apologies," I said, shooting a poor excuse for a smile his way. "Haunts, you said. Well, to be frank about it, yes."

He nodded and glanced beyond me to the valley below. "I wasn't jesting about why I sleep in the cottage."

"I never said you were. Nor thought it." With a sigh, I ran the back of my gloved hand across my face. "Spirits don't trouble me. 'Tis the rest that breeds unease."

"Oh?"

My brows knitted together as I shot a scowl over my shoulder. There was no point in dragging it out. "I've learned that Lord Browne feared her ladyship and thought her in league with a devil."

"Ah." Cormac's jaw clenched. "Well, that's no secret."

"No?" Drawing in a deep breath, I shut my eyes for a brief moment. "Yet no one told me. Should I fear for my life, Mr.

O'Dea? Tell me true now, and don't mince words about it. It won't faze me either which way, but I'd like to know what's coming."

I pulled on the rein and slowed my horse to a stop.

"I don't think yer in danger, but I also don't think o'er much about the future. Knowing what's coming makes the waitin' worse," he said, his voice a gentle lilt on the breeze. "If ye'd known what would befall yer family, would ye have wanted to know?"

"No," I replied, bowing my head as I gave a silent prayer for their souls. "Nor would you have, I assume. And yet when 'tis the happening to me that's in it, the knowing helps a bit."

A beat passed as Cormac glanced out over the sea of limestone.

"There's the house," he said.

I squinted into the distance. "This is the closest we can possibly get from here?" I asked, my heart dropping into my stomach. "I was hoping to make our way toward the house from this spot."

"Unless ye want to dismount and leave the horses," he said with a shrug. "Even so, I can lead ye o'er the crags only to a point. But a few paces in, the ravines grow too large between solid surface, so 'tis likely we could get into difficulty."

I pressed my lips together. "Are you certain?"

"Aye," he said, a note of finality in his tone. "We'd no sooner step in than break our necks. What's all this about, Maggie?"

With a sigh, I shuddered. "It's nothing."

"Couldn't be nothing."

Pursing my lips, I spurred my horse to a fast trot, gently directing her along the green road.

Behind me, Cormac grunted and hurried to catch up.

"Not so fast, Maggie," he called. "The ground is fierce damp."

Fierce damp was one way to put it, all right. I felt the mare tilt each time her hoof squelched into the mud beneath. But I'd churned the turf on many a hunt. If anything, I wanted a little distance to be alone with my thoughts.

If there really wasn't a way through the crags, then I couldn't have seen a group of people out here, running—or riding—along. Not with how far the house appeared in the distance.

With a sigh, I gently tightened the rein and slowed the mare to a walk as Cormac gained our lead.

"Ye can tell me, Maggie," he said, but I stared hard at my horse's groomed neck.

" 'Tis you who needs to be telling me. What is Lady Catherine, and what in the name of God is in store for me?"

He furrowed his brow. "She's a woman that can give ye what ye want."

I sighed. "But at what cost to me? I read it in Lord Browne's journals, Mr. O'Dea. She conjured a Cailleach. And I saw the lights myself, out here, moving over the crags. I needed to see for myself, if it were possible that 'twas naught but people running around in the dark. But now that I've seen it . . . 'tis the féar gortach. Explain all that to me."

"A *Cailleach*?" Eyes widening, Cormac's lips parted in surprise. "No one can conjure an Old God, surely?"

"It *is* an Old God, isn't it?" I asked, heart hammering as I tried to recall all the seanchaí of memory had said about it. "Not a devil?"

He shook his head. "A god for certain. But what would that have to do with the féar gortach?"

"I once heard that the Cailleach could make the féar gortach do its bidding. Either give plenty to the people or take it all away. Once, a seanchaí came to our town, and said 'twas the English controlling the Cailleach, to take everything away from the Irish. To send the fog and turn the spuds to sludge." My words spurted forth in a rush, but once started, I couldn't stop. "Lord Browne thought Lady Catherine was in league with the Cailleach. When he displeased her, the Cailleach sent the féar gortach to destroy his livelihood, and when he pleased her, the Cailleach sent the féar gortach to enrich it. Turning the tide—good to bad, and bad to good."

"Say yer right," Cormac interjected, holding out a palm to still me. "What does any of that have to do with ye fearing for yer life?"

Up until this moment, I hadn't been sure . . . but recounting it aloud and drawing the memory of the seanchaí to mind, my eyes widened.

Though, of course, the féar gortach doesn't always take from the people, he'd said. *Sometimes, when the Cailleach is fed the right kind of energy, it gives abundantly. And that energy? 'Tis vengeance.*

"Remember," I murmured, pulse racing.

"Pardon?"

Is that what Michael had meant? That I had to remember everything—all the emotion, every event—in order to feed the Cailleach, for my vengeance would give her the power to manipulate the féar gortach into providing for the people of Gortacarnaun?

Perhaps the accounting record I had found was not a benign listing of where the tenants' loyalties lay, but of those who chose to benefit from Lady Catherine's sorcery.

My eyes widened. Mayhap then it wasn't I who should be fearful of what came next, but those responsible for destroying my life.

Cormac was right all along. I could fulfill my duty here and walk away once payment was received.

"Are ye all right?" he asked. "Ye've gone three shades paler than a corpse."

I glanced about the terrain with fresh eyes. Not those of a frightened woman, clutching at straws to see a way forward. But of a made woman, independent of owner or landlord, surveying what had been promised to her. The daughter of a land agent, with a keen eye and a sharp ear.

Warmth bloomed from my core, enveloping me in sudden hope.

"I don't know how anyone can make a living here, truth be told," I noted. "Tenant or landlord. I imagine the land promised would be of similar composition."

Cormac's brows arched. "I'm not one to point out contrariness, but I'm unsure how we journeyed from fearing for yer life to surveying yer prospects."

I stiffened, my grip tightening on the rein as I shot a glance his way.

His lips curved upward, their tilt brightening those whiskey-colored eyes, drawing a little color to his cheeks.

"Mayhap I realized how contrary I sounded." There were some things I couldn't—and shouldn't—share with him. Not just yet. If he thought me contrary now, he'd think me fit for the madhouse if I went on about incense and memories.

"Aye. Well . . . 'tis fit for naught more than goats or sheep. But if ye can turn a field and clear it, spuds will grow wherever they're planted." He shook his head. "That's why I turned down her initial offer. I was promised a house and land as well. Enough to have my father and mother live a comfortable life in their winter years."

I hadn't realized I'd stopped breathing until stale air whooshed through my lips.

"A lovely house, with plenty of land for sheep and pigs." He closed his eyes and briefly turned his face upward before opening them again. "But sure, they won't come."

"Why not? Would that not solve the emigration issue?"

Cormac's smile dimmed as he inspected his nails. "Sure, there's a lot of history there, atween her ladyship and me mam."

"They're acquainted?" My brow furrowed as Cormac nodded.

"A long story. Anyway, Lady Catherine will do right by ye,

Maggie. She is many things, but first and foremost she's a woman of her word."

Silence fell for a moment as our horses clopped on.

"That's as far as the road goes," he said at last, pointing ahead. "We should head back. I can bring ye to the other side of the village so ye can get the lay of the land there, if ye'd like."

I nodded, glancing ahead. Sure enough, the carpeted road blended from verdant splendor to rocky gray. But as I switched hands on the rein, ready to turn my mare, a large boulder to the right of the road's end caught my eye.

It was a lighter shade than the dark, slate-like limestone that washed over the Burren. Its ancient, weather-beaten hull stood grand and tall, its edges rounded, decorated with splashes of gull dung as moss grew, barnacled, at its base.

But it wasn't its oddity in such a place or its grandeur that caught my attention.

It was the dull, aged chisel-work on its surface.

"What's that?" I asked, pointing, knowing it was the same symbol etched into the window frame in my own bedroom. The same symbol that hung as a golden charm from the black ribbon at Lady Catherine's throat—three swirls, interconnected.

"A protection symbol," he said, squinting into the distance. "Ye'll find a lot of them hereabouts. There's likely thousands of old burial grounds around here, passage tombs and cairns and things. The Burren is old. A sacred place. That's a triskele."

A hard lump formed in my throat, but I forced it down. "I've seen something like it before."

"Aye. The auld ones knew a thing or two about the Old Gods, I'd say." Tugging his own reins, Cormac turned his gelding around. "Tell you what, though. If ye have a bad dream that sends ye on a hunt like this again, ye should carve a triskele into yer windowsill."

A shudder ran over my shoulders as ice flowed through my veins. "What?" I asked, though it came out as a whisper.

"Oh, for sure. A triskele in the sill keeps demons at bay. Bad dreams too, or so said my mam."

I'd never heard such a thing before.

"Where did you say your family was from?" I asked.

"My mam is from hereabouts, but I was born there between Kildysert and Ennis."

A jolt of pain clutched my chest at those words, and my pulse ignited. "Kildysert . . . and Ennis?"

His eyes met mine, those clear, whiskey-colored windows that had always seemed all-too familiar, yet not at all.

"Do ye remember now?" he asked, voice so gentle I barely heard it above the pounding in my ears.

Remember.

"Have . . . have we met before, Mr. O'Dea?"

He frowned and pulled his horse around.

"It'll come to ye," he said, before digging in his heels and setting off at a trot.

Remember.

Chapter 22

I have always felt a certain horror of political economists
since I heard one of them say he feared the famine . . . in
Ireland would not kill more than a million people, and
that would scarcely be enough to do any good.
—Benjamin Jowett, British economic adviser, 1848

"Michael?" I hissed, throwing my cloak over the armchair
near the fireplace in my bedchamber. The minute we'd returned
to Browne House, I'd raced away from the stables, through the
house, and up the stairs as quickly as possible.

Remember.

"Michael!" I called, glancing around the room. Without
thought, I stomped toward the open curtains and drew them shut,
before lighting a taper with the ever-present flames of the fire. Any
other day, I'd smile and remind myself to compliment Beth on her
dedication to her duties. But this instant, I needed my brother's
spirit to answer some questions. "Michael O'Shaughnessy, show
yerself this instant!"

Cupping the infant flame at the end of the taper, I carefully
shuffled toward my bedside table and touched the flame to the
ready incense box.

"Michael!" I called again, as the incense hissed, sparking as
the flame took hold. I quickly snuffed it, to allow it to smolder.
"What the feck am I supposed to remember? Is it Cormac?"

Each memory reminded me of the hatred I felt, of the fault I placed on the one responsible. But it seemed there were gaps in those memories, and if the Cailleach required my vengeance to feed the féar gortach, then I needed to leave no stone unturned.

"*Michael!*" I screamed his name with all my might before unbuttoning the jacket of my riding habit.

"M'Lady?" Beth's voice filtered through the door, and I whipped around. "Is everything all right?"

"Fine!" I called, heart racing as I shrugged off the jacket. "I'm going to lie down for a while."

"I'll help ye undress—" The door cracked open, but I stopped her cold.

"Nay!" I yelled, fiddling with the ties of my skirt. "I have a megrim and can bear no light!"

"Oh!" Beth quickly shut the door. "Is there anything I can get ye?"

"More incense!" I called, stepping out of my skirts as they pooled to the floor. "I've lit what's here, but if you could refill it in an hour or two, I'd be grateful. It helps with sleep."

Whatever it was I needed to remember, I would remember it all now. No waking in the middle of the night, no spirits causing havoc, no more pondering.

"Yes, m'Lady. I'll see to it," Beth called through the closed door.

"Thank you," I whispered, as I pulled back the duvet and fell into Wilhelmina's bed.

Chapter 23

For our parts, we regard the potato blight as a blessing.
— *The Times* (London), September 1846

November 1846: Before

"Out! Out, I said!" The bailiff clubbed Michael across the shoulders, and Mam shrieked as he fell to the ground outside our door.

"You can't be doing this!" I screamed, pulse racing as I rushed forward to aid Michael, but was stopped short as another club-armed bastard yanked me back by the waist.

"Don't you dare touch her." With a growl, Da balled his fists and took a step in my direction, but Mam reached out to touch his arm, and he glanced at her.

"We knew it would happen, mo chroí," she said softly, and the fight suddenly went out of him.

They knew? That Da would be accused of fiddling with his lordship's accounts? Da would never do such a thing! He was loyal to his lordship and wouldn't do anything to jeopardize his livelihood or the family. Nay, this was all because of what happened last night after the céilí. I never should have gone to the summerhouse—I simply accepted that Teddy had fallen for another woman, one who matched his station. One who brought wealth and connections. I wished them nothing but misery.

"Let me fetch my brother," I begged, and the arm around my waist loosened enough for me to wriggle away.

"We're that sorry, Mr. O'Shaughnessy," said the constable who'd come with the order, but Da said nothing.

I fell to the ground next to Michael and threw my arms around him. "Come on. Quick. Up ye get."

"I'm not fecking moving," he murmured. "This is our house, and Da is innocent!"

"Do ye want them to kill ye?" I hissed. Somewhere behind us, the little ones sniffled and sobbed, and my heart ached that they had to see such a scene. "Think of the babies! We need ye, Michael. You and Da both. Don't do anything stupid!"

With a heavy sigh, Michael righted himself, rose with my help, and without command or signal, the twenty or so bailiffs charged past, into our family home, and set fire to it.

"The O'Shaughnessys are hereby evicted," proclaimed the constable, before running a hand over his face. "Theodore Moore-Vandeleur, acting on behalf of Colonel Moore-Vandeleur, exacts his right as the newly appointed land agent, and as Colonel Moore-Vandeleur's eldest son and heir, to hereby end the good-faith contract signed by his grandfather and your father, and ends your tenure as land agent. Pending investigation of missing money and account irregularities, Colonel Moore-Vandeleur warns that Mr. Michael O'Shaughnessy Senior might incur charges resulting in either termination of life or deportation to the Australian colony at Her Majesty's pleasure."

"He didn't do any of that!" I cried, steadying myself as Michael braced himself against me. Eyes wild and with rage bubbling in my veins, I glanced at Da. *Teddy* did this? "I'll beg an audience with his lordship. Or with Teddy. I can fix this!"

"You will do no such thing," Da snapped, turning toward

the constable as the bailiffs emerged from the house to fire the thatch of our roof. "What do ye think, John? Is it bluster?"

The constable sighed. "I don't know, sir. Rumor has it that the young master found the irregularities himself . . . but surely his lordship will bury such nonsense? D'ye think Master Theodore might have fabricated the evidence?"

But Da simply pressed his lips together, as my lungs stopped working, and the ground rocked beneath my feet.

It was all my fault. From devising the scheme to wed Teddy and lift my family out of poverty, to trusting him in my absence to hold steady in his feelings toward me and against his father. His father, who had given his blessing. His father, who had so thoughtfully sent me away to give birth with all the sustenance I required for a healthy delivery. What had gone wrong? I must have severely overcalculated the hold I had over Teddy's heart, for never would I have believed him capable of such cruelty. Certainly not the sort of cruelty that would incite him to fabricate evidence against Da and sign the declaration that turned us out of our home. My gut roiled at the thought.

"Stop," Michael said with a sigh, placing a gentle hand on my shoulder. I shot a glance over my right shoulder, and there he was, face soot-stained, eyes tearing from the smoke as he stared straight ahead at the house we'd been born in. "I know what yer thinking, and it's not yer fault."

"But—" I began.

"I would've gone there too. Ye needed answers, and ye sure as feck got them. Feck 'em all," Michael said firmly, eyes narrowing as he turned away to find Da.

Da held Mam in his arms, cradling her head into his chest as she cried silent tears.

"What's the plan, Da?" Michael asked.

"Bring yer mam and the children 'round to the neighbors, then meet me back here once they're settled. With luck, we'll be able to make a scalpeen when the fire's out," Da said, pulling back from Mam to glance down at her. "We'll be fine, my Rosie."

"The bailiffs will turn us out of the scalpeen," Mam warned, wiping her tears on her sleeve.

"But not tonight," Da said, straightening as Michael gathered the young ones. A scalpeen was a shelter made in the ruins of a burned house, but as Mam said, we'd be turned out of that too. 'Twas only a matter of time before the bailiff returned to knock down the walls to deny us even that small comfort. "Take them now, Junior. I'm going to head down to the workhouse to get the lie of the land, then visit the church and ask Father Kenny if he knows of any immediate paying work."

"I'll go with you, Da," I said.

"Absolutely not. We've all had a shock, and I'd prefer if you took care of yer—"

"We'll need more than a penny a day to keep us fed, and I have my letters. There's bound to be some business in need of assistance. And if not—" I pointed down at the leather shoes adorning my feet. "I can sell these. They'll fetch a good price. What about Michael's Big House shoes? And yours?"

"Michael sold his off for food after he was let go. I still have mine," Da said with a sigh, watching as Mam and Michael set off down the road with my siblings. "Let's enquire first, then make a shelter, and worry about the rest tomorrow."

I nodded, then pursed my lips. "I'm . . . I'm that sorry, Da. If I had just stayed away—"

"Nonsense," he interrupted.

I nodded, for there was no point in dragging it out. "Let's get to it then. Daylight is wasting."

Without another word, Da and I turned in tandem and strode toward the town—two phoenixes rising from the ash, as the rafters supporting the thatched roof of what was once our home cracked, bowed, and collapsed in a crash of smoke and embers.

*   *   *

A heel of cheese, shared among eleven, was all we had to eat that first week. Baby Crofton still fed at Mam's breast, but her supply had waned to naught but a trickle, mayhap once a day.

Da and I had no luck in the town. The workhouse was at full capacity, thanks to his lordship's evictions in the spring and winter of 1845 and 1846, and Father Kenny broke the news to Da that Theodore Moore-Vandeleur, on behalf of his father, had sent strict instruction to all businesses not to employ the O'Shaughnessys, under pain of legal action.

And they would comply. For who had funded the building of the town? Who had funded the building of the churches and the hall and the workhouse itself?

The Moore-Vandeleurs.

That first night, we'd slept in the ruins of our old home, but as predicted, the bailiffs returned in the morning to demolish the walls, leaving us stranded.

I thought our neighbors might help after all Da had done for them through the years—after we had just sold everything we could to purchase grain for them to last out the winter—but his lordship had made it clear that anyone caught helping us would face eviction themselves.

The only small mercy came when a group of neighbors sent word to Da that morning that they'd dug a scalp for us—a hole in the ground where we could seek shelter from the elements, packed like fish at market. An open grave, where we could lie together, while Da and Michael went off in search of assistance.

That was three weeks ago. With no food, no roof above our heads, and no strength to rally, despair settled thick and heavy. As though time itself had slowed, so we might muse on all the ways we could die in painful silence, stomachs growling, bodies weakening.

The only sound of life from our scalp came from Síofra's lungs, the wheezing rattle of her breath a metronome, tick-tick-ticking as we waited for our men to return.

"Maggie?" Mam's hoarse whisper broke my heart, and I turned to face her, knowing full well what she was about to say. We'd already cried our tears and had none left to shed. "I think he's dead."

I closed my eyes. Baby Crofton had contracted a fever four days ago, and weakened as he was, we feared this might happen. Mam and I had prepared for it, and Mam just held him, surrounding him with comfort and love as she waited for his chest to rise and fall for the last time.

My brother was dead. And it was my fault.

I pulled my aching body into a sitting position, then dragged myself to my feet before climbing out of the scalp.

"Where are ye going?" Mam asked.

I glanced down at her. With Crofton cradled tightly to her chest, Mam's vacant expression struck a chill straight into my heart.

"To dig a grave," I replied. She nodded, and I glanced at my siblings. The little ones all had fevers. "I'll fetch water from the spring. Do ye think ye can build a fire?"

"I can try." Da had instructed us to avoid building a fire, lest the smoke draw the attention of the bailiffs. The land still belonged to his lordship, and we were trespassing, but we had no choice right now. Besides, the fire we'd built three days ago hadn't brought the bailiffs to our hidden location; little good it had done to help poor baby Crofton, but maybe we could still help the others.

I nodded. "I'm also going to head down to the town and try to sell my shoes again."

It was market day. After fetching water and digging a shallow grave, I pulled my good leather shoes from their dry hiding place and walked, barefoot, to the town. I could sit back and wait for the men no longer.

Mam wasn't ready to part with Crofton's corpse just yet, and I hadn't the strength to fight with her.

If I'd held my own babe even once, I wouldn't have let go either, and there wasn't a physician or midwife in the world who would've been able to wrest him from my arms.

A hush had descended over the usual bustle of Kilrush, and market offerings were scarce. Fewer vendors willing to make the trip in these uncertain times, no doubt. With the blight, those who had coin spent every penny they could muster on bulk grain to feed large families for as long as possible. Dainties and fancies would wait until times were better.

"Mistress O'Shaughnessy?" The shocked question jerked me around, and I came face-to-face with Mrs. Moran, the fish seller. "Jesus, Mary, and Joseph! I thought I'd never see ye again!"

A quick glance at my clothes brought a flush to my cheeks. Grime and dirt caked the skirt, and the rest was soaked through with sweat. I hadn't been able to wash—myself, or the clothes— since our eviction. My hair was in a bad state too, but I'd managed to tame it into a braid before setting off for town.

"Hello, Mrs. Moran," I said, my voice hoarse from general misery. "Soft day."

Mrs. Moran pursed her lips, then glanced around the market. "Here," she said, ducking beneath her stall, emerging a few moments later with a package wrapped in a clean rag. "If I'd known I'd meet ye, I'd have more prepared. We heard of yer father's eviction all the way at the island, but I thought ye'd be long gone, what with the accusation."

I stood frozen, staring at the little package, and the briny water soaked through it.

Mrs. Moran followed my gaze and sighed. "It's not a lot, I know. But it doesn't look like I'll have much luck selling today, and ye likely need it more than most."

Tears swam in my eyes, and Mrs. Moran stepped around her stall to close the distance between us. "I don't know what happened, but it must have been serious to evict a land agent and block the family from doing any business in town. Take this to yer family; they must be starving. The babe too. Yer mam has a new babe, doesn't she?"

"Dead," I whispered, staring at the package in Mrs. Moran's hands. "He's dead, and the rest are ill."

Mrs. Moran shoved the package into my hands with a cluck of her tongue, then hurried back to her stall to pluck something from the large bag she used for personal effects on the estuary crossing.

"Here. I have it on me for the pain in me knees," she said, placing a large vial in my skirt pocket. "Only a drop to ease the pain, mind. Too much and ye risk doing more harm than good. It's not much by way of medicine, but it could be a help, and I can fetch more before I leave."

I glanced at her and noticed the burn of coming tears reddening her eyes.

"The light of Heaven to the babe and yer mam," she said, making the sign of the cross. "I'll keep ye in my prayers, but wish I could do more."

I nodded, unable to muster more than a polite, "Thank you."

And with that, I turned, the package held tight in my hands.

"Good luck, Mistress O'Shaughnessy," Mrs. Moran called, but I kept walking.

One foot before the other.

Head down, lest anyone else recognize me.

News I'd been spotted in town would still reach his lordship's ears, regardless, and I wondered if Da would disapprove that I'd risked recognition by making another desperate run to sell the shoes.

Where was Da? My guess was Lissycasey. Surely that was far enough away to ensure some kind of assistance?

With each step, the weight of the shoes, and Mrs. Moran's gifts, settled heavy on my heart. There was still so much kindness in people, so much love. I hoped she sold all her fish and that her family still prospered.

I should've enquired. I should've left her with a blessing. I should've—

"Ooft." The exclamation rushed past my lips as I walked into someone, almost losing my balance. But the stranger's hands shot out to grab my upper arms and steadied me. "Apologies."

"Maggie?"

I froze as the gentle timbre of a voice as familiar as my own washed over me, and I dared glance upward.

From shined leather shoes and fine, full-length trousers. From waistcoat, to tailed overcoat, to the stovepipe hat that stretched above my once-beloved's face.

And something inside, some tiny shred of dignity and pride, shattered.

"T-Teddy?" His name was a breath, an oath, a prayer. But I regretted the greeting in an instant as I finally absorbed the wide-eyed horror that twisted his handsome features.

"Wh-what?" he muttered, his gaze drinking in every ragged inch of me before settling on my dirtied face. "Y-you're . . . is that you? How could this be?"

I stared at him, both brows raised, as his questions rattled around my brain before finding purchase. He thought me far away, fleeing from the lies he'd turned into a declaration in order to be rid of me. Anger swelled in my breast, and before I could think, I spat a question of my own.

"How is your wife?"

I stepped around him, spine straight, and strode away.

One step, two, three.

Teddy's hand clamped down on my shoulder, and he spun me around.

"*How*?" he demanded, voice surer than it was a moment before. "You left—"

"I must have truly meant nothing to you." With a shrug, I held up the package in my hand. "If you don't mind, I must away. My family waits."

"No!" he exclaimed, eyes wild as he stepped forward, but I jerked from his grasp and took a step back. "We must speak. Tonight. The summerhouse. I . . . I'm so very confused right now—"

After everything that had happened that night at the summerhouse, he—and his family—could jump off a cliff for all I cared. Why had he done such things? How could he do such things? Teddy was dead to me, and likely had been from the moment our child had passed away . . . I just needed to see him to realize it.

"Goodbye, Teddy," I said, then shook my head and stared him in the eyes. "Nay. Goodbye, Young Master Theodore. Forgive me. For a moment, I forgot to whom I speak."

Head up. Step after step.

I didn't crumble until I was safely away.

Until I had made my way through the winding trees to reach our scalp.

Until the rumble of male voices set my teeth on edge—had Teddy sent bailiffs already?

Wary, I slowly approached, to find two men kneeling before the fresh mound of baby Crofton's grave.

Da and Michael.

Chapter 24

The hovels which the poor people were building . . .
were of the most abject description . . . floors sunk into
ditches . . . the height scarcely enough for a man to stand
upright . . . a few pieces of grass sods the only covering.
—Isaac Weld, *Statistical Survey of the County of
Roscommon* (1832)

November and December 1846: Before

His lordship's reach was long, and there was no aid to be found for the Moore-Vandeleurs' former land agent.

That left us with only one choice. We had to make the journey to Ennis, by way of Kildysert, in hopes we could find aid there. It was a fine village, Da had said, far enough away from Kilrush, with a market and businesses that might have work for us.

The next morning, Da and Mam mustered the young ones, as Michael and I gathered what little we had for the journey.

"Ye haven't been eating," I said to Michael, staring at the sharpness of his cheekbones. "Ye must be exhausted from journeying."

Michael shrugged and placed an arm around my shoulders. "Doesn't matter."

"Michael. Can ye take Patrick on yer back? Mam will carry Mary. Maggie, ye'll carry Nancy." Da glanced around at us, then summoned a weak smile for the little ones. "We're going on an adventure so we can find food and shelter, my loves. Ye'll all be good for us and do as yer told, won't ye?"

Aoife, Martha, and Síofra leaned against each other—all ill. The youngest babes—Patrick, John, Mary, and Nancy—still raged with fevers, and Da's words likely didn't fully register.

Within a half hour, I had Nancy strapped to my back, and we were on our way.

"Lucky ye ran into Mrs. Moran yesterday," Da said softly, as we reached the Ennis Road and headed toward Lissycasey. "The food was sorely needed."

"Aye," I said, looking out into the distance, before remembering the vial Mrs. Moran had put into my pocket. I reached in to pull it out. "Oh! She gave me this. Said it was medicine."

Da's brows drew together, and he took the vial. "Hmm."

"We should give it to the young ones," I said, glancing behind at our sad little caravan.

"Laudanum," Da mumbled, then squirreled the vial into his own pocket. "Won't help them with what they have right now. It's mostly for pain, not fevers."

"Oh." I sighed, dejected. "How long 'til we branch off for Kildysert?"

"If we can keep a good pace, three days. If not, longer," he said, shifting his grip on John, whose head lolled against Da's shoulder. If I'd had strength, I would've reached out a hand to check his fever, but what little I had needed to be conserved.

"We'll be able to sell the shoes there?" I asked, and Da pursed his lips.

"Hopefully. I want to keep us out of the workhouse if at all possible," he said. So did I. For once a person went into a workhouse, there was no real way out. The minute a poor soul stepped foot inside, the government kept a running tally of what they owed by way of shelter and food consumed, and took that "rent" from the wage earned working. But the "rent" was always higher than what was earned, and so the only way out was death, or sponsorship. If an inmate could find a sponsor to pay off the workhouse debt, then they could freely leave. But if an inmate had a person in their life to do so, they wouldn't have ended up in the workhouse to begin with.

I nodded. There was nothing to say, for the unsaid part hung in the air between us.

If we couldn't sell his pair and mine, we'd have to make our way to Ennis.

And who knew if we'd all make it.

It didn't take three days to branch off for Kildysert. It took a week, and another two to reach the village.

Hunger ate away at the lining of our stomachs, and our bodies shut down 'til we could only shuffle forward a few minutes at a time before resting. We did our best to forage whatever we could as we traveled, but sustenance was scarce in winter.

And on the way we lost little John, and Mary.

Da buried them quietly by the side of the road, and not a single one of us had strength left to cry.

By the time we reached Kildysert proper, Da enquired after a doctor and found one willing to take a look at my siblings in exchange for the shoes. One pair, mind. We still had to use mine for food.

The doctor even allowed us to stay in his stable for two nights while he worked on Nancy, Martha, and Patrick.

But while we worried after the youngest, Síofra quietly succumbed to the miasma attacking her lungs.

Desperate, Da, Michael, and I went in search of a buyer for my shoes at the Kildysert market.

No one would buy. No one needed leather shoes except those who could afford the luxury.

The people here were weak too, and we learned through market gossip that the country was in complete crisis. From coast to coast, famine raged, and the British Crown was doing nothing.

Irish produce and livestock still needed to be exported, and the landed Anglos who ruled over the Irish had to find a way.

"There, maybe," Michael said, his voice weak and hoarse as he pointed toward a storefront that read: Cobbler. "A man who trades in shoes would surely purchase them?"

I nodded and followed in his wake.

A bell tinkled as Michael opened the door, but before he had fully crossed the threshold, a gruff voice barked in Gaeilge: "Out!"

"Sir, we have wares to sell—" Michael began, in Gaeilge.

"I have no business with beggars."

I glanced between Michael and me, at our raggedy clothes and dirty faces, and sighed.

"Sir, we have wares to sell," I repeated, this time in the clipped English I used when paraded before Lady Grace's company. With a gentle shove, I pushed Michael into the establishment and stepped around him. I curtsied. "Forgive our appearance, sir, for we've long been on the road. I have here a fine pair of leather shoes to sell. My own, I assure you."

I glanced across the dim store and spied an elderly man seated behind the counter, his white-gray brows arched high above too-large spectacles.

"Forgive me, Miss," said the cobbler, switching to English as he glanced between us. "They are yer own, ye say?"

I nodded and unhooked the wrapped package from my belt before striding forward to place it on the counter.

The cobbler rose and untied the package, then glanced sharply at me as he beheld my shoes.

"I was a servant of Colonel Moore-Vandeleur, sir," I said by way of explanation. "Unfortunately, we were evicted, and this is all I have left to provide for my family. It would be a mercy if we could do business."

"Aye," said the cobbler, drawing one of the shoes to eye level. "I think we could do business indeed, Ms. O'Shaughnessy."

The blood drained from my face. "I don't recall giving my name, sir."

"Nay," said the cobbler. "But the Moore-Vandeleurs did. Sent word to all the bailiffs to be on the watch for thieves. Servants from the O'Shaughnessy family they once employed, who had stolen from his house. Yer father is a wanted man, apparently. And now that I've confirmed yer identity, I think it's best ye be off."

"Ye bastarding bollocks!" Michael exclaimed, moving to reclaim the shoes.

But the old man was fast and quickly pulled them from Michael's grasp. My pulse quickened, threatening to send me into a faint. This was it—all we had left. Our last hope . . . gone.

"I'll hang onto these to return to the great people ye stole them from, and as an act of Christianity, I'll not alert the bailiffs. God knows times are hard for everyone, but by the looks of ye, ye need no more trouble."

"Thieving prick!" Michael roared, but I held out an arm to still him.

"May God forgive ye, sir. With yer great years, ye should realize that a man as fine as Colonel Moore-Vandeleur wouldn't put so much effort into ensuring we starve to death without something amiss." I spat the words, and the old cobbler had the decency to blush.

"Aye, I know that," he replied. "Which is why I'm not calling the bailiff. Be off with ye now. Best chance ye have is to make it to the Ennis workhouse. I'll say a prayer for ye."

"Ye can take yer prayer and shove it up yer hole," Michael exclaimed.

Aye, he could. But that wouldn't feed us or keep us alive.

Chapter 25

Here you have an Irish hut or cabin, such as millions of
the people of Ireland live in. And some live in worse than
these. Men and women, married and single, old and
young, lie down together, in much the same degradation
as the American slaves. I see much here to remind me of
my former condition.
—Frederick Douglass, African American social reformer
and abolitionist, in a letter to William Lloyd Garrison
outlining his experience in Ireland, February 26, 1846

December 1846: Before

I didn't know how much time had passed, but inquiries along
the road told us we were ten miles from Ennis.

Aoife was dead. So were Nancy, Martha, and Patrick.

The doctor in Kildysert couldn't do much, and the reprieve
Da's shoes had won us wore out quickly.

We left Kildysert the day after the incident with the cobbler,
shuffling along, now barely able to travel a quarter mile a day,
weakened as we were.

The workhouse became a dream, one I now longed for as the
nights stretched on. I never dreamt of food, but of heat. Of a
roof over our heads.

Michael's nose had started dripping some time hence, Da's

too. Even Mam's. But I remained untouched—I suspected due to the good nutrition offered during my eight-month stint in Dublin.

But that didn't make it any easier.

The gnaw of hunger had eased—as it does when one goes without food for quite some time. But the cold? My bones frosted with ice now that my body had started to waste away.

I feared freezing in my sleep, but in the end, the cold took Mam, not me.

And we'd long since lost the strength to bury our losses.

Da, Michael, and I moved her body into the tall grass, then returned to the road to rest, needing respite after the exertion.

We were once twelve, and now we were three.

Three souls who hadn't strength to speak.

Three souls gasping in shallow pants.

"Hello?"

The voice registered, but I couldn't even move to acknowledge it.

"Dad, they're in a terrible state."

"Quick, load them in there."

Arms hoisted me up, and I was laid in a rough-hewn cart.

I'm not dead, I wanted to say, fear niggling at the back of my numb mind that I was being carted off to a mass grave, the kind we'd heard about on our journey. Pits dug where bodies were piled atop another, without grace or dignity in death, for all eternity.

Rumbling.

Cart.

Time . . . pointless.

Wet, my lips.

I parted them, and water dribbled down my throat.

Sleep.

*   *   *

"She's waking."

A woman's voice greeted my opening eyes as something warm trickled into my mouth.

"Hush now," said the woman. "Swallow for me."

My throat had long-since forgotten how to swallow, but I tried, awakening muscles my body had forgotten how to use.

"What's her name?" the woman asked.

"M-Maggie," a hoarse voice responded.

"There ye are, Maggie. Swallow now. Yer da and brother are here, and yer safe."

Safe?

"Another sup," said the woman, as a wooden utensil touched my lips. "That's it, get it in ye now. Ye'll need all yer strength."

The woman fed me a spoonful of broth every two hours until I had strength enough to manage a bowlful by myself.

She'd done the same for Da, and Michael, and when my wits returned, I finally got a good look at where we were.

It was a small, one-roomed house, with a blazing fire roaring at one end, and a man and woman seated at a rough-hewn table before it. Da, Michael, and I were propped against the wall closest to the fire, covered with blankets, bowls in our laps.

"From Kilrush?" the man asked, swiping a hand over his face as he gaped at Da. "Ye came all this way without any aid?"

Da nodded, and the man shook his head as the door to the house opened, sucking a cool rush of air into the warm cavern.

"My son," said the man, as his son quickly shut the door. "I'm Conor, and my wife here, Kitty. We're O'Deas, ourselves. If not for Cormac's sharp eyes, I wouldn't have seen ye hidden in the grass."

"Ye have my thanks." Da's voice croaked, but if I had any propensity for feeling, I'd be glad to hear his returning strength.

"We fared a bit better here. The local landlord, Mr. O'Reilly, opened his own food stores to the tenants. It's not much, but it's keeping most from the workhouse, though the rent is still due. We're lucky too to have fewer mouths to feed. My son there is our one and only. God took the rest as babes. Hard in times past when doing the work for Mr. O'Reilly, but we're grateful for it now. Aren't we, Kitty?" said Conor, gesturing toward his wife.

"That glad," said Kitty, offering a wan smile to her son. "My sisters and brothers have children enough for us to dote on."

"Ye're all local?" Da asked. "We weren't, and neither is— was—my wife. She had a lot of family in Tipperary, but my own was small, and we had none around."

"North and East Clare," Kitty replied, her smile wavering. "We dote from afar, I'm afraid."

Da nodded, and Conor turned toward Da. "Can ye stand a bit to come outside? Kitty and I would like to hear yer story so we can best know how to help ye, if ye'll tell it. But I'd like to keep the memory of it all from yer own children, to save their feelings."

"Aye," said Da, rising with great effort.

I reached out a hand to him, and he squeezed my fingers. "Be back soon, love. Rest up."

I glanced at Michael as Da left with Conor and Kitty, our saviors. He slept, chest rising and falling, and I could swear his color was better.

"Ye'll be fine," said a voice. The son. Right. What did they say his name was? I turned toward him and nodded. He was seated now at the table, spoon poised over a bowl of the same broth Kitty had fed us all.

He was clean, and lean, but definitely far healthier than we.

"Thank ye," I said, closing my eyes as I rested my head against the wall.

"Yer welcome. Had it too rough, ye did," he said, before the clashing clang of a wooden spoon against teeth echoed through the room. "Ow. Feck."

"Slowly," I said with a sigh, eyes still closed. "Careful."

"What's yer name?" he asked.

"Maggie."

"Good to meet ye. Ye look like one of my cousins from up in North Clare, one we only ever get to see in miniatures, so I hope ye stay a while. Mam likely sees it in ye too, so she'll be offering a place to stay and food to eat. She and Da are good folk, so it's best to take what they offer," he said.

I opened my eyes and glanced at him. "We couldn't do that. We're workhouse-bound anyway."

"Ennis?"

"Aye."

"Well, the offer will come, and I hope ye'll stay." He went back to his broth, and I mulled over his words. "I'm heading away off up to North Clare myself, so there'll be one less mouth to feed, if it makes ye feel a bit better about it. I'll be sending money home too, for the rent. Me aunt has work for me."

"Did ye say 'miniatures'?" I asked, brows drawing together. Small paintings sent to family meant money—lots of it.

The son nodded and glanced at me. "Aye. The aunt I mentioned married very well. Too well, if ye ask my mam." He smiled as I cocked my head. "Don't worry, none of it will come my way, so ye needn't scheme a way to marry me."

And for the first time in weeks, in months, a laugh worked its way up my throat.

It burst forth, a cathartic release of every damned thing I'd been through in the last year, of every loss, of every tear . . . and I couldn't stop.

Scheme a way to marry? For money? Never, ever, *ever* again would I entertain the idea, or a union with anyone.

"Jesus, it wasn't that funny," he said, glancing at his clothes as I doubled over, laughter turning to the flood of tears I'd kept at bay all this time. Tears for my siblings, my mam, myself, my life, my babe, my love.

"I'll have ye know I'm the handsomest man in the parish," he mumbled, turning his attention back to his broth as my tears transformed into sobs. He scraped back the stool and rushed to my side. "Are ye crying? Why are ye crying? Arra! Ye can't be doing that! All the good of the broth will pour out through yer eyes. Maggie? Maggie?"

But I couldn't speak.

For I was lost, and had lost.

And this moment brought naught but a brief reprieve.

We didn't stay. After regaling the O'Dea family of everything we'd gone through—every detail, so the family would know exactly how dangerous it was to have us in their home (Da was a wanted man, after all)—Da, Michael, and I recouped some of our strength and were on our way to Ennis two days later.

Mrs. O'Dea, Kitty, packed as much as she could give—which wasn't a lot. There was no flour for bread or milk for cheese, and no way to transport her vegetable stews and broths.

But she conjured up a batch of oat cakes and three small carrots.

It was enough to feed the three of us for one meal, but I figured if we made good time, we could abstain from eating for a few days, then have this feast and rally for the final leg of the journey.

We were going to make it. I knew we would.

Michael was still very weak, and it pained my heart to see my strong brother so desolate. But Da had rejected the O'Dea's offer to have their son drive us in the cart to Ennis—*sure, wouldn't he be on his way to North Clare soon?* Still, Da said he feared for the O'Deas' safety if their assistance was ever discovered.

So, we walked, Michael supported between Da and me.

Rain fell and wind whipped as we trudged along the first

three miles, before Da decided we needed to stop and seek shelter in the trees. Michael was one fever away from death's door, so I willingly complied.

But the rain didn't pass. It stayed that night, the next day, and the next.

"He needs his strength," Da whispered to me on that third night. "He won't make it otherwise."

I nodded and automatically reached for the package of food Mrs. O'Dea had given to us, but Da placed a gentle hand on my arm.

"D'ye understand what awaits us at the workhouse?"

"Separation," I said with a sigh. They'd split up the family, and we'd be lucky to see each other at mealtimes.

"It'll be you and Michael only," Da said softly, and I whipped my head up to look at him. "I made some enquiries while we were in Kildysert, and his lordship used the doctored books to make me a wanted fugitive for rent theft. That means I won't be let into the workhouse. I'll likely be arrested and sent off to the prison colony on the other side of the world."

The blood froze in my veins, but Da smiled warmly.

"Make sure ye both get there safely, love. Rest when ye can, and keep moving when yer able. Mr. O'Dea promised to send word to his sister in Ennis. She's matron of the workhouse, so hopefully she'll be expecting ye." Da put his hand in his pocket and glanced at Michael. "The minute he has a bit of strength, off ye go, and don't look back, ye understand?"

"Da . . . what are ye on about?" I asked. This sounded like goodbye, but he was fine. Well, as fine as circumstances would allow.

Da nodded and reached for the wooden dish we'd brought along. I followed the action with my eyes, sweat pilling along my brow despite the cold. He moved with purpose, as if it was the most natural thing in the world. In one smooth movement, he pulled a knife from his pocket, ran it over the skin of his inner elbow, and allowed the blood to drip into the bowl.

"Get it in him," Da instructed, gasping through the pain.

"Da!" I screamed . . . or tried to. The exclamation erupted on a breath of air.

"There's good iron in blood," Da explained, wincing as he smiled. "Get it down Michael's throat. Then we'll refill it, and you'll take your own share. Save that food for a few more days. There'll be more to share between two, rather than three."

"No, no, no, no, no." My heart raced as Da squeezed his forearm against his bicep to stop the flow before handing me the bowl.

"Quick now, lest it go to waste," he said.

I couldn't move, frozen as I was, mouth open, brows furrowed.

"Maggie!" Da snapped. "Listen, will ye? Feed it to Michael. It gives strength, and mine will soon be gone, given how weakened my body already is. This is my gift to ye, love. Live. Live for me and yer mam. Live as we intended for ye to live when our love brought ye into this world. Take the blood. Do it now."

With shaking hands, I complied, pinching Michael's lips with one hand as I fed him our father's blood with the other.

He sputtered in his deep sleep, but I watched his throat bob.

"Now hand it back, my darlin'," Da said softly, reaching for the dish. "In a little while, take that vial from my pocket—the one Mrs. Moran gave ye—and feed it to me. The whole vial, mind. In large quantities, it should give a painless death."

He took the bowl and released his forearm to allow the blood to flow, to fill it. For me. And again, for Michael.

And I watched, chilled to my soul, as my father slowly, painfully, gave his life for ours, all while cursing the name Moore-Vandeleur.

When Michael awoke, Da was gone, but I'd had no strength to move his corpse—despite the pints of rich, life-giving blood sloshing low in my belly.

I barely had enough strength to articulate what had transpired to Michael, but I wasn't certain he had recovered enough wherewithal to understand what had happened. He just stared at me, then spent a good five minutes staring at Da's stiffening body.

We walked on, Michael leaning heavily on my shoulder. As Da had instructed, I didn't look back. Tears should've come, but they did not, for I was bereft of every—and any—ounce of feeling, both inside and out.

"Four days should bring us to Clareabbey, if we can muster enough strength to make a mile a day," I said, more for the company of words spoken aloud than to Michael himself. "The O'Deas said there's trouble there, so we should try to pass through as quickly as possible."

"What kind . . . of trouble?" Michael asked, panting heavily. I glanced at him, noting the sweat pilling on his brow.

"A public works overseer was shot."

"Shot? With a pistol?"

I nodded, shifting beneath Michael's weight. "The Public Works Board organized around four hundred paying jobs to help with relief, but seven or eight hundred people showed up."

"That'll do it," Michael said with a sigh. "No chance of meeting generous folk like the O'Deas there then. They're all hurtin'. Christ Almighty! Had it been two months earlier we could've poached a little along the way, and I could have tried to find work to avoid the workhouse."

The timing had struck me as particularly cruel too. If we could've trapped a hare or two, how many of us would still be alive?

I shook my head. "No matter. We'll make it. We have to. If you can hold out a few more days, we can eat what Mrs. O'Dea gave us, then make our way into Ennis proper."

A soft chuckle rumbled up Michael's throat. "I'm slipping, Maggie."

Brows furrowing, I shifted his weight, but he shook his head.

"No, you ninny. I mean, I don't think I'll make it."

I scoffed. "Don't even think about it. If you dare die, I'll feckin' haunt you."

"I think you mean *I'll* haunt *you*," he said.

"Ye know what I meant, ye feckin' gobshite."

"Aye," he said softly. "Let's sit a while, Maggie-pie. If ye mean for us both to get there, then we should eat now, lest my fever get any worse."

I nodded, for he was right.

There was no point in forcing him to shuffle on for a few more days if what little food we had wasn't enough to rouse him.

And so, we sat on the side of the road.

And prepared to eat our last meal together—likely, our last meal forever—before entering the workhouse . . . where we might never leave and might never see each other again.

Chapter 26

The children were like skeletons, their features sharpened
with hunger and their limbs wasted, so that there was
little left but bones . . . and the happy expression of
infancy gone from their faces, leaving the anxious look
of premature old age.
—William Forster, a Quaker, 1846

January 1847: Before

No, no, no, no, no, no!

Whatever had numbed my soul to its core thawed two
mornings later, for Michael burned, his skin raging with fever.

"Wake up," I hissed, shaking him. "Michael O'Shaughnessy,
ye wake up this instant!"

We were there—Clareabbey, or about to enter its boundary—
and smoke billowed from chimneys in the distance, promising
people.

I scrambled to my feet, ignoring the pain that gnawed away
my insides. That was the trouble with eating for strength; it
took a few days for the pain to settle, before the stomach forgot
its wants and needs.

"Help. I'll go seek help," I mumbled, eyes wide. This was
different. Before, there'd been no assistance on the road, and
nothing to do but watch each other die.

But here? Chimneys, people, aid.

We had naught to barter, but surely someone would take pity?

"I'll be back as soon as I can," I whispered, removing my cloak despite the cold. Gently, I placed it over Michael before turning on my heel, then paused.

I glanced down at my clothes, so tattered and torn they could hardly be worth anything. Everything swam on me now, and I knew others would see what I did when I looked at Michael—a walking corpse, skin so thin it hugged sharp, protruding bones.

We'd been starving, and on the road close to two months, for what should've been a two-day journey by cart, and ten days by foot, in normal circumstances.

I quickly removed the bodice—it still had all its buttons, so mayhap someone would take it in exchange for a little assistance.

Given what had occurred here, I didn't expect to receive much help, if any, but, God above, I had to try.

As sporadic houses gave way to ordered streets, I was turned away from every door. No one had either the means or the desire to help.

One elderly lady told me to wait at her threshold, before returning with a ladle of broth and instructing that I cup my hands. "Disease-ridden," she'd called me, wanting nothing of hers touching my skin lest such kindness brought death to her door.

My pride had long since vanished, and I cupped my hands to take the broth.

The hours stretched on, but enquiries on the whereabouts of a doctor led me on a goose chase 'round the streets—all merely pointing in random directions to send me away, far from them. For they were "better" than me, not nearly as starved and with rooves over their heads.

"Miss? Did I hear you ask after a physician?"

In a daze, I turned, and came face-to-face with a well-dressed gentleman—finely starched shirt-sleeves rolled to his elbow, wearing both waistcoat and full-length trousers. An Anglo.

Dark eyes widened as they drank in my countenance, and I feared what he saw there.

"My brother, sir," I said, voice barely a whisper. "The fever . . . I fear he's in trouble."

Silence followed as the man stared, but as minutes ticked by, he roused himself with a shake. "Where?"

"I . . ." I wasn't sure. I'd wandered so much I'd lost all sense of direction. Biting my lower lip, I glanced around, hating the telltale sign of tears-to-come stinging my eyes.

"Steady now," said the man. "Where did you come from?"

"The Ennis Road, from Kildysert, just outside Clareabbey, sir."

He nodded and gestured down the street. "Allow me to fetch my bag and a few warm blankets."

"Are ye a doctor, sir?" I asked, not daring to hope.

"Doctor Fitzgibbon, at your service."

Within fifteen minutes, we were on our way—I, bundled atop the fine pony Dr. Fitzgibbon insisted I ride.

"I'm that sorry I had naught to offer by way of food," he said, for the tenth time. "I've been giving all I can to those affected by the pause on the public works project."

I nodded, not caring. All thoughts and energy I had were for Michael.

"No mind, sir. We'll make it to the workhouse soon."

It took over a half hour to return to the spot where I'd left Michael, and Dr. Fitzgibbon went straight to work—leaving me atop the pony in his haste.

It took three tries to gather enough strength to swing my right leg over the beast's rump, and by the time I finally struggled to the ground and shuffled to where Dr. Fitzgibbon knelt over Michael, something told me it was too late.

That I was too late.

"How is he, Doctor?' I whispered, watching as he listened intently to Michael's chest.

Dr. Fitzgibbon shook his head. "I fear naught but a miracle could bring him back. It's incredible he made it thus far."

I clasped my mouth with shaking hands, and sank, wordlessly, to my knees.

"The fever is two-fold," the doctor continued. "When the body enters starvation phase, the humors misalign, causing a susceptibility to catching all kinds of ailments. Night air, cold, exposure to the elements—all cause ailments. Unfortunately, feeding him won't be enough, for something has taken hold in his lungs, I fear. Medicine likely won't work, as the body requires strength to heal. But he needs nutrition to regain strength. There could be a chance if the fever broke—"

"It's broken before," I offered, the words tumbling in a rush. "Twice."

Dr. Fitzgibbon turned to me with brows raised. "How long has he been ill?"

"I . . . I'm not sure. We left our home in November—"

"It's January fifth," he interjected, pursing his lips.

January? I mouthed the word in surprise.

"Has he been ill all that time?"

"Maybe four weeks into the journey," I said, my voice barely audible.

"I'm afraid the best I can do is call the body cart, Miss." Dr. Fitzgibbon laid a hand on my arm, but I jerked away.

"No," I said. "We're going to make it to the workhouse."

"They won't take him in that state."

"They *will*." Reaching out, I tucked the cloak tightly around Michael's shoulders.

"I fear he won't last the night." The words, though gentle, grated against my soul, against the promise I had made Da— that I would get us both safely to the workhouse.

"Then he'll die surrounded by the only family he has left," I said, glaring at the doctor. "Thank ye for coming, Doctor. I'm that sorry it was a wasted trip. For yer trouble."

Slipping the bodice out from beneath Michael's sleeping form, I offered it to him with two hands.

"What?" The doctor's eyes widened.

"Ye could sell it and use the coin to help those ye mentioned earlier," I said, glancing at Michael. He looked so . . . old. Like an elderly man awaiting death.

"Miss, you could use that coin yourself—"

"Nay. It's straight to the workhouse for me. Give it to others who won't have to sell their soul for a bite to eat."

The doctor rose to his feet and took the bodice.

"Here, then," he said, reaching into the pocket of his waistcoat. "If you must remain in vigil, at least build a fire for warmth."

He pulled out a book of matches—a luxury I'd only ever seen at Kilrush House—and placed them in my hand.

"May God bless you and keep you. I'll pray for you both."

"Shh."

I raised my tear-stained face to find Michael's eyes half-open, focused, trained on me. I hadn't notice him turn his head, worried as I was about the rumble in his chest, rattling with the inevitability we all face—but not like this. Too soon, too young, too unfortunate.

"Michael?" I whispered, pushing up to my elbows.

The fire I'd lit—thanks to Dr. Fitzgibbon's match book—slowly waltzed in the breeze, a dance laced with death, in the final minutes of what could be his final hour. The surrounding grass made a comfortable bed, and I was grateful for this one small mercy—soft and damp, but not soaked through.

Michael straightened his head, gaze fixed on the sky above.

"It's clear," he wheezed, lips curling slightly.

I glanced upward, and sure enough, the bright white belt of

glittering stars that oft appeared this time of year lit up the night sky, drawing nearly all attention from the breathtaking view of the usual constellations.

"Perfect," I whispered, lying back in the grass.

Michael's hand reached for mine, and I laced my fingers through his without thought.

"I l-love ye, M-Maggie," Michael whispered.

"And I love ye, Michael."

"Live, will ye?" he said, pausing to cough. "Live to spite them, for living will be the best revenge."

I squeezed my eyes shut and breathed deep.

I couldn't make another promise I might not keep.

"I'll do my best," I said, instead.

"Nay. Ye'll live. Survive. Get revenge for yerself, for me, for everyone. Live, and leave a legacy for those who come after ye. Promise me."

"I . . . I can't promise. I promised Da I'd see us both safe, and I've broken it already."

"That wasn't a promise ye could keep, and Da knew it," Michael said, afore coughs shook his body. "I'll not be here come dawn, so ye'll promise that ye'll avenge us all by living."

"I have a ways to go yet—" I began.

"The stars are so beautiful," Michael whispered, squeezing my hand, before a sudden *fzzt* rent the night air in two.

Michael gasped, and my eyes widened.

"What in the—" I began, but stopped short as the scent of sizzling meat hit the back of my throat, drawing saliva to my mouth.

"P-prom-ise," Michael demanded through clenched teeth. "Take it, eat it, and live, Maggie. My flesh is yours, a parting gift for vengeance. Regain your strength, and bring hellfire to them all."

"Michael?" Eyes wide, my mind finally caught up to the latest chain of events, and I whipped my head around to glance at the fire.

Where Michael had placed his leg.

Calf-down.

Into the flames and embers.

It wasn't meat cooking, it was him, *him*!

"P-promise me," he gasped, squeezing my hand.

"I . . . I—"

"*Promise!*"

"*I promise!*"

And I would follow through. For Michael died not long after.

And, God forgive me, but I ate the flesh he'd so selflessly offered in the name of vengeance, tears streaming down my face as my teeth tore meat from bone.

And my soul, forever blackened, had hardened to steel.

Chapter 27

Ireland must in return behold her best flour, her wheat, bacon, her butter, her live cattle, all going to England day after day.
—*The Chronicle and Munster Adviser*, May 1846

Present: May 1848

I woke with a start, heart and head pounding, surrounded by the haze of incense, and threw off the duvet. Nausea roiled low in my gut as I sat upright, and I slapped a palm over my mouth to keep from retching.

Did ye remember?

Tears stung the back of my eyes as Michael's gentle voice ebbed next to my ear, and I squeezed them shut before nodding.

"I lived it again, all of it. Aye," I whispered, slowly removing my hand as the nausea steadied to a dull emptiness. I lived it again, but not what happened in the summerhouse, not that it mattered. The outcome wouldn't change, nor would what I felt, both then and now.

Then why are ye just sitting there?

My eyes opened and realization squeezed my chest.

"Cormac!" I exclaimed, scrambling from the bed. I'd slept in my underclothes—thank goodness—so I hurried to the chest at the foot of the bed and pulled out the gray day dress.

Dressing quickly, I crossed to the drawn curtains and parted the seam with two fingers. It was full night and raining fit to drown the sea, but this could not wait 'til morning.

With a final adjustment, I crossed the room, plucking my riding cloak from the armchair, and hurriedly threw it over my shoulders afore leaving the bedchamber.

Down the hall, down three flights of stairs, behind and left toward the kitchen, and out the back door. My mind had a single purpose as I stepped into another storm-tossed night.

Thunder rolled in the distance, promising a night awash with sorrow. But thunder meant something else entirely to me, a person who'd lived through the worst years this country might have ever seen: thunder meant heat, a humid summer, and the arrival of yet another blight come October.

I shook my head. Mayhap I had needed to replay it all from beginning to end, to face what once was, in order to fully understand. To grieve. To finally greet the dawn with arms wide open.

My shoes crunched over gravel as I ran through the bower and into the garden. But I cared not a whit about waking the house. I saw, I lived, I remembered.

And Maggie O'Shaughnessy—me, myself, not Wilhelmina—owed a debt so great I'd never be able to repay it.

I set my sights on the gardener's cottage and, without a single thought, turned the knob and stormed right in, to find a startled Cormac, dressed in naught but a sleep shirt.

Lightning flashed somewhere close by, setting the gardener's cottage alight for the space of a breath. Within, a blazing fire roared, dispelling all chill, and I finally drank in the décor. Instead of the stools and rough-hewn table I might expect in a normal cottage, great, fabric-stuffed chairs—with arms—lounged before the hearth. An immaculately sanded and stained table sat behind, a set of finely crafted chairs gathered 'round its beveled edges. White-washed walls and a rug that covered most of the wooden—not slate—floor.

Under other circumstances, I might have complimented the luxury of the home—rungs above even my family's own lauded residence. But now? I couldn't possibly be looking at the son of Conor and Kitty O'Dea, the people who'd saved us miles outside of Clareabbey . . . could I?

I stared at him, open-mouthed, rain dripping from my sleep-mussed, drenched braid.

"It's . . . you?" A crack of thunder rattled the windowpanes, and Cormac startled, eyes widening as he suddenly realized what he wore—or didn't. My cheeks pinked as *I* suddenly realized. "God forgive me, apologies!"

Without a word, he hopped toward a door next to the fireplace as I cursed myself for a fool. A knock would have been courteous, at the very minimum.

He emerged within the space of five breaths, tucking his night shirt into a worn pair of knee breeches, expression awash with both horror and surprise.

"What . . . what is it ye need?" he asked. "What's amiss?"

I shook my head before throwing it back to stare at the ceiling, hands firmly planted on my hips. "Jesus, Cormac. I'm sorry."

"Nay, 'tis grand," he said, taking a step forward as I drew my head back down to look at him. "What has happened?"

"Is it *ye*, Cormac?" I asked, taking two steps toward him.

He furrowed his brow. "Aye. 'Tis me. Myself."

"I knew it's *ye*, but is it *ye*? Are ye *him*?" I asked, frowning as I squinted—as if a narrowed gaze might discern fact from fiction.

His lips curled at the edges as my words sank in, and he gestured for me to join him by the fire. "Tea?"

"I—" Tea? "Nothing stronger?"

He laughed then, a joyful kind of mirth that found purchase deep in the belly.

"Sit down there, my old friend, and get yerself warm."

"I—" Brows furrowing, I pursed my lips as Cormac's clear amber gaze met mine above the rim of his teacup. "That . . . I mean . . . I would have never suspected. Why didn't ye say something?"

"I thought about it, mind. Alas, ye were so weary when under our roof, I didn't expect ye to remember me. But, it is I, the handsomest man in the parish." His lips quirked into a sad smile.

The scoff working its way up my throat converted into a chuckle somewhere between lungs and lips, and I returned his smile. "I have so many questions, but I'm so very glad to meet ye, officially, again. There was so much I wanted to say to ye, yer parents too."

He waved away any thought of thanks before running a rough hand over his face. "Little good any of it did. And I fear my good intentions might have brought ill to ye."

I shook my head and settled into my chair. "Back then, ye gave me more time with my Da and my brother, so thank ye. Our fortune had been ill from the beginning, so think nary of it." I straightened, struck—and not for the first time tonight. "The position in North Clare? It was *here*? But I thought ye had said it was with yer aunt?"

"And it is," he said with a shrug. "Lady Catherine is my aunt—the one who married a little too well. Me mam mentioned it while ye were at our home, but I was setting off in a fortnight to come here. Her ladyship needed the help, and my parents needed the rent money, or they'd have to take ship. Worked out for everyone."

I nodded, turning my attention to the cooling teacup. Heaving a breath, I knocked back its contents.

"Mayhap ye really did need something stronger." Cormac laughed and pushed to his feet. "I have a small jar of poitín here somewhere."

I shook my head before swallowing and replaced the teacup on the lovely mosaic-tiled end table. "No, really. I'm fine. I just . . . what a strange coincidence. All of this."

Amber eyes glittered as flames licked and sparked in the hearth, trained on me. On my very soul. A muscle flickered near his jaw, and he sat back in the armchair.

"Maybe ye don't know, for ye were fair out of it when ye arrived at our home. But yer da was somewhat sharp during yer stay," he began, averting his gaze. "Yer da told mine of all that had troubled ye, so I know more than ye might be comfortable with me knowing. But me mam spoke a bit about her family in return. Connors, that's me mam's family name."

He paused and glanced at me, brows raised and lips thinned. 'Twas the stare of someone expecting a reaction, but I simply looked on and nodded when the pause continued. I'd seen the name mentioned in Lord Browne's journal.

"I suppose ye wouldn't have heard of them, coming from Kilrush yerself." He took a deep breath and leaned forward. "Me grandmother, Ellen, was an Early afore she wed into the Connors. And the Earlys are touched with the Sight, ye know? Mam wanted none of it and wed my father as soon as she could, to escape the stigma of the family legacy. See, everyone knows everyone's business up here, as much as they did in Kilrush, I'm sure. So Mam met Dad at the matchmaking there in Lisdoonvarna, and off she went to his farm in Craggykerivan."

Wondering where all this was going, I picked up my teacup and sipped.

"Thing is, they were dirt poor, the Connors. Poor tenants to a poorer landlord, so conditions were awful. My grandmother died when Mam was fourteen—malnutrition—and my grandfather went with the typhus six months later, so 'twas up to her eldest sister to run the household. But sure, times were bad, and two years later, when they couldn't make rent, the sisters went their separate ways. Mam was glad to get away and rarely spoke of her people. But we were happy enough, and sure, having a small family and a generous landlord meant I never went without much." He paused again and ran a hand over his face. "Thing is, word came when I was very young that Mam's sister, Cate, had wed. But not just anyone."

"Lord Browne," I surmised. Cormac nodded.

"Aye. Her offer to me wasn't the first of its kind. Back then, she'd offered Mam and Dad a grand house fit for a land agent. All she wanted was company, ye see, for the high society she wed into wanted nothing to do with her, or his lordship, as a result of their union. I didn't know the details when I was young, but Mam told me a bit when the offer came, once again, from Lady Catherine. That letter arrived a week before ye did. Lady Catherine wrote that she was in need of someone to see to her affairs—buying, selling, gardening, the accounting books. All the things I was able to do. I knew Mam had cut her off years before, so when I told them I'd take the post if she agreed to a salary, to save them from taking ship, Mam's heart broke."

I took a sip from the cup, watching as his face fell.

"See, I have another aunt, me mam's eldest sister that I mentioned," Cormac continued. "Biddy. And Biddy took my grandmother's maiden name, so she's Biddy Early to all who know her. Auntie Biddy is a rare kind of healer. Whenever Mam felt moved enough to speak of her, she always mentioned the goodness and light that emanated from her. The Sight was strongest with Biddy, and she's earned a fine reputation for good works and communing with the dead. Spirits and the like, ye know. Helping folk to carry out rituals to move them on. Reads minds and fortunes. That kind of person."

" 'Tis blessed ye are, to have such a person in the family," I noted. Though most would give someone of that ilk a wide berth, 'tis that very same person they'd turn to in times of need, and my own da had great respect for those gifted with the Sight.

"Aye," he said, nodding, "I suppose we were, but all me mam saw were the gossiping busybodies and the pelting of salt wherever she went. Anyway, thing was, me mam has a touch of the Sight. Prompting Da to plant this or that, or knowing there was an issue with livestock, and it always true, or a lifesaving endeavor. And Lady Catherine isn't an exception. Though, thing is, Mam always said there was darkness about Lady Catherine, and she didn't want me to come up here, to come near her."

The little hairs on my arms rose as another rumble of thunder shook the gardener's cottage.

"In the beginning, 'twas fine," Cormac said with a shrug. "But the first month or so, I'd see that woman in white and then go into a strange state of remembering."

I froze and straightened my spine.

He glanced at me, cheeks pinking as he rubbed his hands together, before gesturing around the cottage. "I . . . after that, I asked to be given quarters outside the house, and she acquiesced, as ye see. But as time wore on, and ye arrived, and all yer talk of haunts and strange things, I wondered."

My pulse quickened, and I set down the teacup. "What did ye wonder, Mr. O'Dea?"

He rubbed the back of his neck and sat back in the chair. "I don't want to sound uncharitable, but something's just . . . not right. 'Tis like every time I leave the village to go on an errand, I pass through a strange veil. If 'tis raining here, 'tis sunny a half mile down the road. Or whatever weight is pressed on my chest lifts the minute I'm clear of the village boundary. Same thing happens when I return, like everything changes, and suddenly the lightness in my step becomes weighted. I'd even often posted a letter to me parents there at the local pub, but never heard a word in return. So I once sent a letter from Galway, while sending them money by secured coach, and gave the postmaster's address for return. Sure enough, next time I went to Galway to send money home, there was a letter waiting, penned by Dad, scolding me for never writing."

A chill gripped my lungs as his words landed square on my chest.

"That got me thinking, and 'tis odd no one comes to trade in the village, and no one leaves to sell their wares. As if the village mayhap doesn't exist? I don't know . . . but all that to say, 'tisn't ye, Maggie. Ye were right before, and all that talk of other Wilhelminas . . . there might be something to it, and—" He broke off, and slid from the chair to his knees. My eyes widened. "I must beg for yer forgiveness, for I fear I've brought ye to a terrible place."

My brows furrowed, and I quickly joined him on the floor before gripping his shoulders firmly.

"Arra," I said, scoffing. "Sure, what could ye do? 'Tis yer job to drive the carriage and follow her ladyship's—"

"Nay," he said, shaking his head before glancing at me. Our eyes met, and such sadness swam in the depths of his gaze. "For 'twas I who told her ladyship of ye, Maggie. 'Twas I who found ye there on the side of the road, between Clareabbey and Ennis. 'Twas I who loaded ye onto the cart and brought ye to the workhouse, using me da's connection to get ye through the gates. And 'twas I who told yer story—one that wasn't mine to tell—to my aunt, when she mentioned this entire scheme to me. Needing someone who looked like my late cousin, with baggage enough to want some revenge."

"Wh-what?" I asked, eyes widening. He'd saved my life thrice over then. And for the life of me, I couldn't understand why. Why he'd done so. Why me? Nor could I understand why he seemed disturbed by the act. "Ye have my gratitude, Cormac O'Dea. Though 'tis some kind of irony to think the very reason all this began became my saving grace."

He blinked, once slowly, then rapidly, afore running a sleeve over his nose. "But what if—"

"It doesn't matter." I believed them too, those words. What care had I if Lady Catherine was about some dark conjuring? If I was right, the Cailleach she dealt with needed my vengeance, and once she had that and I'd dealt with the solicitors, all would be well. "Whatever yer aunt is up to, ye must see the good in what she's accomplished."

"Aye," he whispered.

I ran my hands from his shoulder to grip his ice-cold fingers. "Neither of us are in any position to question her methods. They work. The village is fed while the world outside burns. And ye're her family through blood. That's no small thing, especially for people like us. She's never forgotten where she comes from. And if that means I have to live with the woman in white 'til all this is accomplished, then so be it."

He glanced at my hands, then laced his fingers through mine. A jolt ran up my arms, straight to my thundering heart, and I swallowed down the lump forming in my throat.

"I'll get ye out of here when the time comes," he whispered, sitting back on his heels, our hands still joined. "We'll take care of this business together, then I'll leave with ye."

'Twas a fine gesture, for certain, but I bit my lip. "I'll see it through, Mr. O'Dea. But I'll not leave my future to the whim of another."

"Are ye not already doing that? Relying on my aunt?" he asked. There was no malice in it, just a simple question, and I took a moment to chew on it.

"Aye," I replied at last. "I suppose I am. But there's a contract in place, and payment at the end. 'Twas my choice to sign that document, and I have my own goals to consider. I owe it to my family."

"May they rest in peace," he intoned with a nod. Then, his gaze found mine once more. "I'll follow yer lead, Maggie

O'Shaughnessy. Whether ye need me or not, I'll be there in the shadows, waiting for yer instruction. If that means living a lifetime within this strange veil, then so be it."

"Why?" I asked, brows furrowing. He had his own life to live, for goodness' sake.

"Because I swore I'd protect ye the moment I lifted yer starved body onto Dad's cart over a year ago and, in my blindness, thought to rescue ye from that godforsaken workhouse through this endeavor," he said.

Tears burned behind my eyes, but I gritted my teeth to prevent from giving them purchase.

I shook my head.

"I want nothing in return," he continued. "But ye can call on me if ever the need may arise."

About to tell him to live his own life to protect himself, we startled apart as rapid knocking shook the door.

"Who is it?" Cormac called, quickly rising to his feet. I scrambled back into my armchair and swiftly plucked up the empty teacup with one hand while smoothing my skirts with the other.

"'Tis Beth, Mr. O'Dea," came the frantic call. "Ye must, that is, ye must come quick to the house. I can't find Lady Wilhelmina, and Lady Catherine is asking for her, and we have a guest, and—"

"A guest?" Cormac called, yanking open the door. Outside, Beth stood, a drowned rat in the downpour, and her eyes widened as she caught sight of me. "M'Lady! Oh, do come quickly!"

I rose to my feet, and rushed toward the door. "What is it, Beth? Who has come?"

"'Tis a man, m'Lady. He was aboard a ship from Galway to Foynes, and 'twas wrecked in the storm. He was barely able to pull himself and his child from the sea, but he saw the house from afar, and came knocking, and—"

"Hush now," I said, glancing at Cormac. I wanted to say

"See? The village is visible. There's naught amiss," but his brows were furrowed so fiercely I thought better of it. "Her ladyship must be in need of ye. I'll follow Beth through the kitchens and change."

He nodded, one sharp slice of the neck, before turning to fetch his coat.

And I grasped Beth's hand as we bolted from the gardens toward the house.

Chapter 28

A woman with a dead child in her arms was begging in the street yesterday and the Guard of the Mail told me he saw a man and three dead children lying by the roadside.
—Major Parker, relief inspector of the Board of Works, December 1846

"Is Mama all right?" I asked Beth, as she finished buttoning up the back of the hastily thrown-on dress made for entertaining company. I braided my hair while she worked and quickly coiled it into a bun at the back of my head.

"Taken aback," Beth said. "But she quickly rallied the staff, and the visitors are bundled before the fire in the parlor. She awaits ye there."

I nodded and whirled on my heel. "Change out of those soaked clothes and warm yerself by a fire. I doubt ye'll be needed."

"Oh no, I must—"

"Ye must do as I tell ye. There's no need to stand on ceremony when strangers turn the house upside down."

Lady Grace would've turned them away at the door, so I was certain sending Beth away was well within the limits of propriety.

Beth nodded, and I hurried from the room, grabbing a shawl and a lamp on the way out the door.

My conversation with Cormac replayed in my mind as I descended each floor, and now, with time between his story and my own strange dreams, I wondered.

If what he said was true—and I was inclined to believe him, given I'd fully embraced the idea of Lady Catherine using sorcery to control the Cailleach—how could a stranger, someone not from this village, find his way to Browne House?

Lightning lit up the entranceway as I stepped onto the marbled floor of the foyer, and a hunched little lump by the door stopped me dead in my tracks.

My pulse ignited, and the rush of blood in my ears drowned out the heavy splash of rain outside the door.

"H-hello?" I whispered, and as the dark lump moved, I extended the lamp with a shaking hand to shed some light on it.

Two big blue eyes, and a shock of damp, curly blond hair, all wrapped up in a blanket. It wasn't a lump at all, but a child.

"Oh!" I exclaimed, cautiously taking a step forward. "Hello there, darling."

The child dropped the blanket, then pointed at a vase that sat upon the console table to the right of the entryway.

"Up. Burdy."

A glance at the child's clothes told me he was a little boy, though, he was breeched far too early. Most little boys wore smocks until at least five years old, but this little lad appeared much younger. Three, perhaps? Two? Only the richest of families breeched their boys so soon.

"Birdy?" I repeated, stepping closer, and noticed the blue birds in flight, brightening the porcelain white of the vase. "Yes, birdy! Do you like birdies?"

The little boy nodded and toddled over to me, before tugging on my skirt. "Up? Up?"

With a smile, I scooped up the child, and brought him level with the vase. "See? Look at the pretty birdies."

He clapped his little hands together, then leaned forward in my arms, reaching and babbling, tugging at a long-forgotten ache in my chest. Would my own babe be this age now, had he lived? Where had it come from, this heavy weight of trust, and love so strong that he'd rely on a stranger to meet his needs?

I inhaled, and the strong tang of sea salt assaulted my nostrils, reminding me that this poor child had undergone an ordeal.

"Are ye all right, lovedy?" I whispered against his damp curls. "Did ye go for a little swim by accident?"

The child nodded and turned in my arms. "Nanny?"

"Nanny?" I repeated, biting my lip. If the child was in search of his minder, and none but he and his father were saved from the wreck, I surely wasn't going to be the one to explain. "I'm sure yer father is in the parlor with Lady Catherine," I said. "Do ye want to find him?"

The child shook his head with a sullen pout, but I hoisted him in my arms, ensuring a solid grip before making my way toward the parlor.

Outside, thunder rumbled, and the babe snuggled into my chest.

"Hush now," I soothed, nearing the parlor door. "The sky goes boom-boom, but yer safe inside, little darlin'."

Turning my back to the door, I bumped it open with my backside and entered rear-first.

"I found this little lad in the hall, admiring your vase, Mama," I announced.

"There you are, Diarmuid."

I froze and glanced at the top of the child's head. Diarmuid? Tears pricked my eyes, but I shook them away with a sigh. My own son's name . . . I hoped the lad bore it well.

"Down ye go," I whispered, gently bending to place him on his feet.

"Ah, my daughter, the Lady Wilhelmina," Lady Catherine announced. I quickly straightened and shut the door before smoothing my dress.

Everything about the child—from finding him in the foyer, to his age, to the healthy weight of him—snuggled its way into my heart. But his name? 'Twas almost too much to bear, that this child shared the name I so desperately wished to give my own babe.

Righting myself, I turned and pasted a polite smile on my face. The fire roared in the hearth, and I applauded whoever had lit it for doing so quickly and efficiently. 'Twas a hard thing to accomplish, to heat a full room on a moment's notice. Lady Catherine had risen to her feet, arm outstretched toward me. It appeared she too was caught unawares tonight and had dressed hastily—evidenced by the simple bun worn at the back of her head, similar to my own.

"Apologies, Mama," I announced, striding forward. "I came as soon as I was able."

"No, Dada!" cried Diarmuid, as he approached his father. "Want Nanny!"

For the first time, I glanced at the back of the man's head and noted a bandage wrapped around it. Poor man. What a dreadful ordeal. And to lose the child's minder in the wreck . . . it would take some time for the child to adjust, and him as well.

But despite the child's estrangement, the gentleman wrapped his arms around the child and pulled him into his embrace, as a great heaving sob racked his shoulders.

"I thank you, Your Ladyship, for your warm hospitality. Truly," he said, voice hoarse, as the hair on my arms rose.

Something about his timbre tickled the recess of memory.

"Fuss and nonsense," Lady Catherine said, waving away his thanks as she gestured for me to sit opposite him.

As the man turned his attention to little Diarmuid, who beat his small fists against his father's chest, Lady Catherine winked at me, then nodded toward him, and I knew without asking what she intended.

I was meant to practice being Wilhelmina before this man.

To speak as if I were her and to act like the heiress of this house, the widow of an earl.

"Tea, dear?" Lady Catherine offered, and I took the cup she held.

"Quite. Thank you, Mama," I said, careful to adopt the upper-class nasal clip expected of me in this moment.

Opposite, father and son held each other—Diarmuid, tired of fighting against what must have been a strange burst of affection from his aristocratic father, now placated his father's wish, while his father buried his injured head in the child's shoulder, clinging with the desperation of one who'd almost lost his own life.

I stiffened then, eyes widening as a thought struck me.

"Sir, forgive me. But the child mentioned his nanny. Was the child's mother also on board—?"

The gentleman didn't look up, but held his son tighter. "L-long d-dead in childbed, I-I'm a-afraid. M-my s-son has been r-raised in Dublin, b-but I f-fetched him, th-thinking to i-introduce him to his g-grandfather. I had b-business in G-galway."

"Oh. I'm so very sorry for your loss." My cheeks pinked, and I glanced at Lady Catherine, who'd chosen to perch on the Chippendale, next to our guests. She pursed her lips, but nodded. It was all right. I hadn't completely made a fool of myself.

Suddenly, the gentleman shook himself and lifted his head in Lady Catherine's direction.

I winced as I realized the man's bandage wrapped not only around his head, but also his eyes. What a terrible accident.

"Lady Wilhelmina, did you say, My Lady?" he asked, as if waking from a stupor.

"Yes. My daughter," said Lady Catherine gesturing toward me, before catching herself. "She's seated immediately opposite."

The poor man must have been shaken to his core, but he

gently moved little Diarmuid from his lap and rose on unsteady legs.

Bedraggled was one word to describe his appearance, I supposed. Though it was clear from the fine buckles on his leather shoes that he was certainly a man of some note.

He bowed deeply, and the sandy curls on his head flopped forward.

I clenched the arm of the chair as those curls stared back at me. So similar. So very—

"Ch-charmed, Lady W-wilhelmina," he said, before clearing his throat, ridding himself of hoarseness and steadying his voice. "I sincerely apologize for the intrusion on this terrible night. Allow me to introduce myself."

My heart stopped beating as the lull of his voice washed over me, and I jerked out of my chair without thought, stepping around it, to place more distance between us.

I glanced at Lady Catherine, wild-eyed, as I fought against the vice that squeezed all air from my lungs.

"I am Theodore Moore-Vandeleur, Esquire," he announced.

And my world went dark.

Chapter 29

Families, when all was eaten and no hope left, took their last look at the sun, built up their cottage doors, that none might see them die nor hear their groans, and were found weeks afterwards, skeletons on their own hearth.
—Journal of John Mitchel (1815–1875), Irish journalist and activist

"Wake up," a voice called, a strange, clear, female voice that floated before me, somewhere between waking and oblivion. I recognized it immediately. It belonged to the woman in white. "All you want is now within your grasp. Yours for the taking, Maggie O'Shaughnessy."

"I didn't want *this*," I said . . . or thought I said. Something deep down told me not to open my eyes. Not to look at whatever it was that spoke. Not to engage.

"Are you not tired of running yet?" it asked.

Yes. Yes, I was.

But then another voice called. A man. Gentle. Lulling. Far away. The taint of my people coloring his English in shades of vibrant familiarity.

"Maggie? Maggie, wake for me."

Cormac.

Cormac!

I tried to call for him, to beg him to drag me from whatever darkness had hold of me.

"I'll run and fetch Dr. Brady. He's tending to our visitors," I heard him say.

"No." This time Lady Catherine's voice filled my ears, muffled. "Give her a few moments. It's naught but a fainting spell. Go see to our guests, please."

"Did ye know?" he demanded, anger dripping from his tongue.

"You give me far too much credit, nephew of mine," said Lady Catherine.

Somewhere, the faint echo of retreating steps permeated my dream. Well, no. 'Twas nay a dream, for there was naught but darkness. A void of nothingness.

"I'll give you some time alone, Maggie," Lady Catherine's voice whispered from that far-off place. "You have much to talk about with my mistress."

A rustle in the distance nailed the coffin on any hope I had of rousing, but still I couldn't open my eyes.

"Take it," said the strange lady.

"Take what?" I asked, voice sure and steady despite the quivering marrow deep within my bones.

"What you seek. I brought it to you."

"I have no idea what yer talking about," I replied, when suddenly an ice-cold finger ran from the top of my forehead, down over the bridge of my nose, only to pause at my lips.

"He took from you, and now you can take from him," said the voice. "And when you do, your vengeance shall fuel the féar gortach for yet another cycle. Don't you want to save the village?"

"Of course," I replied, heart hammering in my chest.

"I am the one summoned to bring protection. The one whose price is vengeance." The cool touch dissipated from my skin, and I shivered. "Do that which you were brought here to accomplish, and the woman with whom I am bound will keep her word to you."

My mind ran a mile a minute, desperately trying to piece together whatever it was this spirit was saying, and it clicked. It wasn't enough to feel vengeance, nor enough to live a comfortable life as an act of revenge. Worse, was he truly, right now, beneath this very same roof, or had it all been but a dream?

"That was no dream you had, child," said the voice, launching my pulse into a canter. "The man who wronged you so deeply is right here, beneath this roof, thanks to me. I, who protect the people, I, who am Ireland itself."

Fear gripped my soul as the woman in white spoke my thoughts back to me.

"You know what I am," the voice purred. "Say it aloud."

"The Cailleach." Once the title left my lips, the being laughed, a deep, harsh sound that scraped against my very soul.

"And yet, ye only save those whom Lady Catherine allows," I spat, emboldened. "Why do ye let the rest of the country fall to ruin?"

"Quiet," the voice hissed.

"Ye said ye were Ireland itself, yet here ye are, haunting the halls of this old house like a rattling spirit with naught to do but petrify the living, doing the bidding of a woman with a bit of the Sight, begging someone like me to do . . . what, exactly?"

Silence fell in the void between us, and I fought the urge to open my eyes. To face her down. But I held firm.

"Why all the strange theatrics?" I snapped into the darkness, rallying for whatever might come next. "Did ye fear I'd cower before the face of the man who killed my entire family? The man who killed *me*, everything I once was? No need, for I'll gladly slit his throat from ear to ear. Just say the word."

"Hmmm," purred the Cailleach, the goddess tasked with turning the tide, the goddess of change, of new beginnings.

"Have I surprised ye?" I asked, with a scoff. "It seems Lady Catherine underestimated the depth of my hatred."

Silence. A step. Silence.

Then . . .

"An eye for an eye," whispered the Cailleach, closer now, as if leaning into my ear. "A tooth for a tooth. The Christ-God might have overtaken the hearts of the people here centuries ago, but this teaching from the older book—from the Jewish texts—I admire. See, brave one, it's no longer vengeance if you truly desire it; it's pleasure. Pleasure won't feed the féar gortach. And if you fail, Lady Catherine will be forced to pay the price."

"What price?"

"If you fail, she must kill you and find another willing to do what's needed before the new moon," said the Cailleach, as though commenting on the weather. "But to find another so quickly . . . impossible."

She'd kill me? End my godforsaken life? I laughed aloud and felt the Cailleach rear back, lightening the weight of her presence—wherever we were.

"Fool," spat the Cailleach.

"Nay," I managed, gasping for breath between chuckles. "More fool ye. Whatever it is ye need, I'll take my vengeance out on Teddy Moore-Vandeleur. That I guarantee. There'll be no need to kill me."

Something like frustration emanated from the Cailleach. "Have you no comprehension at all?"

"What more is there to understand?" I asked. "Ye want me to take vengeance, and I want to kill Teddy so my family can finally be at peace."

"An eye for an eye," the Cailleach repeated, and I cocked my head to the side.

"Ye want me to kill his lordship? Lady Grace? Is that it? His family in exchange for mine?"

I felt it again, the strange heaviness that warned the Cailleach had come close, and my skin crawled with anticipation.

"Nay, girl. For what man like your Teddy would care a whit

for a family that tore the only happiness in his life from him?" said the Cailleach, and I shook my head.

"Happiness?" I spat. "Teddy cast me off—"

"He was told you died, you fool. That childbed took ye. And resigned himself to marrying whomever his father thrust before him."

The blood in my veins froze to ice as her words punched the air from my lungs. I wanted to say "no," to protest with all I had.

But the specter of Teddy's pale face came to mind, that time I had met him by chance at the market, the day baby Crofton had passed away. The way he'd asked "How?" as though seeing a ghost.

But 'twas *his* name on that declaration. *His* name on the document that turned us out of our homes.

I shook my head. "It doesn't matter."

"But it does, and it will, when you realize you were told the same tale," said the Cailleach, and I could envision her smile in my mind's eye.

"What tale?" I demanded.

"An eye for an eye. A tooth for a tooth. For the only family that man cares for now is the child."

"The child?" I asked, slowly, fighting against the tremor of fear that radiated from the deepest recess of my gut. "Ye want me to take his son from him?"

"The child he'd had with his new wife—that I couldn't even think of. That I couldn't even think of. To take a child? An innocent life with naught to do with the sins of the parent?

"He has the look of your brother about him, don't you think?" asked the Cailleach. "The one who hovers near. The brother that protects."

"Who looks like my brother?"

She laughed, then said, clear as day in my ear: "The child. Your son. Your Diarmuid."

*   *   *

I woke, screaming, and bolted upright in the bed.

No. It couldn't be, could it?

"Michael," I whispered, steepling my hands before pressing them together. "Michael, if ye can hear me, I need ye. Protect and guide me. God above, help me."

My voice broke on the last word, and the tears I constantly fought finally won the battle.

The child . . . the *child*?

My child?

Had they lied to me? Had Lady Grace organized for my babe to be taken, while his lordship told Teddy I had perished?

No, they couldn't have. Of all the incredible cruel, brutal—

Remember.

I was meant to be far away in Sligo, working for a new family, never to be seen again.

My child, taken from me to be raised by the woman his lordship found to mend Teddy's broken heart.

Then why . . . *why* had Teddy gone to such lengths to have us evicted?

"Ahhhhhhhhhhh!" I screamed, tossing aside the blankets, swinging my legs over the side of the bed. I rose, grabbed the flower-filled vase that sat on the stand, and tossed it into the fireplace. Pottery shattered, and my breath came hard and heavy. Air, I needed air.

I strode to the curtains and swept them aside before unlatching the window. Pushing, I waited for the pane to give way, but the old hinges simply creaked and didn't yield their hold.

I pushed again—over and over—breaking nails and drawing blood as I fought against the maddening urge to smash it. To shatter it. To—

"Get a hold of yerself!"

Two strong arms came around my waist, pinning mine to my sides.

"Let go of me!" I screamed, the searing smart of it scraping my throat. Good. I welcomed it, the pain.

"Maggie, please. It's me." The words ebbed near my ear, and my body—wound so tight just a moment before—suddenly crumpled.

"Whoa," he murmured, adjusting his grip to hold me upright. "Easy now. Easy. What's the matter? What can I do for ye?"

"Cor-mac," I stuttered, locking my knees so I might stand for myself.

"I'm here," he said.

"We . . ." My eyes widened, and I whirled to face him. "We must go. Now. Away. Can we do that?"

"Of course," he said. Readily. Easily. I watched his face as he glanced around the room. "We'll wait but a few moments, lest anyone else heard yer cries. Then we'll be off."

I nodded and took a step back.

"What happened?" he asked, taking my elbow as he led me toward the bed. "Sit. I'll fetch water from the jug."

Where to start? Where to end? Would it matter? Cormac O'Dea certainly had his own suspicions, but this—whatever it was I just experienced—was beyond the pale.

He busied himself with pouring water into a glass, then opened the door ajar and glanced out into the hallway.

"We might be clear. I heard ye by chance when coming out of the visitors' room," he whispered, handing me the glass. I knocked back its contents, before wiping a hand over my mouth.

"Why were ye there? What time is it?" I asked, offering the empty glass with a shaking hand.

He took it, placed it on the vanity, then returned and grasped my cold hands in his. "'Tis past two in the morning. Dr. Brady instructed he be watched for fear of concussion. Is it true, Maggie? Is it him? My aunt said ye must have been shocked, and she had no idea who he was nor his connection to ye. But surely she knew there was some history between ye and the Moore-Vandeleurs."

I glanced at him, eyes wide. That's right. She knew what poor union I came from, and that Da was land agent to his lordship. And Cormac had relayed the story Da had imparted to him and his family. Surely she had made the connection when he gave his name at the door? It was unfathomable to think Teddy would have failed to introduce himself before I arrived. "Aye. It's him."

Cormac pressed his lips together and nodded. "Get dressed. I'll be back for ye in a short while. I've had a bag ready for such an occasion for months now. We can be on our way within a half hour."

He pushed to his feet, but I reached out with two hands and grasped his arm.

"Wait!" I hissed, unable to keep the desperation from my voice. "The child. We need to bring the child."

"The child?" Cormac sat back down and placed a warm hand over mine.

Taking a deep breath, I told him of my dream—or the dream that may not have been a dream—and he listened. Quietly. Patiently. Until, at last, tears rolled down my cheeks.

"He's my child, the babe I was told had died, Cormac," I whispered. "And she wants me to harm him, this entity your aunt conjured."

"Over my dead body," Cormac hissed, pushing to his feet once more. "Dress warmly, in something practical, and meet me at the cottage as soon as ye can."

"Where are ye going?" I asked, wide-eyed.

"To fetch the lad. I'll bring him straight to the cottage, and we'll leave together. The three of us."

Without another word, Cormac strode from the room, and I stood to follow his instruction.

This once. Surely I could rely on him just this once, couldn't I? The situation had swollen far beyond the bounds of my capabilities, and I needed help.

"Thank ye, Michael," I whispered to the darkness, certain my brother had led Cormac to my room.

Sometimes prayer did work.

Chapter 30

Seventy-five tenants ejected here, and a whole village
in the last stage of destitution there . . . dead bodies of
children flung into holes . . . every field becoming a grave,
and the land a wilderness.
— *The Cork Examiner*, December 1846

My heart leapt with every creak as I tiptoed my way down the
hall, descended three flights of stairs, and snuck through the
kitchen toward freedom. With each step, I expected the woman
in white to appear—to frighten, to halt me in my tracks. Surely
she knew what was afoot? What Cormac and I planned to do?

Then again, perhaps it mattered not. Her pact was with Lady
Catherine, not me. My woes, my vengeance were merely the
means to achieve Lady Catherine's goals, not the woman in
white's.

I'd opted for the simplest dress—lest it was thought I'd cov-
eted and pilfered the fine silks—the day dress peppered with
sunflowers. Beneath, I wore the heaviest petticoat in my coffer,
a fine chemise, and o'er it all, the heaviest woolen cloak I could
find.

The child was alive. The child was mine. Diarmuid.

And Teddy . . . no. Teddy was no victim in this farce. Had
they lied and told him I'd died? Fine, I'd believe it. But that
didn't excuse his defamation of Da, the months of unanswered

letters, and him never deigning to visit. He might claim he'd never received them—may have even told himself so over and over 'til he believed his own lie. Until it became truth, uncontested, to ease his conscience.

The Cailleach was wrong, and I knew it. For contained in those letters, each and every one, was a postscript asking what he thought of the name Diarmuid and whether he'd be amenable to bestowing that name upon our child.

Theodore Moore-Vandeleur had received my letters.

And Theodore Moore-Vandeleur had ignored them.

Because Teddy realized his folly and determined to marry another with inheritance and connections. What father, no matter how supportive of a "love match," would deny his child the opportunity to marry for betterment?

Perhaps his lordship devised the scheme to have me "die" in childbed to ease Teddy's conscience. Keep the child and gain a suitable bride for the family—win, win. But my return jeopardized everything.

Greed destroyed my life and the lives of my family. My greed? Perhaps, in part. But 'twas Teddy's greed, in the end, that set the wheels in motion.

"Ow," I muttered, wincing as a pebble slipped beneath my stockinged feet. Shoes in hand—to avoid crunching through gravel—I wound my way through the storm-tossed garden, grateful the rain had given way to light drizzle.

Leaves and petals lay strewn, in need of raking come morning, but with luck we'd be far from here by the time anyone raised the alarm.

The gardener's cottage loomed in the near distance, and I hopped onto one of the flower beds to save the skin of my feet the indignity of tearing in my haste. They sank into the saturated soil, popping with a *slurp* each time I stepped forward. Not my finest idea to date, but with luck, Cormac might have a spare pair of stockings I could borrow.

Close to the cottage now, I leapt onto the paved path, and within three strides, I was at the door.

I knocked, heart pounding in my chest—from fear, exertion, or exhilaration, I knew not—and in the space of a breath, Cormac opened the door. Well, no. He cracked it, enough to see who stood beyond.

"'Tis ye," he sighed, breath whooshing in a rush as he pulled open the door. "Quick, and in ye come."

I ducked into the cottage, and he glanced down at my filthy stockings.

"Shoes?" he asked, crossing the main room.

"In my hand."

With a nod, he hoisted a sack onto his back. "We'll away, and get ye dry when we're clear."

"Where's Diarmuid?" I asked, eyes wide as I looked around the cottage.

"Asleep. Howld on there." Cormac dipped beneath a low door near the back of the cottage and emerged with the child.

A lump formed in my throat as I equated the little boy with the babe I'd mourned, but I was given no time to think as Cormac deposited the heavy, sleeping weight into my arms.

My eyes widened, and I quickly adjusted my grip, cradling his precious head close to my heart.

"We'll head out the back way. It leads beyond out the garden and toward the stable. I fetched Dr. Brady this evening and returned him to the village in the carriage." Cormac gestured toward a split door on the opposite wall and unlatched it. "I never unharnessed the horses. After confirming him in the guest wing as the man who'd wronged ye, I feared we might need them."

"Won't they come for us?" I whispered, stepping through the door as Cormac opened it.

"With what?" he scoffed, following before closing the door behind us. "They have naught if we take the carriage. We'll be well on our way before any notice our absence."

"What if—" I broke away and glanced at the lad, safe beneath my cloak. What if the Cailleach had lied? What if this child was not, in fact, mine? What if I was simply losing my mind?

Cormac frowned, then took my hand, adjusting the sack on his shoulder with the other. "The what-ifs can wait. Your safety, and the child's, are my only priority."

I nodded and let him lead us toward the stable, where the carriage-and-four waited.

"Ye should sit inside with the lad," Cormac hissed as I mounted the driver's bench and settled beside him. "Ye could take ill in this weather."

"He's safe within," I whispered, pulling my cloak tighter. I'd tucked the babe, securely, onto the floor of the carriage, swaddled in enough blankets to ease the journey. "When we're clear, I can check on him. But I can't sit in there, suffocating, while yer out here doing all the work. We can suffer together."

Suffer the rain, the terror, the fear of being caught.

With a nod, Cormac snapped the reins, and the team of four lurched forward, sending me sprawling into the coach wall at my back.

"Easy," Cormac murmured—to me, or the horses, I knew not.

Righting myself, I glanced right, staring at the house as we wound our way down the eerie, fog-obscured drive, but all seemed well.

No flickering candles in the windows. No shadows staring. In a way, that frightened me more, and my palms turned slick as I gripped the rail afore me. Shouldn't someone have heard? Shouldn't someone have tried to stop us?

I strained my neck as we rode on, leaning out so I could glance back, to keep my eyes on the house, and terror seized my lungs as I squinted into the distance.

What need for shadows or candles haunting the windows, when the house itself stared back? I was right, back then . . .

when I'd first arrived. Now more than ever. For in the dark, with heavy storm clouds obscuring the moon, and the heady scent of rain-churned soil hitting the back of my throat, Browne House truly was alive.

The semicircular windows on the top floor serving as brows above large rectangular eyes . . . in the dim, they seemed wrong. Squinting, perhaps? Nay . . . furrowed, more like. And the wide, stone staircase sweeping from ground to entrance? The one I'd likened to a tongue rolled out afore a hungry, double-doored maw, waiting to devour me whole? Something about the shadows screamed *snarl* and *growl*, no longer a beast awaiting its daily feed, but a predator now, on the hunt, and I its prey.

"Right for Galway, left for Liscannor," Cormac muttered as I tore my gaze from the disappearing house. The entranceway to the drive loomed up ahead, and I made the sign of the cross afore reciting the Lord's Prayer in my mind.

Ár n-Athair, atá ar neamh, go naofar d'ainm, go dtagfadh do ríocht, go ndéantar do thoil ar an talamh mar a dhéantar ar neamh—

One of the horses whinnied, and I glanced up. Ahead, where the great entranceway curved right and left—where Cormac had to make his decision to take us north to Galway or south to Liscannor—the fog roiled. It dipped and flowed, an ocean current awash with whorls, its pale wisps toiling against an absent gale.

A chill wound its way up my spine as we approached. As two, long, dark shapes took form in the mist, reaching to meet a torso, a chest, shoulders, arms, and head.

A figure, but one not of this world.

Maggie, its voice called, resonating somewhere in the depths of my mind.

"Michael?" I breathed, pushing upward in a half stand, bracing myself against the rail.

"Christ, sit back!" Cormac ordered, but I couldn't hear.

Not as the figure held up an arm and pointed toward the village.

South, came the voice again, and my eyes widened.

"Left, Mr. O'Dea. Left to Liscannor, as fast as ye can." My words rang clear, and Cormac gave a sharp nod as I sat back on the bench, watching as the ghostly figure raised a hand—a wave?—and dissipated into the fog.

"Thank ye, Michael," I whispered, dipping my head as Cormac banked left toward the village.

"Eh?" Cormac asked, but I shook my head. He glanced at me as he righted the horses. " 'Tis the right call. I've nay plan but to head for home, and this is the surest route."

"Home?" I echoed.

"My home, that is. Mam and Dad will welcome ye kindly, and we can decide what to do once we're safe and sound."

We?

It had been "I" for so long, that the thought of "we" shook me to the core. Focused solely on surviving, on keeping the promise I'd made to Michael—that had been my only goal.

But now I was a "we" once again—if not with Cormac, then with Diarmuid.

I turned and slid the shutter aside so I could peer through the driver's window. One singular lump lay sleeping on the floor, with one chubby thumb firmly wedged between plump lips.

"Is he all right?" Cormac asked, snapping the reins as the shapes of civilization rolled into view—a spire, a village cross, houses packed close.

"Grand," I replied, closing the shutter once more.

"Christ, what a disaster," said Cormac, and I looked at him— at the clenched lines of his jaw, the furrow of his brow.

"She said I must kill him. Diarmuid." The confession poured from my lips, a drop of tea too hot to swallow, and Cormac glanced at me sharply.

"Then ye made the right choice to get away," he said, turning his attention back to the road. "If I'd known goings-on would end like this, I'd have liberated ye much sooner. And how in the name of God did yer beau wind up here, of all places?"

"In a way, I'm glad." And it was the truth. "For if he hadn't, or if ye'd gotten me away from here before now, I never would've known that Diarmuid lived. That Teddy's deception ran so very deep."

"Aye." With a nod, Cormac slowed the horses as we approached the village square, careful not to rouse the whole place.

We continued in silence, and once we were clear of the village, he turned to me once more.

"Can ye ever forgive me?" he asked. "If not for me, ye never would've had to endure all this."

"Ye saved me, Cormac O'Dea. Once when ye brought us to yer home, once when ye transported me to the workhouse, again when ye brought me to Lady Catherine's attention, and now"—I gestured toward the carriage at our backs—"tonight. I owe ye a great debt."

"Aye, but debt isn't quite the other thing, the forgiveness."

"Ye're forgiven," I said, lips curling into a smile. "And I'll be sure to pay ye back one day."

"An eye for an eye," he said with a laugh, and his words sent a jolt through my body. The Cailleach—the woman in white—had used those very same words. My eyes widened, but by his easy laugh, it seemed he'd meant naught by them. "Ye're wishing near-death on me so ye can save me in return."

"I think we're up to four near-deaths ye must face so I can save ye," I replied, pulling my cloak tight against the sudden chill.

He chuckled, and the sound of it tickled my heart with a feather of "mayhap." Mayhap, one day, I could look back on everything and shake my head. Mayhap, the future held something better, something to grab onto and hope for.

The carriage rolled over a divot, and Cormac and I lurched forward as our team of four whinnied loud enough to call a bean sidhe. We rocked on, the carriage righting itself despite the lead pair rearing as they cantered.

"Woah, woah!" Cormac exclaimed, pulling the reins as I grabbed hold of the rail. "What the Devil has gotten into ye? 'Tis only a pothole."

My pulse thundered, sending blood roaring to my ears, waiting until we'd come to a safe halt before twisting around to check on Diarmuid through the little window.

Bless him, he still slept soundly. Closing my eyes, I inhaled deeply, and thanked God for the resilience of children. Michael would've slept through an onslaught of cannon fire, and I smiled at this little thing that proved, in some way, that the child within was indeed my own blood.

"Jesus, Mary, and Joseph," Cormac breathed, shifting to stand as he secured the reins into the footboard hook. "What in the . . . ?"

My gut roiled, gripped with sudden fear, meted boldly in tandem with the tremor in Cormac's voice.

And I turned. Slowly. Then rose to join him and followed his gaze.

I gasped, knees buckling as a wave of nausea threatened to overtake my senses.

Because there, before us, was the village . . . the same village we'd already traveled through.

With shaking hands, I disembarked, feet and hem disappearing beneath the heavy fog as I stumbled toward the back of the carriage, half-bent as all the blood rushed from head to toe.

One step. Another.

'Til at last I met the rear wheels and dared stare into the darkness beyond.

At what lay there, if the village was, in fact, somehow still before us.

At the curved walls, high as those of the Moore-Vandeleur estate.

The entrance . . . to Browne House.

"How?" I exclaimed—for the fifth time.

"H'ya!" Cormac cried, snapping the reins with fervor. I clutched the rail, knuckles blanching as we raced toward the village, this time not slowing more than necessary as the horses thundered through the main square.

I wasn't going mad—we'd already traveled through and cleared the village boundary. We had . . . hadn't we?

Foolish.

The word came unbidden to my mind's eye, and I bit my lip. Was it my voice or another's? But I supposed the origin was nay as important as the content. Foolish. I was that, aye.

Foolish to think we could escape in the night.

And foolish to think I could somehow change my circumstances.

For when all ye want is presented on a silver platter, things are never what they truly seem. If nothing else, I was grateful for all that had happened at Browne House, for it reminded me of that fact. The memories of what came before my family's death march had subsided to a distant inkling somewhere in those first few weeks, and survival had overtaken all sense.

And here I was again, bound into an agreement from which escape meant fatality. Blinded as I once was by the ends, I knew now the ease by which they could be attained was always presented with false process. Of course, it wasn't as simple as standing in as Wilhelmina. Of course, it wouldn't be as easy as that.

But who could have predicted this? It was beyond imagining. How could we have wound up back at the house . . . unless we'd never left in the first place?

Homes now watered down to naught but gray streaks with each slap of the reins, I glanced at Cormac.

Teeth clenched, his wild amber eyes stared ahead, trained on the horizon.

"Almost clear," he called, snapping the reins once more.

Yes. Almost clear, for this time we were well and truly on our way.

The horses whinnied in unison, and I marveled at the way their thundering hooves cut through the blanket of fog.

"What in the blazes?" Cormac exclaimed, pulling the reins. A vein bulged at his temple, and the *tha-dump* of his pulse juddered against the delicate skin at the base of his throat.

I glanced ahead as the horses slowed, and all the air left my lungs in a whoosh.

For ahead, once more, was the village.

And I knew, without looking, that we were once again outside Browne House.

"No," I whispered, placing my head in my hands as the carriage-and-four rolled to a gentle stop.

"Galway then," Cormac hissed, turning the carriage. "We'll go toward Galway."

I grabbed his arm with sweat-slick palms as an uncontrollable tremor swept from my core to shaking limbs.

"G-Galway." I affirmed his choice with a nod—because the direction we chose was something tangible, something that might make sense . . . somehow. Naturally, south would heave us into a never-ending loop where we somehow wound up where we began. Obviously, we had chosen incorrectly. Somewhere in the world, a scholar would know the whys and hows of it.

Fully turned now, and ready to venture northward, Cormac snapped the reins.

The horses hopped into step, trotting off into the night, and it took me a moment to realize that they were indeed moving.

Pulling us.

Zzzzzp.

Something lashed in the fore, and pain struck my forehead. Time slowed as Cormac exclaimed, throwing an arm across my chest as the carriage rolled forward—while something warm and wet trickled from my hairline.

I reached up a hand and wiped, and only then did I realize that we were alone.

That the horses were . . . gone, their hooves clippetty-cloppetting away up the road.

I froze. They'd somehow become unhooked.

"Are ye all right?" Cormac asked, an edge of fear coloring the question. I nodded, and he quickly dismounted the rolling carriage, grabbed the frontal shaft with both hands and braced himself against it.

The carriage stopped.

"Let me just wedge a few rocks at the wheels, lest we roll again," he said, panting with exertion. "Then I'll tend yer wound."

Wound? I frowned and touched my forehead again. Still wet. Still warm.

That's when the coppery tang hit me.

Blood. I was bleeding.

"What . . . what happened?" I asked.

"Something snapped—breeching, togs, reins, who knows? Whatever it was hit ye in the face."

"Diarmuid," I whispered, sidling to dismount.

"Howld on," said Cormac, popping his head up from beneath the nearest wheel. "Let me secure everything first, and then ye can check the babba."

"No need."

A clear voice rang out in the night, and I flinched, my heart leaping up my throat.

Crunch, crunch.

Step. *Click.* Step. *Click.*

I knew that rhythm, so well 'twas almost as though I'd never lived a day without it.

"What kind of a monster do you think I am?" asked Lady Catherine, rounding the side of the carriage to face me in all her glory.

She'd changed her attire. Immaculate ringlets framed her face, her signature top hat nestled comfortably above. A fine, tailed coat, bright with silver buttons, sat over a frilled shirt, and below, a black satin bustle skirt whispered above high-heeled boots.

"What is it that she wants?" Lady Catherine asked, kicking her walking stick forward so she might lean on it.

She. The Cailleach.

A lump formed in my throat, and it took everything I had to swallow it down.

"It must involve the child if you were prompted you to steal away in the night, and for my nephew to abandon his post." Lady Catherine glanced sharply at Cormac, but he didn't shrink from her the way I wished to. "You'll not be able to get away, I'm afraid. No one can find this place, and no one can leave."

"What are ye talking about?" Cormac spat. "Didn't that jackanapes in the guest wing make his way here from the beach? Don't I leave when ye need? Didn't you and I leave together to fetch Maggie from the workhouse?"

"Maggie no longer exists. She is Wilhelmina!" Lady Catherine exclaimed, words echoing in the quiet surrounds. "And that was different. While the pact is in place, none can leave without Her grace. It's the entire reason I needed you here, Cormac O'Dea, for I lost my last steward to illness—a person who can do business outside the boundary, one who can come and go with the protection of the Cailleach. One who hadn't made the pact. But it extends only to you, not to her. Not to anyone else. That's why you couldn't escape. He, our guest, could only have been led here by Her, to fulfill Her purpose."

My breath came in sharp shallow pants, making it difficult to breathe.

Lady Catherine tutted and reached out a hand to stroke my head. "Wilhelmina's injured and must have had an awful fright. Come, Cormac. Leave the carriage here 'til morning and help her into the house. I need to know what happened."

"I don't trust ye," Cormac hissed, stepping around the front of the carriage to face his aunt.

"Neither did your mother." The words were soft, quiet in a way that set my heart racing. "And I suppose, in the end, she was right."

Lady Catherine turned to me then, the ghost of a smile dancing across her lips. "Let's fix this. Together. You and I."

"That'll be hard," I said, my voice barely a whisper of breath. "For I no longer trust ye either."

Chapter 31

Before our merciful intervention, the Irish nation were a
wretched, indolent, half-starved tribe of savages . . .
notwithstanding a gradual improvement upon the naked
savagery, they have never approached the standard of the
civilized world.
— *The Times* (London), January 1847

Scritch.

The strike of a match sent the hairs on the back of my neck
to attention, and I glanced at Lady Catherine—boots crossed
atop the library desk, chair tipped back as she casually touched
the flame to the bowl of her pipe, tobacco overtaking the musk
of leather and ink that permeated through shadowed rows of
bookshelves.

I sat opposite, in my usual chair, the desk between us, but
this time was different. This time, the sleeping bulk of a child
weighted not only my arms, but my heart, my soul. My son,
my Diarmuid, blond curls crushed against my shoulder as I
cradled his body, chest rising and falling, cheeks pink as sleep
drew bubbles of saliva through pursed, plump lips.

I looked at him, this miracle I'd never dreamt of, this babe
I'd never truly mourned, and I saw Michael in him. In the curve
of juvenile fat protecting high cheekbones. In the downward
slant of his outer eyes. He would look like his uncle, for sure.

And that meant Mam was in him, and Da. Everything, and everyone—every ancestor—who had made me. This was their legacy, this grandchild they'd never held. This babe who'd been cruelly ripped from my torn womb and declared dead. Alive. Well.

And rage became my calling, my vocation, sending a chill up my spine before settling into an unsteady shake that threatened to flay skin from bone. Mine own, Lady Catherine's, Teddy's.

My eyes sliced right, and I caught a flash of callused hand clutching the back of my chair. Cormac, a rock at my rear. My last line of defense in the battle to come.

Blood pounded against my temples, but that hand shifted and came down on my shoulder—a steady heft to lessen the burden.

"So this is yer babe, the one ye thought dead and buried." Dropping the clipped façade of a noble Anglo-born, Lady Catherine fell into the low-born brogue that marked us all. She mulled over the words around the bit of her pipe, and I fixed her with a glare—not that she noticed, for she'd thrown her head back and now stared at the ceiling. "And ye've remembered everything?"

"I have, aye." I barely managed the response, but as Diarmuid whined in his sleep, all rage dissipated as instinct overcame all else. I rocked him, gathering him up before placing my lips against his ear. "Shhh, love. Hush. Mammy's here now. Mammy's here."

"I can take him," Cormac offered, voice low as he bent over my chair.

"Such a pretty painting." *Swish thump.* I shot a glance in Lady Catherine's direction. She'd swept her boots from the table and snapped her chair steady on all four legs. "The three of ye there. Looking like a family. I approve, of course. But yer high horse of a mother might not, nephew dear."

Without a word, Cormac stepped around the chair and bent

to speak to me. I glanced at him. "If ye trust me to take him, I'll not leave this room."

I'd not trust any to *take* him, this child who had already been taken. "I trust ye to hold him."

With a nod, Cormac scooped an arm beneath Diarmuid, and I lifted my precious gift into his arms before rising. He sat in my place, and I stalked toward the desk, placing myself between my child and Lady Catherine.

"How do we fix this?" I asked, slamming my palms on the surface of the desk, leaning over 'til she and I were naught but a nod from collision. "Ye said we could fix this, you and I. Whatever ye put in that incense worked its magic, and I remember all of it. Every last detail. But for the life of me, I can't begin to fathom how killing my child would appease the demon ye convene with."

Lady Catherine smiled, a slow stretch of lips that warned of coming danger, and I jerked away, righting myself to full height.

"It might hurt Teddy, aye. But 'twould hurt me m-more." My voice broke at the last, and the telltale sting of tears burned the backs of my eyes. I shook my head. "No more of this. He's alive, and that's enough. I demand to break our contract. I don't need yer land."

"Unfortunately, breaking that contract means death for us both," Lady Catherine stated, sitting back in her chair. "The Cailleach told ye, did she not? That if ye fail in yer task 'tis you who will pay with blood?"

I nodded.

"I have 'til the new moon to find another if I'm to survive." Rising, Lady Catherine smoothed her skirts and turned to gaze out the window, drawing a deep drag of pipe smoke as she stared out into the night beyond.

"Surely another wouldn't be so difficult to find—" I began, but Lady Catherine whirled on her heel.

"The new moon is two nights from now. Not nearly enough time, and my life will be forfeit without good reason. If I'm to die, it'll be because I decided the hows and whys," she hissed, smoke trailing in the wake of her words, a mythical dragon in all its glory. "If you're to survive, we must fix it all before then. Something has gone sorely amiss."

A mewl from behind drew my attention, and I turned with a start. Diarmuid stretched his little arms over his head, and Cormac shifted the child's weight as he settled back into the chair.

"Then tell me how." The plea was a breath, a charm, as I faced her once more. She who had offered the world, she who would take it all away—like those who had fooled me before.

"They told ye he was dead?" she asked, sitting once more. But the casual indifference she wore but a moment before had vanished, replaced with a veil of exhaustion that hunched her shoulders and drew all brightness from those piercing eyes. Our gazes locked, and she nodded. "I wanted to care for them all, ye know. The villagers. I suppose it came from being dirt poor as a child. Cormac might know something of it, if his mam ever told him. I have the Sight, as ye know, and worked my ways to catch my husband's eye. But he wasn't good for the people. The estate? Aye. He was great at running all that, but we were naught to him, even myself. Animals, he called us. Filthy, flea-bitten, and not worth a penny. But I endured."

She ran a hand over her face, and I pursed my lips.

"At first, I only summoned the Cailleach when needed, and she and I parted ways when the work was done. I had hoped, especially when Wilhelmina came into our lives, that he'd soften, but alas. Bad enough she was half-Irish, he used to say. But witch spawn?" Lady Catherine laughed, and the sound made the blood freeze in my veins. "He embraced her in his heart for a time, but like all things, that didn't last. I suppose I'd had enough when he refused to summon the only doctor for miles when she fell ill. "God's will," he'd said. "The blessed English were never meant to breed with Irish animals." She paused, then locked her glare with mine, and those eyes penetrated deep, straight through to my soul. She continued. "I killed him when she passed away, and that vengeance sealed the bond between my mistress and me, keeping her tethered to this world and this house to me."

Lady Catherine pushed off her chair, and the movement set my heart alight, pounding its warning: run, run away! But I held my ground.

"I didn't know then that our strange coexistence would eat away at my body and mind. That some days I would not be myself, that the guilt of keeping the Cailleach here would make me despise the person I'd become. My village is safe, but what of the country? And yet I couldn't sever the tie. If I did, the village would come to ruin. Ye were not the first," she mused, voice soft as she glanced at me. *Thud, click. Thud, click.* Boot and cane, she stepped around the desk. "Wilhelmina died when she was naught but six summers old, and with Charles cold in the ground, I had need of the Cailleach's help to run things here. To ensure my people prospered. But the price was always steep."

"Ye took in girls like me, to replace yer daughter," I guessed, remembering the vision I'd had.

She nodded. "They all came from hardship, all with rage. Ye see, the Cailleach needs vengeance to manipulate the féar gortach into ensuring the land here flourishes, and a sacrifice is required every few years. But a sacrifice does not always mean blood—revenge comes in many forms. When their vengeance was realized, those girls moved on as promised, each with whatever it was they desired most." She smiled then, and I took a step back. "It was tempting to keep that first girl as my own. Wouldn't life with me be better than any out there? But once her true vengeance was spent, I would've had to turn to the villagers for sacrifice, and that I couldn't do. They'd already paid the price for my protection, so I turned to the outside for willing girls and lured them with a tale. In exchange, I experienced the ghost of motherhood, turning each into the daughter I'd lost . . . if only for a time."

I froze. "Lured them with a tale?"

Lady Catherine scoffed. "No solicitors are coming, Wilhelmina. The inheritance is safe."

"Ye lied to them, to me?" A cold sweat slicked my palms, and I shot a wild-eyed glance over my shoulder to ensure Diarmuid still slept in Cormac's arms—he did.

"Not fully," Lady Catherine countered. "I did promise that a solicitor could arrive at a moment's notice, after all. And did not a storm-tossed solicitor harken our door this very night?"

Teddy. I gave her my full attention once more.

"Ye were a tough one, Maggie O'Shaughnessy." *Thud, click. Thud, click.* Closer and closer she came. "The herbs help with the remembering, but ye fought it so fiercely. And still ye don't recognize the truth of it all. The Cailleach can only decide the punishment based on yer own feelings, yer own conclusions, after ye live those memories once more. Ye have focused on that man upstairs . . . but is that the truth of it?"

I balled my fists and took a step forward to meet her advance. How dare she? Teddy had doctored his lordship's books to have us evicted and Da labeled a felon. Teddy had known I was in Dublin. Teddy hadn't written. Teddy had wed another. If Teddy had talked to me, if someone had explained the gravity of the situation before I'd boarded that coach bound to Kilrush, none of this would have happened. I could have escaped from Lady Grace's Dublin residence before they conspired to take my babe. I could have disappeared so Da could still be land agent, and though things might have been hard, surely my family would have weathered the storm.

Everything was because of Teddy.

Thud, click. Thud, click.

"Are ye certain? Certain enough to wager the life of yer child?" Lady Catherine asked with a sigh, skirts kissing mine as she leaned forward, bringing her lips to the shell of my right ear. "What happened that night, in the summerhouse?"

"The summerhouse?" My brows furrowed as I glanced at her.

"The night of the céilí. The night before ye were all turned out by Moore-Vandeleur."

"I met Teddy . . ." I trailed off and pursed my lips. I had written him a note . . . to meet at eight. To talk. To share our loss and ask what had happened. Where he'd been. And the next day, the bailiffs came.

"Did ye relive that memory?" Lady Catherine asked, her breath tickling my neck. "What really prompted the Moore-Vandeleurs, who undoubtedly knew ye were back in Kilrush, to suddenly cast out yer family?"

"I—" No. I hadn't relived it. Now that I thought about it, my memories had skipped from running toward Kilrush House to suddenly being evicted, and my blood ran cold.

"There are times when good must turn to evil to make things right." The tickle of Lady Catherine's breath startled me back to reality. "And now 'tis your turn."

I reared back, a yelp dying in my throat as an invisible vise squeezed my chest fit to bursting.

"There are some things I can't condone, not only as a mother, but especially as one who's lost her own child, and I'm oh so very tired. 'Tis exhausting, all of this, keeping track of the villagers, drawing power from their payment to have strength enough to control the Cailleach, and I knew this had to be the last arrangement, for it's time to make things right. The key to everything is locked away in that missing memory, Maggie. But it's shoved down so far I fear ye'll need a little help from the power I draw on to remember it. I wish ye a long and happy life with yer child, for this is the last and only thing I can do for ye now," Lady Catherine said, a soft smile lifting her lips as she pressed something hard, with edges, into my hand. "Ye'll find everything ye need in the top drawer. When I realized something was amiss, I took the time to put ink to paper. Remember me fondly, if ye can. I'm afraid this is the only way to fix it."

And without another word, Lady Catherine pulled a dagger from the pocket of her skirt and sliced the blade across the pale white column of her throat.

Chapter 32

The stench was intolerable, and on my complaining of it
the Mother pointed to . . . the putrid—the absolutely
melted away remains of her eldest son. On inquiry why
she did not bury . . . she waited till her other child would
die, and they might bury both together.
—*The Telegraph*, Castlebar, County Mayo,
February 1847

"Do something!" I screamed the order, but the bewildered
Dr. Brady simply stared, wide-eyed, at the scene before him.
At Lady Catherine's dead body, the light of breathtaking dawn
illuminating the heinous scene. At me, bathed as I was in her
blood, chilled to the very marrow of my bones as her life's
essence soaked through layer after layer of clothing. Permeat-
ing the grooves of the hardwood floor. Pooling in coagulated
glory, stains that might never come clean. Dr. Brady was too
late; we were too late. I knew it, but I still couldn't make sense
of it all.

Cormac had whisked Diarmuid from the room the moment
Lady Catherine crumpled to the floor and returned with Dr.
Brady . . . how much time had passed? I knew not.

Wound. Pressure. Stop the bleed. I stared at her lifeless face,
long since warped into a mask of stiffening flesh. No, not *her*

face, not anymore. For that's the verity of death; as the soul departs, the husk of what once was is clearly no more.

Dr. Brady cleared his throat, and my gaze fell to my hands, caked red and cramped, the length of ripped chemise beneath them a mere branch staving off the onslaught of a strong current. But the river no longer ran, and I no longer needed to shore the breach.

And yet, I could not move, nor could I will my tears to dry. Tears that had not come during my darkest of days. Tears that hadn't come since.

But now, the dam had burst.

Something hard bit into the palm of my left hand, and I closed my fingers around it. Slowly. Painfully. The object Lady Catherine had passed to me, once cold, now warm. Warm as Lady Catherine had once been. I slipped it into the pocket of my skirt.

Boots thudded, and a strong pair of arms encircled my waist.

"Come away." Cormac.

I shook my head, but as he plucked me from Lady Catherine's corpse, a scream fit to wake the dead tore from my throat.

"Get this cleaned up," Cormac barked, heaving me over his shoulder. I clawed his back, thumping my bloodied fists as sobs and screams fought for dominance. "Is the bath ready?"

A distant "Aye" met my ears.

"Broth and porridge. A dram of something strong if we have it," Cormac continued, stomping from the library.

"She'll need to rest—" Aggie.

But the last I remembered, before shaking myself to find Beth scrubbing the blood from my hands, was Cormac shouting: "God rot the lot of ye."

We had two days before the new moon. Two days until the Cailleach needed her due. I was exhausted, but rest was the farthest thing from my mind. Now clean and fresh in a new day dress, clarity blossomed as I paced my bedchamber, wearing a path from door to window and back again.

Lady Catherine might be dead, but to feed the Cailleach—and ensure the safety of the villagers—vengeance must still be meted.

My brows drew together as I thought. The only way to fix this . . . it started with Lady Catherine's death.

My eyes widened, and I halted before burrowing a hand into my skirt pocket. I'd somehow gathered the wherewithal to fetch the object Lady Catherine had passed to me before Beth took away my bloodied ensemble for burning. I had even cleaned the blood from the slim metallic rectangle before popping it into my new pocket.

Hurrying toward the window, I pulled it out before turning it over in my hands. A seam . . . a clasp. It was a box. With some fiddling, the seams parted, and inside—

"Her necklace," I whispered, lips parting at the sight of the golden triskele charm, the length of black ribbon wrapped around it. And beneath? That old familiar key to the attic. I glanced over my shoulder at the door. "Michael? What should I do?"

But there was no answer from my dearly departed. Instead, a sudden *knock* startled me to attention.

"Enter!" I called, and in bustled Aggie, face drawn and pale, worry hooked through the lines of her forehead. "Has all been made right?"

"I . . ." Aggie took a breath, then squared her shoulders. "The library has been cleared, m'Lady. Dr. Brady has seen to the gentleman in the guest wing and reports he is sleeping well, thanks to whatever medicine the good doctor administered. I've instructed Beth to serve his evening meal in the guest room—"

"No," I said, placing the empty box on the windowsill before pocketing the necklace and the key to the attic. "There'll be no need to feed him. Where is the child?"

"Ye plan to starve him?" Aggie brought a hand to her chest as her lips tugged downward, melding into the folds that ran from jaw to jowl. "M'Lady, the house may be in mourning, but to not feed him . . . what if he leaves and reports us? We are already in grave danger with Lady Catherine gone—"

"*You* are in grave danger," I hissed, striding forward. "Whatever curse is at work here will undoubtedly come for you all if I do not get to work. He will not eat, is that clear? And he will not leave. No one can, as well ye know."

"Ye know?" Aggie asked, aghast.

"She told me everything, and I will set things to rights," I snapped. "Now, where is the child?"

"I-in the kitchens." Pursing her lips, Aggie straightened her spine. "Safe. Hale and hearty."

I nodded as I neared and paused before her. "Keep him safe."

"Does this mean"—Aggie whipped out a hand and grabbed my arm—"ye'll fix it all? Even all that goes on in the attic?"

Before I could ask what, exactly, went on in the attic, a shadow filled the open doorway, and my heart leapt in my chest as Cormac stepped into the room.

"Mr. O'Dea," I said, by way of greeting. Dark circles painted the delicate skin beneath his eyes, and I knew mine matched.

"I must go to Lahinch and report her death. She left a will," he announced, holding out a folded letter. "And this was with it, in the top drawer. Like she said."

Brow furrowing, I reached out to take whatever it was Lady Catherine had left behind, right as Aggie rounded on Cormac.

"Ye cannot report her death!"

"If the will is to be executed, we must. We need a death certificate," Cormac countered, brow furrowing as I plucked the letter from his grasp. "The constabulary will have to investigate."

"Ye fool. No constabulary in the country would have a current record of this estate, or the village, or the parish. Even if ye report it, none would be able to find it!" Aggie exclaimed, covering her mouth with her hand. "They'd take ye to the Galway asylum."

"Of course he should go and report it," I said with a sigh, unfolding the letter. My eyes scanned the neat script, and with each phrase I read, my pulse ignited. "By the time he returns with the constabulary, it will all be done."

"What will be done? And what are we to do? Without Lady Catherine, our protection payments are lost, with no way to get them back. And if the woman in white isn't appeased, none of it will have mattered, for we'll all perish," Aggie continued, grasping my shoulders the very moment I committed Lady Catherine's sign-off to memory.

"I'll appease her first and figure out the rest," I assured Aggie, placing the letter in my pocket before locking my gaze with hers. "But first, ye must have Beth gather all the incense we have—the kind with the special herbs—and burn the lot in our injured guest's room."

"Incense? But that's for the remembering." Aggie's lower lip trembled, and I squeezed both her shoulders.

"Just do it. When yer done, take everyone—the child included—and assemble the entire village in the parish hall. Yer job is to keep them there 'til tomorrow morning. Can ye do that for me?"

"I . . . but why? How are ye going to set things to rights? Why in the name of God did her ladyship do that awful thing to herself?" Aggie's face crumpled, and tears glistened in her eyes.

"Because it was the only way to do what needs to be done,

and she trusted me to do it. Will ye trust me now, and do as I ask?" I inhaled deeply and waited—one, two—'til Aggie finally nodded.

"Aye," she said, dabbing her eyes with the sleeve of her gown before sweeping from the room.

Releasing my breath, I placed both hands against my hips and kicked a foot against the hem of my gown.

"Did ye read it?" I asked.

"I did, aye. Are ye sure ye can do it? Ye don't have the Sight," Cormac said softly. I glanced at him, and the weight of exhaustion begged me to lean into him, to take solace in his safety for just a moment.

But I simply could not. "Whatever devilry is at work here is contained in the necklace. And only one person can wield it. That's why she did that. So I could wear it and figure out what I'm missing. So I can change the course of the vengeance and have the Cailleach declare a new victim."

A muscle ticked along his jaw as he stared off toward the window. I hadn't noticed before, but he'd washed, as I had, and the faint welting of a straight blade burned red against his neck. But 'twas not his fresh face that gave pause.

"What . . . what are ye wearing?" I asked, gob agape as my mind caught up to my eyes. Fine buckskin pantaloons tucked into tall riding boots, a fine linen shirt, an immaculate cravat woven with brown and gold silk of paisley design, all topped off with a beige-colored clawhammer coat. I'd only seen such an ensemble in the pamphlets Lady Grace ordered in from London. This was not merely the dress of an Anglo, but a landed British aristocrat.

Startled, Cormac turned his attention to his clothing, running his gaze from the toes of his boots, up his legs, before glancing at me, cheeks aflame. With two hands, he adjusted the single-breasted lapels of the clawhammer coat.

"Her ladyship had this made for me long ago, and I refused

to wear it," he admitted, wincing as he placed a finger between cravat and neck. " 'Tis awful uncomfortable, but I supposed today was as good a day as any to put it on . . . honor her in a small way. I thought it best to report her death as a blood relative. The get-up might intimidate them a bit."

"Ye certainly look the part of a countess's nephew," I said, but then pursed my lips. "Better if it were black for mourning, though."

"Beggars can't be choosers," he replied with a shrug. "It'll strengthen the case that we were shocked by her sudden demise. I'll ride myself and switch out the horse along the way."

"Aye." I rounded my shoulders.

"Are ye sure ye can do this by yerself?" he asked, brows furrowing. "It could wait—"

"Go," I said. "Once everything is in motion, there's naught ye could do to help anyway."

"I'll be back as soon as I can," Cormac said. He nodded, resolute. He'd read his aunt's final words, as I had, and knew the truth of it. That the task before me was vast, but only I, and I alone, could take it on.

For the necklace was the charm that tied the Cailleach to Lady Catherine's control and allowed the owner to view others' memories while the incense worked its magic. In viewing the memories, Lady Catherine could determine when the vengeful person had come to their conclusion, before alerting the Cailleach, so the Cailleach could announce what the sacrificial vengeance would be. But with Lady Catherine now gone, and with the necklace now in my possession, I would have the ability to view others' memories.

I glanced at the letter in my hand, eyes scanning the passage that explained the how.

To end it all, Maggie, you must uncover the root of his actions and shift the blame away, thus creating a new path toward vengeance. For the reason it all happened lies elsewhere, and with that truth, you can save the child.

And now it was time.
For Theodore Moore-Vandeleur to remember.

Chapter 33

The time will come when we shall know what the
amount of mortality has been; and though you may
groan, and try to keep the truth down, it shall be known,
and the time will come when the public and the world
will be able to estimate, at its proper value, your
management of the affairs of Ireland.
—Lord Bentwick, addressing the House of
Commons, 1847

I sat, back straight, on the chaise that sat at the end of the hall
of the guest wing. Waiting. Gaze flitting between the haze of
incense escaping through the space at the bottom of Teddy's
door to the darkening sky behind me.

The triskele necklace bit into my palm, slick with sweat as I
clenched my fist around it. It pulsed in my hand, coaxing me to
place it around my neck. To anchor myself to this house, this
village. To shackle myself in its noose.

But I wouldn't. Not yet.

Instead, I'd listened as the clop of hooves clipped down the
gravel drive—Cormac. As Beth coaxed my son outside with the
promise of buttered bread sprinkled with sugar. As the household gathered in the entrance foyer to receive the order to va-
cate—Aggie.

I listened now to the thud of my heart, to the call of a bird beyond the window, to the steady tick of the grand clock that stood sentry on the landing.

I told ye the child wasn't here. That the sins of the father outweigh those of the mother.

The now-familiar wave of ice that meant Michael was near nestled into my left side, but even as his presence urged something primal in me to run, warmth permeated through my chest. I smiled.

"I didn't know what ye meant then," I said, softly, tugging my lips into a sad smile.

I would've brought him to ye if he were.

"I know." I turned to my left, but there was nothing there. No wisp of an apparition. No hint beyond this feeling, and his voice in my head. "I'm glad he's alive."

Silence.

"I'm sorry you're not," I whispered, glancing down at my lap. "I'm sorry all this happened, and that I caused it. I'd planned on making it right, by earning a place to live and land to farm, where I could put up a headstone for ye all. So ye could live on not just in memory, but so those who come after would know ye lived. 'Tis all gone to shite now, though. Lady Catherine is dead, along with any hope of payment."

A cool touch enveloped my hand, and I sighed.

Get it done so ye can live yer life at last, Maggie. Be the mother ye always wanted to be. I can't go until ye're safe.

"Why now, Michael?" I asked, fiddling with the necklace. "Why did ye never come to me before?"

I've always been with ye. But here . . . ye could hear me. See me. Must be the sorcery.

I nodded. Nothing here made any sense, yet it did in the same breath.

It's time. Have ye everything ye need?

Lady Catherine's letter was safely tucked into one skirt pocket, along with the key to the attic—I'd checked ten times. I quickly patted the other pocket, and sighed. I had *that* too, the other thing.

Pursing my lips, I brought the golden triskele to my throat and tied the length of black ribbon at my nape.

And as I did, Michael's icy presence was replaced at once.

By a wave of heat so fierce, I feared the house had caught fire.

The Cailleach wasn't a mere presence, but a melding. The moment I'd secured that necklace around my neck, I could feel her. Inside my thoughts, my body, compelling me. But I was prepared. Lady Catherine had warned me of it in her letter.

Lightning zipped through my veins, as though I had captured a storm and consumed it, channeled it into something else, something other, until I was no longer me.

Steady.

Michael. I nodded. Steady. One foot before the other, as always. Open the door to the guest room.

I strode forward in a daze, pushed in the door, and was met with an outpouring of smoke so fierce I had to cover my nose and mouth with an arm.

The curtains were drawn, but a four-poster bed stood in outline thanks to the still-roaring fire, dead center, a ways into the room.

One foot. The other.

A march toward my past, present, and possible future. Teddy consumed my every waking moment. I recognized that now. He was the past, so dark I had to bury it to keep moving forward. He was the present, so bleak I had to shut my eyes against the spark of what could've been. And the future . . . so unsure that dread had latched onto him as the cause.

But as I looked at him now—head bound, blond curls matted against the stark white of his pillow, chest rising and falling, bathed in the foul fog of Browne House—fear gripped my gut.

I shook my head and circumvented the bed before perching on the edge of the mattress.

I had to face it. For Diarmuid. To save him.

And with a final breath for courage, I lay back and rolled onto my side to face him—the man I'd once loved and cherished—and took his hand in mine.

"Show me. Make him remember," I called, and in the recess of my mind, the Cailleach purred with pleasure.

Chapter 34

At length it was discovered that the best plan would be to get completely rid of those who were so heavy a burden upon them by shipping them to America . . . for the expense of transporting each individual was less than the cost of one year's support in a workhouse.
—Robert Whyte, passenger aboard the coffin ship *Ajax*, 1847

The Night of the Céilí: October 1847: Teddy

Father never struck me. Not once in my twenty years of life. Instead, he deprived—love, safety, comfort—whenever his anger took him to places better kept barred away. They all thought he loved me, his heir, the son for whom he chose a stepmother with utmost care, the son for whom the sun shone in the morning and set at night. But truth be told, it took twelve years, between my mother's death and Lady Grace's arrival, for him to be able to pull his demons together, into the façade of a man, one capable of raising a family.

He would grant me this reprieve, of that I was certain, for the guilt of those early years—locking me away, forgetting me, beating me—ate away at him slowly. Wasn't that why he'd granted my marriage to Maggie to begin with? At least, that's what he had said.

A sharp pain lanced through my chest at even the thought of my dear sweeting, but I fought the urge to wince. For the fire in Father's eyes, sat, as he was now, behind the grand mahogany desk of his study, surrounded by the splendors he'd acquired from abroad, threatened to snap me from wishful thinking and launch me headfirst into a fray.

"Repeat yourself," Father demanded, still as a rock, pen poised above whatever document it was that needed his attention, ink gathering at the tip, perilously close to dripping.

Exhaustion clung to every fiber of my being, the kind that bore weight upon the limb to pressure the soul. Yet somewhere between France and Kilrush, I'd found my voice once more— the one that perished when news arrived. The one that had once questioned why I could not write to my heart, why she must not be burdened with my words, why I could not be there. Or hold her. Or weep as she uttered her final words.

"I cannot marry Miss Fitzgerald," I said, resolute, ensuring solid eye contact with my father. He'd once said the way to make a man give way was to glare him down. To never waver. To establish leadership. I hoped to God he was right.

Father set down the pen and ran a hand over his face before springing from the chair. I swallowed down the lump in my throat as he turned to glance out the window, hands clasped behind his back.

There was nothing wrong with the girl, exactly. She was pretty enough. Pleasing enough, or I thought she likely was. Poor thing came down with fever on our journey from Calais and was indisposed for most of it. Really, she could have just met me here instead of taking a boat all the way to France to escort me home.

I simply didn't love her, nor she me. And I was in mourning. Deepest, darkest mourning, filled with naught but memories of my heart, and regret. Such regret. Regret that our union had resulted in tragedy, and our beloved son would never know her.

Regret that I had been so frightened when last we met that I'd pulled my hand from hers when we stood before her family's home. If only I had been kinder. Warmer.

I clenched my jaw. Tears were for women . . . and men, when safe in their bedchamber. Not now, not when I was taking a stand. For though Father loved me dearly, he would brook no sign of weakness.

"You've been married by proxy. It's already done. You are wed. The banns have been read," Father said, words frosted and clipped where sorrows and prayers had so warmly greeted me upon my return. "And most fortunate of all, her father was willing to overlook the issue of your bastard, and he supports our endeavor to have you enter the political arena."

"Diarmuid," I reminded him, for I had received each of her fervent letters—though I had been cautioned not to reply, lest I inadvertently cause upset that would harm the unborn child—and had named him as she would have wished, though I had not yet laid eyes upon him. By all accounts, he was safely nestled in a wetnurse's embrace, somewhere in Dublin City. "His name is Diarmuid. And he would not be illegitimate had Maggie survived."

"What's done is done, Theodore. The boy *is* illegitimate, and that girl of the Fitzgeralds is your wife. She brings excellent connections, and so long as she agrees, she will be the mother of that child."

My palms went slick at the thought. "And if she refuses?"

"I will find a suitable arrangement for him and provide a stipend for his care. You could see him from time to time, of course, but you cannot raise a bastard if you pursue a political career."

I balled my fists, and Father turned, a sad smile toying at the corners of his lips. "You think me cruel."

"No, sir," I replied, but Father sighed then and absentmindedly pulled my grandfather's watch from his pocket—the watch that would one day be mine. I watched as the golden chain went taut, as Father flicked the latch, as his eyes drifted, not to the clockface within the engraved golden case, but to the custom-made miniature that lined the inside of the cartouche.

The miniature of my mother. The one he had commissioned on their wedding day.

"It's just . . . I haven't even seen him yet, sir," I said. "Mayhap I could fetch him and present him to Ms. Fitzgerald so she sees him, and feels an attachment to him, and cannot in good conscience refuse—"

"Do you know why I raised you with such freedom?" Father asked, interrupting me with a chilled sharpness.

I cleared my throat. The answer was because at times, in his darkest hours, he'd simply forgotten that I'd existed . . . but I knew the question was mere rhetoric.

"Your mother, God rest her, was the love of my life." He smiled at the miniature and ran a gentle thumb over her likeness. "We started much like yourself and our dearly departed Margaret. A gentle sort of romance that kindled for years. My own father welcomed the union. Thought it would bring me closer to the people. Breed empathy, if you will."

With a *snap*, Father shut the watch and shoved it back into his pocket. "But she was no different than them. Broken. Tainted. And in the end, she left me."

Not willingly, I wanted to say, but knew better than to remind him that no one succumbs willingly to death.

He glanced at me, eyes bright as a smile forced my mother's specter into the shadowed depths of the study. "But there you were. My heir. My pride and joy. You would never leave me, my boy. That's why I allowed you free rein. So you could see for yourself how your mother's people are. How they need a strong master in order to survive, how they are bred for servitude. For labor. So you could learn and apply it all when your time comes to take over the estate. So you can gain their favor and be spoken of with kindness so others—those who can vote—would hear of your popularity. Would back you when the time comes. Would heartily place you in Parliament—the beloved landowner who speaks for the people."

I closed my eyes for a moment—just the space of a breath—for there it was, the lie I'd told myself since childhood. That I could have the life I truly wanted. That I didn't have to be my father's ambition, but that I could live among those he reviled, as he had reviled me in my youth. Maggie's people, my people. And what had started as a simple dream grew to such heights that I feared losing her. And I would marry her, as Father had married my mother, and bestow upon my Maggie the greatest gift in my power to give by making her the lady of the house. We would govern over Kilrush and all our land together, and make decisions that would benefit both our pockets and the people.

But I never got to give her that gift. Instead, she'd given one to me—Diarmuid. A gift that now weighed on my chest. Nay, not a gift . . . a burden. For if my new wife would not accept him as her own, I didn't think I'd ever want to see him. How could I look him in the eye or peer upon his face—Maggie's face—and explain that I was too cowardly to stand up to my father?

He was better off without me. Maggie would have been better off without me. I opened my eyes.

"I thank you for that, sir," I intoned—the usual response, as expected.

Father nodded. "I had hoped that you would understand the larger picture, Theodore. That you would require the sort of connections that this union with the Fitzgeralds would bring. But if Margaret was your choice, I was happy to abide by your wishes."

My chest constricted.

He glanced at me then, eyes mournful in a way I'd never seen them before. "I loved your mother once, and I love you. Fiercely, my boy. And this is all I can do for you now. The Fitzgerald girl brings a fine promise for the future, but there's no rule stating that you must immediately jump into your duty. Margaret's passing has affected us all, may she rest in peace."

I wavered then, shutting my eyes against the wave of sadness that threatened tears. "Amen," I whispered.

"Now, to business." Footsteps treaded near, and the reassuring warmth of Father's hand came down on my shoulder. "I may be called to Dublin to report on the situation here. This could be an opportunity for me. For you."

"When do you depart?" I asked. Father had tried, and failed on three separate occasions, to be elected as County Clare's representative in the House of Commons. And I knew it was his greatest wish to see me elevated there one day.

"I await the summons. In the meantime, you'll step into the role of land agent. It will be good to keep your mind off everything."

My heart skipped a beat. "You have a land agent—"

"The O'Shaughnessys have decided to try their luck elsewhere and are finding a new situation for their family. Distraught over Margaret's death, as you can imagine. Fresh start and all that. And"—Father leaned forward to whisper in my ear—"they blame you for her untimely death."

He pulled away and slapped my back. "They claim you led her to her death, then cursed the name Moore-Vandeleur for all to hear. I was going to let them go unmolested, but part of me hopes they do not sully your name wherever they decide to settle."

"Wh-what?" My eyes widened. No, that could not be. They couldn't have possibly believed such a thing—

"I suppose they're right," Father said with a sigh. "Had she not gotten with child, she'd still be with us all."

Ice gripped my heart as each of his words landed a heavy blow.

"Worse, I fear she believed you had abandoned her by the end and wrote such to her father." Father strode toward the window and stared as white clouds billowed over the estuary. "In the end, it's just you and I, my boy. And this new marriage."

Tears stung my eyes as I stared, open-mouthed, at my father.

"What are you saying?" I asked, my voice barely a gruff whisper as this new information clogged my mind.

"It would be a shame if that upstart O'Shaughnessy bad-mouthed your good name and hurt your future political aspirations. All the studying, the hard work to become a solicitor . . . and the hard-won relationship between you and me. My ambitions for you are all you have left, Theodore. What use is this new marriage if Margaret's father chooses to sully her memory, her wishes for you, if he destroys everything we are trying to build? It's what Margaret would have wanted, after all, is it not? A bright, illustrious future for you?"

Something deep in my soul broke as realization washed over me. Maggie was gone, and her father—who had spoken so unkindly to me on the evening when I'd asked for her hand—was now hell-bent on destroying whatever future I would be forced to face.

"What would you have me do, Theodore?" Father asked, returning to his desk. He gestured toward the document he'd been working on when I'd come in.

"What . . . what do you mean?" My brows furrowed. "Are they . . . gone?"

"If you sign it, they can be. It can be your first official act as land agent." Father twisted the document around and slid the inkpot in my direction. "With one signature, you'll be able to preserve Maggie's memory and have the future she would have dreamt for you. What do you say?"

The future she would have dreamt for me? I had wanted . . . what had I wanted? To visit with the O'Shaughnessys. To share memories with them. To mourn with them. To ask how the funeral went. To bring them their grandson, their nephew, and assure them that Maggie would still live. Through Diarmuid. Through my own heart, whose shallow beat now echoed in the empty chamber that was once filled with so much love.

But now? They thought I'd killed her, and it was just as Father said. They wished to sully her memory by destroying the life Maggie would have wanted for me . . . for us both, for our family.

Wrath set my blood to boil as I stared at the document.

"Sign it," Father ordered, eyes narrowing as he glared at me. "Or don't. Their own future now lies in your hands, my son."

Balling my fists, I stepped forward, barely scanning whatever the document pertained to.

Complaint of Fraud, Theft, and Mismanagement of Her Majesty's Share.

Dipping a pen into the inkpot, I signed.

"This one also," Father said, plucking the first document from its place to reveal yet another.

Order of Refusal to Administer Aid.

I signed it.

"Good lad." My father smiled—the slow, cruel curl that always spelled my doom as a child—and a wave of nausea spilled up my throat. Had he tricked me? My heart fluttered in my chest, prompting shallow breaths. Maggie would know if he'd tricked me. Maggie—I wrapped my arms around my stomach as she would have done and told myself to breathe. To stop. To think.

"There's a celebration at the parish hall tonight to announce your marriage," Father announced, smiling—now a bright beam that meant he was happy . . . satisfied.

"Oh? Shall I send word to Ms. Fitzgerald—" I asked, before he interrupted.

"Mrs. Theodore Moore-Vandeleur," Father corrected, pulling the second document beyond my reach. "Nay. The girl is ill, after all. Go and tend to her tonight. Talk a little. She's likely as displeased with this arrangement as you are."

"Yes, Father," I said, bowing slightly. For what else could I do? What had I just signed? What had I just done? "W-we d-dine at the u-usual t-time?"

"Speak properly, Theodore, really. I have a prior engagement this evening, at eight, and your stepmother has decided to take supper in her chamber. You're welcome to do the same."

The same night: Maggie

The summerhouse lay adjacent to the walled garden and was only ever used when the family had company, which was rare. Despite the Moore-Vandeleurs' airs and graces, his "lordship" was naught but a colonel who'd inherited the fruit of his ancestors' legacy—Dutchmen who had settled during Cromwell's reign of terror at that, not even English. But all the landlords were Anglo in station if not by blood. All colored with the same brush, all profiting from the exploitation of a land brutally brought to heel over the course of seven centuries.

Lady Grace must've been fair disappointed to learn that her husband didn't enjoy the social visits she must have envisioned. The Moore-Vandeleurs may have built up the Kilrush area, but it was remote, and the family income wasn't near the class status of the daughter of an earl.

Still, his lordship had always kept the summerhouse in good

order, and it had become a place of refuge for Teddy and me as we grew up together.

I loved the beautiful flowers, blooms from all over the world, thriving in the heat trap of its glass walls, where massive ferns and birds-of-paradise provided shade and shelter from prying eyes. Teddy and I used to play and read on throw blankets when we were children, but when Lady Grace married into the family, she had it decorated with rugs and chaises, ornate tables and gas lamps, building the décor around the foreign feel of our little oasis.

Perhaps that's where it all went wrong, for what two people couldn't imagine a fantastical life—a happy ending I now knew belonged bound in the pages of a rare work of fiction— surrounded as we were by such whimsy.

I shook my head. Eight. I had said eight in my note. Glancing at the door to the walled garden, I balled my fists. Teddy usually made his way from the house and through the garden to meet me. Perhaps I should greet him there, standing tall and proud next to the sundial at its center, where he would have to face me in the open, unable to tug at memories that painted every nook and cranny of the summerhouse or utter sweet words to soften the blow.

Then again, he might not come if he saw me.

With a frustrated sigh, I stomped toward the summerhouse, but then froze.

What if he did not come at all?

What if, now wed to another woman, he felt he no longer owed me a thing?

Pulling my shawl close, I pressed my lips together. No. He would come. He had to.

I grasped the door handle of the summerhouse and slid through with a shiver. It was still warm despite the cool night, its glass surroundings holding tight to every last drop of heat the day had provided.

My pulse raced, from both exertion and anger, and it took me a moment to settle.

I breathed deep, inhaling the scent of soil and earth. There weren't many flowers in bloom this time of year, and the large green plants didn't emit a scent of note. Still, it was familiar, and a few breaths later, my nerves had calmed enough to sit and wait.

I brushed away a large leaf of a bird-of-paradise, and my chest tightened.

Deep in the center of the summerhouse, a light flickered. A lamp, surely. And none would leave a lit lamp so carelessly in a place like this.

Sweat beaded my forehead, from both the sudden heat of the summerhouse and fear. It was one thing thinking of what I must say, and what answers I needed, but quite another when confronted with the immediate opportunity to have said conversation.

He was here.

"Teddy?" I called.

A rustle met my ears, followed by the creak of a chair. I stepped farther into the room, right as a figure stood from their seated position.

"Ah, Maggie. Well met," he said, the voice deeper than Teddy's soft tenor. My heart leapt in my chest as the figure bent to pick up the lamp. "I thought it wise to meet with you, as it wouldn't be polite to have you wait all night."

The blood drained from my head, leaving me dizzy as the light from the lamp lit up the figure's plump face, the mutton-chop beard adorning his jaw casting strange shadows. It most certainly wasn't Teddy.

It was his lordship.

"Sit, sit. Come. How do you fare?" he asked, gesturing me forward.

Eyes wide, I stood, frozen.

"Come, child," he insisted, clucking his tongue. "Is that any way to greet your master?"

Master. He was that. Shaking myself, I approached and took the chair opposite him as he sat, placing the lamp on the table between us.

"Have you recovered from your dreadful ordeal?" he asked. Kind . . . too kind. It reminded me of the audience I'd had with him prior to leaving for Dublin. Then I had been blinded by good faith, but now I noted just the right amount of inflection to *sound* kind. With new perspective, I recognized it for what it was: false pleasantry.

"Yes, m'Lord, I thank you," I replied. Every hair on my body stood to attention, and I fought against the shiver running up my spine. If I were a dog, I'd growl and bark to dispel whatever danger crackled in the air between us.

"Forgive me if my presence gave you a fright. It's only that I found your note, but dear Theodore is not to home, so I thought I'd meet with you to see how you fare."

Lie. I knew Teddy was home. I'd seen him in the carriage with my own two eyes. "How fortuitous, m'Lord. I'm that glad to meet you, and so very humbled that you thought to save me the trouble of waiting."

He nodded, pursing his lips. "I was so very saddened to hear of your loss. Our loss, naturally. I grieved my grandchild, I assure you. And Theodore was so overcome with worry for you that he needed time to recoup his peace of mind, so I sent him to France."

Lie. If Teddy had been so worried about me, he would've at least written or visited. Instead, he had been courting Miss Lila Fitzgerald while I had stared out the window of Lady Grace's townhome, pining for word from him. "Yes, of course, m'Lord."

He stared at me, brows drawing close as he studied my face. "I didn't even realize you were back. Lady Luck must have been on my side when I strolled in here today and stumbled upon your note."

Several lies. The minute I stepped foot in Kilrush, my presence would have been reported, especially if my presence wasn't welcome. To add to that, his lordship never would have strolled into the summerhouse without reason, and there was no feasible way he would've simply found my note without a good rummage. Teddy and I always left correspondence beneath the seedling planter. His lordship would've had to have known and deliberately searched.

"In fact, I thought you'd taken a position with the Gore-Booths of Sligo? My dear wife went to quite some trouble, using family connections to secure it for you."

I had no idea who the Gore-Booths were, nor how far Sligo was from here, but I realized now that I'd made a fool's error. Knowing what I now knew, it was very clear that I was never meant to return. Stilling rumors of an illegitimate child wasn't the only reason I'd been sent away. My presence in Kilrush was no longer desired, and my family's livelihood was now in danger.

I thought back to Michael's anger that morning, and to learning he no longer worked at the Big House. Surely that was a consequence of my union with Teddy. Thank God, Da still held his position . . . but then I mulled over what Da had said when he saw me there in the main room last night: *You're not supposed to be here.* "Forgive me, m'Lord. I'm afraid that, in my own grief and confusion, I misunderstood the offer, and thought to come home for my own peace of mind. Now that I've visited my family, I can of course take it, and I can be on my way to Sligo by this time next week."

"No need," his lordship said, lips curling, smile obscenely warping, dancing in shifting shadows cast by the lamp.

No need. There was nothing and everything in those two words. "No need" because the position was now gone, or "no need" because he would go to the trouble of procuring another?

"I thought you were a clever girl." Bending, his lordship plucked a bottle and two glasses from the floor before placing them on the table. "So clever, my lonely wife, bereft of her social circle, thought she would make a project of you so she might have an educated companion. Time wasted."

He brought the bottle to his mouth, then clasped the cork between his teeth before pulling. *Pop.*

"What use is education if one has no sense? Hmm?" He poured two measures of wine, one per glass, before glancing at me, brow raised as if expecting an answer.

"No use whatsoever, Your Lordship," I murmured, desperately fighting to keep the tremor from my voice. My pulse pounded against temple, wrist, and throat. "I-I apologize, Your Lordship. I was foolish, and couldn't grasp the situation."

"But you do now?"

"Y-yes, Your Lordship." I breathed in, then out, as his lordship swirled the wine in its glass.

"Good. Remember your place," he said, leaving the glass on the table as he sat back, crossing his trousered legs. Embarrassment flushed up the column of my neck. "You are but a trained animal. You may speak like us and look like us to some extent, but that is where the similarity begins and ends. You should have spread your legs without thought when your young master made advances. Marriage, indeed! Theodore told me everything, my dear. How you cajoled him. How you kept that cunny of yours locked up tight, only relinquishing when he made promises."

A vise gripped my chest so hard I couldn't breathe. What? What was his lordship *talking* about?

"Of course, the resulting child was not at fault for your audacity. More's the pity. I would have raised it myself. Don't worry," he said, words muffled as I fought to hear through the roar of blood pounding betwixt my ears. "I've put him in his place. Stupid boy should have set a firm boundary with you from the very beginning. I was too lax with him. Should've reined him in. Marriage with the likes of you, forsooth. Perhaps his own dirty heritage was to blame."

My eyes widened. "Dirty . . . heritage?"

His lordship grinned. "His mother, my dear. One of yours, you know. But, of course, you must have known that. How dare you take such advantage of his empathy? Using his history against him. You selfish idiot! Marriage with you would destroy all chances of Teddy ever setting foot in the House of Commons. I have been working toward that goal since the day he was born!"

"I—" I began, letting out a whoosh of breath as my lungs suddenly sprang back to life. I balled my fists and pushed to my feet. There was no use saying what I wanted to say, to stand up for Teddy, to explain that neither of us thought his lordship would much care who he married, given his own choice of wife. There was no use, because his lordship had been fed lies, lies Teddy had told in defense of his actions. For when cold, hard reality came crashing down the morning he'd gone to beg permission from this man before me, his lordship must have shown his wrath and threatened all the things Da had warned him of. That I had warned him of. And so, I didn't defend Teddy, or myself. It was clear now that Teddy had cast me off of his own free will and told abominable tales in an attempt to patch things up between him and his father.

Instead, I curtsied. "I understand, Your Lordship, and I thank you for your benevolence. I assure you, I'll have naught to do with the young master going forward."

His lordship rose, then plucked both glasses from the table and offered one to me.

"Shall we toast to it?" Though framed as a question, it was an order, so I took the glass and nodded. "Good girl."

"I'll make enquiries as soon as possible to find a position far from here, Your Lordship. You needn't worry. And thanks to you, I can offer some value to an employer."

He laughed, then glanced at me. "Tell me. What makes the best fertilizer?"

I furrowed my brow. "Slurry, Your Lordship."

"And what is slurry?" he prompted.

"Cow shit, begging your pardon, Your Lordship."

He nodded. "Cows are incredible beasts, for they fertilize the land, provide milk and food, and all for the cost of three men's monthly wage. Do you know what that means?"

I shook my head, and he smiled.

"It means one cow is worth more than three Irishmen, my dear. Now, if we divided the cow's equity into parts, I would value the food and milk provided at one man, and its 'shit,' as you so eloquently put it, at two. For that shit ensures a bountiful harvest, feeding hundreds where a single cow might feed twenty. That means two Irishmen are worth a single vat of cow shit, but you, as a filthy calculating whore, are worth far less than that. You could offer value to an employer? Ha!" Reaching out, he clinked his glass with mine. "All that to say, once more, no need. You made your decision when you chose to board a coach bound from Dublin to Kilrush, and any value that remained diminished the moment you arrived home. I have no time, or use, for women without sense, and nor would another be kind or stupid enough to take you on. My only course of action now is to ensure you never cross paths with him again."

"Your Lordship," I snapped, instantly biting down on my tongue. Colonel Moore-Vandeleur was not the person to speak back to in any way, shape or form. I had to swallow the words, the retort, that burned the back of my throat. "Thank you for the wine."

I raised the glass in the air, then slowly drew it toward my mouth, and with each inch closer, his lordship's smile widened a fraction. It was worrisome, as though he waited for me to take a sip. He hadn't even raised his arm to drink his own, and a shudder of fear took hold in my gut.

But just as the cool glass made contact with the skin of my lips, the door to the summerhouse opened with a bang, sending a jolt of fear from my head to my toes, and I dropped the wine. It shattered with a crash, and I glanced down to find hundreds of blood-stained glittering shards reflecting the light from the lamp.

"Maggie?!" Michael. Whatever mettle had held my back straight this entire time snapped upon hearing my brother's voice. I was frightened, had been since the moment I'd found his lordship there in place of Teddy.

Michael brushed aside the leaves of the bird-of-paradise with all the grace one might muster to bat away a cobweb.

"My, my," his lordship said with a chuckle. "It seems my old valet is loath to part ways as cleanly as was assured to me. Come, Michael. We were just about to have a glass of wine. Though—" He glanced from the glass in his hand to the one shattered at his feet.

"Don't drink that," Michael hissed, lunging for my arm before jerking me back. "What the hell are ye doing here?"

"Having a nice chat," his lordship said, offering the glass in his hand to me. "Here, Maggie. Let's finish the toast. Michael, you don't mind drinking straight from the bottle, do you?"

"We need to get out of here. *Now*!" Michael hissed the words into my ear, and I grasped in the dark for his hand. If Michael said we needed to go, go we would.

As I laced my fingers with his, he quickly pulled me close and pushed me toward the door, without even a "by your leave" to his lordship.

"I don't want to know how ye wound up alone with that man," Michael huffed, dragging me along as we raced toward the entrance gate. "But ye can pay me back later."

"For what?" I asked, struggling to keep up.

"For saving yer fecking life!"

And something inside, something deep and dark, something I had stuffed down and ignored when it was just his lordship and me, alone, knew—without a shadow of doubt—that when his lordship had said "no need," he meant I wouldn't *have* need.

Because I would be dead.

The cause? Whatever he had put in that wine.

Chapter 35

The "land of song" was no longer tuneful; or, if a human
sound met the traveler's ear, it was only that of the feeble
and despairing wail for the dead.
—George Petrie, Irish artist, 1855

Present: May 1848

My eyes fluttered open as I slowly came to, only to find a
bright blue, wide-eyed stare trained on my face, the hazy remnants of now-spent incense bathing us both in shades of gray. I
froze, fear gripping my gut as Teddy—my Teddy—lay there,
gazing at me, the bandage once wrapped over his eyes bunched
up over his forehead.

He smiled, that same beautiful smile that could light up the
entire summerhouse even on the darkest of days.

"A most wonderful dream," he murmured, settling further
into his pillow. "I fear I don't wish to wake, dear heart. There's
so much I must say."

Christ above, he thought he was still dreaming. This man I'd
once loved. This man who—I now knew—allowed his father to
manipulate his every action. This man, so controlled by his father that his father would rather see me and my family dead
than have my presence deprive his precious heir's chances of a
glittering political career.

Yes. There it is. The Cailleach's voice reverberated through my mind, and I smiled—a terrible, sad smile that tore at my heart. At Teddy, at her. *Do you realize it at last?*

"Teddy," I whispered, reaching out a hand to gently push a wayward curl from his forehead. He relaxed at my touch and covered my hand with his before gently coaxing it toward his mouth. "Why did you tell your father that I cajoled you into a relationship? That I would not lie with you unless you offered marriage? Why did you sign those documents without reading them? Did you have any idea what the consequences would be?"

He stiffened, lips but a breath from my palm, before placing a gentle kiss in its center. "If you had been there, it never would have happened. He bullied me, Maggie. You know how he is! Without you there, I couldn't stand up to him. You know that."

"You let them all die. You let me die," I hissed. "Because you couldn't stand up for me. For yourself!"

Even now, he would lay the decimation of my family at my feet? I ground my teeth as he laced his fingers through mine. "You can't blame me for your stupidity, Teddy. I've told you time and again to stop. To breathe. To think."

"No, no . . . that's not true, Maggie. I did my best! But your father was angry when I asked for your hand, remember? He told me I'd be cast off, and mocked me, and despised me. He was right. Father threatened everything, and I had no strength left to fight him." In the past, the pout he now flashed might have made me crumble, made me weak. "Don't be angry with me. Tell me, how is it there? On the other side?"

"Peaceful," I said with a sigh. Best he was like this. Relaxed. Completely at ease. Best he thought me a dream, a specter visiting in sleep.

"I thought I saw you once, you know," he whispered. "In the market. At home. But when I told Father, he assured me it could not be. He even had me seen by a doctor. They said I hallucinated it. That I missed you so dearly that I had willed you before my eyes. But I know that's not true. You came to me, my Maggie. As a spirit. And I have feared ever since that you are not at rest. That you resent me for what I did to Diarmuid."

My chest tightened.

"What did you do to Diarmuid?" The question lashed from my tongue before I could soften the blow, and his eyes widened a fraction.

"I love him, but my wife refused to raise him as our own, and Father refused to have a bastard in the house. So I left him there, in Dublin. I thought . . . I thought one day the guilt would lessen, and I could find the courage to finally be a father to him. Better abandoned with strangers than treat him as my father did me. I was right to do so, wasn't I, lovedy?"

My child, my son, abandoned in a strange city with naught but strangers to care for him? It was all I could do to restrain myself from slapping him.

"And now? You thought it time to be a father? You said you were bringing him to meet his grandfather."

Teddy shook his head. "Father stopped providing a stipend for his care, and he has full control over my own purse. He said it was time to cut Diarmuid loose and move on. But how could I do such a thing? I thought a forced meeting with his grandchild might soften his heart. Do you think it will? I think it unlikely, but I must try before returning him to the city."

"You plan on returning him to Dublin after? What if his lordship won't release the funds needed for his care?" My heart raced, and I fought against the rising tide to breathe. To stop. To think.

"Then I'll give him into the care of the church."

"An orphanage?" I cried, horror gripping my soul. We all heard stories of those left in the care of the church. Of the missing children. The mysterious pits. The suddenly empty dormitories.

"Are you angry, dear heart?" he asked, searching my eyes

with his. "I am not his father without you here as his mother. I cannot do it. Not yet. In truth, I am relieved. I feared your spirit would be more angered by my moving on so soon. But I had no choice. Father—"

"Shhh." With every last ounce of strength I still possessed, I swallowed my rage, pulled my hand free of his, and placed a finger against his lips. "I know, Teddy."

"Is she there with you?" he asked, suddenly alert—too alert for comfort.

"Who?"

"Lila. My . . . my wife. She died perhaps three months after we arrived at Kilrush together. Caught a fever aboard the ship and never shook it."

The light of heaven to her. Tears glistened in his eyes, and I had to bite my tongue to keep from screaming.

"Yes, she's here. She's safe. With me." I pulled back my hand.

"Thank you, Maggie," he said with a sigh. "Thank you for loving me. For giving birth to Diarmuid. For caring for Lila there in Heaven. I deserve none of your love. None of your kindness."

"I know. You deserve none of it," I replied, and Teddy's brows twitched. "Your family don't deserve the luck they've enjoyed. They don't deserve the people who depend upon them. My family didn't deserve the cruel death you and your father gifted to them. Nor did I deserve to wander, broken and shattered from all I endured."

"What?" The corners of Teddy's mouth took a downward dive, but before he could fully rouse himself into a seated position, I quickly threw a leg over his torso and straddled him.

Say the name of the one who wronged you, purred the Cailleach. *Announce it.*

"His Lordship, Colonel Crofton Moore-Vandeleur!" I exclaimed. Teddy's eyes widened. "I thought it was you all along, that you had lied and schemed to have my da accused of theft, to have us evicted, to have them all die on the side of the road. That you had cast me off because you grew tired of me, but the truth is much more terrifying. Your father schemed it all. Told me Diarmuid had died at birth, and told you I had perished in childbed. All to secure your future, and you . . . you never fought for me, never insisted on visiting me, never asked to see my body, and condemned my family to death! You nodded your head and did everything your father commanded. If it weren't for your father, my family would have had a chance. Maybe even survived. If it weren't for him, I would have held our son in my arms and never abandoned him to a nanny or left him with the church. If it weren't for him, his ambition, his lies, maybe we could have salvaged some sliver of happiness together. And if it weren't for him, *you wouldn't have become the insidious idiot that you are, and would have never been born to begin with!*"

"What—?" Teddy bucked beneath my thighs, but I bore down, grasping his wrists with hands that held the strength of the Cailleach, and pinned him to the bed.

Give the verdict. Mete out the punishment.

"I curse him," I said softly, lips curling as Teddy screwed his eyes shut.

"Wake up, wake up, wake up," he muttered, a prayer to the sandman, beseeching him for mercy.

"I curse him," I repeated. "And your family. May your estate burn, consumed by the fires of hell. May you—the only joy in your father's wretched life, the one he pushes to achieve heights he never could—be forever forgotten by everyone but him. May he wallow in memory, while the world around him crumbles. While madness consumes him. While he claims he did have another son. An heir. My vengeance is you! Taking you from him. Because he took everything away from me!"

Yesssss, hissed the Cailleach. *Seal it.*

"I loved you with all my heart, Teddy, but you broke it when you could not find the strength to protect the family you and I created together." And I meant it. Perhaps the softness of my voice stilled him, or mayhap he heard sincerity in the breathy sob that broke over his name. For he ceased to thrash and opened his eyes—those beautiful blue eyes that had been a part of my life for so long. That promised comfort in times of trouble, that promised love in times of joy.

"Maggie, you are my strength," he murmured, tears glistening in his glassy gaze. "I love you still."

"This is the only way, T-teddy." My voice broke over his name, for I knew—*knew*—that, when alone with his father, he couldn't hold his own. I knew that he'd been fooled into signing those orders, but it didn't matter. His weakness spelled the decimation of my family. I knew that he believed me dead and gone . . . but I could have never known that he would abandon our child or even think to throw that precious babe onto the mercy of the church. No. I couldn't even stomach the thought of reconciling with a man like that. I had to do this. For Diarmuid had never even known his father, or his lordship, and this was the only way to give my son the life he deserved. "I must save Diarmuid."

Releasing one of Teddy's wrists, I reared back and whipped the hidden blade from my skirt pocket.

And the last my love, my dearest, saw before the warm rush of blood soaked the sheet beneath him was the glint of my knife.

As I screamed my wrath.

As my curse was sealed.

All to the sound of the Cailleach . . . laughing.

Chapter 36

The streets are daily thronged with moving skeletons.
The fields are strewn with dead . . . the curse of Russell,
more terrible than the curse of Cromwell, is upon us.
—Eyewitness in Ballinrobe, County Mayo, 1849

The Cailleach's fiery presence dissipated in the wake of what I had done, despite the fact that I was still wearing the triskele charm—satiated, calm, retreating in euphoric bliss. Through searing tears, my stomach heaved as I stumbled from the bed. There was only one last thing to do. One final instruction in Lady Catherine's letter.

"Michael!" I called, stumbling out into the hallway, not daring to glance back at the carnage I'd wrought.

It wasn't a clean death. Blood had spurted and gushed from the wound in Teddy's throat, and the gargling rattle of Teddy's last struggling breaths would likely haunt me for the rest of my days. He didn't deserve this end—no one did. It had been easier to paint him as the villain incarnate, but to know the whole truth at last? I shook my head. I had no other choice. Diarmuid was the only option.

Steady. My brother's gentle voice ebbed somewhere near, drawing a sob up my throat.

"I d-did i-it," I whispered, gripping my skirts to keep my hands from shaking.

Ye did.

"Why did ye never tell me? That I wasn't meant to return?"

Would you have believed us if we'd told ye? Would things have gone any differently if we had?

I shook my head, for what was done was done. He was right. I still would have tried to meet with Teddy, to hear it from his mouth, and everything would have unfolded as it had.

But a new dream awaited—a new life. One where I would raise my son, and watch him grow, and provide for him as best I could.

Finish it now, Maggie. Or that new life of yers might not happen.

I nodded and strode down the hall, sweeping up the flight of stairs that led to the third floor, then the fourth.

Catching my breath on the landing, I homed in on my target—the hidden door to the attic. The final piece to all this. The last hurdle.

You'll need to set her free if you ever wish to leave this place, Lady Catherine had written. *She is bound to the one who owns the triskele, and the triskele is bound to the land. The choice, of course, is yours. You could always don the mantel of Wilhelmina proper and continue to provide for the village if you so choose. But, if you do not, the window to untether the Cailleach from our earthly plane opens the moment a sacrifice is made and closes soon after, so you must make haste. Please, no matter which path you select, provide for my people as best you can . . .*

I had no interest in staying here longer than necessary, and no matter how strange and cruel I found the Cailleach's methods, no being deserved imprisonment without means of release.

For I—former inmate 1-3-4-0, O'Shaughnessy, Margaret—would have never been able to pay back the debt that accumulated daily in the workhouse. Not on my own. Not without a sponsor like Lady Catherine. Likewise, the Cailleach was in a similar position—fixed in an endless cycle of sacrifice and providing for this small group of people, unable to assist what was left of the rest: the people she'd watched over for millennia. Ireland.

Aye. It was time to let her go.

As I hooked the velveteen drape to the side, the door to the attic revealed itself, and I got to work.

One by one, I slid each bolt to the side, then placed the old key in the final lock. It was full night now, and naught but moonlight illuminated the dark hallway, but no mind. If memory served, Lady Catherine had hung a lamp inside this slab of rotting wood and decaying hinges, and I'd place my hand on it soon enough.

"Now or never," I muttered, glancing over my shoulder as an icy breeze ruffled the little hairs on the back of my neck.

I turned the key and winced as the grating of metal against rust-eaten mechanisms set my teeth on edge. It clicked, and taking a deep breath, I pushed the door open.

A stray moonbeam, from the landing above, guided me toward the glinting glass case of the lamp, nestled neatly upon a dust-ridden shelf, and I made quick work of lighting it.

"I'm coming," I called, trying to keep the lamp steady as I hurried up the narrow staircase. My heart thundered in my chest, unsure of what might greet me above. For this was the place, the sanctum, in which Lady Catherine had practiced all her conjuring. Or so her letter had said.

But when I reached the landing and stepped into the near-barren room, my eyes widened. Given the size of the house, the attic's dimensions were surprisingly spare. Mayhap the length and breadth of my own bedchamber.

The window where I'd oft spied shadows from outside now lay ahead, sitting proudly in the wall at the back of the room, the almost-full moon in a perfect landscape beyond. Before it, a

worktable stood—rough-hewn but sturdy—with neatly labeled jars of ground lavender and sage carefully placed together
at one end, a hand-cranked grinder next to them.

Row upon row of drying racks, filled to the brim with those
unusual, trumpet-shaped white blooms lining the walls, creating an aisle—dead center—that led toward the table. An intruder might think her ladyship industrious, with a mind to
provide perfumed sachets to every noblewoman in Ireland.

A sad smile twisted my lips, and I took a deep breath to
steady my nerves.

"Are ye ready?" I asked, aloud, unsure if my intent would be
welcomed or scorned.

But my answer drifted along the icy draft that spelled a
spirit's presence, and the Cailleach's voice washed over me—
warm, inviting.

Please, she said.

And I nodded, before striding toward the worktable.

"I release ye," I announced, my stare fixed on the grinder.
No doubt it had pulverized pounds upon pounds of dried herbs
and flowers over the years, but tonight, it would serve a different purpose.

Wait. The Cailleach's order stilled me, and my attention was
drawn down, down, below the table, to the freshly swept, un-
varnished floor.

"What is it?" I asked aloud.

Beneath.

Brows furrowing, I plucked the lamp from the table and
squatted, only to find a large wooden chest under the table, an
open lock looped through its hinges.

You must do this first, or I'll not go.

"What is it?"

*The source of her power, the power you could now take for
yourself if you wished. You must give back what they paid for*

her protection, or I will remain to ensure that protection is given.

"But if yer released, I could do naught with it." Even as I said the words, I placed the lamp on the floor and reached out to pull the chest by the handle. Whatever this was, I'd do it, for she'd done enough for the people of Gortacarnaun.

I might be gone, but that wouldn't stop you from drawing on what's inside to work a new conjuring. A new magic.

"I wouldn't mess with that stuff." With a final yank and the chest clearing the table, and I unhooked the lock before pushing up the lid. My brows furrowed. "What's all this?"

Hundreds of small glass jars lay nestled within, each clearly labeled with a person's name. I held up the first toward the lamp—*Paddy MacNamara*—but the jar appeared empty.

"There's nothing inside."

Open it.

Pursing my lips, I unscrewed the tin lid, and as soon as it came free in my hand, a tiny spark of light shot out.

"Oh!" I reeled back, landing unceremoniously on my behind, as I watched the light dance from the ceiling, to the table, until it finally settled in one of the windows, darting from side to side.

Let it out.

And I knew then that I must open the window.

"What is it?" I whispered, scrambling to my feet, surprised my pulse did not stir. Perhaps it was the Cailleach's influence . . . or perhaps there was simply no danger.

I strode toward the window and pulled the latch before pushing the pane. It gave way easily—unlike the window in my bedchamber—and the light darted out into the night, flitting in the direction of the village.

The price they paid for protection. A piece of their souls.

My eyes widened. That was the payment Aggie had mentioned? I would have been desperate to see it returned to me too! "The villagers?"

Yes. She drew on the power of their combined souls to control me. Release them now.

I did, hands aching as I unscrewed almost four hundred jars. Four hundred sparks of light. Four hundred streaks flying out into the night.

Payment returned.

You'll find another way to care for them?

"I will," I replied, pushing up from the ground. Placing two fists against the small of my spine, I stretched backward, then straightened. "Are ye ready now?"

Yes.

I blew out a heavy breath and stepped toward the table.

"I know I didn't seem very grateful before, but I do thank ye. For guiding Diarmuid to me. For helping me work through my own pain so I could move forward. For closure." I reached across the table and pulled the grinder toward me. "Thank ye for helping those other Wilhelminas do the same. And thank ye for keeping the people here safe all this time. The methods might have been strange, but they're alive and well because of ye. I release ye now."

Reaching up and around, I unknotted the black ribbon at my nape before placing the triskele charm in the well of the grinder.

"Take care of the country. Help it heal," I whispered, before cranking the handle to destroy it.

The cogs screeched against the golden charm, resisting, but my second hand joined the first, and with all my strength, I rotated the crank.

Thank you . . .

A chill wound up my spine as the Cailleach's distant voice echoed in the shadowed attic, and as the shards of the destroyed charm dropped into the waiting bowl below, a boom reverberated somewhere within the house, shaking the foundation for the space of a heartbeat.

Inexplicable tears welled in my eyes as my chest constricted, and I bent over the grinder to catch my breath. In. Out. Breathe.

Ye did well. Michael.

A sob tore from my throat, sending a wracking shudder through my shoulders.

Ye did very, very well, my Maggie-pie.

The cool touch of his spirit form stroked my back, and we stood there, together, in the attic of Browne House, until I was ready to face the world.

"Ye should go now, Michael. I'll be fine. Go to Da and Mam and the others. Tell them all is well, and that I'm sorry. I don't need ye anymore."

Chapter 37

We can feel again that it is an Irish strength to celebrate
the people in our past, not for power, not for victory, but
for the profound dignity of human survival. We can
honor that survival best, it seems to me, by taking our
folk-memory of this catastrophe into the present world
with us, and allowing it to strengthen and deepen our
identity with those who are still suffering.
—Mary Robinson, president of Ireland, December 1990
to September 1997

As though in a dream, I had descended the attic stairs, changed
from my bloodied clothes, fetched a cloak, and walked to the
village in the dead of night. Through the square, into the tavern,
through to the hall beyond. True to her word, Aggie had gathered all the villagers, and they lay in every spare corner of the
floor, their gentle snores music to liven the twilight, the heat
from their bodies enough to warm the heart.

I found Diarmuid snuggled with Beth near the far wall—
close to where I had passed time in the village not long before,
waiting for the storm to pass—and promptly plucked him from
his makeshift bed so he might sleep cradled in my chest.

I didn't sleep. Though I had been awake now for a day and a
half, something akin to anticipation kept me from slumber. So I

sat, my son sound in my arms, until the dawn's first rays penetrated the darkness. Until the villagers stirred.

Until we'd broken our fast on yesterday's bread.

No one spoke. But hundreds of eyes bored into my soul as I quietly nibbled and supervised Diarmuid's meal.

It was Aggie who took charge.

"Is it done?" She appeared from seemingly nowhere and startled me into turning to my right. Her face had weathered in the night, stress and worry wreaking havoc the only way it could—pale, drawn, fingers twirling in knots.

"Aye," I said, clearing my throat as I glanced around. They all stared—brows furrowed, lips pressed together. "And yer payment has been returned. Yer souls are safe. It was time the Cailleach went to help everyone else, in whatever way she could. I'll take care of ye now."

"How?" An angry call ground out from the crowd, igniting a murmured chorus that set my teeth on edge, but the door that led from the hall to the village square beyond slammed open, drawing everyone's attention away.

"M'Lady!" A wild-eyed Beth filled the doorway, chest heaving with exertion. "M'Lady, come quick! 'Tis Mr. O'Dea! He's brought the Lahinch constabulary! There are people here! Outsiders!"

"Ye really did do it," Aggie whispered.

And my eyes closed briefly as the warm weight of her reassuring hand gently squeezed my shoulder.

"We're that sorry for yer loss, Yer Ladyship."

I nodded, lips pursed, as four strong officers removed Lady Catherine's now shrouded corpse on a handheld gurney.

We stood in the foyer, Cormac and I, grim-faced as the constable before us removed his hat out of respect for the dead.

My heart raced in my chest, for it was only a matter of time before the officers searching the house found Teddy's body.

They'd arrived too soon. Too early! I hadn't thought through what needed to be done before they arrived. Yes, I knew they would come eventually, but I'd had no sense of urgency. Stupid, *stupid*!

Instead, Diarmuid—getting to him—had been my sole focus. And now, the mother he'd lost, and regained, would be taken away for murder.

"Ye should go lie down," Cormac said gently, and I turned into him. I'd immediately pulled him aside when I'd exited the hall to greet the visitors and hastily hissed that Teddy's body was still in the house.

I'd never seen a person's face pale with such haste.

"I can't," I replied.

"And had Lady Catherine suffered from any malaise? Melancholia?" asked the constable, placing his hat back atop his head. He adjusted his belt, and I noted that even he appeared gaunt—clothes loose-fitting, the look of a few skipped meals about him. If even the likes of the well-paid constabulary were hurting, what did that say for the rest of the people?

"She was given to fits of fancy," Cormac replied, and I glanced at him. "It's awful isolated here, as ye can see."

The constable peered at Cormac's fine attire and arched a brow. "Ye don't sound like ye'd be a nephew of this house."

"My aunt was a Connors. Elevated through marriage, sir. She took care of her own." With a wide sweep of his arm, Cormac gestured toward the entrance of the library. "All her legal documents are archived within, sir. Ye'll find the truth of it there. And the solicitor from Ennistymon should be arriving this afternoon with the will I provided. I brought it directly to him after alerting you of the death."

"Aye. Of course. No offense meant, sir." With a nod, the constable glanced at me, and blood rushed in my ears. "And you, Yer Ladyship. How did ye find yer mother's mind? When exactly did ye return to the house?"

And just like that, everything I'd prepared for poured from

my lips—the rehearsed story of Wilhelmina's marriage, her life, her mourning period, down to the minute of Wilhelmina's return to Browne House. And I wondered then . . . if she knew. If she had predicted this. If she'd grilled me—despite the lies she'd told to trap me here—because she knew this moment would come. That I would need this information for this very occasion.

"Third floor is clear!"

I almost snapped my neck as I whipped my head toward the staircase.

"Thank you, Mahony," the constable yelled.

The third floor was not clear! Teddy's body was there in the guest bedroom.

I gathered breath to demand to know if they had truly checked, but Cormac pinched my arm, and I quickly turned my attention to the checkered marble floor.

"A moment please, constable," I said. "I would like to fetch a shawl from my chamber."

And before anyone could stop me, I crossed the foyer and hurried up the stairs. I half-expected Cormac to follow, but as I reached the second-floor landing, a quick glance found him engaging the constable in conversation, as though my contrariness was the most natural thing in the world.

Good. Gathering my skirts, I rounded the banister and flew up the next flight of stairs, heart pounding as a thin layer of sweat coated my brow. I could hear the officers above, their shouts echoing from the fourth floor to the third-floor landing.

"All clear."

"They said 'twas this room, Lady Browne's."

Panting heavily, I swept to the right, toward the room where Teddy had met his demise at my hands.

The chaise where I'd sat so patiently the night before still stood beneath the window at the end of the hall, the rug before it slightly disturbed.

My brows drew together—someone had certainly come in this direction, but—

My heart ceased beating as I halted, blood turning to ice before I quickly rubbed my eyes.

"What?" I whispered.

Where once there had been a door . . . now there was not. Scurrying forward, my hands swept over the wall, fingers brushing over its papered surface for any sign of a door beneath, but there was . . . nothing.

They hadn't found Teddy . . . because there was nary a room for them to check.

"There ye are. Tea's ready in the parlor, m'Lady." Beth appeared on the landing, and I whirled, eyes wide.

"What happened to the door?" I hissed, storming toward her as I pointed toward the offending wall. "Where did it go?"

Beth pursed her lips as she glanced over my shoulder, then gave a little shrug. "A final gift from the woman in white?"

My jaw slackened, but as a shout rang out from the floor above, I shook myself.

"All clear!"

"Let's go," I whispered, leading the way down the staircase. Whether 'twas a gift, or a trick, the door was hidden from the constabulary, and that's all that mattered in this moment. For if it reappeared once they'd left, Cormac and I would deal with the mess within.

Mustering a deep breath, I schooled my face as I reached the second-floor landing and cleared my throat as my shoe tapped against the checkered marble of the foyer.

"Would you care to continue our conversation in comfort, Constable?" I asked, sweeping an arm toward the open door of the parlor.

"Don't mind if I do," he replied. And with all the hauteur I'd practiced the last few months, I strode ahead and led them through to the parlor, as the lady of the house I'd been taught to be.

* * *

Morning stretched to afternoon. The constable had drunk his fill and devoured the sandwiches provided, and I sent the kitchen staff to work, preparing something the others could take with them when they left—which would be soon, I hoped.

The investigation of the house continued, and every fiber of my being itched for them to be gone.

The solicitor from Ennistymon had arrived an hour since, and he and Cormac were settled in the library, discussing particulars while I stared into the fireplace, watching as the flames leapt and danced.

"More tea, m'Lady?" Beth.

Startled, I pulled the shawl draped over my shoulders closer and turned in the direction of her voice.

"Where is Diarmuid?" I asked.

Glancing over her shoulder, she scurried closer and bent to whisper in my ear. "Safe. The publican's wife placed him in with her own children, and he's fine."

I nodded and sank further into the chair as she righted herself.

"What's taking them so long?"

"Them constables are checking every nook and cranny, m'Lady," Beth said, snatching the poker from its stand to build up the fire. Then whispered: "The door is still gone, m'Lady. I've gone up there twice now to check."

"Thank God," I murmured.

"Maybe it really was the woman in white," Beth said, turning her attention back to the fire. The pieces of burning turf within crackled and sparked as she spread their ashy remnants around the grate, before piling new bricks atop them. "She had the kind of power to do such a thing."

"Perhaps. I just want them all to leave—"

"Cousin?" Cormac's voice from the door set my heart alight, and I slapped a palm to my chest as I turned.

"Y-yes?" I called.

"They're ready for ye."

Swallowing the lump that formed in my throat, I quickly rose to my feet and smoothed my crumpled dress.

"*I* am ready for *them*," I snapped, straightening my spine. "They are welcome to join me here, for I shan't step a foot inside that library. Mama's soul has barely departed, and we shan't speak business over the rug that became her deathbed."

"As ye wish." With a wink, Cormac left to fetch the solicitor and the constable, and I moved from my place at the fireside to a grand Queen Anne armchair that stood in-round with the fine suite of furniture placed carefully for entertaining.

"Tea, Beth," I commanded, descending into the plush safety of the chair, back rigid, chin up. Ready. Able. The daughter of an earl. The widow of an earl. Wilhelmina.

"Cousin, dear." Cormac announced his arrival with a bow, before ushering the legal party into the parlor. "This is the Right Honorable Jonathan Plunkett, Esquire. Aunty's will was addressed to him."

"Thank you for coming all this way," I said, fighting to keep my voice steady. I hoped they would confuse fear for shock, given the circumstances.

He was a reed of a man, clean-shaven, and wearing a fine tweed suit. Well-to-do, but not wealthy, as expected of a countryside solicitor. He bowed. "Your Ladyship."

"Mama must have held you in high esteem," I offered, by way of flattery.

"Indeed. I've done business with her ladyship for decades, though I haven't seen her in society for a few years now. She wrote often to Lords Belmont and O'Brien, however, so I had news of her from them." He stepped forward, and I indicated the chair to my right. He sat. "I was, needless to say, shocked by this news. Such a terrible thing."

"It was quite the shock to us all," I replied, sweeping a hand toward the Chippendale opposite. "Do make yourself comfortable, Constable. Cormac, I've asked Beth to bring tea."

"Let's get to business, gentlemen," Cormac urged, flopping onto the chair at my left side. "As exhausted as I am from the hasty journey, my cousin here was so perturbed by events that she deigned to spend the night on the floor of the village hall, afeared as she was to spend a night in this house, alone with her mother's body."

"Dreadful," murmured Mr. Plunkett, smoothing the papers he carried on his lap.

"Who shall begin?" I asked, gently massaging my temples—both for show and to offset the ache of exhaustion that threatened to undo me.

"Ah. That be me," said the constable. "The official cause of death is—Roy? Where's that doctor?"

A young officer popped his head through the open parlor door and ducked out again.

I let loose a long-suffering sigh, but the lad returned a moment later with an older gentleman sporting spectacles and a disheveled shirt tucked into knee breeches that had seen better days.

"Your Ladyship," he mumbled, bowing far lower than was necessary.

"Doctor Kelly," said the constable, jerking a thumb over his shoulder. "What's the cause of death, Seán?"

"Exsanguination," replied the doctor.

"Right, that thing," said the constable. "It's clear her ladyship took her own life, but we'll make sure the death certificate reflects the verbiage ye'd prefer."

Aye. So she could have a proper burial and a mass said with the grace of the church.

"Please list it as an accidental fall," I called, addressing Dr. Kelly.

He nodded and swept from the room.

"No foul play," said the constable, nodding toward the solicitor. "Yer in the clear to execute the will."

The constable took his leave, and Mr. Plunkett began.

I sat, frozen, as he read the particulars.

Cormac was endowed with a sizable amount, enough to live comfortably for the rest of his life and care for his aging parents.

But the estate—the house and all the land—were now mine. Well, no. Wilhelmina's. In death, Lady Catherine had fulfilled her promise, and shock settled in, hard and heavy.

The next half hour flew by in a daze—as Mr. Plunkett had me sign the will, and the deed, as he went over the hows and wheres with Cormac.

As we all rose and shook on it.

As I led them from the parlor, to meet the constables and the doctor in the foyer.

As we sauntered outside, into the late-afternoon air, sun shining for the first time in what felt like months—the first true sign of summer, birdsong chirping, the scent of blooming flowers heavy on the gentle breeze.

As they boarded coaches and mounted horses.

Until I suddenly came to, as Dr. Kelly cleared his throat next to me.

"Begging your pardon, Your Ladyship. But I found a sizable amount of this toxin in the attic." Reaching inside the pocket of the coat he now wore, the doctor pulled a sprig of the dried white, trumpet-shaped flower from within and presented it to me.

My eyes widened.

"Toxin?"

"Aye. It's angel's trumpet, m'Lady. Causes hallucinations—makes ye see things that aren't really there. Ghouls, ghosties, people, conversations that never happened and the like." He pursed his lips. "The flowers themselves give off very little of the damaging miasma, but when dried and burned . . . well, I did notice incense burners throughout the house, and given the way her ladyship passed, it's possible that this might be the cause."

My lungs ceased functioning as I stared at the sprig in his hand.

"You mean, Mama might have been driven to such an act through hallucinations?" I asked, voice tinny even to my own ears.

"It's possible. I suggest opening all the windows to clear any remnants, and scrub the place from top to bottom to rid every surface of residue, just in case. If ye'd like, I can return next week and take the stock from the attic, to dispose of it for ye."

"Y-yes. Yes." I nodded, and he placed the sprig back into his pocket.

"Next week then, m'Lady," he said, bowing before boarding the closest coach.

Cormac came to my side and placed a steadying hand against my elbow, waving as the drivers spurred the horses forward.

"Ye didn't imagine it," he murmured, words passing through clenched teeth as the second coach passed by.

"I couldn't have," I whispered. There was no way . . . "Diarmuid is here? In the village?"

"He is. I saw him with my own two eyes earlier."

Whatever knot that had twisted my gut suddenly released, and I was suddenly able to breathe once more.

"The room is gone. I don't know how, or if some magic kept it hidden until they all left . . . but there's no door. We should check again in the morning," I said.

"Gone?" Cormac's eyes widened, but Aggie's crisp voice cut across the drive.

"This young lad is asking for buttered bread," she called, and I damn near broke my neck as I whirled, eyes wide, to spy Diarmuid skipping along beside her, his little hand in hers.

"Then he shall have it!" I exclaimed, delighted as they neared. "Take him straight to the kitchen, and I'll join ye in a moment."

"Ye did well," Aggie said, smiling as she guided Diarmuid up the steps of Browne House. "Come along now, Young Master. We'll get ye a treat."

"What now?" Cormac asked, as Aggie and Diarmuid disappeared into the entrance. "Ye got what ye wanted in the end. A house. Land."

But I didn't even have to think about it.

"Sell it. I'll continue as Lady Wilhelmina until it's done, then we'll parse what we earn among the villagers. They can try their luck elsewhere, with enough money to get them by, or take ship to the Americas."

I glanced at him to find him smiling, and my lips twitched in tandem. "What? What is it?"

"And ye? What'll ye do, after freeing some four hundred people from the bonds of the land war?"

"I—" My brows furrowed. "Diarmuid doesn't know me as his mother yet, and it'll likely take some time. But I should keep enough from the sale of Browne House to buy a small place. Maybe put my learning to good use and find a position in a city. Limerick?"

"Limerick?" Cormac turned his face toward the sun, eyes closing as a grin near split his cheeks. "I suppose I could get used to it."

With a scoff, I smacked his arm, and he crumpled in on himself with a laugh. "Yer not coming with me. We'll be fine on our own."

"And so yer just going to go live in the city, unwed, with a small child?" he asked, straightening, those amber eyes alight with mischief.

"Yes!"

"Ye know . . . I'm not only the handsomest man in the parish now, but the richest."

"Cormac O'Dea!" I scolded, but the joy on his face drew a laugh from the depths of my belly.

"I thought ye said ye owed me four near-deaths so our life debt could be even? How will ye save me four times if I'm not with ye?"

"Arra now. It's ahead of yerself yer getting." I exclaimed, a spark of "perhaps" blooming across my chest. Not now. But maybe, when time had healed my heart, Cormac O'Dea could have a place by my side. At the very least, he'd earned the opportunity to try.

"All right, all right." He chuckled, raising his arms in surrender. "No need to worry about all that right now. Come on, let's go."

He held out a hand, and I eyed it with suspicion.

"Where are we going?"

"To feed yer son as much buttered bread as he can stomach, Maggie O'Shaughnessy. Let's go into yer home."

My son. My home. My *name*.

Finally, the life I always wanted was there for the taking.

And no one—above or below—would have a say in the choices I made from this day forth.

With a smile, I placed my hand in Cormac's, and as the gulls of North Clare squawked from the rocky shore, I strode along the path I had made for myself.

Toward the bright dawning of a brilliant future.

Author's Note

We (the Irish) don't talk much about An Gorta Mór (the Great Hunger). Even coming up through secondary school, we barely scratched the surface of what really happened. It's dealt with as a footnote in history class, the ultimate result of the Land Wars, the Irish Confederate Wars, the Glorious Revolution, and so on. "The potatoes rotted, the country was devastated by death and emigration, and now on to how we kicked out the Brits!"

And believe it or not, I didn't learn the truth of the atrocities committed until my junior (third) year of college, when I took a mandatory year abroad and wound up in Kentucky, USA. There, I took what I thought would be an "easy A" of a class— Irish History—but imagine my confusion when the Great Hunger was taught as an entire module. In that class, Dr. Hebert opened my eyes to everything we glossed over in secondary school and introduced me to the realization that it was never a famine—potato crops failed all over the world, at the same time, and no other country went through what Ireland did. It was the purposeful and intentional starvation of a people that the British Empire had long tried to bring to heel. It was genocide.

Until I took that class, I had no idea that I was born in a part of the country that was devastated from 1845 to 1850, nor had I any idea that I lived but a stone's throw from a town that was so cruelly dealt with that the plight of its people was brought up in the British Parliament. That town was (and is) Kilrush, County Clare.

I didn't want to write this book. I know now why surviving generations don't like to talk about it, and I was terrified that I wouldn't be able to portray it in a respectful way that not only educates but also entertains. It seemed like a paradox—to turn this trauma into entertainment—but I knew I had to do it. Not only for those who should be forgiven for not knowing the history, but for those who should—my fellow Irish people, who weren't given the full story in school.

As *This House Will Feed* is a work of fiction, liberties were taken, but though Maggie, Cormac, Lady Catherine, and Teddy are figments of my imagination, Colonel Crofton Moore-Vandeleur is not. One of the worst of the landowners during the Great Hunger, he reigned over seventeen townlands and parishes in County Clare. Directly responsible for the eviction and deaths of countless tenants and people under his care during the crisis, he was reported to the House of Commons by Poor Law inspector Captain (later Sir) Edward Kennedy (who at one point in time challenged Moore-Vandeleur to a duel). A public reprimand took place via a seven-part admonishing in the London *Times*, but nothing was ever "done" about it. Moore-Vandeleur was despised, but his heir, Hector, was worse. Instead of rallying to mend relations and commerce in the town of Kilrush once his father passed, Hector opted to spend all his time partying in London while those under his care floundered in the wake of such profound loss.

Their home, Kilrush House, burned to the ground in 1897, and the Land Commission confiscated the demesne from the family in an effort to aid the people. The house and grounds were forgotten about until restoration efforts resurrected the gardens into a premier tourist destination that now bolsters the local economy.

But not all landlords of the time treated their people like chattel. I made mention of the Gore-Booths of Sligo in the book, referencing the fifth baronet, Sir Henry. During the Great Hunger, the family opened their food stores to the people and created jobs (the building of unnecessary walls and roads) so tenants could earn a wage and afford to purchase lifesaving grains. He instilled such a love of Ireland and compassion for its people in his children that his daughter, Countess Constance Markievicz, became one of the most famous revolutionaries in Ireland's history. Deeply involved in the planning and execution of the Easter 1916 Rising, she received the death penalty, but the sentence was later commuted, leading to her release in 1917. She went on to become the first woman ever elected to the United Kingdom House of Commons, but in protest, she never took her seat. She continued as Éamon de Valera's right hand as the Irish revolutionary war commenced and eventually passed away in a free and independent Ireland in 1927.

As for some of the more extreme elements recorded in this book, I wish I could say they were fictionalized. Many official accounts of cannibalism were recorded in the counties of Cork, Galway, Kerry, and Mayo, and these accounts survive in the writings of priests begging their bishops for aid, in court records, and in newspapers.

Even the idea of a village that no one would find on a map or villages that were completely deserted isn't entirely fiction, as whole villages and townlands were wiped out from existence.

That said, all faith in humanity was not lost. Thanks to foreign observers present in the country at the time, advocates, like American abolitionist Frederick Douglass, were able to get the word out. As a result, attempts at aid were made by foreign leaders (though those attempts were blocked by the British government).

But perhaps the most beautiful and long-enduring triumph of humanity can be seen in the relationship that developed between the Irish people and the people of the Choctaw Nation. Having heard of Ireland's condition, the recently displaced Choctaw pooled what little money and resources they had to ease Ireland of its plight. That relationship endures to this day with the erection of the *Kindred Spirits* sculpture in County

Cork, the meeting of our leaders, and university scholarships for Choctaw Nation students to study in Ireland. In 2020, the Irish government paid the kindness forward by sending aid to the Navajo Nation and the Hopi Reservation during the COVID-19 crisis.

To that end, thank you to the people of the Choctaw Nation: Without your elders, mine would have never survived.

And finally, I wouldn't be much of a Clare woman if I didn't mention the legend herself: Biddy Early. Though fictionally portrayed here as Cormac's aunt, Biddy was a very real wise-woman and seer that was well-respected in County Clare and beyond. Born into extreme poverty in 1798, she made her living by healing the sick, tending to the poor, lifting curses . . . and casting a few. In 1865, she was put on trial for witchcraft in the town of Ennis, but so many of those she'd healed and helped testified on her behalf that the Catholic Church had no choice but to acquit her.

In folklore, it was said that she placed a curse on the Clare hurling team so they'd never win another All-Ireland championship, but given that Biddy died in 1874 and whispers of this "curse" emerged only after 1914, that rumor has been fully laid to rest.

Biddy's legacy was preserved by authors and poets like Lady Gregory and W.B. Yeats, and more recently by one of the last seanchaithe left in Ireland—who is also a Clare man—a national treasure: Eddie Lenihan.

Further Reading

Paddy's Lament by Thomas Gallagher
The Great Hunger: Ireland 1845–1849 by Cecil Woodham-Smith
The Famine Plot by Tim Pat Coogan
Peig by Peig Sayers

Websites of Interest

Learn about the relationship between the Irish and the
Choctaw: https://www.choctawnation.com/about/history/
irish-connection/

Learn about the Vandeleur Walled Garden: https://www.
vandeleurwalledgarden.ie/

Resources for Further Study

A complete resource for those interested in learning more
about the Great Hunger:
https://www.irishfamine.ie/greatirishfamineonline/
https://ucc.maps.arcgis.com/apps/MapSeries/index.html?
appid=83617870f2624735b4f5cae21077ea36

Pronunciation Guide

Place Names: Their Pronunciation
Caherbannagh — Kah-hurr-bann-ah
Clareabbey — Clare-abbey
Craggykerivan — Craggy-ker-ih-van
Ennis — En-iss
Ennistymon — En-niss-tie-mun
Faha — Fah-ha
Formoyle — Furr-moyle
Foynes — Foins (like "loins")
Gortacarnaun — Gurt-ah-cawr-nawn
Hag of Beara — Hag of Barr-ah
Kildysert — Kill-die-surt
Kilrush — Kill-rush
Liscannor — Liss-can-urr
Lisdoonvarna — Liss-doon-var-nah
Lissycasey — Lizzy-case-ee (sometimes Liss-ee-case-ee)
Moyarta — Moy-arta
Toonagh — Too-nah

Character Names
Aoife — Ee-fah
Cormac O'Dea — Korr-mock Oh Day
Diarmuid — Deer-mwid
Maggie O'Shaughnessy — Maggie Oh Shock-nissy
Síofra — Shee-ah-frah

From the Text (pronunciation, followed by the meaning in English)
Amadán — O (as in "orange")-mah-dawn. Idiot.
Ár n-Athair, atá ar neamh, go naofar d'ainm, go dtagfadh do

ríocht, go ndéantar do thoil ar an talamh mar a dhéantar ar neamh—Awr nah-hurr at-aw err nav, guh nai-fur dan-im, go dog-ah duh ree-ockt, guh nain-turr duh hull err on tall-iv mawr ah yane-turr err nav. Our Father who art in Heaven, hallowed be thy name, thy kingdom come, thy will be done.

Ba mhaith leat a eitilt?—Bah wah lee-yat ah ett-ilt. Do you want to fly?

Bean draíochta dorcha—Bann dree-ock-tah durr-kah. Woman of the dark magic; dark sorceress.

Bean sidhe—Bann shee (also known as the "banshee"). Woman of the fairy mound; fairy woman—a harbinger of death in Irish mythology.

Bilé—Bill-ai. God of Death.

Cailleach—Ky-lock. Old goddess of winter/change/change of fortune.

Céilí—Kay-lee. A party or social gathering that includes traditional music and dance.

Cillín—Kill-een. An unconsecrated burial site.

Daoine Uaisle—Dee-nah (sometimes Dee-nee) Oosh-ah-lah. Esteemed People; used to refer to the Other Crowd, beings from beyond the veil, elementals, folkloric beings, fae.

Eitilt—Ett-ilt. Fly, to fly.

Fanann an diabhal i mo dhiaidh—Fonn-un onn dee-vul ih muh yee-g. The Devil follows me; the Devil is behind me; the Devil travels behind me.

Féar gortach—Fare gurth-ock. Starving grass; hungry grass.

Gaeilge—Gway-ill-geh. The Irish language, aka Irish Gaelic, Irish.

Poitín—Putch-een. An alcohol derived from distilling potatoes.

Púca—Poo-kah. A bringer of good or bad fortune; generally a mix: a quarter human and three-quarters some other animal.

Puiseóg—Pwish-oge (like ogre). A charm/spell with ill intent.

Rith amach as seo—Rih ah-mock oss shyuh. Run away from
here.

Seanchaí—Shan-kee (traditional Irish storyteller in the oral
tradition)

Seanchaithe—Shan-kah-ha (plural of seanchaí)

Tír na nÓg—Teer nah Noe-g. Land of Youth/Land of
Everlasting Youth; a mythological place where the Tuatha
De Danann (old golds) reside, located off the west coast of
Ireland, in the Atlantic Ocean.

Tusa agus mise—Tuss-ah o(as in orange)-guss mish-ah. You
and me.

From the Epigraphs

Aodh Buí—Ai Bwee (name).

Acknowledgments

This is always the hardest part—thanking everyone who helped shape this book—so I'll start with thanking my agent, Amy Giuffrida, and the entire team at the Belcastro Agency. You all are awesome!

To my editor, Elizabeth Trout—thank you, and the entire team at Kensington for believing in this book. It damn near killed me to write, so it means the world that you all recognized the value of this story, and that you championed it into the book it's become.

To Jeni Chappelle—my forever cheerleader—thank you for always being there for me.

To my early readers and pitch perfecters—Paulette Kennedy, Teagan King, Megan Peterson, Justine Manzano, Kimberly Imbert, Jenny Lane, Natasha Hanova, Taylor Kemper, Sasa Hawk, Haley Hwang, Aoife Doyle, Jenny Adams—thank you for being such incredible peers. And thank you to all the other authors who've been a part of this very long journey.

To my son, Devon—you are the brightest rainbow after every rain shower, and I love you to the moon and back.

And to my family—your support has always meant the world to me.

Here's to many more books, and to the stories still left untold. Cheers.

THIS HOUSE
WILL FEED

ABOUT THIS GUIDE

The suggested questions are included to enhance your group's
reading of Maria Tureaud's *This House Will Feed*.

Discussion Questions

1. How do Maggie's actions—past and present—reflect the historical context that she lives in?

2. If you plucked Maggie from 19th-century Ireland and deposited her into the 21st century, how would her choices differ?

3. In the book, Maggie does not seem to fear the supernatural things around her as much as we might. How does this purposeful choice by the author tie into the historical context of the book?

4. Was there a specific moment that particularly frightened or disturbed you? If so, why? How does it relate to your modern experiences? Does this history reflect the current political climate where you live?

5. In keeping with traditional Irish storytelling, no character is inherently bad—or good—as every protagonist could be another person's antagonist. How did this unusual aspect of Irish storytelling shape your view of characters like Lady Catherine and Teddy?

6. In a similar vein, some of the "good" characters, like Cormac and Maggie herself, also made choices that could be considered antagonistic. How did you reconcile these thought processes and decisions as a modern reader, unfamiliar with these aspects of traditional Irish storytelling?

7. As a character, Cormac could be seen as a green-flagged cheerleader, but the author might argue that he is the conductor and catalyst of events in the book. Discuss.

8. In the timeline of the past, we see a snapshot of what life was like at the Big House and for those who lived on and worked the land. Compare and contrast the classes and their status. In what other ways are these differences portrayed in the book?

9. In Lord Browne's journal, could comparisons be drawn between how the Anglos viewed the native Irish and excessive fear of that which they didn't understand? Discuss.

10. In the book, Maggie's goal is to honor her family in a way that will allow their memories to live on—by acquiring land. This need was perpetuated in the Irish psyche for generations after the Great Hunger, spurring those who successfully landed in America (alive and healthy enough to be admitted) to take the fool's journey west to settle the land the government offered. How did this trauma shape countries like the United States, Canada, the United Kingdom, and Australia?

11. The Great Hunger was the culmination of centuries of war and the hope that joining the United Kingdom would finally afford the Irish people stability—and personhood—within the borders of the Commonwealth. After reading this book, how would you describe this great deception and its aftermath?

12. Ingrained in the Irish consciousness, folklore—the Other Crowd (fae and the like), elementals, the Old Gods and Goddesses—and the superstitions surrounding it permeate the modern Irish psyche to this day. In your country, do superstition and tradition play a role in how your culture was shaped? If so, how do these nods to your elders play a role in your everyday life?